GORDON R. DICKSON *In the Bone*
Earth's finest technology made the universe his for the taking... until he ran into someone one step up from mankind.

DAMON KNIGHT *What Rough Beast*
He could twist time and events, heal the sick, create wealth beyond imagining... but could he ever find a world to call home?

POUL ANDERSON *Un-man*
Un-man was a legend. Killed a thousand times, he never died.

ROBERT SILVERBERG *After the Myths Went Home*
In the Hall of Man they called forth the greatest from Earth's history, then from its legends. But what would happen when they grew bored with these myths?

From a troubled mutant to a barbarian gladiator with the strength to topple insterstellar empires, here in short novels and stories are the **SUPERMEN**, all inhabitants of Isaac Asimov's World of Science Fiction.

Isaac Asimov's World of Science Fiction

SUPERMEN

Edited by Isaac Asimov, Charles G. Waugh and Martin H. Greenberg

Robinson Publishing
London

Robinson Publishing
11 Shepherd House
Shepherd Street
London W1Y 7LD

First published in the UK by Robinson Publishing in 1988

Collection copyright © Nightfall Inc.,
                    Charles G. Waugh and
                    Martin H. Greenberg, 1984

Cover illustration © Robin Hidden

ISBN 0 948164 98 0

Printed by Cox & Wyman Ltd., Reading

Contents

Acknowledgments

'Angel, Dark Angel' by Roger Zelazny. Copyright © 1967 by Galaxy Publishing Corporation. Reprinted by permission of the author.

'Worlds to Kill' by Harlan Ellison. Copyright © 1968 by Galaxy Publishing Corporation: copyrights reassigned 7 July 1980 to the Kilimanjaro Corporation. Copyright © 1980 by the Kilimanjaro Corporation. Reprinted with permission of and by arrangement with the Author and the Author's agent Richard Curtis Associates, Inc., New York. All rights reserved.

'In the Bone' by Gordon R. Dickson. Copyright © 1966 by Galaxy Publishing Corporation. Reprinted by permission of the author.

'What Rough Beast' by Damon Knight. Copyright © 1959 by Mercury Press, Inc. From THE MAGAZINE OF FANTASY AND SCIENCE FICTION. Reprinted by permission of the author.

'Death by Ecstasy' by Larry Niven. Copyright © 1969 by Galaxy Publishing Corporation. Reprinted by permission of Kirby McCauley Ltd.

'Un-man' by Poul Anderson. Copyright © 1953 by Street & Smith Publications, Inc.: copyright renewed © 1981 by Poul Anderson. Reprinted by permission of the author and his agents, the Scott Meredith Literary Agency, Inc., 845 Third Avenue, New York, New York 10022.

'Muse' by Dean R. Koontz. Copyright © 1969 by Mercury Press, Inc. From THE MAGAZINE OF FANTASY AND SCIENCE FICTION. September, 1969, reprinted by permission of the author.

'Resurrection' by A. E. van Vogt. Copyright © 1948 by Street & Smith Publications, Inc., copyright renewed 1976 by A. E. van Vogt. Reprinted by permission of Forrest J. Ackerman, 2495 Glendower Avenue, Hollywood, California 90027-1110.

'Pseudopath' by Philip E. High. Copyright © 1960 by Great American Publications, Inc., for new worlds science fiction. Reprinted by permission of the author and E. J. Carnell Literary Agency.

'After the Myths Went Home' by Robert Silverberg. Copyright © 1969 by Mercury Press, Inc. From THE MAGAZINE OF FANTASY AND SCIENCE FICTION. Reprinted by permission of Agberg, Inc.

'Before the Talent Dies' by Henry Slesar. Copyright © 1957 by Fantasy House, Inc. From THE MAGAZINE OF FANTASY AND SCIENCE FICTION. Reprinted by permission of the author.

'Brood World Barbarian' by Perry A. Chapdelaine. Copyright © 1969 by Galaxy Publishing Corporation. Reprinted by permission of Forrest J. Ackerman, 2495 Glendower Avenue, Hollywood, California 90027-1110.

Introduction

Once, some 40,000,000 years ago, there lived a little creature named Eohippus. (Its proper name is Hyracotherium, according to the paleontologists, but I like Eohippus better.)

It was a delicate little creature, with a stubby little horse face, that browsed on leaves and scampered away as fast as it could when a meat-eater showed up. It was about the size of a fox, and weighed perhaps as much as 9 kilograms. It was a hoofed animal with four little hooves on each foreleg and three on each hind leg.

If we suppose that the Eohippus could think after our fashion, we might ask him: "What do you suppose a Supereohippus would be like?"

It seems to me the little creature would answer, "Well, first it would have to be large and strong so that it wouldn't be afraid of these rotten predators that are always chasing me. It ought to weigh a lot, maybe as much as 1,300 kilograms, so that it would be 140 times as big as I am.

"Then it would have to be tall, so that it could look far out over the plains and see predators if they come. It shouldn't be a quarter of a meter high at the shoulders as I am, but perhaps as much as two meters higher—nine times my height—and it should have a long neck that would raise its eyes higher still.

"Oh, yes, and it should be fast, so that if predators happened by that were large enough to be dangerous, or that hunted in packs, it could run like the wind and get away. It should run maybe as fast as 55 kilometers per hour, at least for short distances—just long enough to get away. Now *that* would be a Supereohippus."

Well, an Eohippus capable of saying all that would display a really active imagination, but even more so, real prescience, for such a Supereohippus actually lives today. Some of them are as massive, some as tall, and some as fast as Eohippus' dreams would have them. Supereohippus is what we, today, call a horse, and Eohippus is itself from Greek words that mean "dawn-horse." That dawn-horse slowly evolved over the millions of years into today's supercreature.

Another example . . .

About three and a half million years ago, there were animals living in Africa that looked a little bit like small apes, about 1.2 meters tall and delicately built. They walked erect as we do. The animal is called *Australopithecus afarensis* by paleontologists. The first word is from the Greek and means "southern ape," because the first specimens were found in South Africa. The second word is from the name of a region in eastern Ethiopia where a particularly early skeletal specimen was discovered in 1974. Creatures belonging to this and to related species are lumped together as "australopithecines."

The australopithecines are examples of "hominids" (from a Greek word for "man"), since their ability to walk erect puts them closer to modern human beings than to apes.

If an australopithecine could reason as we do, we might ask it to describe its notion of a Superaustralopithecine. It might answer thus:

"Well, first of all, I'd want it bigger and stronger than I am so it could defend itself better and be a better hunter than I am. I suppose that if it were, say, 1.6 meters tall, instead of 1.2 as I am, and if it weighed about 70 kilograms, instead of 30 as I do, it would be tall enough and strong enough to be a Superaustralopithecine.

"It would be no use making it even bigger and stronger, because that's not the chief advantage it ought to have. Some extra height, mass, and muscle are all right, but what it would mainly need is brains. My brain is pretty big for my size. It's bigger than that of the apes, which are stronger than I am. I'm doing better than they are because I'm smart enough to chip rock against rock and use sharpened rocks along with tree branches and thighbones as tools and weapons. The apes just use their nails and teeth.

"Now, then, it seems to me that if you really want a Superaustralopithecine, what you mainly need, therefore, is a larger brain; one that weighs, say 1.5 kilograms, or four times the size of mine. I realize that would mean Super-australopithecine's skull would have to be huge and swollen and he would look ugly, but there's no way out, if you want someone who is super. A big-brained Superaustralopithecine—well, who can possibly tell what he would be capable of?''

The Australopithecines were extinct by about a million years ago, but by that time there were hominids that were larger and bigger-brained, and, eventually, still other hominids that were even larger and still bigger-brained. Indeed, about 50,000 years ago, a creature that was precisely the Superaustralopithecine described by our mythical australopithecine thinker made its appearance in Europe. We call him *Homo sapiens sapiens* or ''modern man.'' *We* are Superaustralopithecine.

Well, then, now it's our turn. We are actually the first species on Earth capable of deducing the evolutionary process that produced us, and the first capable of imagining a further evolutionary advance over ourselves. What would a superman be like? (Let me assure you that I am using the term ''superman'' here, and in the title of this anthology, as a generic term to include all superhuman beings—women and children, as well as men.)

The classic Superman, the person who first appeared in *Action Comics* nearly half a century ago, is a good example of what I mean. He is not grossly different from us; indeed, he can masquerade as a ''mild-mannered reporter'' named Clark Kent. However, he is incredibly strong, has X-ray vision, can fly through the air, and displays many other remarkable abilities. His great deficiency is that he is not particularly brighter than we are. In fact, he resembles the Siegfried of Wagner's operas, who, according to Anna Russell, is ''very handsome, very strong, very brave, and very *very* stupid.''

That is not exactly what we want. We want superman to have a better brain than we have, to think and reason more efficiently; we would want him to have faster reflexes than we have, sharper senses, perhaps some senses we lack altogether. Then, if on top of that he is also stronger, fine—but that doesn't come first.

However, why puzzle it out? Here we have an anthology of a number of excellent stories in which human beings are described who, in one way or another (and no two stories exactly duplicate the particular way), are markedly superior to ourselves. Sometimes the superiority rests upon the cooperation of a human being with another species, sometimes as the result of education and training, sometimes as a result of mutation—

It doesn't matter. The result is, in each case, that the vision is of something like ourselves, but more remarkable. You can decide for yourself if each particular vision resembles what *you* would consider super—or even endurable.

It may be, for all I know, that there are as many different kinds of supermen as there are dreamers who wish they were something better than they are. My own idea of a superman, for instance, would be someone who could write as well as Shakespeare, and who didn't need sleep, so that he could write *a lot*, and—oh, yes, who would be infinitely attractive to the ladies (at such time as he wasn't writing, and when his wife was willing to be cooperative—which isn't likely).

Angel, Dark Angel

by Roger Zelazny

An agent of death, he kept the peace by killing. Then he fell in love with a victim.

He entered the kiosk and escalated down to the deck that stood beside the rumbling strip. He was fifty-five years of age and he bore a briefcase in his right hand.

As he crossed toward the conveyor belt, a dozen heads turned in his direction because of the flash of light which occurred immediately before him.

For one bright instant, a dark figure stood in his path.

Then there came the *crack* of imploding air, as the figure vanished and the man fell to the deck.

Later that day, the death record read, "Natural causes."

Which was true. Quite, quite true.

It slithered along the moist tunnel, heading toward the river.

It knew that its life had ended the moment that the blaze occurred; and the facets of its eyes held sixty-four images of the tall, leather-masked figure, garbed all in black, with its hard, dark hand upraised.

The hand extended toward it, offering that which it could not refuse.

The gift was thunder and pain, and the medical record prepared later that day said, "Natural causes."

Putting down his champagne glass, he unfastened her negligee and pushed it back over her shoulders. His hands molded her, described her sex, drew her down onto the bed. She sighed as he raised himself onto an elbow and touched her lips.

She felt him stiffen, in the glare that came from the corner of the suite. She screamed within the thunderclap that followed, having glimpsed the Angel of Death for a single, dark moment as she felt her lover stop his loving, forever.

This, too, was the result of natural causes.

The man called Stain was in his greenhouse, where he had spent some part of almost every day for the past two years, plucking dead leaves and taking cuttings.

He was slightly under six feet in height, and his eyes were iodine-dark within his sharp-cornered, sunbaked face beneath black hair salted lightly at the temples.

His left shoulder brushed against an earthenware pot on the shelf at his back, and he felt its movement and departure.

Turning, he caught it at waist level and replaced it on the shelf.

He began repotting a geranium, and then the instrument strapped to his left wrist buzzed and he pressed a button on its side and said, "Yes?"

"Stain," said the voice, which could have been coming from the red flowers in his hand, "do you love the human races and all other living things within the universe?"

"Of course," he replied, recognizing the crackling sibilance that was the voice of Morgenguard.

"Then please prepare yourself for a journey of some duration and report to your old cubicle in Shadowhall."

"But I am retired, and there must be many others whose speed now exceeds my own."

"Your last medical report shows that your speed is undiminished. You are still one of the ten best. You were retired at the proper age because it is your right to enjoy the rest of your days as you see fit. You are not ordered to do the thing I now say. You are requested to do it. So you may refuse if you see fit. Should you accept, however, you will be compensated, and you will have served the things you profess to love."

"What would you have of me?"

"Come not in uniform, but in civil garb. Bring with you your gauntlets and your daily requirements in all things, save nourishment, for a period of approximately two weeks."

"Very well. I will attend directly."

The communication ended, and he finished potting the geranium and returned to his quarters.

To his knowledge, none such as himself had ever been recalled from retirement, nor was his knowledge inaccurate.

Her name is Galatea, and she has red hair and stands to slightly over five and a half feet in height. Her eyes are green and her complexion pale, and men call her lovely but generally avoid her company. She lives in a big, old house which she has remodeled, on the outskirts of Cyborg, an ancient city on Ankus in the Ceti System. She keeps to herself and runs up large bills with the Cyborg Power Co.

She lives alone, save for mechanical servants. She favors dark colors in her garb and her surroundings. She occasionally plays tennis or else fences at the local sports center. She always wins. She orders large quantities of chemicals from local wholesalers. Men who have dated her say that she is stupid, brilliant, oversexed, a prude, fascinated with her deathwish, full of *joie de vivre*, an alcoholic, a teetotaler and a wonderful dancer. She has had many dates/few friends/no suitors, and her lovers be unknown. It is suggested that she maintains a laboratory and perhaps engages in unknown researches.

"We do not know the answer," said Simule. "There is no defense against him, save here. I cannot remain here if I am to serve my function. Therefore, I must leave soon, and secretly."

"Wait," she said. "You are not yet ready to survive on your own. Another month, perhaps . . ."

"Too long, too long, we fear," Simule replied.

"Do you doubt my power to protect you?"

Simule paused, as if to consider, then, "No. You can save this body, but the question 'Is it worth it?' comes forth. Is it worth it? Preserve yourself, lady. We love you. There remains yet more that you may do."

"We shall see," she said. "But for now, you remain."

She replaced him, upon the reading stand in her library, and she left him there with *Lear*.

His name was Stain, and he came to her door one day and announced himself, saying, "Stain, of Iceborg."

After a time, the door let him in.

She appeared and asked, "Yes?"

"My name is Stain," he replied, "and I have heard that you play tennis, and are very good. I am looking for a partner in the Cyborg Open Mixed Doubles. I am good. Will you play with me?"

"How good?" she asked him.

"They don't come much better."

"Catch," she said, and picked up a marble figurine from off an inlaid table and hurled it toward him.

He caught it, fumbling, and set it on the ledge at his side.

"Your reflexes are good," she replied. "Very well, I'll play with you."

"Will you have dinner with me tonight?"

"Why?"

"Why not? I don't know anyone here."

"All right. Eight o'clock."

"I'll pick you up then."

"Till then."

"Till then."

He turned, and headed back toward the town and his hotel.

Of course, they took the tournament. They won hands down. And Stain and Galatea danced that night and drank champagne, and she asked him as he held her, both of them all in black, "What do you do, Stain?"

"Nothing but enjoy myself," he said. "I'm retired."

"In your thirties?"

"Thirty-two."

She sighed and softened within his arms.

"What do *you* do?" he asked.

"I, too, am retired. I enjoy my hobbies. I do as I would."

"What does that come to?"

"Whatever I please."

"I've brought you a Hylagian orchid to wear in your hair, or anywhere else you may choose. I'll give it to you when we return to the table."

"They're very expensive," she said.

"Not so if you raise them yourself."

"And you do?"

"*My* hobby," he replied.

At their table, they finished their champagne and smoked and she studied the flower and her companion. The club was done all in silver and black, and the music was soft—and as the dancers seated themselves it lost all semblance of a theme. Her smile was the candle of their table, and he ordered them a dessert and liqueurs to accompany it, and she said, "Your poise defies description."

"Thank you, but yours is superior."

"What did you do, before you retired?"

"I was a paymaster. What of yourself?"

"I dealt in accounts receivable, for a large concern."

"Then we have something else almost in common."

"So it would seem. What will you do now?"

"I'd like to continue seeing you, for so long as I am in town."

"How long might that be?"

"For so long as I might wish, or you desire."

"Then let us finish our sherbet; and since you wish me to have the trophy, we will take it home."

He brushed the back of her hand, lightly, and for an instant their eyes met, and a spark that might have been electric leapt between them and they smiled at precisely the same instant.

After a time, he took her home.

The bat-thing quivered and dipped, on the way to the council of its people.

As it passed by a mountaintop, there came a flash of light. Though its speed was virtually inconceivable and its movement unpredictable, it knew that it would fall in an instant; and it did, as the thunder roared above it.

He held her very closely and their lips met. They stood in the foyer of her big old remodeled house on the outskirts of Cyborg City on Ankus, of the Ceti System, and one of her mechanical servants had taken their cloaks and another the double-handled golden tennis trophy, and the front door had closed behind them and the night lights had come on dim as they had entered.

"You'll stay awhile," she said.

"Fine."

And she led him into a long, sunken living room filled with soft furniture, with a fresco upon one wall. They faced it as he seated himself on the green divan, and she stared at the wall as he lit two cigarettes and she handed him a final drink and joined him there.

"Lovely," he said.

"You like my fresco?"

"I hadn't noticed it."

". . . And you haven't tasted your drink."

"I know."

Her hand came to rest upon his arm, and he put his drink aside and drew her to him once again, just as she put hers to rest.

"You are quite different from most men," she said.

". . . And you from most women."

"Is it growing warm in here?"

"Very," he said.

Somewhere it is raining. Controlled or artificial—somewhere it is always raining, any time you care to think about it. Always remember that, if you can.

A dozen days had passed since the finale of the Cyborg City Mixed Open. Every day Stain and Galatea moved together somewhere. His hand upon her elbow or about her waist, she showed him Cyborg City. They laughed often, and the sky was pink and the winds were gentle and in the distance the cliffs of Ankus wore haloes of fog prismatic and crowns of snow and ice.

Then he asked her of the fresco as they sat in her living room.

"It represents the progress of human thought," she said. "That figure—far to the left, contemplating the birds in flight—is Leonardo da Vinci, deciding that man might do likewise. High at the top and somewhat to the left, the two figures ascending the ziggurat toward the rose are Dante and Virgil, the Classic and the Christian, joined together and departing the Middle Ages of Earth into a new freedom—the place where Leonardo might contemplate. That man off to the right is John Locke. That's the social contract in his hand. That man near the middle—the little man clutching the figure-eight—is Albert Einstein."

"Who is the blinded man far to the left, with the burning city at his back?"

"That is Homer."

"And *that* one?"

"Job, on a heap of rubble."

"Why are they all here?"

"Because they represent that which must never be forgotten."

"I do not understand. I have not forgotten them."

"Yet the final five feet to the right are blank."

"Why?"

"There is nothing to put there. Not in a century has there been anything worth adding. Everything now is planned, prescribed, directed—"

"And no ill comes of it, and the worlds are managed well. Do not tell me how fine were the days of glorious discontent, days through which you never lived yourself. The work done then has not gone to waste. Everything is appreciated, used."

"But what new things have been added?"

"Size, and ease of operation within it. Do not preach to me of progress. Change is not desirable for its own sake, but only if it offers improvement. I could complete your fresco for you—"

"With a gigantic machine guarded by the Angel of Death! I know!"

"You are wrong. It would end with the Garden of Eden."

She laughed.

"Now you know the story of my fresco."

He took her hand. "You may be right," he said. "I don't really know. I was only talking about how things seem to me."

"And *you* may be right," she said. "*I* don't really know . . . I just feel there should be something to counterbalance that wonderfully flexible mechanism which guides us so superbly that we are becoming the vegetables in that garden you would draw me."

"Have you any suggestions?"

"Have you read any of my papers?"

"I'm afraid not. I fool around with my own garden and I play tennis. That's about it."

"I have proposed the thesis that man's intelligence, extruded into the inanimate, has lost all that is human. Could you repair the machine that mixes our drinks, if it ceased to function?"

"Yes."

"Then you are very unusual. Most people would call in a robot which specializes in small appliance repairs."

Stain shrugged.

"Not only have we given up this function of intelligent manipulation—but divorced from us and existing elsewhere, it turns and seeks to suppress what remains of it within ourselves."

"What do you mean?"

"Why has life become a horizontal line, rather than an upward curve? One reason is that men of genius die young."

"This I cannot believe."

"I purposely published my most important papers recently and I was visited by the Angel of Death. This proved it to me."

He smiled.

"You still live, so this could not be so."

She returned his smile, and he lit two cigarettes and said, "On what subjects were the papers?"

"The Preservation of Sensibility."

"An innocuous-seeming subject."

"Perhaps."

"What do you mean 'perhaps'? Perhaps I misunderstand you."

"It would seem that you do. Sensibility is a form of esthetic consciousness cultivated by intelligence. This is lacking today and I proposed a method whereby it might be preserved. The fruits of my work were then threatened."

"And what may these be?"

She tilted her head slightly, studied his face, then, "Come with me, and I will show you," she said, and she rose and led him into her library. As he followed her, he removed from an inner pocket his black gauntlets and drew them onto his hands. Then he jammed his hands into his side pockets to cover them and entered the room at her back.

"Simule," she called out, and the tiny creature that sat before a reading machine upon her desk leapt into her extended hand, ran up her right arm and sat upon her shoulder.

"What is it?" he questioned.

"The answer," she said. "Pure, mechanistic intelligence can be countered by an infinitely mobile and easily concealed organic preserver of sensibility. This is Simule. He and others like him came to life in my laboratory.''

"Others?''

"There are many, upon many worlds already. They share a mass mind. They learn constantly. They have no personal ambition. They wish only to learn and to instruct any who wish to learn from them. They do not fear the death of their bodies, for they continue to exist thereafter as a part of the mind they all share. They—or it—are—or is—lacking in any other personal passion. The Simule could never represent a threat to the human races. I know this, for I am their mother. Take Simule into your hand, consider him, ask him anything, Simule, this is Stain; Stain, this is Simule.''

Stain extended his right hand, and the Simule leaped into it. Stain studied the tiny, six-legged creature, with its disquietingly near-human face. Near. Yet not quite. It was unmarked by the physical conversions of those abstract passion-producers men call good and evil, which show in some form upon every human countenance. It ears were large, doubtless for purposes of eavesdropping, and its two antennae quivered upon its hairless head as it raised a frail limb as if to shake hands. An eternal smile played upon its lips, and Stain smiled back.

"Hello,'' he said, and the Simule replied in a soft but surprisingly rich voice, "The pleasure is mine, sir.''

Stain said, "What is so rare as a day in June?'' and the Simule replied, "Why, the lady Galatea, of course, to whom I now return,'' and leaped and was upon her suddenly extended palm.

She clutched the Simule to her breast and said, "Those gauntlets—!''

"I put them on because I did not know what sort of creature the Simule might be. I feared it might bite. Please give him back that I might question him further—''

"You fool!'' she said. "Point your hands in another direction, unless you wish to die! Do you not know who I am!''

Then Stain knew.

"I did not know . . .'' he said.

In Shadowhall in Morgenguard the Angel of Death stands within ten thousand transport cubicles. Morgenguard, who controls the destinies of all civilized worlds, briefs his agents for anything from ten seconds to a minute and a half—and then, with a clap of thunder, dispatches them. A second later—generally—there is a flash of light and a brief report, which is the word "Done," and there then follows another briefing and another mission.

The Angel of Death is, at any given moment, any one of ten thousand anonymous individuals whose bodies bear the mark of Morgenguard, after this fashion:

Selected before birth because of a genetic heritage which includes heightened perception and rapid reflexes, certain individuals of the *Homo sapiens* variety are given a deadly powerful education under force-fed conditions. This compensates for its brevity. At age fourteen, they may or may not accept employment in the service of Morgenguard, the city-sized machine created by the mutual efforts of all civilized peoples over a period of fifteen years and empowered to manage their worlds for them. Should any decline, these individuals generally proceed to excel in their chosen professions. Should they accept, a two-year period of specialized training follows. At the end of this time, their bodies have built into them an arsenal of weapons and numerous protective devices and their reflexes have been surgically and chemically stimulated to a point of thoughtlike rapidity.

They work an eight-hour day, five days a week, with two daily coffee breaks and an hour for lunch. They receive two vacations a year and they work for fourteen years and are retired on full salary at age thirty, when their reflexes begin to slow. At any given moment, there are always at least ten thousand on duty.

On any given workday, they stand in the transport cubicles in Shadowhill in Morgenguard, receive instructions, are transported to the worlds and into the presence of the individuals who have become superfluous, dispatch these individuals and depart.

He is the Angel of Death. Life lasts long, save for him; populations would rise up like tidal waves and inundate worlds, save for him; criminals would require trials and sentencing, save for him, and of course history might reflect unnecessary twistings and turnings, save for the Angel of Death.

One dark form might walk the streets of a city and leave that city empty of life at its back. Coming in lightning and departing in thunder, no world is foreign, no face unfamiliar, and the wearer of the black gauntlets is legend, folklore and myth; for, to a hundred billion people, he is but one being with a single personality.

All of which is true. Quite, quite true.

And the Dark Angel cannot die.

Should the near-impossible occur, should some being with speed and intrepidity be standing accidentally armed at the moment his name on the roll yonder and up is being shouted, then the remains of the stricken Dark Angel vanish as, with a simultaneous lightning-and-thunder effect, another takes his place, rising, as it were, out of ashes.

The few times that this has occurred, the second has always finished the job.

But this time things were different; and what little remained of seven agents of Morgenguard had lain in cubicles, smoldered, bled, been dead.

"You are the Dark Angel, the Sword of Morgenguard," she said. "I did not mean to love you."

"Nor I you, Galatea, and were you only a mortal woman, rather than a retired Angel yourself—the only being whose body would throw back the charge upon me and destroy me, as it did the others—please believe that I would not raise my hand against you."

"I would like to believe that, Stain."

"I am going now. You have nothing to fear of me."

He turned and headed toward the door.

"Where are you going?" she asked him.

"Back to my hotel. I will be returning soon, to give a report."

"What will it say?"

He shook his head and left.

But he knew.

He stood in Shadowhall within the thing called Morgenguard. He was the Angel of Death, Emeritus, and when the old familiar voice crackled over the loudspeaker and said, "Report!" he did not say, "Done." He said, "Extremely confidential," for he knew what that meant.

There came a flash of lightning, and he stood in a larger hall before a ten-story console, and he advanced toward it and heard the order repeated once more.

"One question, Morgenguard," he said, as he halted and folded his arms upon his breast. "Is it true that you were fifteen years in the building?"

"Fifteen years, three months, two weeks, four days, eight hours, fourteen minutes and eleven seconds," Morgenguard replied.

Then Stain unclasped his arms, and his hands came together upon his breast.

Morgenguard may have realized in that instant what he was doing: but then, an Angel's body has built into it an arsenal of weapons and numerous protective devices and his reflexes have been surgically and chemically stimulated to a point of thoughtlike rapidity; also, Stain had been recalled from retirement because he was one of the ten fastest who had ever served Morgenguard.

The effect was instantaneous. The clap of thunder was not Morgenguard's doing, for he did not remove Stain in time.

The Dark Angel might never strike itself. The seven who had approached the lady Galatea had suffered from a recoil-effect from her own defense system. Never before had the power of the Dark Angel been turned upon himself, and never in the person of one. Stain had worked it out, though.

Death and destruction meeting automatic defense meeting recoil meeting defense recoil defense recoil breakthrough, and a tremendous fireball blooming like an incandescent rose rose within the heart of the city-sized machine Morgenguard.

Right or wrong, Simule will have some years to grow, he knew, in that instant, and—

—and somewhere the sun is shining, and its heart is the mobius-burn of the Phoenix Action/Reaction. Somewhere the sun is always shining, any time you care to think about it. Try to remember that, if you can. It is very important.

She remembers. Her name is Galatea. And we remember. We always remember. . . .

Worlds To Kill

by Harlan Ellison

Unimagined power leads to a godlike feeling. Must it also end in corruption?

I

Clasping the jeweled hilt of the stone kris with both hands, the Rt. Rev. Mr. Push, exalted high priest of the One Authentic Temple of God, Inc., raised it slowly heavenward, point downward, perfectly straight and parallel to his naked and painted body. When his extended elbows formed the outside points of a diamond, and the brown-stained blade was just above his head, he began to intone the sacred litany. The sound of it was picked up by the loudspeaker mike hanging around his neck, and was thrown out across the great stadium.

Even so, it was difficult making out the words where the cripple sat, across the huge tiered bowl, in the 2.50 seats. A candy butcher was shrieking. "Koola! Frynuts! Cold Koola! Hot Frynuts!" at the end of his row, and the high priest's sacred sing-song was drowned out by the commercial.

Hunkered down, legless, on his rolling cart, the leather-tanned man lifted the binoculars to his eyes again, and sighted across the bowl to the sacrificial altar, trying to lip-synch the few words he was able to make out, with the precise mouth movements of the high priest.

The litany came to an end and the crowd shouted its responses with religious enthusiasm. The legless man on the cart tracked the binoculars rapidly across the crowd, and then brought their unblinking sight back to the high priest as he arched back slightly, rib cage suddenly becoming prominent with the effort, and drove straight down, hard, with the kris, into the red circle that had been painted over the naked girl's heart.

As the kris sank in to the jeweled hilt the crowd roared, leaping to its feet, throwing sacrificial roses into the air.

On his cart, the cripple holstered his binoculars and finished his popcorn. The crowd blocked off his view of everything but their straining bodies. The voices went up and seemed to become too shrill to have emanated from human throats.

When the bedlam quieted, the legless man asked two of the nearest enthusiasts if they would lift his cart down off the seat. When they had set him in the aisle, he propelled himself with difficulty up the aisle to the exit portal, and down the ramp. Behind him another virgin was being sacrificed.

Outside the stadium, scooting along smoothly with a pair of padded wooden blocks strapped over his hands, the cripple made for a freight expressway moving like quicksilver through the suburban stadium section.

Crates of goods, force-locked in position to avoid theft or spillage, hissed past him on the maximum-speed strip, as he came abreast of a checkloading station. The clocker, a man of indeterminate age chewing on a chocolate ring, did not bother to look up as the cripple propelled himself up the short metal ramp with a forceful rowing motion. But when the little cart stopped in front of the clocker's bubble—a pie-wedge opened in its force-field so he could get the dubious benefits of the sticky moist breeze blowing across the expressways—he looked down from his seat and his eyes narrowed.

"Excuse me," the cripple asked politely, "would you do me a kind of a favor, please?"

The clocker did things with his mouth, cleaning out the bits of nuts the chocolate ring had deposited between his teeth. "What?"

A short, harsh syllable.

"I, uh, can't afford a passenger slipway, and I was wondering if you'd let me ride the freightway down to the 147th Street Oval . . .?"

The clocker was shaking his head. "No."

"You wouldn't even have to lock me on," the cripple insisted. "I can do a thing with the wheels, they've got a vacuum base. It wouldn't be any bother."

The clocker turned away.

"I'd really appreciate it," the cripple pressed him.

The clocker turned back, eyes narrowed again, mouth hard.

"Against the rules, bo, you know that. Don't wanna discuss't. Just slipaway."

The cripple's deeply tanned face grew tense, jaw muscles moved softly, and his anger extended itself through his features to his nose, which quivered like an animal's. "Some helluva way to treat a bo," he snapped. "How the hell you think I got shortn'd this way, you bastard! I worked the slips, same's you. Now I give both my legs and I come an' ask another workman same's I was, an' what I get? Dumped on, is what it is. You bastard, all I asked was for a ride down'ta the Oval, that such a big damn thing?"

The clocker looked shocked, and suddenly chagrined.

"Hey, I'm sorry, bo."

The cripple did not reply. He slipped the wooden blocks back on his hands and started to turn himself around. The clocker got down off his seat, which regained its original shape sighing softly. The clocker came and stood in front of the little cart. "No, hey, I'm really sorry, bo. It's, you know, they get you locked in with rules. Hell, I'll put you on a slip, just gimme a minute."

The cripple nodded brusquely, as though only now getting his due.

The clocker opened the access lock and walked ahead of the cart as the cripple rolled after him. The elevator dropped them down just below the level of the works, and they moved across under the maximum-speed and mid-range slipways. They came up through the loading lock between the mid-range and slow-speed slips, and the clocker got down on his knees and made ready to shove the cart onto the slowest slipway.

"Thanks," the cripple said with a smile.

The clocker made a forget-it motion with his hand, and nudged him onto the slipway. As the cripple slid away, the clocker stood up and called after him, "Hey, sorry, bo!"

Three miles down the slipway, the cripple shifted slips more adroitly than the clocker would have thought possible. He held his position on the mid-range slipway for a quarter mile, then shifted again. Now on the maximum-speed freightway, with the whining of the works making it impossible for any spy equipment of the priest's police to pick up his words, he rubbed back the flap of flesh on his right bicep that concealed the communications device, and began to report:

"Okay. Final stuff. Feed it directly to the machine. The preliminary judgments seem to be accurate. They've reached a seven stage in technology, but socially they're doing maybe four. Strong myth and religious ties. Wide open for a crash-in tactic, I think. No, make that a certainty. Couch the attack in a religious way, maybe the fall of a sun god, or a second coming kind of thing. That'll put them into a temporary panic and first penetration can be effected with minimal losses. Now I'm going to feed you the coded stuff for precision, but the one thing I couldn't code-up is the barbarism thing they've got going here. Really a bunch of animals, just under the surface. That may be our strongest weapon, so code what you can of it, and let the analyzer extrap the rest. You can get Arnak's troops ready, and tell Folger we'll need light to medium armor on the cruisers, probably nothing any heavier. Except I've got a long list of special stuff Nord'll have to rig up for particular jobs. Okay now, I'll wait for your signal for clear on the machine . . ."

He rode the express freightway another three miles, in silence, waiting.

When it came, it was a sharp jamming buzz, and he began to speak in a flat, emotionless voice, into his bicep:

"Invasion ET commence ourtime five slant two five slant zero nine-er slant thirteen hundred hours . . ."

He had long-since passed the 147th Street Oval by the time he had finished transmitting; his words had gone out through the atmosphere, directed through space in a line as straight as a thought, which was by no means straight. Curlicued and doubled-back, the transmission had been picked up by doggie stations and boosted even farther.

In another star-system altogether, the transmission had been received, and acknowledged.

On the freightway, the legless cripple rose from his cart, stretched his legs and changed his clothes quickly. When he shifted slips, back down to the low-speed strip, he was dressed as a kelp fisherman in from the fields, wearing country bumpkin clothing.

He disappeared without a trace into the amusement suburb. It was twelve days histime till the planet was scheduled to die.

II

Natives called the planet Reef. Its origins in slang went back to the first Terran explosion outward, when the immigrants, sick to death of space and wandering, had foundered on that bright planet of a blue-white star. Reef, on which they had built a world for themselves. Reef, on the verge of being invaded.

A manta was dropped down first. It sowed the winds with an alienation dust that drove every man from every other man, that sent husbands quivering from their wives and mothers from their children. The people of Reef broke into tiny communities of one frightened soul each. Then the fireballs came down, and the people trembled in fear and superstition.

Then came Folger's cruisers. The medium class stock took out the military installations and the railheads, the shipping ports and the single space center. The lightweights ranged up and down the planet slicing communications lines, blacking out television and radian, playing search-and-destroy with any pockets of possible organized resistance (as reported by the advance scout, the legless cripple, the man known as Jared). Then the troop platforms were skimmed in, and Arnak's commandos spun their spiderwebs down, waiting for the word to downdrop. Through the early morning sky the great circular black platforms rode the winds, the cilia-thin spiderwebs hanging down like sensory-feelers of some gigantic sea creature.

The commandos waited.

The psycheprobe stations were dropped in seventy previously specified locations, hit the planet at full acceleration and shucked their protective hulls on impact. They drove straight down through the crust of the planet; linking up in a network of overriding thought-patterns, the broadcast went out, jamming normal brain-signals.

In varying intensities the psycheprobes washed the minds of the invaded with hopelessness, shame, cowardice, depression, terror, paranoia, nausea, weariness, hunger, a desire to return to the womb, a realization that there was never, ever any such return possible for them . . . and back through the cycle again.

The commandos dropped.

ET of Commencement was 5/25/09/1300 hours.

In the flagship *Tempest*, Jared received the Planetary Secure signal on 5/27/09/0644 hours. It had taken forty-one hours and forty-four minutes to initiate, execute and complete the subjugation of the planet called Reef. It was the one hundred and seventy-fourth planet Jared had conquered for a client.

On the bridge of the *Tempest*, the circular hull was studded with two hundred highly sophisticated two-way viewing screens showing every phase of the securing operation.

Jared had been watching the screens; now he turned to the humanoid with the squid's head, and said softly, "Pay me."

Ram, unquestioned ruler of thirty million squid humanoids existing on a dark planet of Reef's sun, a being who had lived his life in various kinds of darkness, turned to the leathery-tanned man and his one great eye blinked quickly.

The tentacles that draped down over his chest and back twirled and fretted. "You do a magnificent job, Jared," his tentacle-semaphore twined.

"Pay me," Jared repeated.

Ram twined. "The job is not completed."

"You heard the Secure signal. You owe me the final half of your payment. Make it, Ram."

The squid-creature's rear tentacles made a plaited statement to a second squid-being near the dropshaft. Ram's lieutenant saluted with a roil, and stepped off into the dropshaft.

"He will return in a moment with the cases."

"Thank you, Ram." Jared turned back to his screens.

Ram watched him for long moments, then stepped up beside him. Jared was not a tall man; the squid-being stood a full head above him. Ram was barely capable of forming human speech, his vocal apparatus composed almost entirely of vibrating membranes. Yet he fancied himself a cosmopolite, and it pleased him to make the attempt. With a hideous parody of the speech of men, he ventured, "Yooo errr fummmm Earssss orrrginnnyyy, hiiii mmmm towwww?"

Jared kept his eyes on screen 113, where commandos were separating women from men into force-screened compounds. "Yes. I'm an Earthman. Originally."

But his tone was not one to encourage conversation. Had Ram been of Earth, he would have recognized the tone. But as he was not, "Whudddizzziddd lygggonnnn Earssss?"

Jared turned slowly.

He stared at Ram until the alien's tentacles began a reflexive twining. He did not answer, and in a few moments Ram moved away, twining behind Jared's back, "Arrogant polyp! Mercenary!"

Ram's lieutenant lifted into view, followed by two alien squids carrying metal cases. They were set down at Ram's feet, and he was just looking up, focusing the great eye, when Jared came to him. "Open them," the leathery spacer said. Ram waggled to his lieutenant.

The lieutenant undulated the command to the two squid troopers with the caskets, at the same time handing an unscrambler to one of them. The instrument was used on the force-bead locks and the caskets hissed open pneumatically.

Jared looked down into the cases, first one, then the other.

"Thank you, Ram," he said.

"One year's production of The Metal," Ram said softly, slowly, with movements like seaweed in a gentle warm ocean current. "Enough of The Metal to light a planet for a thousand years. Enough to power a million cruisers to the edge of infinity. Enough to buy a world."

"It bought you Reef," Jared said.

"This half . . . and the other half . . . two years' production of my world. The most valuable export we have ever had. What will you do with all of it?"

Jared looked at him coldly. The silence grew. Ram turned away.

Jared took the unscrambler and thumbed in a new setting. Then without another look at The Metal within the cases, he sealed them, the lids lowering on their pneumatic rods. "Aren't you curious whether I short-changed you?" Ram waggled, his interpretation tentacle signaling wry good humor.

Jared smiled at him with a noticeable lack of warmth. "You wouldn't cheat me, Ram. You want to hire me again. To conquer Signa II."

Ram's lieutenant made a frantic movement. A movement of consternation. Ram silenced him with a wave.

The squid-creature took a step toward Jared.

"Yes. Yes, I do."

Jared turned back the screens. He pointed to screen 50. "Look, Ram. The end is coming to Reef."

On the screen the sky of Reef had turned yellow with day. In the distance the red sun was a blur. Down out of that crimson sky Ram's chosen Governor was dropping, his human body drawn up inside the soft ruff of its squid head. The one great eye, its central orb gleaming green and bright, the Governor was dropping down from a squid cruiser riding safely within an attack wedge of Jared's invasion force.

The Governor was descending to take control of the conquered planet from Jared's mercenaries. His squid flesh glowed with the black and red tints of joy.

Ram's tentacles touched Jared on the shoulder.

The man who conquered worlds for a price turned half to him. Ram spoke with the intentness pattern.

"Now I have two worlds in this system. Signa II is next. Then Gola, Karthes, Vale and Kalpurnika. My people will rule the system. We lie in the center of the hub of the trade lanes. Half of everything is yours as payment. Jared?"

The mercenary wore a garment very much like a tunic. His arms were bare. Now he rubbed one muscular forearm with the stiffened fingers of his other hand. He did not respond to Ram's words; there was something of unliving stone in his expression.

"I know you've done it for other worlds," Ram pressed on. "My reports on your work were thorough. That is why I came to you. I know you've done jobs for clients several times in the same system. I *need* the other five to strengthen my position in this galaxy. They'll take Reef back if—"

Jared spoke with no intonation, flat and final. "No."

"But why?"

Jared walked away from him, then.

Ram stared after him for a few moments, then stalked after him, suddenly lashing out with tentacles that encircled the mercenary's waist and chest. He spun him around and hissed, "Yooo doooo sissss forrrr meeee!"

Jared's movements were almost too quick to see; grasping the thick ropes of the tentacles circling his waist in one hand, and the tentacles around his chest with the other, he dipped and spun out of their encircling grasp. Then he planted himself firmly, and contracted his body in a peculiar manner, literally lifting the squid creature off his feet, whirling and hurling him across the bridge. It was an unexpected and artful maneuver, and Ram careened through the air toward a bulkhead. At the beginning of the movement his legs and arms and tentacles had been a twisted mass, but instinctively he withdrew his body into the ruff of the squid head, and as he struck the wall his tentacles touched first, absorbing the shock. The humanoid body dropped down out of the squid head and he touched down on the deck no more unsettled than he had been before Jared had thrown him.

Jared aimed a finger at the alien. "I took your commission for one job, one job only, Ram. I've done my job, you've paid me. The contract is fulfilled. Go take possession of your conquered province."

Ram betrayed no sign of fury at the Earthman's words. He walked quickly to the dropshaft and disappeared. The remaining squids stood immobile, as though waiting for a command from the Earthman. He did not speak.

Then the lieutenant signaled his men and they went downship after Ram.

Not long after, Jared saw the shuttle ship of Ram and his group drop out of the *Tempest*. He followed it down on screens 71-5, his face frozen without expression.

But much later, when Arnak's commandos had been withdrawn and Ram's Governor had brought in his own holding forces, Jared's face was a field of emotions, watching the wholesale slaughter in the force-screened compounds.

In a matter of hours three-fourths of the population of Reef was dead. The remaining millions already being routed to work-areas.

Jared fed the coursecomp a route back, and went away from there.

He left the screens burning, showing space and not-space, showing stars and whirling pinwheels of galaxies.

He drenched himself in the loneliness of darkness.

The cases of The Metal remained unmoved on the bridge.

Jared took no calls on the bridge; alone, watching nothing as the *Tempest* stretched itself between the scene of his last commission and the return base.

Downship, the staff found it difficult to speak to one another. They were loyal, but there were times when their employer took on assignments they could not reconcile with even their basest motives.

It was night.

It was always night.

There was seldom anything but silence in the night.

III

Pocked, but faceless, the bulk of Jared's moon grew ever greater. Somehow, it was less a home than a return base for him. He watched it emptily, two hundred times in two hundred screens. He was compelled to close his eyes.

As they approached the snuff-out barrier that invisibly closed Jared's moon off from the rest of the universe, there on the dark edge of nowhere, he coded the signals for entry.

The crust of the blasted moon-surface rolled back and the *Tempest* entered. The moon closed over the flagship. The rest of the rolling stock was already berthed. Jared left the ship, entered one of the dropshafts ranked to one side of the mooring docks, and was sucked up to the city level.

The core of Jared's moon had been artificially-hollowed. The machine had been planted in the center. Around the core of the machine Jared's city had been built. An impregnable fortress.

He went straight to his town house, where he tore off his clothes, bathed and let the mecks massage and relax him. Then he slept for twenty-six hours.

When he arose, he punched out breakfast, though it was artificial night in the city. All around him, above and below him, the sound of the machine, vague and satisfied, hummed in the walls. The machine was thinking. He sat on the edge of a chair and ate the breakfast.

Then he turned off the air-jets that had been his bed, bathed again, and went downstairs to check what his staff had put on the memorycorders. There were six items, all coded priority.

One: a delegation from the Galactic Sodality had arrived two months previous with formal complaints to be lodged.

Two: a client from Kim. Commission: to conquer the sea-world Wah-whiting in the same solar system.

Three: a client from the Clan of Seven. Commission: to conquer the three remaining worlds in the String of Ten who would not join the Clan.

Four: an ex-client, the Ragish of Tymalle, seeking return of a portion of his payment due to an almost successful insurrection. Payment: the miracle drug Y-Kappa.

Five: a client from Bunyan IV. Commission: to conquer the woman-ruled world of Khaine in the nearby star-system.

Six: a representative of the conquered planet EElax. Commission: regain the planet for the deposed government.

He programmed them Four, Six, Three, Two, One, Five. The memorycorder assured him each of the delegations had been thoroughly searched and okayed; they had been billetted comfortably, waiting for Jared's return from the Reef job.

He sat in the office of his town house, amid the heavy oak furniture transshipped from Earth years before. He sat silently, smoking, thinking about Reef.

The slaughter had been ghastly, even greater than he had supposed—but not greater than the machine had predicted. Having fed Ram's nature, and the nature of the invasion rationale, into the machine, the prediction had been on the decimal point. The machine was always right.

Jared remembered when he had begun organizing his invasion and conquest project. The first job, a small one, utilizing ancient (and nearly forgotten) guerrilla techniques had netted him enough capital to begin the construction of the machine. It had purchased the services of the scientific staff he needed. The first prototype of the machine had been workable enough to provide plans for the second job. And from that conquest had come the first base, and troops. The organization had expanded steadily, its reputation spreading throughout the star-groups. Ten years before, he had begun the core job on the moon of this dark star's only planet. Now, closed off and untouchable, he was sought out by hundreds of clients every year. Some he interviewed, most he turned away. Of the ones seen, only a handful ever had their propositions fed into the machine. And of those scant few, only one or two were ever taken on as clients.

But when the bargain had been struck, Jared had carried off his end without failure. One hundred and seventy-four worlds had changed hands through the world-killing talents of Jared, his troops and his machine.

The city was now a large city, the machine had restructured itself and added to its own bulk; his equipment was the most advanced, his techniques the most effective. For hire. Jared, the world-killer. At first his price had been staggering sums in Galactic Funds. But as the years had passed, less and less he had accepted money.

One job might bring huge stores of an anti-death drug, another ownership of an ore planetoid, still another the placement of a certain government official. Random payments, random selection of clients, totally without form or direction. Only the name of Jared persisted, cloaked almost in legend, feared and hated.

Jared heard the sound of footsteps coming through the reception hall. He looked up as Denna Gill appeared at the head of the short flight of stairs leading down into the oak-beamed living room.

"Welcome back," the alien said.

He came down the stairs, his furball body atop its three long ostrich legs bobbing up and down. The two great, limpid eyes looked at Jared with concern. The alien's "face" was roughly humanoid in arrangement, but more closely approximated that of an intelligent bird in demeanor.

"You don't look well."

Jared slumped in the big armchair. He shoved the memory-corder pickup away from him. It rolled to its niche in the paneled wall, the wall opened, the machine rolled in, the panel closed. It was an Eighteenth Century living room again. "I'm just a little tired."

"How did it go?"

"Well enough, I suppose."

"I take it the machine was correct?"

"Ram brought it right out on the decimal point."

Gill settled down his legs till his perfectly round fuzzy head was on a level with Jared's. "You expected it."

"Doesn't mean I had to enjoy watching it."

"No. It doesn't mean that."

They sat in silence for a moment. Then Jared drew in a deep breath, shifted the conversation, and asked, "This delegation from the Sodality. Who's on it?"

"Becker from Earth, Stieglitz from Alpha C Nine, that young one, what's his name, Mosey, Morrissey . . ."

"Mosier, French I think; from the Crab?"

"That's the one."

"Anyone else?"

"The usual. Representatives of frightened planets."

"You don't sound particularly worried."

"I fed it to the machine."

"And?"

Gill bobbled his head in a movement of dismissal. "Un-important."

"I see we finally got Bunyan IV to come in."

"We've been pushing them for three years. When you bought the cake for Cooper they had to do something It was a nice maneuver."

"Don't remind me of the cost."

"But they're here, that's what counts. Think we can get what we want from them?"

"They want Khaine. They have to have it. I think they'll bite. What does the machine say?"

"No extrap on it yet."

Jared rose. "Let's start the clown-show."

The human and his companion walked out through the living room. Down a passage behind a concealed panel, to a monorail whose single track vanished in the dimness of a tunnel carved from the dead heart of the moon. In the little car, Jared passed his hand across a glowing plate and the monorail vehicle shot out of its berth. The trip lasted only seventy seconds, ending in a low cave where a dropshaft hissed softly.

Jared and Gill descended in the dropshaft and stepped off at the vacuum-lock behind the reception chamber. They passed through the lock and Jared swung the center-pin panel around. They entered the reception chamber.

A hundred million million reflections of themselves flooded back at them, washed in the silvery light of the incredible diamond that was the reception chamber.

In a position where every delegate or potential client might truly be an assassin sent by a conquered world to rid the universe of the man who hired himself out to kill worlds for a price, Jared had made it as difficult as possible for the dispensers of vengeance.

His payment for the conquest of Isopia had been the nearly impossible delivery of a diamond one-eighth of a mile in diameter. A diamond from the Glass Mountains of Isopia, selected by his geologists for this purpose. Who could kill a man when there were a hundred million million possibilities?

Jared and Gill seated themselves behind the interview consoles, and Gill signaled for the first client to be dropped down.

The Ragish of Tymalle and his group entered from the far end of the diamond, through a panel similar to the one Jared and Gill had used. They were a long way off, but their images cascaded and slipped and bounced across the chamber. Inside a diamond, they faced Jared.

It took Jared three minutes to explain clearly why even a partial return of the payment for the conquest the Ragish had commissioned was impossible. Jared made it forcefully apparent that he took no responsibilities for the inability of a client to hold what had been won for him. The Ragish and his group departed.

He took one minute to turn down the commission of the EElaxian government-in-exile.

One minute to turn down the commission from the Clan of Seven. With a ray of hope: come see me again in four years Earthtime.

One minute to dispatch the delegation from Kim. A bogus client that had somehow passed inspection. The kill attempt was a clever one, but the three aliens were vaporized even as they released the search/seek/kill missiles from their ornate brocaded clothing.

Then the neatly-tailored group from the Galactic Sodality entered.

Becker, their spokesman, was a large-bodied man with a full white beard. He instinctively impelled thoughts of kindness, wisdom, honesty, Santa Claus.

Jared knew him, and distrusted him.

Though they were at the far end of the diamond, pickups in the walls bounced their voices clearly to Jared.

"Good evening," Becker began.

"I understand you have a complaint to lodge, Mr. Becker." Jared spoke softly, but the dismissal of protocol obviously shocked Becker.

"Why, uh, that's why we've come."

"Then let's get to it."

Becker called for some files from a young man behind him, apparently Mosier of the Crab Nebula. He extended them toward Jared, far down the glimmering chamber. It was a ludicrous gesture, and Becker drew back his hand. "We have specifics enumerated herein."

"Say it, Mr. Becker. My time is short."

"This policy of conquest of yours must end. We of the Galactic Sodality have banded together in a spirit of peace and harmony, our purpose is to bring unity to the known universe. There has been war and conquest since man left Earth . . ."

"I know my history, Mr. Becker. Perhaps better than you. I've made so much of it, after all."

"Arrogance can be the death of you!"

"Hypocrisy can be yours!"

Becker stammered for a moment.

"Let me put it to you bluntly, Mr. Becker.You and your Sodality, from which in the past two years I've received applicants from nine worlds. Your spoken wish for peace is a laudable one. It may not be the best thing for me personally or commercially, but I can sympathize with it intellectually. If you get what you say you want, I'm out of business. That doesn't appeal to me particularly. But it's still a lofty concept.

"Unfortunately, you're a fraud, Mr. Becker, as is your Galactic Sodality. The nomenclature doesn't matter. Galactic Sodality. United Worlds. Planetary Nexus. I've seen them come and go. Under stress, any one of the signatories to your pact would turn on the rest of you and employ me, if they thought they had a chance of taking over the starways. Not the least of them is Earth, for which we are all supposed to harbor a deep and instinctive affection. Your ball of mud is no more honest and valuable than any other, Becker. In fact, I've had feelers from clients on Earth as regards Alpha C Nine. Mr. Stieglitz, are you there in the group . . .?"

A tall, thin Niner stepped forward. His bright red flesh was pulsing with fury. "I'm here!"

"You might inquire of Mr. Becker about that. The most recent feeler was from President Spaak himself. It was done through a Swiss Neutrality Combine on Proxima C One."

There was an immediate and heated exchange between Becker and the Niner. Jared ordered them out of the diamond.

With the warning that any attempt at mounting an attack on Jared's moon would be greeted with the same enthusiasm Jared brought to any commission he undertook.

When they were gone, the Earthman sank back in his chair. Gill watched him closely.

"Do you want to break for a while?"

Jared shook his head. "Let's get to the meat."

The delegation from Bunyan IV was dropped in, and made its application. Jared listened and when the delegate had concluded he fed the additional facts into the machine through the console. It came back, as he had hoped, affirmative.

"I'll take the job."

"At what cost?" the client asked.

"The highest possible, of course," Jared replied.

IV

It was not that Khaine was an amazon world, nor even that women dominated. It had been made obvious, however, centuries before, that women ruled better than men. Thus, the government of Khaine was almost entirely female, with "the High" a woman elected by a combination of popular vote and computer selection. The High Irina was the current ruler of the planet: part president, part queen, part spokesman of a senate; very much a woman.

She discovered the presence of Jared on Khaine only three months histime after he had arrived.

They trapped him in the Park of Cats, there in the center of the capital city of Khaine, Jerusalem.

A mixed male and female unit of intelligence rangers staked out the park and began moving toward the center. Jared had been posing as a night club comedian, a fat man with a fluffy ring of white hair that circled his head. The disguise deflated and peeled easily. He was stripped down to a skinsuit, night-black and oiled, by the time the first of the rangers found him. They were under orders to take him alive. He swung up into a tree, sending the Khainesque cats shrieking from the branches. He hurled himself forward, from tree to tree, as they tried to make out his direction in the dark.

Then they brought in the kliegs and the flamers, and burned down the trees in the direction he was heading. They had him trapped in the feather-topped trees, the lights on him, when he vanished.

High above them, against the night sky, a bright blue dot appeared, flickered for a moment, then winked out.

Jared reappeared on the left bank of the Ganges River that divided Jerusalem in two parts. He now wore a breathing apparatus over his face, and a weapons belt was slung around his waist.

He took a reading from an instrument on his wrist, then he

dove into the river. Down into its polluted darkness he swam, the special light goggles allowing only the most inadequate view through the water.

Near the bottom of the River, one of the guards from the intelligence rangers caught him blipping on his screen and came up to meet him. Jared met the man with an extended trident-spear. The guard caught the steel in his chest and disappeared tumbling awkwardly into the darkness.

Jared found the waterlock to the chamber without difficulty, and blew it with equal ease. When he had pumped out the access chamber, he unshipped his weapon and undogged the entry portal. There was silence in the chamber. Jared consulted the instrument on his wrist and turned to his right, feeling along the solid metal wall. Suddenly, it slipped back, and he was looking into a control room floor-to-ceiling with dials and circuit indicators. The woman had her back to him.

"It can't do what my machine can do," Jared said.

The woman turned suddenly, dropping a group of thin metal strips on a ring.

"You dropped your phasers."

The woman was lovelier than the dossier photo-block Jared had studied. Lovelier, but not prettier. Just lovelier, in a way no facsimile could capture. Hers was a face that had been pretty in youth, but as she had grown older the prettiness had fought a battle with the accumulation of wisdom, the encroachment of character. Merely pretty had lost. Now she was lovelier.

"Who are you . . . how did you . . .?"

"The source that let you know I was on Khaine is the same source that told me where your control chamber was to be found." He added, after a moment, "I've always felt espionage was a two-edged sword. It usually cuts both ways at the same time. Jeopardy is the operable word, I believe."

She went for a button on a wall. He caught her before she had reached it. She spun him around as he grabbed her arm. He felt her apply the leverage and tried to check himself, but she used his inertia against him and he went up against the wall, and rebounded.

She went for the button again.

He fired and the beam sizzled past her, blowing the button, the circuit, and half the wall out.

The concussion pitched her sidewise and she struck her

neck on the edge of a components cabinet. Her eyes rolled up and she fell to the deck.

Jared rose slowly, and went to her.

She was only unconscious.

He snapped a breather on her, hoisted her over his shoulder and left the control chamber.

Rising up through the river, he could not tell if she had stopped breathing. It was not till he had disassembled them, beamed them, and reassembled them in the observation center of the *Tempest* that he called in the surgeon and was told she would be all right.

They were three days out from Khaine, heading for the moon, when she came up from under the sedatives.

She looked around, instantly grasped where she was, and tried to escape. Jared had her put under again. It would not to do to have the High Irina of Khaine die in the airless, colorless spaces of not-space.

Gill was waiting. He looked worried. It was not an expression a human would hold if he were worried, but Gill was a Mexla and Jared knew his moods. He was worried.

"What if she won't cooperate?"

"I don't expect her to want to."

Gill sank and rose on his legs. "Then how the hell—"

"No, not a brainscan; and not drugs. I've got to make her want to do it."

"How the hell—"

"You said that: if you haven't something constructive, pass off and let me get on with it."

"Jared, my God, what if . . . what if . . ." He could not even frame the thought. It was much too dangerous, much too horrible a thought.

Jared touched the alien gently. "Gill, we've come this far. If we're wrong now, if all of your 'what ifs' are so . . . if somewhere along the way it went bad and we never knew it . . . then we are what they say we are. If we've done it right, then it'll work out all right."

Gill bobbled in a resigned manner. "You going to see the machine now?"

Jared nodded. "Is it programmed?"

Gill walked him to the dropshaft. "Up to the top."

Jared touched him again, gently ruffling his fur. "Be at peace, old friend." Then said, "No way back now."

He dropped down through the center of the moon, till he came to the force-locks that separated men from the machine. He unscrambled them, with the only unit that worked—a unit phased in with his brain wave patterns.

The great port opened, and Jared passed in to speak to the machine. It had been many years since he had been summoned down for a consultation.

Now he stood before it, as it rose up out of sight in the gut of the moon. He stood before the metal brain he had caused to be built, to serve him as he killed worlds for profit.

"Hello, Jared," the machine said.

"It's been a long time," Jared answered. He went to the formfit chair the machine kept for him. He sat down and oddly, for the first time in years, he was totally relaxed. Talking to the machine was exactly like talking to Gill, for the machine had selected the voiceprints of the little alien as his own. The gentle warmth of Gill's tones came from the air around Jared, but it was the voice of the machine, faintly oiled and cool in the caverns.

"Did you bring the High?"

"Yes, I brought her. You're certain it was a necessity for the invasion?"

"Have I ever been wrong?"

Jared chuckled softly. "If you have, I've no way of checking you."

The machine chittered to itself as though considering. "Is it that you think perhaps you've given too much power to a machine, mine creator?"

"It isn't seemly for a machine to mock its master."

"Sorry. Only asking."

"No, it's not that I think you have too much power, it's that I'm afraid if you blow a circuit somewhere, and reroute buggy, we may all wind up saying, 'Yes, massa' to the robots."

"I have no desire to rule men. I am content."

Jared let it lie. The machine could not lie, it could not obfuscate. But it might program itself for a specious truth.

"You're worried about the invasion of Khaine." The machine pinpointed Jared's problem.

"You haven't told me much this time."

"There are reasons. You set me only one chore, Jared. I am directed to the fulfillment of that chore. I have to do what is necessary. Till now we have been in the first phase of the program. Now we are about to enter the second, the most difficult phase. There was only one weak link."

"And that was . . .?"

The machine waited. "You."

Jared's eyes widened. Many things suddenly became clear to him. He sank down in the formfit, his mind a whirling cyclone of disorder.

Finally, he said, "So now we need the High Irina."

The machine answered quickly. "Yes. *We* need her, and *you* need her. Men often become too much like their machines, Jared. Then they blame the machines for dehumanizing them. For fifteen years I have worked on the program with you. And you worked on it alone for seven years before I was built. Twenty-two years, Jared, a large part of any man's life. Larger than most for yours, because the task you've set yourself is destined to kill you. You've become too much like me. Yes, we need the High."

They talked on, for many hours.

Then Jared dropped up to his city, where Gill met him. Jared looked exhausted. He was able to smile at the alien for a moment before he whispered, "Take me home, Gill. I need sleep."

Then he slumped down and the Mexla took him through the tunnels to the town house, where he stripped him and sent him to sleep on the restful jets of warm air.

And then the alien went to his own home.

But he did not sleep.

V

Gill could not understand it. After the machine had made it an imperative that Jared, himself, personally, run the recon mission to Khaine, and personally capture the High Irina himself, there was no place in the incredibly simple invasion plan for her use.

The machine had only told them that much, at the outset of the commission. *Capture the High Irina.* So Jared had risked his life and had done it. Then Jared had gone down below and had his talk with the machine, and said nothing about it.

But the next day they had had their battle plan, and the High

Irina's only place in it was that the machine insisted she be on board the *Tempest* to witness the invasion in all of its phases.

Gill was nervous, worried. It seemed wrong. There *was* something wrong, terribly wrong.

Now, as they watched the final stages of the mop-up, as the client from Bunyan IV chuckled like a madman beside them, Gill checked the force-bonds on the High, and wished they had never accepted the commission.

She had not spoken throughout the campaign. It had been a one-day affair; Khaine was terribly vulnerable. Now it was killed, even as she watched.

Jared had paid no attention to her, but had taken his position before the two hundred screens and supervised the slaughter. She had not spoken when they turned the skyline of Jerusalem glowing red, nor when the city winked out of existence. She had not spoken when they ran the strafing missions with the stukas across the plandar refineries, nor when they made a glass-sided crater of the mountain armaments base. She watched silently, and when the Planetary Secure signal came through, she closed her eyes and sank back against her bonds.

The client from Bunyan IV—tall and thin as something out of an Earth legend, with knobs at the joints, a nose sharp as a letter opener, and eyes slitted and green—turned to Jared as the world-assassin said, "That's it, Seventeen. The job is done."

"Fine, just fine," said the alien, snapping his joints with delight. He had laughed hysterically throughout the operation. Jared despised him.

"One more tiny thing, though," Seventeen said, palming out a razor-disc. He turned to the High, where she sat force-shackled. "Goodbye, my Irina."

He cracked back in three sharp stages cocking his arm to spin off the disc. Irina stared at him coldly. She was not frightened.

"No!"

The word cracked as sharply as had Seventeen's joints. Seventeen swiveled his long head in stages. Jared was staring at him evenly. The wire-thin arm with the razor-disc did not lower.

"I said: no."

Seventeen laughed with the shrieking high sound of a

lunatic. "This is the High Irina, assassin. She is the only one who could lead a counter-attack against me. It is that she must die. Now!" He jerked back.

"I haven't been paid yet, Seventeen."

"In good time, assassin."

"Now."

"First I attend myself to final things first."

"Don't make me kill you, Seventeen," Jared said, behind him. The client from Bunyan IV snapped back in stages, and saw the weapon in Jared's hand.

"What is this?"

"I want to be paid now. Right now."

Seventeen tried to keep his eyes on both Gill and Jared at the same time. The fuzzy alien was working his way around the bridge slowly. Seventeen could tell he was being stalked, but he did not know why.

"You never told me what it is that is payment."

Jared nodded toward the woman.

"No!" The word was Jared's word, said as loud and with as much imperativeness as the world-killer had said it, a moment before.

Jared moved closer, aiming the weapon and realigning himself so the beam would miss vital instruments behind Seventeen. "She's mine. That's my payment. Kill her and I call back my units. In three days we can be at Bunyan IV; what you saw here can be repeated there."

Seventeen lowered the disc.

"She is yours."

Jared's reply was pleasant. "Thank you, Seventeen. Now go take possession."

The client from Bunyan IV dropped out of sight, and in the screens a few minutes later the shuttleship dropped out of the *Tempest* in a similar manner. Then Jared spoke to Gill.

"Relay the transfer affirmative. Let them take it now."

Gill rose on his legs and went to pass ownership of Khaine to the Bunyan IV fleet hanging just outside the detector range of the conquered planet.

Irina watched as the alien ships dropped down through the atmosphere of her planet. Now . . . she averted her eyes.

Finally, when she looked up, Jared was watching her. "You should have let him kill me," she said in a low and level voice. "You'll never have a secure moment while I live." Jared put away his weapon.

"You'll talk to a friend of mine," Jared said.

And he turned away from her.

When they returned to Jared's moon, she tried to kill him as the force-bonds were removed. It was an abortive effort, and Gill managed to get the sedative-spray into her skull without too much thrashing around.

When she woke, she was in the caverns, in the formfit, in the presence of the machine.

Then the machine proved to her that Jared paid a far higher price for his conquests than did any of his clients. The machine opened channels in her brain that had always been blocked by environment and loyalties and age.

Then she knew who Jared really was, and what he was doing . . .

"It was a futile, noble idea," the machine said. "It was doomed from the start; until I was created. Then it stood a chance. Twenty-two years. Now it is a possibility. Order in the known universe. Worlds linked to worlds by mutual respect and mutual ethic. Now it is a possibility. We have conquered each world in a manner to give Jared's clients possession—but not permanent possession. When the time comes, because of the manner of conquest and because of the stresses we have set up in a master program, all the parts will fall into place. Each invader will fall, but in a way that will link the worlds in reliance upon one another. Cogs in a great galactic machine. Not like their petty Sodalities and Unions, but a great humanistic structure that will serve all men as individuals and all worlds as entities."

Irina, no longer the High, listened to it all, her mind absorbing the truth of the machine because it had been at last opened to truth.

"Jared's loneliness is that he knows he must do this job alone, for it is the only way it *can* be done. And if he fails, or if he dies in the process, his name will live on in the memory of the million worlds as the greatest villain the universe ever spawned. It is now an additional part of my task to keep him sane, keep him honest, keep him alive, so the job can be done. Each payment he took was an aid to getting the master program implemented. Even you. Most importantly, you."

Irina rose.

The machine added only, "Not just as his woman, if you decide to stay. But to learn all he knows, to take over for him if he dies. And if there is time, to give him children who can do the job after him. This is one secret that must be shared with silence. Only the alien Gill knows, and he cannot help Jared."

She left the chamber, dropped up, and was met by the fuzzy Mexla. "Will you stay?" he asked her.

"I'll stay," she said, and then paused, as if she wanted to say something else. "Not now," she finally said. "Another time, when I can say what I have to say."

Gill took her to him, where he slept. And he left her there, watching him as he turned in his sleep, thinking awful thoughts of death and futility. And she looked at him, not loving him, perhaps never loving him, not really liking him, for she could never like the man who had showed her the sights in the two hundred screens, but willing to stay; wondering in the silent words she had not been able to speak to Gill:

Why should this god be any more successful than all the other gods who have failed?

But across the empty reaches of space there was no answer, only silent attention from the million worlds that waited to become parts of a master universe, or to curse till eternity the names of those who killed planets for profit.

In The Bone

by Gordon R. Dickson

The illusion of power often leads to hubris *(false pride). But the acceptance of powerlessness often promotes determination.*

I

Personally, his name was Harry Brennan.

Officially, he was the *John Paul Jones*, which consisted of four billion dollars' worth of irresistible equipment—the latest and best of human science—designed to spread its four thousand-odd components out through some fifteen cubic meters of space under ordinary conditions—designed also to stretch across light-years under extraordinary conditions (such as sending an emergency messenger-component home) or to clump into a single magnetic unit in order to shift through space and explore the galaxy. Both officially and personally—but most of all personally—he represents a case in point.

The case is one having to do with the relative importance of the made thing and its maker.

It was, as we know, the armored horseman who dominated the early wars of the Middle Ages in Europe. But, knowing this, it is still wise to remember that it was not the iron shell that made the combination of man and metal terrible to the enemy—but rather the essentially naked man inside the shell. Later, French knights depending on their armor went down before the cloth-yard shafts of unarmored footmen with bows, at Crécy and Poitiers.

And what holds true for armor holds true for the latest developments of our science as well. It is not the spacecraft or the laser on which we will find ourselves depending when a time of ultimate decision comes, but the naked men within and behind these things. When that time comes, those who rank the made thing before its maker will die as the French knights died at Crécy and Poitiers. This is a law of nature as

47

wide as the universe, which Harry Brennan, totally unsuspecting, was to discover once more for us, in his personal capacity.

Personally, he was in his mid-twenties, unremarkable except for two years of special training with the *John Paul Jones* and his superb physical condition. He was five-eleven, a hundred seventy-two pounds, with a round, cheerful face under his brown crew-cut hair. I was Public Relations Director of the Project that sent him out; and I was there with the rest to slap him on the back the day he left.

"Don't get lost, now," said someone. Harry grinned.

"The way you guys built this thing," he answered, "if I got lost the galaxy would just have to shift itself around to get me back on plot."

There was an unconscious arrogance hidden in that answer, but no one marked it at the time. It was not the hour of suspicions.

He climbed into the twelve-foot-tall control-suit that with his separate living tank were the main components of the *John Paul Jones* and took off. Up in orbit, he spent some thirty-two hours testing to make sure all the several thousand other component parts were responding properly. Then he left the solar system.

He clumped together his components, made his first shift to orbit Procyon—and from there commenced his explorations of the stars. In the next nine weeks, he accumulated literally amazing amounts of new information about the nearby stars and their solar systems. And—this is an even better index of his success—located four new worlds on which men could step with never a spacesuit or even a water canteen to sustain them. Worlds so like Earth in gravity, atmosphere and even flora and fauna, that they could be colonized tomorrow.

Those were his first four worlds. On the fifth he encountered his fate—a fate for which he was unconsciously ripe.

The fact was the medical men and psychologists had overlooked a factor—a factor having to do with the effect of Harry's official *John Paul Jones* self upon his entirely human personal self. And over nine weeks this effect changed Harry without his ever having suspected it.

You see, nothing seemed barred to him. He could cross light-years bv touching a few buttons. He could send a sensing element into the core of the hottest star, into the most poisonous planetary atmospheres or crushing gravities, to look around as if he were down there in person. From orbit, he could crack open a mountain, burn off a forest or vaporize a section of icecap in search of information just by tapping the energy of a nearby sun. And so, subtly, the unconscious arrogance born during two years of training, that should have been noted in him at take-off from Earth, emerged and took him over—until he felt that there was nothing he could not do; that all things must give way to him; that he was, in effect, master of the universe.

The day may come when a man like Harry Brennan may hold such a belief and be justified. But not yet. On the fifth Earthlike world he discovered—World 1242 in his records— Harry encountered the proof that his belief was unjustified.

II

The world was one which, from orbit, seemed to be the best of all the planets which he had discovered were suitable for human settlement; and he was about to go down to its surface personally in the control-suit, when his instruments picked out something already down there.

It was a squat, metallic pyramid about the size of a four-plex apartment building; and it was radiating on a number of interesting frequencies. Around its base there was mechanical movement and an area of cleared ground. Further out, in the native forest, were treaded vehicles taking samples of the soil, rock and vegetation.

Harry had been trained for all conceivable situations, including an encounter with other intelligent, space-going life. Automatically, he struck a specific button, and immediately a small torpedo-shape leaped away to shift through alternate space and back to Earth with the information so far obtained. And a pale, thin beam reached up and out from the pyramid below. Harry's emergency messenger component ceased to exist.

Shaken, but not yet really worried, Harry struck back instantly with all the power his official self could draw from the GO-type sun, nearby.

The power was funneled by some action below, directly

into the pyramid itself; and it vanished there as indifferently as the single glance of a sunbeam upon a leaf.

Harry's mind woke suddenly to some understanding of what he had encountered. He reached for the controls to send the *John Paul Jones* shifting into the alternate universe and away.

His hands never touched the controls. From the pyramid below, a blue lance of light reached up to paralyze him, select the control-suit from among the other components and send it tumbling to the planetary surface below like a swatted insect.

But the suit had been designed to protect its occupant, whether he himself was operative or not. At fifteen hundred feet, the drag chute broke free, looking like a silver cloth candle-snuffer in the sunlight; and at five hundred feet the retro-rockets cut in. The suit tumbled to earth among some trees two kilometers from the pyramid, with Harry inside bruised, but released from his paralysis.

From the pyramid, a jagged arm of something like white lightning lashed the ground as far as the suit, and the suit's outer surface glowed cherry-red. Inside, the temperature suddenly shot up fifty degrees; instinctively Harry hit the panic button available to him inside the suit.

The suit split down the center like an overcooked frankfurter and spat Harry out; he rolled among the brush and fernlike ground cover, six or seven meters from the suit.

From the distant pyramid, the lightning lashed the suit, breaking it up. The headpiece rolled drunkenly aside, turning the dark gape of its interior toward Harry like the hollow of an empty skull. In the dimness of that hollow Harry saw the twinkle of his control buttons.

The lightning vanished. A yellow lightness filled the air about Harry and the dismembered suit. There was a strange quivering to the yellowness; and Harry half-smelled, half-tasted the sudden, flatbite of ozone. In the headpiece a button clicked without being touched; and the suit speaker, still radio-connected with the recording tank in orbit, spoke aloud in Harry's voice.

"Orbit . . ." it said. ". . . into . . . going . . ."

These were, in reverse order, the last three words Harry had recorded before sighting the pyramid. Now, swiftly gain-ing speed, the speaker began to recite backwards, word for word, everything Harry had said into it in nine weeks. Faster it went, and faster until it mounted to a chatter, a gabble, and finally a whine pushing against the upper limits of Harry's auditory register.

Suddenly, it stopped.

The little clearing about Harry was full of silence. Only the odd and distant creaking of something that might have been a rubbing branch or an alien insect, came to Harry's ears. Then the speaker spoke once more.

"Animal . . ." it said flatly in Harry's calm, recorded voice and went on to pick further words from the recordings, ". . . beast. You . . . were an animal . . . wrapped in . . . made clothing. I have stripped you back to . . . animal again. Live, beast. . . ."

Then the yellowness went out of the air and the taste of ozone with it. The headpiece of the dismembered suit grinned, empty as old bones in the sunlight. Harry scrambled to his feet and ran wildly away through the trees and brush. He ran in panic and utter fear, his lungs gasping, his feet pounding the alien earth, until the earth, the trees, the sky itself swam about him from exhaustion; and he fell tumbling to earth and away into the dark haven of unconsciousness.

When he woke, it was night, and he could not quite remember where he was or why. His thoughts seemed numb and unimportant. But he was cold, so he blundered about until he found the standing half-trunk of a lightning-blasted tree and crept into the burned hollow of its interior, raking frill-edged, alien leaves about him out of some half-forgotten instinct, until his own body-warmth in the leaves formed a cocoon of comfort about him; and he slept.

From then on began a period in which nothing was very clear. It was as if his mind had huddled itself away somehow like a wounded animal and refused to think. There was no past or future, only the endless now. If now was warm, it had always been warm; if dark—it had always been dark. He learned to smell water from a distance and go to it when he was thirsty. He put small things in his mouth to taste them. If they tasted good he ate them. If he got sick afterwards, he did not eat them again.

Gradually, blindly, the world about him began to take on a

certain order. He came to know where there were plants with portions he could eat, where there were small creatures he could catch and pull apart and eat and where there was water.

He did not know how lucky he was in the sheer chance of finding flora and fauna on an alien world that was edible—let alone nourishing. He did not realize that he had come down on a plateau in the tropical highlands, with little variation in day and night temperature and no large native predators which might have attacked him.

None of this, he knew. Nor would it have made any difference to him if he had, for the intellectual center of his brain had gone on vacation, so to speak, and refused to be called back. He was, in fact, a victim of severe psychological shock. The shock of someone who had come to feel himself absolute master of a universe and who then, in a few short seconds, had been cast down from that high estate by something or someone inconceivably greater, into the state of a beast of the field.

But still, he could not be a true beast of the field, in spite of the fact his intellectual processes had momentarily abdicated. His perceptive abilities still worked. His eyes could not help noting, even if incuriously, the progressive drying of the vegetation, the day-by-day shifting in the points of setting and rising of the sun. Slowly, instinctively, the eternal moment that held him stretched and lengthened until he began to perceive divisions within it—a difference between *now* and *was*, between *now* and *will be*.

III

The day came at last when he saw himself.

A hundred times he had crouched by the water to drink and, lowering his lips to its surface, seen color and shape rising to meet him. The hundredth and something time, he checked, a few inches above the liquid plane, staring at what he saw.

For several long seconds it made no sense to him. Then, at first slowly, then with a rush like pain flooding back on someone rousing from the anesthesia of unconsciousness, he recognized what he saw.

Those were eyes at which he stared, sunken and dark-circled

under a dirty tangle of hair. That was a nose jutting between gaunt and sunken cheeks above a mouth, and there was a chin naked only because once an ultrafine laser had burned out the thousand and one roots of the beard that grew on it. That was a man he saw—*himself*.

He jerked back like someone who has come face-to-face with the devil. But he returned eventually, because he was thirsty, to drink and see himself again. And so, gradually, he got used to the sight of himself.

So it was that memory started to return to him. But it did not come back quickly or all at once. It returned instead by jerks and sudden, partial revelations—until finally the whole memory of what had happened was back in his conscious mind again.

But he was really not a man again.

He was still essentially what the operator of the pyramid had broken him down into. He was still an animal. Only the memory and imaginings of a man had returned to live like a prisoner in a body that went on reacting and surviving in the bestial way it had come to regard as natural.

But his animal peace was broken. For his imprisoned mind worked now. With the control-suit broken up—he had returned to the spot of its destruction many times, to gaze beastlike at the rusting parts—his mind knew he was a prisoner, alone on this alien world until he died. To know that was not so bad, but remembering this much meant remembering also the existence of the someone or something that had made him a prisoner here.

The whoever it was who was in the pyramid.

That the pyramid might have been an automated, mechanical device never entered his mind for a moment. There had been a personal, directed, living viciousness behind the announcement that had condemned him to live as a beast. No, in that blank-walled, metallic structure, whose treaded mechanical servants still prospected through the woods, there was something alive—something that could treat the awesome power of a solar tap as a human treated the attack of a mosquito—but something *living*. Some being. Some Other, who lived in the pyramid, moving breathing, eating and gloating—or worse yet, entirely forgetful of what he had done to Harry Brennan.

And now that he knew that the Other was there, Harry

began to dream of him nightly. At first, in his dreams, Harry whimpered with fear each time the dark shape he pursued seemed about to turn and show its face. But slowly, hatred came to grow inside and then outside his fear. Unbearable that Harry should never know the face of his destroyer. Lying curled in his nest of leaves under the moonless, star-brilliant sky, he snarled, thinking of his deprivation.

Then hate came to strengthen him in the daylight also. From the beginning he had avoided the pyramid, as a wild coyote avoids the farmyard where he was once shot by the farmer. But now, day after day, Harry circled closer to the alien shape. From the beginning he had run and hidden from the treaded prospecting machines. But now, slowly, he grew bolder, standing close enough at last to touch them as they passed. And he found that they paid no attention to him. No attention at all.

He came to ignore them in turn, and day by day he ventured closer to the pyramid. Until the morning came when he lay, silently snarling, behind a bush, looking out across the tread-trampled space that separated him from the nearest copper-colored face of the pyramid.

The space was roughly circular, thirty meters across, broken only by a small stream which had been diverted to loop inwards toward the pyramid before returning to its original channel. In the bight of the loop a machine like a stork straddled the artificial four-foot-wide channel, dipping a pair of long necks with tentacle-clustered heads into the water at intervals. Sometimes Harry could see nothing in the tentacles when they came up. Occasionally they carried some small water creature which they deposited in a tank.

Making a perfect circle about the tramped area, so that the storklike machine was guarded within them, was an open fence of slender wands set upright in the earth, far enough apart for any of the machines that came and went to the forest to pass between any two of them. There seemed to be nothing connecting the wands, and nothing happened to the prospecting machines as they passed through—but the very purposelessness of the wands filled Harry with uneasiness.

It was not until after several days of watching that he had a chance to see a small native animal, frightened by something in the woods behind it, attempt to bolt across a corner of the clearing.

As it passed between two of the wands there was a waveriness in the air between them. The small animal leaped high, came down and lay still. It did not move after that, and later in the day, Harry saw the indifferent treads of one of the prospecting machines bury it in the trampled earth in passing.

That evening, Harry brought several captive, small animals bound with grass up to the wand line and thrust them through, one by one at different spots. All died.

The next night he tried pushing a captive through a small trench scooped out so that the creature passed the killing line below ground level. But this one died also. For several days he was baffled. Then he tried running behind a slow-moving machine as it returned and tying a small animal to it with grass.

For a moment as the front of the machine passed through, he thought the little animal would live. But then, as the back of the machine passed the line, it, too, died.

Snarling, Harry paced around outside the circle in the brush until the sun set and stars filled the moonless sky.

In the days that followed, he probed every gap in the wand-fence, but found no safe way through it. Finally, he came to concentrate on the two points at which the diverted stream entered and left the circle to flow beneath the storklike machine.

He studied this without really knowing what he was seeking. He did not even put his studying into words. Vaguely, he knew that the water went in and the water came out again unchanged; and he also wished to enter and come out safely. Then, one day, studying the stream and the machine, he noticed that a small creature plucked from the water by the storklike neck's mass of tentacles was still wriggling.

That evening, at twilight, while there was still light to see, he waded up the two-foot depth of the stream to the point where the killing line cut across its watery surface and pushed some more of his little animals toward the line underwater.

Two of the three surfaced immediately, twitched and floated on limply, to be plucked from the water and cast aside on the ground by the storklike machine. But the third swam on several strokes before surfacing and came up living to scramble ashore, race for the forest and be killed by wands further around the circle.

Harry investigated the channel below the killing line. There was water there up to his mid-thigh, plenty to cover him completely. He crouched down in the water and took a deep breath.

Ducking below the surface, he pulled himself along with his fingertips, holding himself close to the bottom. He moved in as far as the tentacled ends. These grabbed at him, but could not reach far enough back to touch him. He saw that they came within a few inches of the gravel bottom.

He began to need air. He backed carefully out and rose above the water, gasping. After a while his hard breathing stopped, and he sat staring at the water for a long while. When it was dark, he left.

The next day he came and crept underwater to the grabbing area of the storklike machine again. He scooped out several handfuls of the gravel from under the place where the arms grabbed, before he felt a desperate need for air and had to withdraw. But that day began his labors.

IV

Four days later the bottom under the grasping tentacles was scooped out to an additional two feet of depth. And the fifth twilight after that, he pulled himself, dripping and triumphant, up out of the bend of the diverted stream inside the circle of the killing wands.

He rested and then went to the pyramid, approaching it cautiously and sidelong like a suspicious animal. There was a door in the side he approached through which he had seen the prospecting machines trundle in and out. In the dimness he could not see it; and when he touched the metallic side of the structure, his fingers, grimed and toughened from scrabbling in the dirt, told him little. But his nose, beast-sensitive now, located and traced the outline of the almost invisible crack around the door panel by its reek of earth and lubricant.

He settled down to wait. An hour later, one of the machines came back. He jumped up, ready to follow it in; but the door opened just before it and closed the minute it was inside—nor was there any room to squeeze in beside it. He hunkered down, disappointed, snarling a little to himself.

He stayed until dawn and watched several more machines enter and leave. But there was no room to squeeze inside, even with the smallest of them.

During the next week or so he watched the machines enter and leave nightly. He tied one of his small animals to an entering machine and saw it pass through the entrance alive and scamper out again with the next machine that left. And every night his rage increased. Then, wordlessly, one daytime after he had seen a machine deep in the woods lurch and tilt as its tread passed over a rock, inspiration took him.

That night he carried through the water with him several cantaloupe-sized stones. When the first machine came back to the pyramid, in the moment in which the door opened before it, he pushed one of the rocks before the right-hand tread. The machine, unable to stop, mounted the rock with its right tread, tilted to the left and struck against that side of the entrance.

It checked, backed off and put out an arm with the grasping end to remove the rock. Then it entered the opening. But Harry was already before it, having slipped through while the door was still up and the machine busy pulling the stone aside.

He plunged into a corridor of darkness, full of clankings and smells. A little light from the opening behind him showed him a further, larger chamber where other machines stood parked. He ran toward them.

Long before he reached them, the door closed behind him, and he was in pitch darkness. But the clanking of the incoming machine was close behind him, and the adrenalized memory of a wild beast did not fail him. He ran, hands outstretched, directly into the side of the parked machine at which he had aimed and clambered up on it. The machine entering behind him clanked harmlessly past him and stopped moving.

He climbed cautiously down in the impenetrable darkness. He could see nothing; but the new, animal sensitivity of his nose offered a substitute for vision. He moved like a hunting dog around the chamber, sniffing and touching; and slowly a clear picture of it and its treaded occupants built up in his mind.

He was still at this when suddenly a door he had not seen opened almost in his face. He had just time to leap backwards as a smaller machine with a boxlike body and a number of upward-thrusting arms entered, trundled to the machine that had just come back and began to relieve the prospecting machine of its sample box, replacing it with the one it carried itself

This much, in the dim light from the open door, Harry was able to see. But then, the smaller machine turned back toward the doorway; and Harry, waking to his opportunity, ducked through ahead of it.

He found himself in a corridor dimly lit by a luminescent strip down the center of its ceiling. The corridor was wide enough for the box-collecting machine to pass him; and, in fact, it rolled out around him as he shrank back against one metal wall. It went on down the corridor, and he followed it into a larger room with a number of machines, some mobile, some not, under a ceiling lit as the corridor had been with a crossing translucent strip.

In this area all the machines avoided each other—and him. They were busy with each other and at other incomprehensible duties. Hunched and tense, hair erect on the back of his neck and nostrils spread wide, Harry moved through them to explore other rooms and corridors that opened off this one. It took him some little time; but he discovered that they were all on a level, and there was nothing but machines in any of them. He found two more doors with shallow steps leading up to them, but these would not open for him; and though he watched by one for some time, no machine went up the steps and through it.

He began to be conscious of thirst and hunger. He made his way back to the door leading to the chamber where the prospecting machines were parked. To his surprise, it opened as he approached it. He slipped through into darkness.

Immediately, the door closed behind him; and sudden panic grabbed him, when he found he could not open it from this side. Then, self-possession returned to him.

By touch, smell and memory, he made his way among the parked machines and down the corridor to the outside door. To his gratification, this also opened when he came close. He slipped through into cool, fresh outer air and a sky already graying with dawn. A few moments later, wet but free, he was back in the woods again.

From then on, each night he returned. He found it was not

necessary to do more than put any sizable object before a returning machine. It would stop to clear the path, and he could enter ahead of it. Then, shortly after he was inside, a box-collecting machine would open the inner door.

Gradually, his fear of the machines faded. He came to hold them in a certain contempt. They always did the same thing in the same situation, and it was easy to trick or outmaneuver them

But the two inner doors of the machine area with the steps would not open to him; and he knew the upper parts of the pyramid were still unexplored by him. He sniffed at the cracks of these door, and a scent came through—not of lubricating medium and metal alone, but of a different musky odor that raised the hairs on the back of his neck again. He snarled at the doors.

He went back to exploring minutely the machine level. The sample boxes from the prospecting machines, he found, were put on conveyorbelt-like strips that floated up on thin air through openings in the ceiling—but the openings were too small for him to pass through. But he discovered something else. One day he came upon one of the machines taking a grille off the face of one of the immobile devices. It carried the grille away, and he explored the opening that had been revealed. It was the entrance to a tunnel or duct leading upward; and it was large enough to let him enter it. Air blew silently from it; and the air was heavy with the musky odor he had smelled around the doors that did not open.

The duct tempted him, but fear held him back. The machine came back and replaced the grille; and he noticed that it fitted into place with a little pressure from the outside, top and bottom. After the machine had left he pressed, and the grille fell out into his hands.

After a long wait, he ventured timorously into the tube— but a sudden sound like heavy breathing mixed with a wave of a strong, musky odor came at him. He backed out in panic, fled the pyramid and did not come back for two days.

When he came back, the grille was again neatly in place. He removed it and sat a long time getting his courage up. Finally, he put the grille up high out of reach of the machine which had originally removed it and crawled into the duct.

He crept up the tube at an angle into darkness. His eyes

were useless, but the musky odor came strongly at him. Soon, he heard sounds.

There was an occasional ticking, then a thumping or shuffling sound. Finally, after he had crawled a long way up through the tube, there was a sound like a heavy puffing or hoarse breathing. It was the sound that had accompanied the strengthening of the musky odor once before; and this time the scent came strong again.

He lay, almost paralyzed with terror in the tube, as the odor grew in his nostrils. He could not move until sound and scent had retreated. As soon as they had, he wormed his way backward down to the lower level and freedom, replaced the grille and fled for the outside air, once again.

But once more, in time, he came back. Eventually returned to explore the whole network of tubes to which the one he had entered connected. Many of the branching tubes were too small for him to enter, and the biggest tube he could find led to another grille from which the musky-smelling air was blasted with force.

Clearly it was the prime mover for the circulation of air through the exhaust half of the pyramid's ventilating system. Harry did not reason it out to himself in those intellectual terms, but he grasped the concept wordlessly and went back to exploring those smaller tubes that he could crawl into.

These, he found, terminated in grilles set in their floors through which he could look down and catch a glimpse of some chamber or other. What he saw was mainly incomprehensible. There were a number of corridors, a number of what could be rooms containing fixed or movable objects of various sizes and shapes. Some of them could be the equivalent of chairs or beds—but if so, they were scaled for a being plainly larger than himself. The lighting was invariably the low-key illumination he had encountered in the lower, machine level of the pyramid, supplied by the single translucent strip running across the ceiling.

Occasionally, from one grille or another, he heard in the distance the heavy sound of breathing, among other sounds, and smelled more strongly the musky odor. But for more than a week of surreptitious visits to the pyramid, he watched through various grilles without seeing anything living.

V

However, a day finally came when he was crouched, staring down into a circular room containing what might be a bed shape, several chair shapes and a number of other fixed shapes with variously spaced and depthed indentations in their surfaces. In a far edge of the circular room was a narrow alcove, the walls of which were filled with ranked indentations, among which several lights of different colors winked and glowed.

Suddenly, the dim illumination of the room began to brighten. The illumination increased rapidly, so that Harry cringed back from the grille, lifting a palm to protect his dimness-accustomed eyes. At the same moment, he heard approaching the sound of heavy breathing and sniffed a sudden increase in the musky odor.

He froze. Motionless above the grille, he stopped even his breathing. He would have stopped his heart if he could, but it raced, shaking his whole body and sounding its rapid beat in his ears until he felt the noise of it must be booming through the pyramid like a drum. But there was no sign from below that this was so.

Then, sliding into sight below him, came a massive figure on a small platform that seemed to drift without support into the room.

The aperture of the grille was small. Harry's viewpoint was cramped and limited, looking down directly from overhead. He found himself looking down onto thick, hairless brown-skinned shoulders, a thick neck with the skin creased at the back and a forward-sloping, hairless brown head, egg-shaped in outline from above, with the point forward.

Foreshortened below the head and shoulders was a bulging chinline with something like a tusk showing; it had a squat, heavy, hairless, brown body and thick short forearms with stubby claws at the end of four-fingered hands. There was something walruslike about the tusks and the hunching—and the musky odor rose sickeningly into Harry's human nostrils.

The platform slid level with the alcove, which was too narrow for it to enter. Breathing hoarsely, the heavy figure on it heaved itself suddenly off the platform into the alcove, and the stubby hands moved over the pattern of indentations. Then, it turned and heaved itself out of the alcove, onto the flat, bed surface adjoining. Just as Harry's gaze began to get a full-length picture of it, the illumination below went out.

Harry was left, staring dazzled into darkness, while the heavy breathing and the sound of the figure readjusting itself on the bed surface came up to his ears. After a while, there was no noise but the breathing. But Harry did not dare move. For a long time he held his cramped posture, hardly breathing himself. Finally, cautiously, inch by inch, he retreated down the tube, which was too small to let him turn around. When he reached the larger tubes, he fled for the outside and the safety of the forest.

The next day, he did not go near the pyramid. Or the next. Every time he thought of the heavy, brown figure entering the room below the grille, he became soaked with the clammy sweat of a deep, emotional terror. He could understand how the Other had not heard him or seen him up behind the grille. But he could not understand how the alien had not *smelled* him.

Slowly, however, he came to accept the fact that the Other had not. Possibly the Other did not have a sense of smell. Possibly . . . there was no end to the possibilities. The fact was that the Other had not smelled Harry—or heard him—or seen him. Harry was like a rat in the walls—unknown because he was unsuspected.

At the end of the week, Harry was once more prowling around back by the pyramid. He had not intended to come back, but his hatred drew him like the need of a drug addict for the drug of his addiction. He had to see the Other again, to feed his hate more surely. He had to look at the Other, while hating the alien, and feel the wild black current of his emotions running toward the brown and hairless shape. At night, buried in his nest of leaves, Harry tossed and snarled in his sleep, dreaming of the small steam backing up to flood the interior of the pyramid, and the Other drowning—of lightning striking the pyramid and fire racing through it—of the Other burning. His dreams became so full of rage and so terrible that he woke, twisting and with the few rags of clothing that still managed to cling unnoticed to him, soaked with sweat.

In the end, he went back into the pyramid.

Daily he went back. And gradually, it came to the point

where he was no longer fearful of seeing the Other. Instead, he could barely endure the search and the waiting at the grilles until the Other came into sight. Meanwhile, outside the pyramid in the forest, the frill-edged leaves began to dry and wither and drop. The little stream sank in its bed—only a few inches, but enough so that Harry had to dig out the bottom of the streambed under the killing barrier in order to pass safely underwater into the pyramid area.

One day he noticed that there were hardly any of the treaded machines out taking samples in the woods any more.

He was on his way to the pyramid through the woods, when the realization struck him. He stopped dead, freezing in midstride like a hunting dog. Immediately, there flooded into his mind the memory of how the parking chamber for the treaded machines, inside the base of the pyramid, had been full of unmoving vehicles during his last few visits.

Immediately, also, he realized the significance of the drying leaves, the dropping of the water level of the stream. And something with the urgency of a great gong began to ring and ring inside him like the pealing of an alarm over a drowning city.

Time had been, when there had been no pyramid here. Time was now, with the year fading and the work of the collecting machines almost done. Time would be, when the pyramid might leave.

Taking with it the Other.

He began to run, instinctively, toward the pyramid. But, when he came within sight of it, he stopped. For a moment he was torn with indecision, an emotional maelstrom of fear and hatred all whirling together. Then, he went on.

He emerged a moment later, dripping, a fist-sized rock in each hand, to stand before the closed door that gave the machines entrance to the pyramid. He stood staring at it, in broad daylight. He had never come here before in full daylight, but his head now was full of madness. Fury seethed in him, but there was no machine to open the door for him. It was then that the fury and madness in him might have driven him to pound wildly on the door with his stones or to wrench off one of the necks of the storklike machine at the stream and try to pry the door open. Any of these insane things he might have done and so have attracted discovery and the awesome power of the machinery and killing weapons at the command of the Other. Any such thing he might have done if he was simply a man out of his head with rage—but he was no longer a man.

He was what the Other had made him, an animal, although with a man locked inside him. And like an animal, he did not rave or rant, any more than does the cat at the mousehole, or the wolf waiting for the shepherd to turn in for the night. Instead, without further question, the human beast that had been Harry Brennan—that still called himself Harry Brennan, in a little, locked-away, back corner of its mind—dropped on his haunches beside the door and hunkered there, panting lightly in the sunlight and waiting.

Four hours later, as the sun was dropping close to the treetops, a single machine came trundling out of the woods. Harry tricked it with one of his stones and, still carrying the other, ran into the pyramid.

He waited patiently for the small collecting machine to come and empty out the machine returned from outside, then dodged ahead of it, when it came, into the interior, lower level of the pyramid. He made his way calmly to the grille that gave him entrance to the ventilating system, took out the grille and entered the tube. Once in the system, he crawled through the maze of ductwork, until he came at last to the grille overlooking the room with the alcove and the rows of indentations on the alcove walls.

When he looked down through the grille, it was completely dark below. He could hear the hoarse breathing and smell the musky odor of the Other, resting or perhaps asleep, on the bed surface. Harry lay there for a number of slow minutes, smelling and listening. Then he lifted the second rock and banged with it upon the grille.

For a second there was nothing but the echoing clang of the beaten metal in the darkness. Then the room suddenly blazed with light, and Harry, blinking his blinded eyes against the glare, finally made out the figure of the Other rising upright upon the bed surface. Great, round, yellow eyes in a puglike face with a thick upper lip wrinkled over two tusks stared up through the grille at Harry.

The lip lifted, and a bubbling roar burst from the heavy

fat-looking shape of the Other. He heaved his round body off
the bed surface and rolled, waddling across the floor to just
below the grille.

Reaching up with one blunt-clawed hand, he touched the
grille, and it fell to the floor at his feet. Left unguarded in the
darkness of the ductwork, Harry shrank back. But the Other
straightened up to his full near six and a half feet of height
and reached up into the ductwork. His blunt clawed hand
fastened on Harry and jerked. Off balance, Harry came tumbling to the floor of the chamber.

A completely human man probably would have stiffened up
and broken both arms, if not his neck, in such a fall. Harry,
animal-like, attempted to cling to the shape of the Other as he
fell, and so broke the impact of his landing. On the floor, he
let go of the Other and huddled away from the heavy shape,
whimpering.

The Other looked down, and his round, yellow eyes focused on the stone Harry had clung to even through his fall.
The Other reached down and grasped it, and Harry gave it up
like a child releasing something he has been told many times
not to handle. The Other made another, lower-toned, bubbling roar deep in his chest, examining the rock. Then he laid
it carefully aside on a low table surface and turned back to
stare down at Harry.

Harry cringed away from the alien stare and huddled into
himself, as the blunt fingers reached down to feel some of the
rags of a shirt that still clung about his shoulders.

The Other rumbled interrogatively at Harry. Harry hid his
head. When he looked up again, the Other had moved over to
a wall at the right of the alcove and was feeling about in some
identations there. He bubbled at the wall, and a second later
Harry's voice sounded eerily in the room.

". . . You are . . . the one I . . . made a beast . . ."

Harry whimpered, hiding his head again.

"You can't . . ." said Harry's voice, ". . . even speak
now. Is . . . that so . . ."

Harry ventured to peek upward out of his folded arms, but
ducked his head again at the sight of the cold, yellow eyes
staring down at him.

". . . I thought . . . you would be . . . dead by now,"
said the disembodied voice of Harry, hanging in the air of the
chamber. ". . . Amazing . . . survival completely without

. . . equipment. Must keep you now . . ." The eyes, yellow as topaz, considered Harry, huddled abjectly on the floor, ". . . cage . . . collector's item . . ."

The alien revolved back to the indentations of the wall a little way from the alcove. The broad, fleshy back turned contemptuously on Harry, who stared up at it.

The pitiful expression of fear on Harry's face faded suddenly into a soundless snarl. Silently, he uncoiled, snatched up the rock the Other had so easily taken from him, and sprang with it onto the broad back.

As he caught and clung there, one arm wrapped around a thick neck, the stone striking down on the hairless skull, his silent snarl burst out at last into the sound of a scream of triumph.

The Other screamed too—a bubbling roar—as he clumsily turned, trying to reach around himself with his thick short arms and pluck Harry loose. His claws raked Harry's throat-encircling arm, and blood streamed from the arm; but it might have been so much stage makeup for the effect it had in loosening Harry's hold. Screaming, Harry continued to pound crushingly on the Other's skull. With a furious spasm, the alien tore Harry loose, and they both fell on the floor.

The Other was first up; and for a second he loomed like a giant over Harry, as Harry was scrambling to his own feet and retrieving the fallen rock. But instead of attacking, the Other flung away, lunging for the alcove and the control indentations there.

Harry reached the alcove entrance before him. The alien dodged away from the striking rock. Roaring and bubbling, he fled waddling from his human pursuer, trying to circle around the room and get back to the alcove. Half a head taller than Harry and twice Harry's weight, he was refusing personal battle and putting all his efforts into reaching the alcove with its rows of indented controls. Twice Harry headed him off; and then by sheer mass and desperation, the Other turned and burst past into the alcove, thick hands outstretched and grasping at its walls. Harry leaped in pursuit, landing and clinging to the broad, fleshy back.

The other stumbled under the added weight, and fell, face down. Triumphantly yelling, Harry rode the heavy body to the floor, striking at the hairless head . . . and striking . . . and striking . . .

VI

Sometime later, Harry came wearily to his senses and dropped a rock he no longer had the strength to lift. He blinked around himself like a man waking from a dream, becoming aware of a brilliantly lit room full of strange shapes—and of a small alcove, the walls of which were covered with rows of indentations, in which something large and dead lay with its head smashed into ruin. A deep, clawing thirst rose to take Harry by the throat, and he staggered to his feet.

He looked longingly up at the dark opening of the ventilator over his head; but he was too exhausted to jump up, cling to its edge and pull himself back into the ductwork, from which he could return to the stream outside the pyramid and to the flowing water there. He turned and stumbled from the chamber into unfamiliar rooms and corridors.

A brilliant light illuminated everything around him as he went. He sniffed and thought he scented, through the musky reek that filled the air about him, the clear odor of water. Gradually, the scent grew stronger and led him at last to a room where a bright stream leaped from a wall into a basin where it pooled brightly before draining away. He drank deeply and rested.

Finally, satiated, he turned away from the basin and came face-to-face with a wall that was all-reflecting surface; and he stopped dead, staring at himself, like Adam before the Fall.

It was only then, with the upwelling of his returning humanness, that he realized his condition. And words spoken aloud for the first time in months broke harshly and rustily from his lips like the sounds of a machine unused for years.

"My God!" he said, croakingly. "I've got no clothes left!"

And he began to laugh. Cackling, cackling rasping more unnaturally even than his speech, his laughter lifted and echoed hideously through the silent, alien rooms. But it was laughter all the same—the one sound that distinguishes man from the animal.

He was six months after that learning to be a complete human being again and finding out how to control the pyramid. If it had not been for the highly sophisticated safety devices built into the alien machine, he would never have lived to complete that bit of self-education.

But finally he mastered the controls and got the pyramid into orbit, where he collected the rest of his official self and shifted back through the alternate universe to Earth.

He messaged ahead before he landed; and everybody who could be there was on hand to meet him as he landed the pyramid. Some of the hands that had slapped his back on leaving were raised to slap him again when at last he stepped forth among them.

But, not very surprisingly, when his gaunt figure in a spare coverall now too big for it, with shoulder-length hair and burning eyes, stepped into their midst, not one hand finished its gesture. No one in his right senses slaps an unchained wolf on the back; and no one, after one look, wished to risk slapping the man who seemed to have taken the place of Harry.

Of course, he was still the same man they had sent out—of *course* he was. But at the same time he was also the man who had returned from a world numbered 1242 and from a duel to the death there with a representative of a race a hundred times more advanced than his own. And in the process he had been pared down to something very basic in his human blood and bone, something dating back to before the first crude wheel or chipped flint knife.

And what was that? Go down into the valley of the shades and demand your answer of a dead alien with his head crushed in, who once treated the utmost powers of modern human science as a man treats the annoyance of a buzzing mosquito.

Or, if that once-mighty traveler in spacegoing pyramids is disinclined to talk, turn and inquire of other ghosts you will find there—those of the aurochs, the great cave bear and the woolly mammoth.

They, too, can testify to the effectiveness of naked men.

What Rough Beast

by Damon Knight

Having power is one thing. Controlling it is quite another.

> *Surely some revelation is at hand;*
> *Surely the Second Coming is at hand. . . .*
>
> *And what rough beast, its hour come round at last,*
> *Slouches toward Bethlehem to be born?*

—William Butler Yeats, *"The Second Coming"*

Mr. Frank said to me, "Hey, you. Get that corner cleaned up." He was big man with red face, mouth always open little bit, wet lips always pulling back quick over little yellow teeth. This I remember, late at night, just after rush from theaters and before bars close. Place was empty, all sick light on the tiles and brown tabletops. Outside, dark and wet. People going by with coat collars turned up and faces blue-gray like rain.

On corner table was some dishes, some food spilled. I cleaned up, put dishes in kitchen sink on top of big stack, then came back to Mr. Frank. He was cutting tomato for sandwiches, using his knife too quick and hard. The end of his big thumb was white from holding knife.

I said to him, "Mr. Frank, I work here three weeks and you call me, 'Hey, you.' My name is Kronski. If is too hard to remember, say Mike. But not 'hey, you.' "

He looked down on me, with lips pulling away from yellow teeth. The sides of his nose turned yellow-white, like I saw before when he was mad. And his knife went cut. He sucked air between teeth, and grabbed his hand. I saw the blood coming out dark as ink from the side of his thumb. Blood was dripping dark on board and pieces of tomato. It was deep cut, bleeding hard. He said through teeth, "Now look what you made me do. Christ!"

69

From other end of counter, Mr. Harry called out, "What's the matter?" He started toward us—a thin man, bald, with big eyes blinking all time like afraid.

Was my fault. I went quickly to Mr. Frank, but he pushed me away with his elbow. "Get off of me, you creep!"

Now Mr. Harry looked on Mr. Frank's thumb and he whistled, then turned and went to the medicine box on wall. Mr. Frank was holding his wrist and swearing. From the cashier's desk at front of cafeteria, Mr. Wilson the night manager was coming. I heard his footsteps on the tiles.

Mr. Harry was trying to put bandage on, but it would not stick. Mr. Frank pushed him out of the way, shouting, "God damn it!" and pulled the medicine box off wall. Always bleeding.

I got quickly a fork and handkerchief, not clean, but best I could do. I tied a knot in the handkerchief, and tried to put it around Mr. Frank's wrist, but he pushed me away again.

"Give me that," said Mr. Harry, and he took from me the fork and the handkerchief. Now Mr. Frank was leaning back against coffee machine looking white, and Mr. Harry slipped the handkerchief over his wrist.

Always was blood, over counter, duckboards, steam tables, everything. Mr. Harry tried to tighten the fork, but he dropped it and picked up. He took it saying, "Get out of the way, will you?" and started to turn the handkerchief.

"Better call a hospital," said Mr. Wilson's voice behind me. Then, "Look out!"

Mr. Frank had his eyes turned up and mouth open. His knees started to bend and then he was falling, and Mr. Harry tried to catch, but too late, and he also went down.

Mr. Wilson was going around end of counter, so I went the other way to telephone.

Was in my pocket, no dimes. I thought to go back and ask, but it would take minute. I thought maybe Mr. Frank would die, because I was not quick. So I put fingers in the metal hole where coin is supposed to come back, and was no coin there; but I felt deeper, down where turning place was, and I found it and I turned. Then, was a dime lying in coin hole. So I took it and put in top of telephone. I called ambulance for Mr. Frank.

Then I went back to where he was lying, and they were by his side squatting, and Mr. Wilson looked up and said, "Did you call the hospital?'' I said yes, but without listening he said, ''Well, get out of the way then. Harry, you take the feet and we'll straighten him out a little.''

I could see Mr. Frank's red shirt front, and hand wrapped now in gauze, also red, with tourniquet around his wrist. He was lying without moving.

I went to stand at end of the counter, out of way. I was feeling very bad for Mr. Frank. I saw he was mad, and I knew he was cutting with knife, so it was my fault.

After long while came a policeman, and he looked on Mr. Frank, and I told how it happened. Mr. Harry and Mr. Wilson also told, but they could not tell all, because they did not see from beginning. Then came ambulance, and I asked Mr. Wilson could I go with Mr. Frank to hospital. So he said, ''Go on, I don't care. We won't need you here after tonight, anyhow, Kronski.'' He looked on me from bright glasses. He was gray-haired man, very neat, who alway spoke cheerful but thought suspicious. I liked Mr. Harry, and even Mr. Frank, but him I could never like.

So I was fired. Not new feeling for me. But I thought how in year, two years, or even sooner, those men would forget I was ever alive.

I was working in place three weeks, night shift, cleaning up tables and stacking dishes in sink for dishwasher. It is not enough to make a place different because you are there. But if you make no difference, you are not living.

At the hospital, they wheeled Mr. Frank up indoors and took him in elevator. Hospital woman asked me questions and wrote down on a big paper, then policeman came again, and was more questions.

''Your name is Michael Kronski, right? Been in this country long?''

''Since twenty years.'' But I told a lie, was only one month. Policeman said, ''You didn't learn English very good, did you?''

''For some is not easy.''

''You a citizen?''

''Sure.''

''When naturalized?''

I said, ''Nineteen Forty-one.'' But it was a lie.

He asked more questions, was I in army, how long belong

to union, where I worked before, and always I would lie. Then he closed book.

"All right, you stick around till he comes to. Then if he says there was no assault, you can go on home."

In hospital was quiet like grave. I sat on hard bench. Sometimes doors opened, doctor shoes squeaked on floor. Then telephone went *brr* very quiet, hospital woman picked up and talked so I could not hear. She was blonde, I think from bottle, with hard lines in cheeks.

She put down telephone, talked to policeman for minute, then he came over to me. "Okay, they fixed him up. He says he did it himself. You a friend of his?"

"We work together. *Did* work. Is something I can do?"

"They're going to let him go, they need the bed. But somebody ought to go home with him. I got to get back on patrol."

"I will take him to his home, yes."

"Okay." He sat down on bench, looked on me. "Say, what kind of an accent is that, anyhow? You Chesky?"

"No." I would say yes, but this man had the face of a Slav. I was afraid he should be Polish. Instead, I told different lie. "Russian. From Omsk."

"No," he said slow, looking on me hard, and then spoke some words in Russian. I did not understand, it was too different from Russiche, so I said nothing.

"Nyet?" asked policemen, looking on me with clear gray eyes. He was young man, big bones in cheeks and jaw, and lines of smiling around mouth.

Just then came down the elevator with Mr. Frank and nurse. He had a big white bandage on hand. He looked on me and turned away.

Policeman was writing in his book. He looked on me again. He said something more in Russian. I did not know the words, but one of them was like word for "pig" in Russiche. But I said nothing, looked nothing.

Policeman scratched his head. "You say you're from Russia, but you don't understand the language. How come?"

I said, "Please, when we leave Russia, I was young boy. In house was speaking only Yiddish."

"Yeah? Ir zent ah Yidishe' yingl?"

"Vi den?"

Now was better, but still he did not look happy. "And you only spoke Yiddish in the home?"

"Sometimes French. My mother spoke French, also my aunt."

"Well—that might account for it, I guess." He closed book and put away. "Look, you got your naturalization papers on you?"

"No, is home in box."

"Well, hell, you ought to carry them on you. Times like these. You remember what I said. All right, take it easy now."

I looked up, and was no Mr. Frank. I went quickly to desk. "Where did he go?"

Woman said very cold, "I don't know what you mean." Each word separate, like to child.

"Mr. Frank, was just here."

She said, "Down the hall, the payment office." And pointed with yellow pencil over her shoulder.

I went, but in hall I stopped to look back. Policeman was leaning over desk to talk with woman, and I saw his book in pocket. I knew there would be more questions, maybe tomorrow, maybe next week. I took long breath, and closed eyes. I reached down where turning place of book was. I found it, and turned. I felt it happen.

Policeman never noticed; but next time he would look in book, would be no writing about me. Maybe would be empty pages, maybe something else written. He would remember, but without writing is no good.

Mr. Frank was by window in hall, pale in face, arguing with man in office. I came up, I heard him say, "Twenty-three bucks, ridiculous."

"It's all itemized, sir." Man inside pointed to piece of paper in Mr. Frank's hand.

"Anyway, I haven't got that much."

I said quickly, "I will pay." I took out purse.

"I don't want your money," said Mr. Frank. "Where would you get twenty-three bucks? Let the workmen's pay for it."

"Please, for me is pleasure. Here, you take." I pushed money at man behind window.

"All right, give him the God damn money," said Mr. Frank, and turned away.

"That's it," said Mr. Frank. Was street of old thin houses, with stone steps coming down like they would stick out all their gray tongues together. I paid the taxi driver, and helped Mr. Frank up steps. "What floor you live?"

"Fourth. I can make it."

But I said, "No, I help you," and we went up stairs. Mr. Frank was very weak, very tired, and now his lips did not pull back over teeth any more.

We went down long hall into kitchen and Mr. Frank sat down by table under the sour yellow light. He leaned his head on hand. "I'm all right. Just let me alone now, okay?"

"Mr. Frank, you are tired. Eat something now, then sleep."

He did not move. "What sleep? In three hours I got to be on my day job."

I looked on him. Now I understood why was cutting so hard with knife, why was so quick anger.

"How long you worked two jobs?" I said.

He leaned back in chair and put his hand with white bandage on the table. "Year and a half."

"Is no good. You should quit one job."

"What the hell do you know about it?"

I wanted to ask more, but then behind me the door opened and someone came in. I looked, and it was young girl in a blue bathrobe, pale without makeup, holding bathrobe closed at her neck. She looked on me once, then said to Mr. Frank, "Pop? What's the matter?"

"Ah, I cut my damn hand. He brought me home."

She went to table. "Let me see."

"It don't amount to nothing. Come on, Anne, don't fuss, will you?"

She stepped back, once more looking on me. She had good face, thin, with strong bones. She said, like talking to herself, "Well, don't let me bother you." She turned and went out, and door closed.

Mr. Frank said after minute, "You want a drink or anything? Cup of coffee?" He was still sitting same way at table.

"No, no thanks, thanks just same. Well, I think now I will go."

"All right. Take care yourself. See you at work."

I went out, and for minute could not remember which end of hall was door. Then I remembered we turn right to go in kitchen, so I turned left, and found door at end of hall and went outside.

In little light, Anne was standing part bent over, looking on me with big eyes. I stood and could not move. It was not outside hall, it was some other room—I could see part of dressing table, and bed, and then I saw she had bathrobe pulled down from shoulder and was leaning to look in mirror. Then she covered up shoulder quickly, but not before I saw what was there.

She said in hard quiet voice, "Get out of here. What's the matter with you?"

And I wanted to move away, but could not. I took instead one step toward her and said, "Let me see it."

"What?" She could not believe.

"The burn. Let me see, because I know I can help you."

She had hand tight at her neck, holding the bathrobe together, and she said, "What do you know about—"

"I can do it," I said. "Do you understand? If you want, I will help." I stopped, and stood waiting and looking on her.

In the small light I could see that her face got pink, and the eyes very bright. She said very hard, "You can't," and looked away. She was crying.

I said, "Believe me."

She sat down and after minute she took hard breath and opened the bathrobe from shoulder. "All right, look then. Pretty?"

I took one more step and was close. I could see her neck, smooth and like cream. But on the shoulder and across the chest was skin hard and white, standing up in strings and lumps, like something that would melt and boil, and then harden.

She had her head down, and eyes shut, crying. I was crying also, and inside was big hurt trying to get out. I touched her with my hand, and I said, "My dear."

She jumped when hand touched her, but then sat still. I felt under my fingertips cold skin, touch like lizard. Inside me was big hurt jumping, I could not hold in very long. I rubbed her very easy, very slow with my fingers, looking and feeling where was inside the wrong kind of skin. Was not easy to do. But if I did not do it this way, then I knew I would do it without wanting, all at once, and it would be worse.

To make well all at once is no good. Each cell must fit

with next cell. With my fingertips I felt where down inside
the bottom part of bad skin was, and I made it turn, and
change to good skin, one little bit at a time.

She sat still and let me do it. After while she said, "It was
a fire, two years ago. Pop left a blowtorch lit, and I moved it,
and there was a can of plastic stuff with the top off. And it
went up—"

I said, "Not to talk. Not necessary. Wait. Wait." And
always I rubbed softly the bad skin.

But she could not bear to have me rub without talking, and
she said, "We couldn't collect anything. It said right on the
can, keep away from flame. It was our fault. I was in the
hospital twice. They fixed it, but it just grew back the same
way. It's what they call keloid tissue."

I said, "Yes, yes, my dear, I know."

Now was one layer on the bottom, soft skin instead of
hard; and she moved a little in the chair, and said small
voice, "It feels better."

Under my fingertips the skin was still hard, but now more
soft than before. When I pushed it, was not like lizard any
more, but like glove.

I worked, and she forgot to be ashamed until came a noise
at door opening at front of apartment. She sat up straight,
looking around and then on me. Her face got pink again, she
grabbed my wrist. "What are you *doing?*"

In minute I knew she would jump up and pull her bathrobe,
and then maybe she would yell, so whatever happened, it
would not be her fault.

But I could not let her do it. I was also ashamed, and my
ears like on fire, but to stop now was impossible. I said loud,
"No, sit down." I held her in the chair, and kept my fingers
on her skin. I did not look up, but I heard Mr. Frank's feet
come into room.

I heard him say, "Hey, you. What do you think you're up
to?"

And the girl was trying to get up again, but I held her still,
and I said, "Look. Look." With tears running down my
cheeks.

Under my fingers was a little place of good, soft skin,
smooth like cream. While I moved my fingers, slowly this
place got bigger. She looked down, and she forgot to breathe.

From corner of my eye, I saw Mr. Frank come nearer, with

face mad and wondering. He said once more. "Hey," with lips pulling back hard over teeth, and then he looked on shoulder of his daughter. He blinked eyes like not believing, and then looked again. He put his hand on it, quick, hard, and then took away like burned.

Now was changing more fast the rest of skin. Was like rubbing from a window the frost. Still they were not moving, the daughter and Mr. Frank, and then he went down on knees beside chair with arm around her and arm around me holding so hard that it hurt, and we were all three tight together, all three hot wet faces.

Since I was small boy in Novo Russie—what they call here Canada, but it is all different—always I could see where beside this world is many other worlds, so many you could not count. To me is hard thing to understand that other people only see what is here.

But then I learned also to reach, not with hands but with mind. And where this world touches other world, I learned to turn so that little piece of it would be different. At first I did this without knowing, when I was very sick, and frightened that I would die. Without knowing it I reached, and turned, and suddenly, I was not sick. Doctor was not believing, and my mother prayed a long time, because she thought God saved my life by a miracle.

Then I learned I could do it. When I learned badly in school, or if something else I would not like would happen, I could reach and turn, and change it. Little by a little, I was changing pieces of world.

At first was not so bad, because I was young boy and I only did things for myself, my own pleasure.

But then I was growing up, and it was making me sad to see how other people were unhappy. So then I would begin to change more. My father had a bad knee, I made it well. Our cow broke her neck and died. And I made her alive again.

First I was careful, then not so careful. And at last they saw that I did it.

Then everyone said I was going to be a great rabbi, they prayed over me, and they talked to me so much that I believed it.

And I worked miracles.

Then one day I began to see that what I did was bad. I

made so many patches in world that it was not world any more, but mistake. If you would try to make chair better by many patches, putting a piece oak wood here, and piece cherry wood there, until all was patches, you would make a worse chair than before.

So I saw every day that I was only making more patches, but I would not let myself know it was bad. And at last I could not bear it, and I reached back far, I changed not little bit, but whole country. I reached back before I was born, and I turned, and I changed it.

And when I looked up, all world around me was different— houses, fields, people.

My father's house was not there. My mother, my brothers, my sisters, they were all gone; and I could not bring them back.

After I fixed Anne's shoulder, it was like party, with wine on table, and Italian bread and sweet butter, and salami, and what they call here bagels, and from radio in next room, music playing loud and happy. Pretty soon from across hall came a lady named Mrs. Fabrizi to complain from noise, and in two minutes she was also one of party, hugging Anne and crying, then talking and laughing louder than the rest of us. Next from upstairs it was young man, Dave Sims, painter, and also joined us. Mrs. Fabrizi went back to her apartment and brought some lasagna, which is with pasta and cheese, and very good, and from upstairs Dave brought bottle of whiskey. We all loved each other, and to look on each other made us laugh because we all were so happy. Anne was now with lipstick and her hair combed, and she was wearing a blue evening dress with no top. She could not keep her hand from touching smooth place on her shoulder and chest, and every time she would touch it, she would stop like surprised. But she was worried because new skin was brown, not white like cream, and it made a patch you could see.

But I explained to her, "Is because if you would not have accident, then you would go often to beach and get brown. So when I turn where you do not have accident, that skin is brown, you see?"

"I don't get it, at all," said Dave, and I could see from their faces, they did not understand either. So I said, "Look. From time God made the world, if a thing was possible, it must happen. Right? Because otherwise it would not be

God." I looked on Mrs. Fabrizi, I knew she was religious woman, but in her eyes was no understanding.

Dave said slowly, "You mean, wait a minute— You mean, if a thing is possible, but doesn't happen, that would limit God's powers, is that it? His powers of creation, or something?"

I nodded. "Yes, that is it."

He leaned over table. On one side Anne and Frank were also leaning, and on other side Mrs. Fabrizi, but still only Dave understanding.

"But look," he said, "plenty of things that could happen, don't. Like this pickle—I *could* throw it on the floor, but I'm not going to, I'm going to eat it." And he took a bite, and grinned. "See? It didn't happen."

But I said, "It did. It happened that you threw it on floor. Look." And while I said it, I reached and turned, and when they looked where I pointed, there was pickle on the floor.

Then they all laughed like joke, and Frank slapped Dave on back, saying, "That's a good one on you!" And it was a minute before I saw they thought it was only joke, and that I threw pickle on floor myself.

Dave was also laughing, but waving at me the piece of pickle in his hand. "I've got the trump card," he said. "Right here—see? I didn't throw it, I ate it."

But I said, "No, you didn't." And once more I turned, and in his fingers was no pickle.

Then they all laughed more than ever, except Dave, and after minute Anne touched her chest and stopped laughing too. Frank was poking Dave in shirt, and saying, "Where is it? Hah? Where is it?" Then he also stopped and looked on me. Only Mrs. Fabrizi laughed, and her high voice sounded like hen until Frank said, "Pipe down a second, Rosa, for Pete's sake."

Dave looked on me and said, "How did you do that?"

I was warm inside from the wine and whiskey, and I said, "I try to explain to you. If a thing is possible, somewhere it happens. It must happen, otherwise God is not God. Do you see? It is like each world is a card in a deck of cards. Each one, little bit different. Annie, in some worlds you had accident, and in some worlds you did not have it. So I reach, and turn, one little place at a time. Wherever I turn, it can be a little place like head of match, or it can be a big like a building.

And it can be from a long time ago, hundred years, five hundred years, or only minute. So always I think of place I turn like this: it is a shape like ice-cream cone. Here on top is what we see now, then down here at bottom is little dot, week ago, or year ago. If long time ago, cone is long—if short time ago, cone is short. But from little sharp dot at the bottom comes all this cone, and makes here at the top all things different.''

"Let me get this straight," said Dave, running had through hair. "You mean, if you change any little thing in the past, then everything that happened afterward has to be different?"

I said, "Yes. Only I do not really change, because all these things exist already. I cannot make another world, but I can reach, and take piece of another world where it already is, and bring here so that you see it. So with Anne, before—I turn one little bit of skin, then another little bit of skin. And I make good skin come where bad skin was. So it is colored brown, because in worlds where you did not have accident, you went to beach and became brown.''

They all looked on me. Frank said, "This is still too deep for me. What do you mean, you turn—?" He made twisting motion with his fingers.

I said, "It is like revolving door. Suppose should be little tiny revolving door—or I can make it big, any size—but suppose on one side is one world, on other side, another world. So I turn—" I showed them with my hands—"until little piece of this world is here, and little piece of that world there. That's what I mean when I turn.''

Frank and Dave sat back and looked on each other, and Frank made blowing sound with his lips. "Hell, you could do anything," he said.

"Not anything. No.''

"Well, damn near. Jesus Christ, when I start to thinking about—" Then he and Dave were talking all together. I heard ". . . cure every sick person . . ." ". . . water into wine . . ." ". . . wait a minute, what about . . ." After while Mrs. Fabrizi yelled, "Wait. Waita, you men. Can you fixa my kitch' a-ceiling?"

Then they all began to laugh and shout, and I did not know why it was a joke, but I laughed too, and we all went to Mrs. Fabrizi's apartment, laughing and hanging on to each other not to fall down.

Next morning before I was awake, they were in living room talking, and when I came out, they could not wait to tell me ideas. From remembering the night before I was ashamed, but they made me sit down and drink coffee, and then Anne brought eggs, and not to make her feel bad, I eat.

Always, if I do good for someone, I should do it in secret like a robber. I know this. So, if I would have climbed in window when Anne was sleeping and fix shoulder, then would be no trouble. But no, I let myself be sad for her, I fix it with big scene, and then worse, I am full of wine, I talk big, and I fix kitchen ceiling. So now I was in trouble.

They were looking on me with such love in eyes that I was inside like butter melting. First it was, "Mike you are so wonderful," and "Mike how can we ever thank you," and then pretty soon they wanted to see some trick, because they still could not believe. So like a fool, I threw a nickel on table, and showed them where it was possible nickel should land here, here, or here. And each place, I turned, and was another nickel until was on table ten of them in a row. And to them it was if I should make water flow from the rock.

Then Anne was pink and holding hands tight together, but she said to me, "Mike, if you wouldn't mind—Mrs. Fabrizi has an old gas stove that—"

Then Mrs. Fabrizi began to shout no, no, and Frank also said. "No, let him eat his breakfast," but Anne would not stop and said, "Honestly, it's dangerous, and the landlord won't do anything." I said I would go and look.

In the apartment across the hall I saw clean new ceiling in kitchen where should be old one falling down in pieces, but I looked away quickly. The gas stove was like Anne said, old, with leaky pipes, everywhere rust and with one side on bricks because leg was gone. "She might have an explosion any day," Anne said, and I saw it was true. So I reached, and turned to where was new gas stove.

They could not understand that whatever I give, I must take away. To this Mrs. Fabrizi I gave a new ceiling, yes, and new stove too, but from some other Mrs. Fabrizi I took away new ceiling, new stove, and gave old ones instead. With Anne's shoulder it was different, because I took from each other Anne only one little cell; and the nickels I took from myself. But again I was a fool, and to me Mrs. Fabrizi's gasp of wonder was like food to starving.

So when Anne said, "Mike, how about new furniture?" and again Mrs. Fabrizi shouted no, but with joy in her eyes, I could not refuse her. We went into living room, and where each piece of old furniture with wrinkled slip covers was, I turned, and there was new furniture, very ugly but to Mrs. Fabrizi beautiful. And she tried to kiss my hand.

Then we all went back to breakfast table, and now they had bright faces and hard eyes, and they licked their lips. They were thinking of themselves.

Dave said, "Mike, I'll lay it on the line. I need five hundred bucks to last out till the beginning of September. If you can do it with nickels—"

"There's no serial numbers on nickels," Frank said. "What do you want him to do, counterfeiting?"

I said, "I can do it." I got wallet, put one dollar bill on table. They watched me.

Dave said, "I wouldn't ask, Mike, but I just don't know where else—"

I told him, "I believe you. Please don't tell me, I know it is truth." Now I could not stop. I reached and turned where instead of dollar bill, someone could have given me five dollar bill by mistake. Always this could happen, even if only one time out of thousand. Then I turned this five dollar bill into one dollar bills, and so on table was five of them. And each one I again turned to a five, and then fives to ones, and so on, while they watched without breathing.

So in little while was on table one hundred five dollar bills, and Dave counted them with fingers that trembled, and put them in his pocket, and looked on me. I could see that he wished now he had asked for more, but he was ashamed to say it.

Then I said, "And for you, Frank, nothing?"

He looked on me and shook his head. He said, "You already done something for me," and put his arm around Anne's waist.

She said to him, "Pop—maybe about that stroke of yours?"

"No, now forget it, will you? That was a year ago."

"Well, but you might have another one sometime. But suppose Mike could fix you up—"

I was shaking my head. "Anne, some things I cannot do.

How would I fix a weak heart? Could I take from somebody else the heart out of his body, and put inside Frank?''

She thought about it. "No, I guess not. But couldn't you kind of change it a little bit at a time, like you did to me?''

"No, it is not possible. If I was doctor, maybe, if I could cut open and reach in, to feel where is everything. And also if I would know all about what is wrong with heart. But I am not doctor. If I would try it, I would only make bad mistake.''

She did not quite believe, but I told her, "To change skin is one thing, is like a game for little child with paper and scissors. But to change living heart, that is different thing altogether. It is like for mechanics, he must take engine from your car apart, and put back together, while it is still going.''

Then I thought I saw what would happen. But was nothing I could do about it. So I waited, and in half hour Frank fell over table where was reaching for match, and rolled from table to floor. His face was turning purple, and eyes turned up under lids. He was not breathing.

Anne fell on her knees beside him, and looked up on me with white face. "Mike!"

Was nothing else to do. I reached and turned; and Frank got to his feet red-faced, shouting, "God damn it, Anne, why don't you tack that carpet down?''

She looked up on him and tried to speak, but at first could not make words. Then she whispered, "Nothing wrong with the carpet.''

"Well, I tripped over something. Almost broke my neck, too." Frank was looking around floor, but carpet was smooth and nothing to trip over. Then he saw she was crying, and said, "What the hell's the matter?''

"Nothing," she said. "Oh, Mike.''

So then I was bigger hero than before, but had a bad feeling, and not until after dinner, when we again drank too much whiskey, could I laugh and talk like the rest. And I made for Frank two new suits in place of old ones, and for Anne and Mrs. Fabrizi all new dresses in their closets. Dave we did not see all day after breakfast.

In the morning I was again ashamed and feeling bad, but others happy and talking all together. When we were finishing meal, door banged open and in came Dave with another man, thin, with dark hair and skin like girl, and small mustache. He was carrying package under his arm.

"Put it down there," said Dave, with eyes bright. "Friends, now you're going to see something. This is Grant Hartley, the collector. Grant, this is Miss Curran, Mrs. Fabrizi, Mr. Curran, and this is Mike. Now."

Mr. Hartley was nodding, with cold smiles, "How do you do. How do you do." He took from watch chain a small knife, and began to cut open rope around package. It was sitting in middle of breakfast table, between toaster and jam jar, and rope went tick, tick when he cut it. And we all sat and watched.

Inside brown paper was cotton, and Mr. Hartley pulled it away in big pieces, and inside was little statue in gold. A dancer made of gold, with skirt flaring out wide and legs graceful.

"There!" said Dave. "What do think of that?"

When we did not answer, he leaned over table. "That's a Degas. It was cast in Eighteen Eighty-two from his wax model—"

"Eighteen Eighty-three," said Mr. Hartley, with small smile.

"All right, Eighteen-Eighty-three—cast in gold, and there was only one copy made. Grant owns it. Now this is the pitch. There's another collector who wants this statuette the worst way, and Grant has been turning him down for years. But it hit me yesterday, if Mike could make a copy, an exact copy—"

"This I want to see with my own eyes," said Mr. Hartley.

"Sure. So I put it up to Grant, and he agreed, if Mike will make *two* copies, he'll keep one, sell one to the other collector—and the third one is ours!"

Mr. Hartley rubbed his mustache, looking sleepy.

I said, "From this no good will come, Dave."

He looked surprised. "Why not?"

"First, it is dishonest—"

"Now wait, just a minute," said Mr. Hartley. "The way Sims represented it to me, this copy will be so exact, that no expert examination could ever tell the difference between them. In fact, what he told me was that one would be just as much the original as the other. Now then, if I sell one as the original. I fail to see where there's anything dishonest involved. Unless, of course, you can't do it?"

I said, "I can do it, but in second place, if I would make you something big and expensive like this, it would bring only trouble. Believe me, I have seen it so many times already—"

Dave said to Mr. Hartley in low voice, "Let me talk to him a minute." His face was pale, and eyes bright. He led me over in the corner and said, "Look, Mike, I didn't want to say this in front of him, but you can make *any* number of copies of that thing, can't you, even after Grant takes his and goes away? What I mean is, once it's been there, it's just like money in the bank—I mean you can draw on it any time."

I said, "Yes, this is true."

"I thought it was. I couldn't sleep all last night for thinking about it. Look, I don't want that copy because it's beautiful. I mean, it *is*, but what I want to do is melt it down. Mike, it'll keep us all, for years. I'm not selfish, I don't want it all for myself—"

I tried to say, "Dave, this way is too easy, believe me when I tell you."

But he was not listening, "Look, Mike, do you know what it's like to be an artist without money? I'm young, I could be turning out my best work now—"

"Please," I said, "Don't tell me, I believe you. So all right, I will do it."

He went back to table, and golden dancer was still standing there, but they had cleared away toaster and plates and it was alone. They were all looking on statue, and then on me, and no one spoke a word.

I sat down, and when Mr. Hartley was watching me with cold smile on his face, I reached and turned. And on table was two golden dancers, both the same. One turned partly away from other, facing Anne; and she looked on it as if she could not look away.

I saw Mr. Hartley jump, and put out his hand. But even before he could touch statue, I turned again, and on table was three.

Mr. Hartley pulled back his hand again like stung. He was very pale. Then he put out hand and picked up one of the statues, and then took another one. And holding both up and looking on them hard, he went away to the window. Then

Dave picked up the third one and stood smiling and holding it close to his chest.

From window, Mr. Hartley said in loud voice, "By God, it's true!" He came back part way into room and said, "Have you got some newspaper—?"

Frank got up and handed him Sunday paper and sat down again, saying nothing. Mr. Hartley knelt down on floor and wrapped up first one statue, then other. His hands were shaking, and he did not do good job, but he finished quickly and stood up holding packages in his arms. "You've got the other one, that's all right," he said. "Goodbye." He went out walking quickly.

Dave had on his face a hard smile, and his eyes looking somewhere else, not here. He held statue away from his chest, and said, "Ten pounds anyhow, and gold is worth twenty dollars an ounce."

He was not talking to us, but I said, "Gold is nothing. If you want gold, is easier ways." And I reached in my pocket to where could be a gold coin, and turned, and threw coin on the table. Then I turned where it would hit different places, here, here, or there, and in a minute was little pile of coins shining on tablecloth.

Dave was watching like dizzy. He picked up some of the coins and looked on them, both sides, with eyes big, and then scooped up a handful. He counted them, stacked them, and finally after Frank and Anne also looked, he put them in his pocket. "Let me take these down to a jeweler," he said, and went out quick.

Frank sat back in chair and shook his head. After while he said, "This is getting to be too much for me. Who was that guy, anyhow?"

Anne said, "Mr. Hartley? He's just some art collector that—"

"No, no, not him, the other one. The one that just went out."

She looked on him. "Pop, that was Dave."

"All right, Dave who? I ask a simple question around here—"

"Dave *Sims*. Pop, what's the matter with you? We've known Dave for years."

"We have like hell." Frank stood up very red. I tried to say something, but he was too mad. "What am I, supposed to think I'm crazy or something? What are you pulling on me?'' He made his hands in fists, and Anne was leaning away frightened. "I figured I'd keep my mouth shut a while, but— What the hell did you do with the carpet? Where's the picture of my old man that used to hang on that wall? What is this Dave business now, why is everything all different, what are you trying to do to me?''

She said, "Pop, there's nothing different—I don't know what you mean about—''

"Damn it, don't give me that, Katie!''

She was looking on him with mouth open and face very white. "What did you call me?''

"Katie! That's your name, isn't it?''

I put my face in hands, but I heard her whisper, "Pop, my name is Anne—''

I heard sound when he hit her. "I told you stop giving me that! I took about enough of this—wait till Jack gets home, I'll find out what you got rigged up here—I know damn well I can count on my own son, anyway—''

I looked and she was in chair crying. "I don't know what you're talking about! Who's Jack? What do you mean your son—?''

He leaned down and began to shake her. "Cut it out—I told you cut it out, didn't I, you bitch!''

I tried to get between them. "Please, is my fault, let me explain—''

Suddenly she screamed and got out of chair like a cat, and he could not stop her. She took hold of my coat and looking on me from few inches away, said, "You did it. You did it, when he had the heart attack.''

"Yes.'' On my face was tears.

"You changed him—you made him different. What did you do, what did you do?''

Frank came up saying, "What, what's this about a heart attack?''

I said, "Anne, he was dying. There was nothing I could do about it. So I turned where was another Frank, not same one, but almost like.''

"You mean this isn't *Pop*?''

"No.''

"Well, where is he?''

I said, "Anne, he died. He is dead.''

She turned away, with hands on face, but Frank came and took hold of my shirt. "You mean you did something to me, like you done to her shoulder? Is that what this is all about?"

I nodded. "Here is not where you belong. Not same apartment, not even same family."

"What about my boy Jack?"

I said, hurting, "In this world, not born."

"Not born." He took harder hold of shirt. "Listen, you get me back there, understand?"

I said, "I can't do it. Too many worlds, I can never find same one again. Always I reach, I can find something. But it would be little different, just like here."

He was red, and eyes very yellow. He said, "Why, you lousy little—"

I twisted, and got away when he would hit me. He came after me around table, but stumbled over chair, and got to the door. "Come back here, you—" he shouted, and just as I opened door I saw him pick up the gold statue from table, and swing it in air. Inside me was a hurt jumping to be free, but I held it back.

Then I was out, and standing in hall was Mr. Hartley and two men about to ring bell. And one of them reached for me, but just then gold statue hit wall, and fell on floor. And while they looked on it, and one man began to pick it up, I went past and started down stairs, still holding back the thing inside me that was trying to get loose.

I heard shout, "Hey, wait! Don't let him get away!" So I ran faster.

Still they were coming down faster than me, and my heart was bumping like it would break out of chest, and on my forehead was cold sweat. My feet would not run good because I was so frightened, and I could not hold back the bad thing much longer, and so I reached in pocket where it could happen that I would have put pile of coins from table. And I turned, and took out handful of gold coins, and threw them on landing behind me. And first man stopped, other two ran into him, with swearing.

I went down rest of stairs weak in knees, and out to street, and I could not think, only to run.

Behind me came shouts and bangings. It was the two men, with heads down, running hard, and behind them Mr. Hartley. I saw they would catch me, and so I reached again in my pocket where I could have put statue, and I turned, but it was so heavy I almost fell down. But I took it out and threw it on street and kept running, and I heard them shouting back and forth to each other, to take it, not to take it, and so on. And I reached, and turned, and threw another statue on street. It made a sound like lead pipe falling.

Now from the sidewalk between cars came a man with his arms out, and I reached in pocket and threw at him some coins. I saw him stop, looking at coins hopping by his feet, and then I was past, running.

Next at corner where I turned there was three men standing by street sign, one with newspaper, and I heard shout, "Hey! Stop that guy!" When they began to move, I reached in pocket again, and to nearest man I handed statue. He took, in both hands, and I was around other ones and still running, but breath like cutting in my throat.

Then I looked back and saw them in street coming, like a fan of people—first a few, then behind them more, and more and more, all running together, and from both sides of street still others coming. I saw in their hands the gold statues, bright in sunlight, and their faces ugly. All this I saw like a picture, not moving, and it made me afraid like a big wave that stands up, and stands up behind you, and still does not fall.

Still it was really not stopped—all this was in an instant—and then I could again hear the noise of their footsteps and their voices like one big animal, and I was running but legs too weak to keep up with me. And I saw doorway, and I went across sidewalk in two big falling steps, and then in doorway I fell.

And across street came that wave of people, fast as a train. And I could not move.

Inside I was all fear, like a knot. I was crying, and sick, and I took from my pockets golden statues and I threw them out in front of me like a fence, two, six, eight—and then the wave burst over me.

Then I felt inside me a movement I could not stop—a reaching and turning. And all was quiet.

I opened my eyes. In front of me was no more people, no street. Under where I was lying in doorway was only big hole, very deep, so deep, I could not see bottom in shadow. I heard a noise of tires, and I saw a car stop sideways, just in time not to fall in. Then I looked up, and where should be other buildings across street, was ruins. Halfway down block, all the buildings had no fronts. Inside rooms the people were still sitting, with all their faces turned like pink dots, and still it was quiet. Then I heard some bricks fall with small hollow sounds; and then down in the hole, I heard noise of water rushing from a pipe.

I hold on to side of the doorway, not to fall; and then I began to hit my head against the side of doorway.

All those people who a minute ago were here, running, breathing, I had put them I could not tell where. Maybe falling through air, screaming—maybe drowning in deep ocean. Maybe burning in fire.

That child inside me had reached back to where was a world with ground lower down than this one—so when I turned it, a piece of the street went to that world, and only air, emptiness, came to this one.

After long time I lifted my head and looked on this destruction that I had made. A hole in street, buildings half gone, innocent people dead, no different than if I would have thrown a bomb.

All because I was frightened—because the frightened child inside me could not hold himself back when he felt in danger. So, now it was all over for me in this world.

Always the same, always the same, no matter how hard I tried . . .

Now I saw police cars pull up, and ambulance, and then fire truck close behind. Crowds were so thick that cars could hardly move. I saw a taxi stop at edge of the crowd, and I thought it was Anne and Frank that got out, but I could not tell for sure. It did not seem to matter. Now already they were far away and long ago.

I sat on my doorstep and I wished I should be dead. If it were not a sin, I would try to kill myself. But even then I know it would not work. Because that frightened child inside me would always turn to where it could not happen—where the bullet would not fire, or would miss, or rope break, or poison would be water.

Once only, for almost a year, I lived in a world where was no man. I lived in forest, and that world was beautiful, but always, when I would sleep, in my dream I would turn myself out of that world, and would wake up in world of men, and have to go back again to different forest.

Until at last I gave it up, and stayed in city afterward. Where I was going I did not know, but I knew that I must go. I was worst man in the creation, I was evil, but even for me I knew God had made a place.

I stood up, and dried my face on sleeve, and then took deep breath.

If I must wander, then, I said to myself, let me go far. I reached back deep, deep, farther than ever before—two thousand years. I found a place where one man was not born, and so all was different. And I turned.

The street disappeared. Up leaped a new city, of cold gray buildings climbing one behind another. All had peaked doors and windows, very big, and with domes of yellow stone, or powdery blue copper. Across the sky was airplane drifting—not cross-shaped, but round. The street was of cobblestones.

Because I had made one man not born two thousand years ago, here now, all world was different—all two thousand years of history different, all cities and all men living, different.

Here at least I would not make all old mistakes, here I could start new. And I thought to myself, *Now if I will only do one right thing, maybe it will wipe out all mistakes of before.*

I was standing inside a little park, with a railing of stone carved like loops of cloth. Behind me was a pedestal of stone, and two statues, one of a handsome young man in a hat with no brim, carrying a torch in his arms. And the other just the same, but with torch upside down. I remembered I had seen once in a book statues like these. It was a book about a god named Mithra of old times, and these statues that I now saw were statues of Mithra the morning star, and Mithra the evening star. They looked down on me with blank stone eyes.

Is it you? they seemed to say.

And I, looking back on them, said, *Is it here?*

But we could not answer one another; and I left them standing there, and went into the city.

Death by Ecstasy

by Larry Niven

What good is an invisible telekinetic arm to a cop? It can help put the squeeze on a suspect.

First came the routine request for a Breach of Privacy permit. A police officer took down the details and forwarded the request to a clerk, who saw that the tape reached the appropriate civic judge. The judge was reluctant, for privacy is a precious thing in a world of eighteen billion; but in the end he could find no reason to refuse. On November 2, 2123, he granted the permit.

The tenant's rent was two weeks in arrears. If the manager of Monica Apartments had asked for eviction he would have been refused. But Owen Jennison did not answer his doorbell or his room phone. Nobody could recall seeing him in many weeks. Apparently the manager only wanted to know that he was all right.

And so he was allowed to use his passkey, with an officer standing by.

And so they found the tenant of 1809.

And when they had looked in his wallet, they called me.

I was at my desk at ARM Headquarters, making useless notes and wishing it were lunchtime.

At this stage the Loren case was all correlate-and-wait. It involved an organlegging gang, apparently run by a single man, yet big enough to cover half the North American west coast. We had considerable data on the gang—methods of operation, centers of activity, a few former customers, even a tentative handful of names—but nothing that would give us an excuse to act. So it was a matter of shoving what we had into the computer, watching the few suspected associates of the ganglord Loren, and waiting for a break.

The months of waiting were ruining my sense of involvement.

My phone buzzed.

I put the pen down and said, "Gil Hamilton."

A small dark face regarded me with soft black eyes. "I am Detective-Inspector Julio Ordaz of the Los Angeles Police Department. Are you related to an Owen Jennison?"

"Owen? No, we're not related. Is he in trouble?"

"You do know him, then."

"Sure I know him. Is he here, on Earth?"

"It would seem so." Ordaz had no accent, but the lack of colloquialisms in his speech made him sound vaguely foreign. "We will need positive identification, Mr. Hamilton. Mr. Jennison's ident lists you as next of kin."

"That's funny. I—back up a minute. Is Owen dead?"

"Somebody is dead, Mr. Hamilton. He carried Mr. Jennison's ident in his wallet."

"Okay. Now, Owen Jennison was a citizen of the Belt. This may have interworld complications. That makes it ARM's business. Where's the body?"

"We found him in an apartment rented under his own name. Monica Apartments, Lower Los Angeles, room 1809."

"Good. Don't move anything you haven't moved already. I'll be right over."

Monica Apartments was a nearly featureless concrete block, eighty stories tall, a thousand feet across the edges of its square base. Lines of small balconies gave the sides a sculptured look, above a forty-foot inset ledge that would keep tenants from dropping objects on pedestrians. A hundred buildings just like it made Lower Los Angeles look lumpy from the air.

Inside, a lobby done in anonymous modern. Lots of metal and plastic showing; lightweight, comfortable chairs without arms; big ashtrays; plenty of indirect lighting; a low ceiling; no wasted space. The whole room might have been stamped out with a die. It wasn't supposed to look small, but it did, and that warned you what the rooms would be like. You'd pay your rent by the cubic centimeter.

I found the manager's office, and the manager, a soft-looking man with watery blue eyes. His conservative paper suit, dark red, seemed chosen to render him invisible, as did the style of his brown hair, worn long and combed straight back without a part. "Nothing like this has ever happened here," he confided as he led me to the elevator banks. "Nothing. It would have been bad enough without his being a Belter, but *now*—" He cringed at the thought. "Newsmen. They'll *smother* us."

The elevator was coffin-sized, but with the handrails on the inside. It went up fast and smooth. I stepped out into a long, narrow hallway.

What would Owen have been doing in a place like this? Machinery lived here, not people.

Maybe it wasn't Owen. Ordaz had been reluctant to commit himself. Besides, there's no law against picking pockets. You couldn't enforce such a law on this crowded planet. Everyone on Earth was a pickpocket.

Sure. Someone had died carrying Owen's wallet.

I walked down the hallway to 1809.

It was Owen who sat grinning in the armchair. I took one good look at him, enough to be sure, and then I looked away and didn't look back. But the rest of it was even more unbelievable.

No Belter could have taken that apartment. I was born in Kansas; but even I felt the awful anonymous chill. It would have driven Owen bats.

"I don't believe it," I said.

"Did you know him well, Mr. Hamilton?"

"About as well as two men can know each other. He and I spent three years mining rocks in the main asteroid belt. You don't keep secrets under those conditions."

"Yet you didn't know he was on Earth."

"That's what I can't understand. Why the blazes didn't he phone me if he was in trouble?"

"You're an ARM," said Ordaz. "An operative in the United Nations Police."

He had a point. Owen was as honorable as any man I knew; but honor isn't the same in the Belt. Belters think flatlanders are all crooks. They don't understand that to a flatlander, picking pockets is a game of skill. Yet a Belter sees smuggling as the same kind of game, with no dishonesty involved. He balances the thirty percent tariff against possible confiscation of his cargo, and if the odds are right he gambles.

Owen could have been doing something that would look honest to him but not to me.

"He could have been in something sticky," I admitted.
"But I can't see him killing himself over it. And . . . not
here. He wouldn't have come here."

1809 was a living room and a bathroom and a closet. I'd
glanced into the bathroom, knowing what I would find. It
was the size of a comfortable shower stall. An adjustment
panel outside the door would cause it to extrude various
appurtenances in memory plastic, to become a washroom, a
shower stall, a toilet, a dressing room, a steam cabinet.
Luxurious in everything but size, as long as you pushed the
right buttons.

The living room was more of the same. A King bed was
invisible behind a wall. The kitchen alcove, with basin and
oven and grill and toaster, would fold into another wall; the
sofa, chairs, and tables would vanish into the floor. One
tenant and three guests would make a crowded cocktail party,
a cozy dinner gathering, a closed poker game. Card table,
dinner table, coffee table were all there, surrounded by the
appropriate chairs; but only one set at a time would emerge
from the floor. There was no refrigerator, no freezer, no bar.
If a tenant needed food or drink he phoned down, and the
supermarket on the third floor would send it up.

The tenant of such an apartment had his comfort. But he
owned nothing. There was room for him; there was none for
his possessions. This was one of the inner apartments. An age
ago there would have been an air shaft; but air shafts took up
expensive room. The tenant didn't even have a window. He
lived in a comfortable box.

Just now the items extruded were the overstuffed reading
armchair, two small side tables, a footstool, and the kitchen
alcove. Owen Jennison sat grinning in the armchair. Naturally he grinned. Little more than dried skin covered the
natural grin of his skull.

"It's a small room," said Ordaz, "but not too small. Millions of people live this way. In any case a Belter would
hardly be a claustrophobe."

"No. Owen flew a singleship before he joined us. Three
months at a stretch, in a cabin so small you couldn't stand up
with the airlock closed. Not claustrophobia, but—" I swept
my arm about the room. "What do you see that's his?"

Small as it was, the closet was nearly empty. A set of
street clothes, a paper shirt, a pair of shoes, a small brown

overnight case. All new. The few items in the bathroom medicine chest had been equally new and equally anonymous.

Ordaz said, "Well?"

"Belters are transients. They don't own much, but what they do own, they guard. Small possessions, relics, souvenirs. I can't believe he wouldn't have had *something*."

Ordaz lifted an eyebrow. "His space suit?"

"You think that's unlikely? It's not. The inside of his pressure suit is a Belter's home. Sometimes it's the only home he's got. He spends a fortune decorating it. If he loses his suit, he's not a Belter anymore.

"No, I don't insist he'd have brought his suit. But he'd have had *something*. His phial of Marsdust. The bit of nickel-iron they took out of his chest. Or, if he left all his souvenirs home, he'd have picked up things on Earth. But in this room—there's *nothing*."

"Perhaps," Ordaz suggested delicately, "he didn't notice his surroundings."

And somehow that brought it all home.

Owen Jennison sat grinning in a water-stained silk dressing gown. His space-darkened face lightened abruptly beneath his chin, giving way to normal suntan. His blond hair, too long, had been cut Earth style; no trace remained of the Belter strip cut he'd worn all his life. A month's growth of untended beard covered half his face. A small black cylinder protruded from the top of his head. An electric cord trailed from the top of the cylinder and ran to a wall socket.

The cylinder was a droud, a current addict's transformer.

I stepped closer to the corpse and bent to look. The droud was a standard make, but it had been altered. Your standard current addict's droud will pass only a trickle of current into the brain. Owen must have been getting ten times the usual charge, easily enough to damage his brain in a month's time.

I reached out and touched the droud with my imaginary hand.

Ordaz was standing quietly beside me, letting me make my examination without interruption. Naturally he had no way of knowing about my restricted psi powers.

With my imaginary fingertips I touched the droud in Owen's head, then ran them down to a tiny hole in his scalp, and further.

It was a standard surgical job. Owen could have had it

done anywhere. A hole in his scalp, invisible under the hair, nearly impossible to find even if you knew what you were looking for. Even your best friends wouldn't know, unless they caught you with the droud plugged in. But the tiny hole marked a bigger plug set in the bone of the skull. I touched the ecstasy plug with my imaginary fingertips, then ran them down the hair-fine wire going deep into Owen's brain, down into the pleasure center.

No, the extra current hadn't killed him. What had killed Owen was his lack of will power. He had been unwilling to get up.

He had starved to death sitting in that chair. There were plastic squeezebottles all around his feet, and a couple still on the end tables. All empty. They must have been full a month ago. Owen hadn't died of thirst. He had died of starvation, and his death had been planned.

Owen my crewmate. Why hadn't he come to me? I'm half a Belter myself. Whatever his trouble, I'd have gotten him out somehow. A little smuggling—what of it? Why had he arranged to tell me only after it was over?

The apartment was so clean, so clean. You had to bend close to smell the death; the air conditioning whisked it all away.

He'd been very methodical. The kitchen was open so that a catheter could lead from Owen to the sink. He'd given himself enough water to last out the month; he'd paid his rent a month in advance. He'd cut the droud cord by hand, and he'd cut it short, deliberately tethering himself to a wall socket beyond reach of the kitchen.

A complex way to die, but rewarding in its way. A month of ecstasy, a month of the highest physical pleasure man can attain. I could imagine him giggling every time he remembered he was starving to death. With food only a few footsteps away . . . but he'd have to pull out the droud to reach it. Perhaps he postponed the decision, and postponed it again . . .

Owen and I and Homer Chandrasekhar, we had lived for three years in a cramped shell surrounded by vacuum. What was there to know about Owen Jennison that I hadn't known? Where was the weakness we didn't share? If Owen had done this, so could I. And I was afraid.

"Very neat," I whispered. "Belter neat."

"Typically Belter, would you say?"

"I would not. Belters don't commit suicide. Certainly not this way. If a Belter had to go, he'd blow his ship's drive and die like a star. The neatness is typical. The result isn't."

"Well," said Ordaz. "Well." He was uncomfortable. The facts spoke for themselves, yet he was reluctant to call me a liar. He fell back on formality.

"Mr. Hamilton, do you identify this man as Owen Jennison?"

"It's him." He'd always been a touch overweight, yet I'd recognized him the moment I saw him. "But let's be sure." I pulled the dirty dressing gown back from Owen's shoulder. A near-perfect circle of scar tissue, eight inches across, spread over the left side of his chest. "See that?"

"We noticed it, yes. An old burn?"

"Owen's the only man I know who could show you a meteor scar on his skin. It blasted him in the shoulder one day while he was outside the ship. Sprayed vaporized pressure-suit steel all over his skin. The doc pulled a tiny grain of nickel-iron from the center of the scar, just below the skin. Owen always carried that grain of nickel-iron. Always," I said, looking at Ordaz.

"We didn't find it."

"Okay."

"I'm sorry to put you through this, Mr. Hamilton. It was you who insisted we leave the body *in situ*."

"Yes. Thank you."

Owen grinned at me from the reading chair. I felt the pain, in my throat and in the pit of my stomach. Once I had lost my right arm. Losing Owen felt the same way.

"I'd like to know more about this," I said. "Will you let me know the details as soon as you get them?"

"Of course. Through the ARM office?"

"Yes." This wasn't ARM business, despite what I'd told Ordaz; but ARM prestige would help. "I want to know why Owen died. Maybe he just cracked up . . . culture shock or something. But if someone hounded him to death, I'll have his blood."

"Surely the administration of justice is better left to—" Ordaz stopped, confused. Did I speak as an ARM or as a citizen?

I left him wondering.

The lobby held a scattering of tenants, entering and leaving elevators or just sitting around. I stood outside the elevator for a moment, searching passing faces for the erosion of personality that must be there.

Mass-produced comfort. Room to sleep and eat and watch tridee, but no room to *be* anyone. Living here, one would own nothing. What kind of people would live like that? They should have looked all alike, moved in unison, like the string of images in a barber's mirrors.

Then I spotted wavy brown hair and a dark red paper suit. The manager? I had to get close before I was sure. His face was the face of a permanent stranger.

He saw me coming and smiled without enthusiasm. "Oh, hello, Mr. . . . uh . . . Did you find . . ." He couldn't think of the right question.

"Yes," I said, answering it anyway. "But I'd like to know some things. Owen Jennison lived here for six weeks, right?"

"Six weeks and two days, before we opened his room."

"Did he ever have visitors?"

The man's eyebrows went up. We'd drifted in the direction of his office, and I was close enough to read the name on the door: JASPER MILLER, *Manager*. "Of course not," he said. "Anyone would have noticed that something was wrong."

"You mean he took the room for the express purpose of dying? You saw him once, and never again?"

"I suppose he might . . . no, wait." The manager thought deeply. "No. He registered on a Thursday. I noticed the Belter tan, of course. Then on Friday he went out. I happened to see him pass."

"Was that the day he got the droud? No, skip it, you wouldn't know that. Was it the last time you saw him go out?"

"Yes, it was."

"Then he could have had visitors late Thursday or early Friday."

The manager shook his head, very positively.

"Why not?"

"You see, Mr., uh . . . ."

"Hamilton."

"We have a holo camera on every floor, Mr. Hamilton. It takes a picture of each tenant the first time he goes to his room, and then never again. Privacy is one of the services a tenant buys with his room." The manager drew himself up a little as he said this. "For the same reason, the holo camera takes a picture of anyone who is *not* a tenant. The tenants are thus protected from unwarranted intrusions."

"And there were no visitors to any of the rooms on Owen's floor?"

"No, sir, there were not."

"Your tenants are a solitary bunch."

"Perhaps they are."

"I suppose a computer in the basement decides who is and is not a tenant."

"Of course."

"So for six weeks Owen Jennison sat alone in his room. In all that time he was totally ignored."

Miller tried to turn his voice cold, but he was too nervous. "We try to give our guests privacy. If Mr. Jennison had wanted help of any kind he had only to pick up the house phone. He could have called me, or the pharmacy, or the supermarket downstairs."

"Well, thank you, Mr. Miller. That's all I wanted to know. I wanted to know how Owen Jennison could wait six weeks to die while nobody noticed."

Miller swallowed. "He was dying all that time?"

"Yah."

"We had no way of knowing. How could we? I don't see how you can blame us."

"I don't either," I said, and brushed by. Miller had been close enough, so I had lashed out at him. Now I was ashamed. The man was perfectly right. Owen could have had help if he'd wanted it.

I stood outside, looking up at the jagged blue line of sky that showed between the tops of the buildings. A taxi floated into view, and I beeped my clicker at it, and it dropped.

I went back to ARM Headquarters. Not to work—I couldn't have done any work, not under the circumstances—but to talk to Julie.

Julie. A tall girl, pushing thirty, with green eyes and long hair streaked red and gold. And two wide brown forceps marks above her right knee; but they weren't showing now. I looked into her office, through the one-way glass, and watched her at work.

She sat in a contour couch, smoking. Her eyes were closed.

Sometimes her brow would furrow as she concentrated. Sometimes she would snatch a glance at the clock, then close her eyes again.

I didn't interrupt her. I knew the importance of what she was doing.

Julie. She wasn't beautiful. Her eyes were a little too far apart, her chin too square, her mouth too wide. It didn't matter. Because Julie could read minds.

She was the ideal date. She was everything a man needed. A year ago, the day after the night I killed my first man, I had been in a terribly destructive mood. Somehow Julie had turned it into a mood of manic exhilaration. We'd run wild through a supervised anarchy park, running up an enormous bill. We'd hiked five miles without going anywhere, facing backward on a downtown slidewalk. At the end we'd been utterly fatigued, too tired to think. . . . But two weeks ago it had been a warm, cuddly, comfortable night. Two people happy with each other; no more than that. Julie was what you needed, anytime, anywhere.

Her male harem must have been the largest in history. To pick up on the thoughts of a male ARM, Julie had to be in love with him. Luckily there was room in her for a lot of love. She didn't demand that we be faithful. A good half of us were married. But there had to be love for each of Julie's men, or Julie couldn't protect him.

She was protecting us now. Each fifteen minutes, Julie was making contact with a specific ARM agent. Psi powers are notoriously undependable, but Julie was an exception. If we got in a hole, Julie was always there to get us out . . . provided some idiot didn't interrupt her at work.

So I stood outside, waiting, with a cigarette in my imaginary hand.

The cigarette was for practice, to stretch the mental muscles. In its way my "hand" was as dependable as Julie's mind-touch, possibly because of its very limitations. Doubt your psi powers and they're gone. A rigidly defined third arm was more reasonable than some warlock ability to make objects move by wishing at them. I knew how an arm felt, and what it would do.

Why do I spend so much time lifting cigarettes? Well, it's the biggest weight I can lift without strain. And there's another reason . . . something taught me by Owen.

At ten minutes to fifteen Julie opened her eyes, rolled out of the contour couch, and came to the door. "Hi, Gil," she said sleepily. "Trouble?"

"Yah. A friend of mine just died. I thought you'd better know." I handed her a cup of coffee.

She nodded. We had a date tonight, and this would change its character. Knowing that, she probed lightly.

"Jesus!" she said, recoiling. "How . . . how horrible. I'm terribly sorry, Gil. Date's off, right?"

"Unless you want to join the ceremonial drunk."

She shook her head vigorously. "I didn't know him. It wouldn't be proper. Besides, you'll be wallowing in your own memories, Gil. A lot of them will be private. I'd cramp your style if you knew I was there to probe. Now if Homer Chandrasekhar were here, it'd be different."

"I wish he were. He'll have to throw his own drunk. Maybe with some of Owen's girls, if they're around."

"You know what I feel," she said.

"Just what I do."

"I wish I could help."

"You always help." I glanced at the clock. "Your coffee break's about over."

"Slave driver." Julie took my earlobe between thumb and forefinger. "Do him proud," she said, and went back to her soundproof room.

She always helps. She doesn't even have to speak. Just knowing that Julie has read my thoughts, that someone understands . . . that's enough.

All alone at three in the afternoon, I started my ceremonial drunk.

The ceremonial drunk is a young custom, not yet tied down by formality. There is no set duration. No specific toasts must be given. Those who participate must be close friends of the deceased, but there is no set number of participants.

I started at the Luau, a place of cool blue light and running water. Outside it was fifteen-thirty in the afternoon, but inside it was evening in the Hawaiian Islands of centuries ago. Already the place was half full. I picked a corner table with considerable elbow room and dialed for Luau grog. It came, cold, brown, and alcoholic, its straw tucked into a cone of ice.

There had been three of us at Cubes Forsythe's ceremonial

drunk, one black Ceres night four years ago. A jolly group we were, too; Owen and me and the widow of our third crewman. Gwen Forsythe blamed us for her husband's death. I was just out of the hospital with a right arm that ended at the shoulder, and I blamed Cubes and Owen and myself, all at once. Even Owen had turned dour and introspective. We couldn't have picked a worse trio, or a worse night for it.

But custom called, and we were there. Then as now, I found myself probing my own personality for the wound that was a missing crewman, a missing friend. Introspecting.

Gilbert Hamilton. Born of flatlander parents, in April, 2093, in Topeka, Kansas. Born with two arms and no sign of wild talents.

Flatlander: a Belter term referring to Earthmen, and particularly to Earthmen who had never seen space. I'm not sure my parents ever looked at the stars. They managed the third largest farm in Kansas, ten square miles of arable land between two wide strips of city paralleling two strips of turnpike. We were city people, like all flatlanders, but when the crowds got to be too much for my brothers and me, we had vast stretches of land to be alone in. Ten square miles of playground, with nothing to hamper us but the crops and automachinery.

We looked at the stars, my brothers and I. You can't see stars from the city; the lights hide them. Even in the fields you couldn't see them around the lighted horizon. But straight overhead, they were there: black sky scattered with bright dots, and sometimes a flat white moon.

At twenty I gave up my UN citizenship to become a Belter. I wanted stars, and the Belt government holds title to most of the solar system. There are fabulous riches in the rocks, riches belonging to a scattered civilization of a few hundred thousand Belters; and I wanted my share of that, too.

It wasn't easy. I wouldn't be eligible for a singleship license for ten years. Meanwhile I would be working for others, and learning to avoid mistakes before they killed me. Half the flatlanders who join the Belt die in space before they can earn their licenses.

I mined tin on Mercury and exotic chemicals from Jupiter's atmosphere. I hauled ice from Saturn's rings and quicksilver from Europa. One year our pilot made a mistake pulling up to a new rock, and we damn near had to walk home. Cubes Forsythe was with us then. He managed to fix the com laser and aim it at Icarus to bring us help. Another time the mechanic who did the maintenance job on our ship forgot to replace an absorber, and we all got roaring drunk on the alcohol that built up in our breathing-air. The three of us caught the mechanic six months later. I hear he lived.

Most of the time I was part of a three-man crew. The members changed constantly. When Owen Jennison joined us he replaced a man who had finally earned his singleship license, and couldn't wait to start hunting rocks on his own. He was too eager. I learned later that he'd made one round trip and half of another.

Owen was my age, but more experienced, a Belter born and bred. His blue eyes and blond cockatoo's crest were startling against the dark of his Belter tan, the tan that ended so abruptly where his neck ring cut off the space-intense sunlight his helmet let through. He was permanently chubby, but in free fall it was as if he'd been born with wings. I took to copying his way of moving, much to Cubes' amusement.

I didn't make my own mistake until I was twenty-six.

We were using bombs to put a rock in a new orbit. A contract job. The technique is older than fusion drives, as old as early Belt colonization, and it's still cheaper and faster than using a ship's drive to tow the rock. You use industrial fusion bombs, small and clean, and you set them so that each explosion deepens the crater to channel the force of later blasts.

We'd set four blasts already, four white fireballs that swelled and faded as they rose. When the fifth blast went off we were hovering nearby on the other side of the rock.

The fifth blast shattered the rock.

Cubes had set the bomb. My own mistake was a shared one, because any of the three of us should have had the sense to take off right then. Instead, we watched, cursing, as valuable oxygen-bearing rock became near-valueless shards. We watched the shards spread slowly into a cloud . . . and while we watched, one fast-moving shard reached us. Moving too slowly to vaporize when it hit, it nonetheless sheared through a triple crystal-iron hull, slashed through my upper arm, and pinned Cubes Forsythe to a wall by his heart.

A couple of nudists came in. They stood blinking among the booths while their eyes adjusted to the blue twilight, then converged with glad cries on the group two tables over. I watched and listened with an eye and an ear, thinking how different flatlander nudists were from Belter nudists. These all looked alike. They all had muscles, they had no interesting scars, they carried their credit cards in identical shoulder pouches, and they all shaved the same areas.

. . . We always went nudist in the big bases. Most people did. It was a natural reaction to the pressure suits we wore day and night while out in the rocks. Get him in a shirtsleeve environment, and your normal Belter sneers at a shirt. But it's only for comfort. Give him a good reason and your Belter will don shirt and pants as quickly as the next guy.

But not Owen. After he got the meteor scar, I never saw him wear a shirt. Not just in the Ceres domes, but anywhere there was air to breathe. He just had to show that scar.

A cool blue mood settled on me, and I remembered . . .

. . . Owen Jennison lounging on a corner of my hospital bed, telling me of the trip back. I couldn't remember anything after that rock had sheared through my arm.

I should have bled to death in seconds. Owen hadn't given me the chance. The wound was ragged; Owen had sliced it clean to the shoulder with one swipe of a com laser. Then he'd tied a length of fiberglass curtain over the flat surface and knotted it tight under my remaining armpit. He told me about putting me under two atmospheres of pure oxygen as a substitute for replacing the blood I'd lost. He told me how he'd reset the fusion drive for four gees to get me back in time. By rights we should have gone up in a cloud of starfire and glory.

"So there goes my reputation. The whole Belt knows how I rewired our drive. A lot of 'em figure if I'm stupid enough to risk my own life like that, I'd risk theirs too."

"So you're not safe to travel with."

"Just so. They're starting to call me Four Gee Jennison."

"You think you've got problems? I can just see how it'll be when I get out of this bed. 'You do something stupid, Gil?' The hell of it is, it *was* stupid."

"So lie a little."

"Uh huh. Can we sell the ship?"

"Nope. Gwen inherited a third interest in it from Cubes. She won't sell."

"Then we're effectively broke."

"Except for the ship. We need another crewman."

"Correction. *You* need *two* crewmen. Unless you want to fly with a one-armed man. I can't afford a transplant."

Owen hadn't tried to offer me a loan. That would have been insulting, even if he'd had the money. "What's wrong with a prosthetic?"

"An iron arm? Sorry, no. I'm squeamish."

Owen had looked at me strangely, but all he'd said was, "Well, we'll wait a bit. Maybe you'll change your mind."

He hadn't pressured me. Not then, and not later, after I'd left the hospital and taken an apartment while I waited to get used to a missing arm. If he thought I would eventually settle for a prosthetic, he was mistaken.

Why? It's not a question I can answer. Others obviously feel differently; there are millions of people walking around with metal and plastic and silicone parts. Part man, part machine, and how do they themselves know which is the real person?

I'd rather be dead than part metal. Call it a quirk. Call it, even, the same quirk that makes my skin crawl when I find a place like Monica Apartments. A human being should be all human. He should have habits and possessions peculiarly his own, he should not try to look like or to behave like anyone but himself, and he should not be half robot.

So there I was, Gil the Arm, learning to eat with my left hand.

An amputee never entirely loses what he's lost. My missing fingers itched. I moved to keep from barking my missing elbow on sharp corners. I reached for things, then swore when they didn't come.

Owen had hung around, though his own emergency funds must have been running low. I hadn't offered to sell my third of the ship, and he hadn't asked.

There had been a girl. Now I'd forgotten her name. One night I was at her place waiting for her to get dressed—a dinner date—and I'd happened to see a nail file she'd left on a table. I'd picked it up. I'd almost tried to file my nails, but remembered in time. Irritated, I had tossed the file back on the table—and missed.

Like an idiot I'd tried to catch it with my right hand.

And I'd caught it.

I'd never suspected myself of having psychic powers. You

have to be in the right frame of mind to use a psi power. But who had ever had a better opportunity than I did that night, with a whole section of brain tuned to the nerves and muscles of my right arm, and no right arm?

I'd held the nail file in my imaginary hand. I'd felt it, just as I'd felt my missing fingernails getting too long. I had run my thumb along the rough steel surface; I had turned the file in my fingers. Telekinesis for lift, esper for touch.

"That's it," Owen had said the next day. "That's all we need. One crewman, and you with your eldritch powers. You practice, see how strong you can get that lift. I'll go find a sucker."

"He'll have to settle for a sixth of net. Cubes' widow will want her share."

"Don't worry. I'll swing it."

"Don't worry!" I'd waved a pencil stub at him. Even in Ceres' gentle gravity, it was as much as I could lift—then. "You don't think TK and esper can make do for a real arm, do you?"

"It's better than a real arm. You'll see. You'll be able to reach through your suit with it without losing pressure. What Belter can do that?"

"Sure."

"What the hell do you want, Gil? Someone should give you your arm back? You can't have that. You lost it fair and square, through stupidity. Now it's your choice. Do you fly with an imaginary arm, or do you go back to Earth?"

"I can't go back. I don't have the fare."

"Well?"

"Okay, okay. Go find us a crewman. Someone I can impress with my imaginary arm."

I sucked meditatively on a second Luau grog. By now all the booths were full, and a second layer was forming around the bar. The voices made a continuous hypnotic roar. Cocktail hour had arrived.

. . . He'd swung it, all right. On the strength of my imaginary arm, Owen had talked a kid named Homer Chandrasekhar into joining our crew.

He'd been right about my arm, too.

Others with similar senses can reach further, up to halfway

around the world. My unfortunately literal imagination had restricted me to a psychic hand. But my esper fingertips were more sensitive, more dependable. I could lift more weight. Today, in Earth's gravity, I can lift a full shot glass.

I found I could reach through a cabin wall to feel for breaks in the circuits behind it. In vacuum I could brush dust from the outside of my faceplate. In port I did magic tricks.

I'd almost ceased to feel like a cripple. It was all due to Owen. In six months of mining I had paid off my hospital bills and earned my fare back to Earth, with a comfortable stake left over.

"Finagle's Black Humor!" Owen had exploded when I told him. "Of all places, why Earth?"

"Because if I can get my UN citizenship back, Earth will replace my arm. Free."

"Oh. That's true," he'd said dubiously.

The Belt had organ banks too, but they were always undersupplied. Belters didn't give things away. Neither did the Belt government. They kept the prices on transplants as high as they would go. Thus they dropped the demand to meet the supply, and kept taxes down to boot.

In the Belt I'd have to buy my own arm. And I didn't have the money. On Earth there was social security, and a vast supply of transplant material.

What Owen had said couldn't be done, I'd done. I'd found someone to hand me my arm back.

Sometimes I'd wondered if Owen held the choice against me. He'd never said anything, but Homer Chandrasekhar had spoken at length. A Belter would have earned his arm or done without. Never would he have accepted charity.

Was that why Owen hadn't tried to call me?

I shook my head. I didn't believe it.

The room continued to lurch after my head stopped shaking. I'd had enough for the moment. I finished my third grog and ordered dinner.

Dinner sobered me for the next lap. It was something of a shock to realize that I'd run through the entire lifespan of my friendship with Owen Jennison. I'd known him for three years, though it had seemed like half a lifetime. And it was. Half my six-year lifespan as a Belter.

*   *   *

I ordered coffee grog and watched the man pour it: hot, milky coffee laced with cinnamon and other spices, and high-proof rum poured in a stream of blue fire. This was one of the special drinks served by a human headwaiter, and it was the reason they kept him around. Phase two of the ceremonial drunk: blow half your fortune, in the grand manner.

But I called Ordaz before I touched the drink.

"Yes, Mr. Hamilton? I was just going home for dinner."

"I won't keep you long. Have you found out anything new?"

Ordaz took a closer look at my phone image. His disapproval was plain. "I see that you have been drinking. Perhaps you should go home now, and call me tomorrow."

I was shocked. "Don't you know *anything* about Belt customs?"

"I do not understand."

I explained the ceremonial drunk. "Look, Ordaz, if you know that little about the way a Belter thinks, then we'd better have a talk. Soon. Otherwise you're likely to miss something."

"You may be right. I can see you at noon, over lunch."

"Good. What have you got?"

"Considerable, but none of it is very helpful. Your friend landed on Earth two months ago, arriving on the *Pillar of Fire*, operating out of Outback Field, Australia. He was wearing a haircut in the style of Earth. From there—"

"That's funny. He'd have had to wait two months for his hair to grow out."

"That occurred even to me. I understand that a Belter commonly shaves his entire scalp, except for a strip two inches wide running from the nape of his neck forward."

"The strip cut, yah. It probably started when someone decided he'd live longer if his hair couldn't fall in his eyes during a tricky landing. But Owen could have let his hair grow out during a singleship mining trip. There'd be nobody to see."

"Still, it seems odd. Did you know that Mr. Jennison has a cousin on Earth? One Harvey Peele, who manages a chain of supermarkets."

"So I wasn't his next of kin, even on Earth."

"Mr. Jennison made no attempt to contact him."

"Anything else?"

"I've spoken to the man who sold Mr. Jennison his droud and plug. Kenneth Graham owns an office and operating room on Gayley in Near West Los Angeles. Graham claims that the droud was a standard type, that your friend must have altered it himself."

"Do you believe him?"

"For the present. His permits and his records are all in order. The droud was altered with a soldering iron, an amateur's tool."

"Uh huh."

"As far as the police are concerned, the case will probably be closed when we locate the tools Mr. Jennison used."

"Tell you what. I'll wire Homer Chandrasekhar tomorrow. Maybe he can find out things—why Owen landed without a strip haircut, why he came to Earth at all."

Ordaz shrugged with his eyebrows. He thanked me for my trouble and hung up.

The coffee grog was still hot. I gulped at it, savoring the sugary, bittery sting of it, trying to forget Owen dead and remember him in life. He was always slightly chubby, I remembered, but he never gained a pound and he never lost a pound. He could move like a whippet when he had to.

And now he was terribly thin, and his death-grin was ripe with obscene joy.

I ordered another coffee grog. The waiter, a showman, made sure he had my attention before he lit the heated rum, then poured it from a foot above the glass. You can't drink that drink slowly. It slides down too easily, and there's the added spur that if you wait too long it might get cold. Rum and strong coffee. Two of these and I'd be drunkenly alert for hours.

Midnight found me in the Mars Bar, running on scotch and soda. In between I'd been barhopping. Irish coffee at Bergin's, cold and smoking concoctions at the Moon Pool, scotch and wild music at Beyond. I couldn't get drunk, and I couldn't find the right mood. There was a barrier to the picture I was trying to rebuild.

It was the memory of the last Owen, grinning in an armchair with a wire leading down into his brain.

I didn't know that Owen. I had never met the man, and never would have wanted to. From bar to nightclub to restaurant I had run from the image, waiting for the alcohol to break the barrier between present and past.

So I sat at a corner table, surrounded by 3D panoramic views of an impossible Mars. Crystal towers and long, straight blue canali, six-legged beasts and beautiful, impossibly slender men and women, looked out at me across never-never land. Would Owen have found it sad or funny? He'd seen the real Mars, and had not been impressed.

I had reached that stage where time becomes discontinuous, where gaps of seconds or minutes appear between the events you can remember. Somewhere in that period I found myself staring at a cigarette. I must have just lighted it, because it was near its original two-hundred-millimeter length. Maybe a waiter had snuck up behind me. There it was, at any rate, burning between my middle and index fingers.

I stared at the coal as the mood settled on me. I was calm, I was drifting, I was lost in time. . . .

. . . We'd been two months in the rocks, our first trip out since the accident. Back we came to Ceres with a holdful of gold, fifty percent pure, guaranteed suitable for rustproof wiring and conductor plates. At nightfall we were ready to celebrate.

We walked along the city limits, with neon blinking and beckoning on the right, a melted rock cliff to the left, and stars blazing through the dome overhead. Homer Chandrasekhar was practically snorting. On this night his first trip out culminated in his first homecoming: and homecoming is the best part.

"We'll want to split up about midnight," he said. He didn't need to enlarge on that. Three men in company might conceivably be three singleship pilots, but chances are they're a ship's crew. They don't have their singleship licenses yet; they're too stupid or too inexperienced. If we wanted companions for the night—

"You haven't thought this through," Owen answered. I saw Homer's double take, then his quick look at where my shoulder ended, and I was ashamed. I didn't need my crewmates to hold my hand, and in this state I'd only slow them down.

Before I could open my mouth to protest, Owen went on.

"Think it through. We've got a draw here that we'd be idiots to throw away. Gil, pick up a cigarette. No, not with your left hand—"

I was drunk, gloriously drunk and feeling immortal. The attenuated Martians seemed to move in the walls, the walls that seemed to be picture windows on a Mars that never was. For the first time that night, I raised my glass in toast.

"To Owen, from Gil the Arm. Thanks."

I transferred the cigarette to my imaginary hand.

By now you've got the idea I was holding it in my imaginary fingers. Most people have the same impression, but it isn't so. I held it clutched ignominiously in my fist. The coal couldn't burn me, of course, but it still felt like a lead ingot.

I rested my imaginary elbow on the table, and that seemed to make it easier—which is ridiculous, but it works. Truly, I'd expected my imaginary arm to disappear after I got the transplant. But I'd found I could dissociate from the new arm to hold small objects in my invisible hand, to feel tactile sensations in my invisible fingertips.

I'd earned the title Gil the Arm, that night in Ceres. It had started with a floating cigarette. Owen had been right. Everyone in the place eventually wound up staring at the floating cigarette smoked by the one-armed man. All I had to do was find the prettiest girl in the room with my peripheral vision, then catch her eye.

That night we had been the center of the biggest impromptu party ever thrown in Ceres Base. It wasn't planned that way at all. I'd used the cigarette trick three times, so that each of us would have a date. But the third girl already had an escort, and he was celebrating something; he'd sold some kind of patent to an Earth-based industrial firm. He was throwing money around like confetti. So we let him stay. I did tricks, reaching esper fingers into a closed box to tell what was inside, and by the time I finished all the tables had been pushed together and I was in the center, with Homer and Owen and three girls. Then we got to singing old songs, and the bartenders joined us, and suddenly everything was on the house.

Eventually about twenty of us wound up in the orbiting mansion of the First Speaker for the Belt Government. The goldskin cops had tried to bust us up earlier, and the First

Speaker had behaved very rudely indeed, then compensated by inviting them to join us. . . .

And that was why I used TK on so many cigarettes.

Across the width of the Mars Bar, a girl in a peach-colored dress sat studying me with her chin on her fist. I got up and went over.

My head felt fine. It was the first thing I checked when I woke up. Apparently I'd remembered to take a hangover pill.

A leg was hooked over my knee. It felt good, though the pressure had put my foot to sleep. Fragrant dark hair spilled beneath my nose. I didn't move. I didn't want her to know I was awake.

It's damned embarrassing when you wake up with a girl and can't remember her name.

Well, let's see. A peach dress neatly hung from a door-knob. . . . I remembered a whole lot of traveling last night. The girl at the Mars Bar. A puppet show. Music of all kinds. I'd talked about Owen, and she'd steered me away from that because it depressed her. Then—

Hah! Taffy. Last name forgotten.

"Morning," I said.

"Morning," she said. "Don't try to move, we're hooked together. . . ." In the sober morning light she was lovely. Long black hair, brown eyes, creamy untanned skin. To be lovely this early was a neat trick, and I told her so, and she smiled.

My lower leg was dead meat until it started to buzz with renewed circulation, and then I made faces until it calmed down. Taffy kept up a running chatter as we dressed. "That third hand is strange. I remember you holding me with two strong arms and stroking the back of my neck with the third. *Very* nice. It reminded me of a Fritz Leiber story."

"*The Wanderer*. The panther girl."

"Mm hmm. How many girls have you caught with that cigarette trick?"

"None as pretty as you."

"And how many girls have you told that to?"

"Can't remember. It always worked before. Maybe this time it's for real."

We exchanged grins.

A minute later I caught her frowning thoughtfully at the back of my neck. "Something wrong?"

"I was just thinking. You really crashed and burned last night. I hope you don't drink that much all the time."

"Why? You worried about me?"

She blushed, then nodded.

"I should have told you. In fact, I think I did, last night. I was on a ceremonial drunk. When a good friend dies it's obligatory to get smashed."

Taffy looked relieved. "I didn't mean to get—"

"Personal? Why not. You've the right. Anyway, I like—" *maternal types*, but I couldn't say that. "People who worry about me."

Taffy touched her hair with some kind of complex comb. A few strokes snapped her hair instantly into place. Static electricity?

"It was a good drunk," I said. "Owen would have been proud. And that's all the mourning I'll do. One drunk and—" I spread my hands. "Out."

"It's not a bad way to go." Taffy mused reflectively. "Current stimulus, I mean. I mean, if you've got to bow out—"

"Now drop that!" I don't know how I got so angry so fast. Ghoul-thin and grinning in a reading chair, Owen's corpse was suddenly vivid before me. I'd fought that image for too many hours. "Walking off a bridge is enough of a cop-out," I snarled. "Dying for a month while current burns out your brain is nothing less than sickening."

Taffy was hurt and bewildered. "But your friend did it, didn't he? You didn't make him sound like a weakling."

"Nuts," I heard myself say. "He didn't do it. He was—"

Just like that, I was sure. I must have realized it while I was drunk or sleeping. Of *course* he hadn't killed himself. *That* wasn't Owen. And current addiction wasn't Owen either.

"He was murdered," I said. "Sure he was. Why didn't I see it?" And I made a dive for the phone.

"Good morning, Mr. Hamilton." Detective-Inspector Ordaz looked very fresh and neat this morning. I was suddenly aware that I hadn't shaved. "I see you remembered to take your hangover pills."

"Right. Ordaz, has it occurred to you that Owen might have been murdered?"

"Naturally. But it isn't possible."

"I think it might be. Suppose he—"

"Mr. Hamilton."

"Yah?"

"We have an appointment for lunch. Shall we discuss it then? Meet me at Headquarters at twelve hundred."

"Okay. One thing you might take care of this morning. See if Owen registered for a nudist's license."

"Do you think he might have?"

"Yah. I'll tell you why at lunch."

"Very well."

"Don't hang up. You said you'd found the man who sold Owen his droud-and-plug. What was his name again?"

"Kenneth Graham."

"That's what I thought." I hung up.

Taffy touched my shoulder. "Do—do you really think he might have been—killed?"

"Yah. The whole setup depended on him not being able to—"

"No. Wait. I don't want to know about it."

I turned to look at her. She really didn't. The very subject of a stranger's death was making her sick to her stomach.

"Okay. Look, I'm a jerk not to at least offer you breakfast, but I've got to get on this right away. Can I call you a cab?"

When the cab came I dropped a ten-mark coin in the slot and helped her in. I got her address before it took off.

ARM Headquarters hummed with early morning activity. Hellos came my way, and I answered them without stopping to talk. Anything important would filter down to me eventually.

As I passed Julie's cubicle I glanced in. She was hard at work, limply settled in her contour couch, jotting notes with her eyes closed.

Kenneth Graham.

A hookup to the basement computer formed the greater part of my desk. Learning how to use it had taken me several months. I typed an order for coffee and donuts, then: INFORMATION RETRIEVAL. KENNETH GRAHAM. LIMITED LICENSE: SURGERY. GENERAL LICENSE: DIRECT CURRENT STIMULUS EQUIPMENT SALES. ADDRESS: NEAR WEST LOS ANGELES.

Tape chattered out of the slot, an instant response, loop after loop of it curling on my desk. I didn't need to read it to know I was right.

*   *   *

New technologies create new customs, new laws, new ethics, new crimes. About half the activity of the United Nations Police, the ARMs, dealt with control of a crime that hadn't existed a century ago. The crime of organlegging was the result of thousands of years of medical progress, of millions of lives selflessly dedicated to the ideal of healing the sick. Progress had brought these ideals to reality, and, as usual, had created new problems.

1900 A.D. was the year Karl Landsteiner classified human blood into four types, giving patients their first real chance to survive a transfusion. The technology of transplants had grown with the growing of the twentieth century. Whole blood, dry bone, skin, live kidneys, live hearts could all be transferred from one body to another. Donors had saved tens of thousands of lives in that hundred years, by willing their bodies to medicine.

But the number of donors was limited, and not many died in such a way that anything of value could be saved.

The deluge had come something less than a hundred years ago. One healthy donor (but of course there was no such animal) could save a dozen lives. Why, then, should a condemned murderer die to no purpose? First a few states, then most of the nations of the world had passed new laws. Criminals condemned to death must be executed in a hospital, with surgeons to save as much as could be saved for the organ banks.

The world's billions wanted to live, and the organ banks were life itself. A man could live forever as long as the doctors could shove spare parts into him faster than his own parts wore out. But they could do that only as long as the world's organ banks were stocked.

A hundred scattered movements to abolish the death penalty died silent, unpublicized deaths. Everybody gets sick sometime.

And still there were shortages in the organ banks. Still patients died for the lack of parts to save them. The world's legislators had responded to steady pressure from the world's people. Death penalties were established for first, second, and third degree murder. For assault with a deadly weapon. Then for a multitude of crimes: rape, fraud, embezzlement, having children without a license, four or more counts of false advertising. For nearly a century the trend had been growing, as the world's voting citizens acted to protect their right to live forever.

Even now there weren't enough transplants. A woman with kidney trouble might wait a year for a transplant: one healthy kidney to last the rest of her life. A thirty-five-year-old heart patient must live with a sound but forty-year-old heart. One lung, part of a liver, prosthetics that wore out too fast or weighed too much or did too little . . . there weren't enough criminals. Not surprisingly, the death penalty *was* a deterrent. People stopped committing crimes rather than face the donor room of a hospital.

For instant replacement of your ruined digestive system, for a *young* healthy heart, for a whole liver when you'd ruined yours with alcohol . . . you had to go to an organlegger.

There are three aspects to the business of organlegging.

One is the business of kidnap-murder. It's risky. You can't fill an organ bank by waiting for volunteers. Executing condemned criminals is a government monopoly. So you go out and *get* your donors: on a crowded city slidewalk, in an air terminal, stranded on a freeway by a car with a busted capacitor . . . anywhere.

The selling end of the business is just as dangerous, because even a desperately sick man sometimes has a conscience. He'll buy his transplant, then go straight to the ARMs, curing his sickness and his conscience by turning in the whole gang. Thus the sales end is somewhat anonymous, but as there are few repeat sales, that hardly matters.

Third is the technical, medical aspect. Probably this is the safest part of the business. Your hospital is big, but you can put it anywhere. You wait for the donors, who arrive still alive; you ship out livers and glands and square feet of live skin, correctly labeled for rejection reactions.

It's not as easy as it sounds. You need doctors. Good ones.

That was where Loren came in. He had a monopoly.

Where did he get them? We were still trying to find out. Somehow, one man had discovered a foolproof way to recruit talented but dishonest doctors practically en masse. Was it really one man? All our sources said it was. And he had half the North American west coast in the palm of his hand.

Loren. No holographs, no fingerprints or retina prints, not

even a description. All we had was that one name, and a few possible contacts.

One of these was Kenneth Graham.

The holograph was a good one. Probably it had been posed in a portrait shop. Kenneth Graham had a long Scottish face with a lantern jaw and a small, dour mouth. In the holo he was trying to smile and look dignified simultaneously. He only looked uncomfortable. His hair was sandy and close-cut. Above his light gray eyes his eyebrows were so light as to be nearly invisible.

My breakfast arrived. I dunked a donut and bit it, and found out I was hungrier than I'd thought.

A string of holos had been reproduced on the computer tape. I ran through the others fairly quickly, eating with one hand and flipping the key with the other. Some were fuzzy; they had been taken by spy beams through the windows of Graham's shop. None of the prints were in any way incriminating. Not one showed Graham smiling.

He had been selling electrical joy for twelve years now.

A current addict has an advantage over his supplier. Electricity is cheap. With a drug, your supplier can always raise the price on you; but not with electricity. You see the ecstasy merchant once, when he sells you your operation and your droud, and never again. Nobody gets hooked by accident. There's an honesty to current addiction. The customer always know just what he's getting into, and what it will do for him—and to him.

Still, you'd need a certain lack of empathy to make a living the way Kenneth Graham did. Else he'd have had to turn away his customers. Nobody becomes a current addict gradually. He decides all at once, and he buys the operation before he has ever tasted its joy. Each of Kenneth Graham's customers had reached his shop after deciding to drop out of the human race.

What a stream of the hopeless and the desperate must have passed through Graham's shop! How could they help but haunt his dreams? And if Kenneth Graham slept well at night, then—

Then, small wonder if he had turned organlegger.

He was in a good position for it. Despair is characteristic of the would-be current addict. The unknown, the unloved, the people nobody knew and nobody needed and nobody missed, these passed in a steady stream through Kenneth Graham's shop.

So a few didn't come out. Who'd notice?

I flipped quickly through the tape to find out who was in charge of watching Graham. Jackson Bera. I called down through the desk phone.

"Sure," said Bera, "we've had a spy on him about three weeks now. It's a waste of good salaried ARM agents. Maybe he's clean. Maybe he's been tipped somehow."

"Then why not stop watching him?"

Bera looked disgusted. "Because we've only been watching for three weeks. How many donors do you think he needs a year? Two. Read the reports. Gross profit on a single donor is over a million UN marks. Graham can afford to be careful who he picks."

"Yah."

"At that, he wasn't careful enough. At least two of his customers disappeared last year. Customers with families. That's what put us on him."

"So you could watch him for the next six months without a guarantee. He could be just waiting for the right guy to walk in."

"Sure. He has to write up a report on every customer. That gives him the right to ask personal questions. If the guy has relatives, Graham lets him walk out. Most people do have relatives, you know. Then again," Bera said disconsolately, "he could be clean. Sometimes a current addict disappears without help."

"How come I didn't see any holos of Graham at home? You can't be watching just his shop."

Jackson Bera scratched at his hair. Hair like black steel wool, worn long like a bushman's mop. "Sure we're watching his place, but we can't get a spy beam in there. It's an inside apartment. No windows. You know anything about spy beams?"

"Not much. I know they've been around awhile."

"They're as old as lasers. Oldest trick in the book is to put a mirror in the room you want to bug. Then you run a laser beam through a window, or even through heavy drapes, and bounce it off the mirror. When you pick it up it's been distorted by the vibrations in the glass. That gives you a perfect recording of anything that's been said in that room. But for pictures you need something a little more sophisticated.''

''How sophisticated can we get?''

''We can put a spy beam in any room with a window. We can send one through some kinds of wall. Give us an optically flat surface and we can send one around corners.''

''But you need an outside wall.''

''Yup.''

''What's Graham doing now?''

''Just a sec.'' Bera disappeared from view. ''Someone just came in. Graham's talking to him. Want the picture?''

''Sure. Leave it on. I'll turn it off from here when I'm through with it.''

The picture of Bera went dark. A moment later I was looking into a doctor's office. If I'd seen it cold I'd have thought it was run by a podiatrist. There was the comfortable tilt-back chair with the headrest and the footrest; the cabinet next to it with instruments lying on top, on a clean white cloth; the desk over in one corner. Kenneth Graham was talking to a homely, washed-out-looking girl.

I listened to Graham's would-be-fatherly reassurances and his glowing description of the magic of current addiction. When I couldn't take it any longer I turned the sound down. The girl took her place in the chair, and Graham placed something over her head.

The girl's homely face turned suddenly beautiful.

Happiness is beautiful, all by itself. A happy person is beautiful, per se. Suddenly and totally, the girl was full of joy and I realized that I hadn't known everything about droud sales. Apparently Graham had an inductor to put the current where he wanted it, without wires. He *could* show a customer what current addiction felt like, without first implanting the wires.

What a powerful argument that was!

Graham turned off the machine. It was as if he'd turned off the girl. She sat stunned for a moment, then reached frantically for her purse and started scrabbling inside.

I couldn't take any more. I turned it off.

Small wonder if Graham had turned organlegger. He had to be totally without empathy just to sell his merchandise.

Even there, I thought, he'd had a head start.

So he was a little more callous than the rest of the world's billions. But not much. Every voter had a bit of the organ-legger in him. In voting the death penalty for so many crimes, the law makers had only bent to pressure from the voters. There was a spreading lack of respect for life, the evil side of transplant technology. The good side was a longer life for everyone. One condemned criminal could save a dozen deserving lives. Who could complain about that?

We hadn't thought that way in the Belt. In the Belt survival was a virtue in itself, and life was a precious thing, spread so thin among the sterile rocks, hurtling in single units through all that killing emptiness between the worlds.

So I'd had to come to Earth for my transplant.

My request had been accepted two months after I landed. So quickly? Later I'd learned that the banks always have a surplus of certain items. Few people lose their arms these days. I had also learned, a year after the transplant had taken, that I was using an arm taken from a captured organlegger's storage bank.

That had been a shock. I'd hoped my arm had come from a depraved murderer, someone who'd shot fourteen nurses from a rooftop. Not at all. Some faceless, nameless victim had had the bad luck to encounter a ghoul, and I had benefited thereby.

Did I turn in my new arm in a fit of revulsion? No, surprising to say, I did not. But I had joined the ARMs, once the Amalgamation of Regional Militia, now the United Nations Police. Though I had stolen a dead man's arm, I would hunt the kin of those who had killed him.

The noble urgency of that resolve had been drowned in paperwork these last few years. Perhaps I was becoming callous, like the flatlanders—the *other* flatlanders around me, voting new death penalties year after year. *Income-tax evasion. Operating a flying vehicle on manual controls over a city.*

Was Kenneth Graham so much worse than they?

Sure he was. The bastard had put a wire in Owen Jennison's head.

I waited twenty minutes for Julie to come out. I could have sent her a memorandum, but there was plenty of time before noon, and too little time to get anything accomplished, and . . . I wanted to talk to her.

"Hi," she said. "Thanks," taking the coffee. "How went

the ceremonial drunk? Oh, I *see*. Mmmmm. Very good. Almost poetic.'' Conversation with Julie has a way of taking shortcuts.

Poetic, right. I remembered how inspiration had struck like lightning through a mild high glow. Owen's floating cigarette lure. What better way to honor his memory than to use it to pick up a girl?

''Right,'' Julie agreed. ''But there's something you may have missed. What's Taffy's last name?''

''I can't remember. She wrote it down on—''

''What does she do for a living?''

''How should I know?''

''What religion is she? Is she a pro or an anti? Where did she grow up?''

''Dammit—''

''Half an hour ago you were very complacently musing on how depersonalized all us flatlanders are except you. What's Taffy, a person or a foldout?'' Julie stood with her hands on her hips, looking up at me like a short schoolteacher.

How many people is Julie? Some of us have never seen this Guardian aspect. She's frightening, the Guardian. If it ever appeared on a date, the man she was with would be struck impotent forever.

It never does. When a reprimand is deserved, Julie delivers it in broad daylight. This serves to separate her functions, but it doesn't make it easier to take.

No use pretending it wasn't her business, either.

I'd come here to ask for Julie's protection. Let me turn unlovable to Julie, even a little bit unlovable, and as far as Julie was concerned, I would have an unreadable mind. How, then, would she know when I was in trouble? How could she send help to rescue me from whatever? My private life *was* her business, her single, vastly important job.

''I *like* Taffy,'' I protested. ''I didn't care who she was when we met. Now I like her, and I think she likes me. What do you want from a first date?''

''You know better. You can remember other dates when two of you talked all night on a couch, just from the joy of learning about each other.'' She mentioned three names, and I flushed. Julie knows the words that will turn you inside out in an instant. ''Taffy is a person, not an episode, not a symbol of anything, not just a pleasant night. What's your judgment of her?"

I thought about it, standing there in the corridor. Funny: I've faced the Guardian Julie on other occasions, and it has never occurred to me to just walk out of the unpleasant situation. Later I think of that. At the time I just stand there, facing the Guardian/Judge/Teacher. I thought about Taffy . . .

"She's nice," I said. "*Not* depersonalized. Squeamish, even. She wouldn't make a good nurse. She'd want to help too much, and it would tear her apart when she couldn't. I'd say she was one of the vulnerable ones."

"Go on."

"I want to see her again, but I won't dare talk shop with her. In fact . . . I'd better not see her till this business of Owen is over. Loren might take an interest in her. Or . . . she might take an interest in me, and I might get hurt . . . have I missed anything?"

"I think so. You owe her a phone call. If you won't be dating her for a few days, call her and tell her so."

"Check." I spun on my heel, spun back. "Finagle's Jest! I almost forgot. The reason I came here—"

"I know, you want a time slot. Suppose I check on you at oh nine forty-five every morning?"

"That's a little early. When I get in deadly danger it's usually at night."

"I'm off at night. Oh nine forty-five is all I've got. I'm sorry, Gil, but it is. Shall I monitor you or not?"

"Sold. Nine forty-five."

"Good. Let me know if you get real proof Owen was murdered. I'll give you two slots. You'll be in a little more concrete danger then."

"Good."

"I love you. Yeep, I'm late." And she dodged back into the office, while I went to call Taffy.

Taffy wasn't home, of course, and I didn't know where she worked, or even what she did. Her phone offered to take a message. I gave my name and said I'd call back.

And then I sat there sweating for five minutes.

It was half an hour to noon. Here I was at my desk phone. I couldn't decently see any way to argue myself out of sending a message to Homer Chandrasekhar.

I didn't want to talk to him, then or ever. He'd chewed me

out but good, last time I'd seen him. My free arm had cost me my Belter life and it had cost me Homer's respect. I didn't want to talk to him, even on a one-way message, and I most particularly didn't want to have to tell him Owen was dead.

But someone had to tell him.

And maybe he could find out something.

And I'd put it off nearly a full day.

For five minutes I sweated, and then I called long distance and recorded a message and sent it off to Ceres. More accurately, I recorded six messages before I was satisfied. I don't want to talk about it.

I tried Taffy again; she might come home for lunch. Wrong.

I hung up wondering if Julie had been fair. What had we bargained for, Taffy and I, beyond a pleasant night?

And we'd had just that, and would have others, with luck.

But Julie would find it hard not to be fair. If she thought Taffy was the vulnerable type, she'd taken her information from my own mind.

Mixed feelings. You're a kid, and your mother has just laid down the law. But it *is* a law, something you can count on . . . and she *is* paying attention to you . . . and she *does* care . . . when, for so many of those outside, nobody cares at all.

"Naturally I thought of murder," said Ordaz. "I always consider murder. When my sainted mother passed away after three years of the most tender care by my sister Maria Angela, I actually considered searching for evidence of needle holes about the head."

"Find any?"

Ordaz' face froze. He put down his beer and started to get up.

"Cool it," I said hurriedly. "No offense intended." He glared a moment, then sat down half mollified.

We'd picked an outdoor restaurant on the pedestrian level. On the other side of a hedge (a real live hedge, green and growing and everything) the shoppers were carried past in a steady one-way stream. Beyond them, a slidewalk carried a similar stream in the opposite direction. I had the dizzy feeling that it was we who were moving.

A waiter like a bell-bottomed chess pawn produced steaming dishes of chili from its torso, put them precisely in front of us, and slid away on a cushion of air.

"Naturally I considered murder. Believe me. Mr. Hamilton, it does not hold up."

"I think I could make a pretty good case."

"You may try, of course. Better, I will start you on your way. First, we must assume that Kenneth Graham the happiness peddler did not sell a droud-and-plug to Owen Jennison. Rather, Owen Jennison was forced to undergo the operation. Graham's records, including the written permission to operate, were forged. All this we must assume, is it not so?"

"Right. And before you tell me Graham's escutcheon is unblemished, let me tell you that it isn't."

"Oh?"

"He's connected with an organlegging gang. That's classified information. We're watching him, and we don't want him tipped."

"That is news." Ordaz rubbed his jaw. "Organlegging. Well. What would Owen Jennison have to do with organlegging?"

"Owen's a Belter. The Belt's always drastically short of transplant materials."

"Yes, they import quantities of medical supplies from Earth. Not only organs in storage, but also drugs and prosthetics. So?"

"Owen ran a good many cargos past the goldskins in his day. He got caught a few times, but he's still way ahead of the government. He's on the records as a successful smuggler. If a big organlegger wanted to expand his market, he might very well send a feeler out to a Belter with a successful smuggling record."

"You never mentioned that Mr. Jennison was a smuggler."

"What for? All Belters are smugglers, if they think they can get away with it. To a Belter, smuggling isn't immoral. But an organlegger wouldn't know that. He'd think Owen was already a criminal."

"Do you think your friend—" Ordaz hesitated delicately.

"No, Owen wouldn't turn organlegger. But he might, he just *might* try to turn one in. The rewards for information leading to the capture and conviction of, et cetera, are substantial. If someone contacted Owen, Owen might very well have tried to trace the contact by himself.

"Now, the gang we're after covers half the west coast of this continent. That's big. It's the Loren gang, the one Graham may be working for. Suppose Owen had a chance to meet Loren himself?"

"You think he might take it, do you?"

"I think he did. I think he let his hair grow out so he'd look like an Earthman, to convince Loren he wanted to look inconspicuous. I think he collected as much information as he could, then tried to get out with a whole skin. But he didn't make it.

"Did you find his application for a nudist license?"

"No. I saw your point there," said Ordaz. He leaned back, ignoring the food in front of him. "Mr. Jennison's tan was uniform except for the characteristic darkening of the face. I presume he was a practicing nudist in the Belt."

"Yah. We don't need licenses there. He'd have been one here, too, unless he was hiding something. Remember that scar. He never missed a chance to show it off."

"Could he really have thought to pass for a—" Ordaz hesitated—"flatlander?"

"With that Belter tan? No! He was overdoing it a little with the haircut. Maybe he thought Loren would underestimate him. But he wasn't advertising his presence, or he wouldn't have left his most personal possessions home."

"So he was dealing with organleggers, and they found him out before he could reach you. Yes, Mr. Hamilton, this is well thought out. But it won't work."

"Why not? I'm not trying to prove it's murder. Not yet. I'm just trying to show you that murder is at least as likely as suicide."

"But it's not, Mr. Hamilton."

I looked the question.

"Consider the details of the hypothetical murder. Owen Jennison is drugged, no doubt, and taken to the office of Kenneth Graham. There, an ecstasy plug is attached. A standard droud is fitted, and is then amateurishly altered with soldering tools. Already we see, on the part of the killer, a minute attention to details. We see it again in Kenneth Graham's forged papers of permission to operate. They were impeccable."

"Owen Jennison is then taken back to his apartment. It would be his own, would it not? There would be little point in moving him to another. The cord from his droud is shortened, again in amateurish fashion. Mr. Jennison is tied up—"

"I wondered if you'd see that."

"But why should he not be tied up? He is tied up, and allowed to waken. Perhaps the arrangement is explained to him, perhaps not. That would be up to the killer. The killer then plugs Mr. Jennison into a wall. A current trickles through his brain, and Owen Jennison knows pure pleasure for the first time in his life.

"He is left tied up for, let us say, three hours. In the first few minutes he would be a hopeless addict, I think—"

"You must have known more current addicts than I have."

"Even I would not want to be pinned down. Your normal current addict is an addict after a few minutes. But then, your normal current addict asked to be made an addict, knowing what it would do to his life. Current addiction is symptomatic of despair. Your friend might have been able to fight free of a few minutes' exposure."

"So they kept him tied up for three hours. Then they cut the ropes." I felt sickened. Ordaz' ugly, ugly pictures matched mine in every detail.

"No more than three hours, by our hypothesis. They would not dare stay longer than a few hours. They would cut the ropes and leave Owen Jennison to starve to death. In the space of a month the evidence of his drugging would vanish, as would any abrasions left by ropes, lumps on his head, mercy needle punctures, and the like. A carefully detailed, well-thought-out plan, don't you agree?"

I told myself that Ordaz was not being ghoulish. He was just doing his job. Still, it was difficult to answer objectively.

"It fits our picture of Loren. He's been very careful with us. He'd love carefully detailed, well-thought-out plans."

Ordaz leaned forward. "But don't you see? A carefully detailed plan is all wrong. There is a crucial flaw in it. Suppose Mr. Jennison pulls out the droud?"

"Could he do that? Would he?"

"Could he? Certainly. A simple tug of the fingers. The current wouldn't interfere with motor coordination. Would he?" Ordaz pulled meditatively at his beer. "I know a good deal about current addiction, but I don't know what it *feels* like, Mr. Hamilton. Your normal addict pulls his droud out as often as he inserts it, but your friend was getting ten times normal current. He might have pulled the droud out a dozen times, and instantly plugged it back each time. Yet Belters are supposed to be strong-willed men, very individualistic. Who knows whether, even after a week of addiction, your friend might not have pulled the droud loose, coiled the cord, slipped it in his pocket, and walked away scot free?

"There is the additional risk that someone might walk in on him—an automachinery serviceman, for instance. Or someone might notice that he had not bought any food in a month. A suicide would take that risk. Suicides routinely leave themselves a chance to change their minds. But a murderer?

"No, even if the chance were one in a thousand, the man who created such a detailed plan would never have taken such a chance."

The sun burned hotly down on our shoulders. Ordaz suddenly remembered his lunch and began to eat.

I watched the world ride by beyond the hedge. Pedestrians stood in little conversational bunches; others peered into shop windows on the pedestrian strip, or glanced over the hedge to watch us eat. There were the few who pushed through the crowd with set expressions, impatient with the ten-mile-per-hour speed of the slidewalk.

"Maybe they *were* watching him. Maybe the room was bugged."

"We searched the room thoroughly," said Ordaz. "If there had been observational equipment, we would have found it."

"It could have been removed."

Ordaz shrugged.

I remembered the spy-eyes in Monica Apartments. Someone would have had to physically enter the room to carry a bug out. He could ruin it with the right signal, maybe, but it would surely leave traces.

And Owen had had an inside room. No spy-eyes.

"There's one thing you've left out," I said presently.

"And what would that be?"

"My name in Owen's wallet, listed as next of kin. He was directing my attention to the thing I was working on. The Loren gang."

"That is possible."

"You can't have it both ways."

Ordaz lowered his fork. "I *can* have it both ways, Mr. Hamilton. But you won't like it."

"I'm sure I won't."

"Let us incorporate your assumption. Mr. Jennison was contacted by an agent of Loren, the organlegger, who intended to sell transplant material to Belters. He accepted. The promise of riches was too much for him.

"A month later, something made him realize what a terrible thing he had done. He decided to die. He went to an ecstasy peddler and he had a wire put in his head. Later, before he plugged in the droud, he made one attempt to atone for his crime. He listed you as his next of kin, so that you might guess why he had died, and perhaps so that you could use that knowledge against Loren."

Ordaz looked at me across the table. "I see that you will never agree. I cannot help that. I can only read the evidence."

"Me too. But I knew Owen. He'd never have worked for an organlegger, he'd never have killed himself, and if he had, he'd never have done it that way."

Ordaz didn't answer.

"What about fingerprints?"

"In the apartment? None."

"None but Owen's?"

"Even his were found only on the chairs and end tables. I curse the man who invented the cleaning robot. Every smooth surface in that apartment was cleaned exactly forty-four times during Mr. Jennison's tenancy." Ordaz went back to his chili size.

"Then try this. Assume for the moment that I'm right. Assume Owen was after Loren, and Loren got him. Owen knew he was doing something dangerous. He wouldn't have wanted me to get onto Loren before he was ready. He wanted the reward for himself. But he might have left me something, just in case.

"Something in a locker somewhere, an airport or spaceport locker. Evidence. Not under his own name, or mine either, because I'm a known ARM. But—"

"Some name you both know."

"Right. Like Homer Chandrasekhar. Or—got it. Cubes Forsythe. Owen would have thought that was apt. Cubes is dead."

"We will look. You must understand that it will not prove your case."

"Sure. Anything you find, Owen could have arranged in a fit of conscience. Screw that. Let me know what you get," I said, and stood up and left.

I rode the slidewalk, not caring where it was taking me. It would give me a chance to cool off.

Could Ordaz be right? Could he?

But the more I dug into Owen's death, the worse it made Owen look.

Therefore Ordaz was wrong.

Owen work for an organlegger? He'd rather have been a donor.

Owen getting his kicks from a wall socket? He never even watched tridee!

Owen kill himself? No. If so, not that way.

But even if I could have swallowed all that . . .

Owen Jennison, letting me know he'd worked with organleggers? Me, Gil the Arm Hamilton? Let *me* know *that?*

The slidewalk rolled along, past restaurants and shopping centers and churches and banks. Ten stories below, the hum of cars and scooters drifted faintly up from the vehicular level. The sky was a narrow, vivid slash of blue between black shadows of skyscraper.

Let *me* know *that?* Never.

But Ordaz' strangely inconsistent murderer was no better.

I thought of something even Ordaz had missed. Why would Loren dispose of Owen so elaborately? Owen need only disappear into the organ banks, never to bother Loren again.

The shops were thinning out now, and so were the crowds. The slidewalk narrowed, entered a residential area, and not a very good one. I'd let it carry me a long way. I looked around, trying to decide where I was.

And I was four blocks from Graham's place.

My subconscious had done me a dirty. I wanted to look at Kenneth Graham, face to face. The temptation to go on was nearly irresistible, but I fought it off and changed direction at the next disk.

A slidewalk intersection is a rotating disk, its rim tangent to four slidewalks and moving with the same speed. From the center you ride up an escalator and over the slidewalks to reach stationary walks along the buildings. I could have caught a cab at the center of the disk, but I still wanted to think, so I just rode halfway around the rim.

I could have walked into Graham's shop and gotten away with it. Maybe. I'd have looked hopeless and bored and hesitant, told Graham I wanted an ecstasy plug, worried loudly about what my wife and friends would say, then changed my mind at the last moment. He'd have let me walk out, knowing I'd be missed. Maybe.

But Loren had to know more about the ARMs than we knew about him. Some time or other, had Graham been shown a holo of yours truly? Let a known ARM walk into his shop, and Graham would panic. It wasn't worth the risk.

Then, dammit, what *could* I do?

Ordaz' inconsistent killer. If we assumed Owen was murdered, we couldn't get away from the other assumptions. The care, the nitpicking detail—and then Owen left alone to pull out the plug and walk away, or to be discovered by a persistent salesman or a burglar, or—

No. Ordaz' hypothetical killer, and mine, would have watched Owen like a hawk. For a month.

That did it. I stepped off at the next disk and got a taxi.

The taxi dropped me on the roof of Monica Apartments. I took an elevator to the lobby.

If the manager was surprised to see me, he didn't show it as he gestured me into his office. The office seemed much roomier than the lobby had, possibly because there were things to break the anonymous-modern decor: paintings on the wall, a small black worm track in the rug that must have been caused by a visitor's cigarette, a holo of Miller and his wife on the wide, nearly empty desk. He waited until I was settled, then leaned forward expectantly.

"I'm here on ARM business," I said, and passed him my ident.

He passed it back without checking it. "I presume it's the same business," he said without cordiality.

"Yah. I'm convinced Owen Jennison must have had visitors while he was here."

The manager smiled. "That's ridic—impossible."

"Nope, it's not. Your holo cameras take pictures of visitors, but they don't snap the tenants, do they?"

"Of course not."

"Then Owen could have been visited by any tenant in the building."

The manager looked shocked. "No, certainly not. Really, I don't see why you pursue this, Mr. Hamilton. If Mr. Jennison had been found in such a condition, it would have been reported!"

"I don't think so. Could he have been visited by any tenant in the building?"

"No. No. The cameras would have taken a picture of anyone from another floor."

"How about someone from the same floor?"

Reluctantly the manager bobbed his head. "Ye-es. As far as the holo cameras are concerned, that's possible. But—"

"Then I'd like to ask for pictures of any tenant who lived on the eighteenth floor during the last six weeks. Send them to the ARM Building, Central L.A. Can do?"

"Of course. You'll have them within an hour."

"Good. Now, something else occurred to me. Suppose a man got out on the nineteenth floor and walked down to the eighteenth. He'd be holoed on the nineteenth, but not on the eighteenth, right?"

The manager smiled indulgently. "Mr. Hamilton, there are no stairs in this building."

"Just the elevators? Isn't that dangerous?"

"Not at all. There is a separate self-contained emergency power source for each of the elevators. It's common practice. After all, who would want to walk up eighty stories if the elevator failed?"

"Okay, fine. One last point. Could someone tamper with the computer? Could someone make it decide not to take a certain picture, for instance?"

"I . . . am not an expert on how to tamper with computers, Mr. Hamilton. Why don't you go straight to the company? Caulfield Brains, Inc."

"Okay. What's your model?"

"Just a moment." He got up and leafed through a drawer in a filing cabinet. "EQ 144."

"Okay."

That was all I could do here, and I knew it . . . and still I didn't have the will to get up. There ought to be *something* . . .

Finally Miller cleared his throat. "Will that be all, sir?"

"Yes," I said. "No. Can I get into 1809?"

"I'll see if we've rented it yet."

"The police are through with it?"

"Certainly." He went back to the filing cabinet. "No, it's still available. I'll take you up. How long will you be?"

"I don't know. No more than half an hour. No need to come up."

"Very well." He handed me the key and waited for me to leave. I did

The merest flicker of blue light caught my eye as I left the elevator. I would have thought it was my optic nerve, not in the real world, if I hadn't known about the holo cameras. Maybe it was. You don't need laser light to make a holograph, but it does get you clearer pictures.

Owen's room was a box. Everything was retracted. There was nothing but the bare walls. I had never seen anything so desolate, unless it was some asteroidal rock, too poor to mine, too badly placed to be worth a base.

The control panel was just beside the door. I turned on the lights, then touched the master button. Lines appeared, outlined in red and green and blue. A great square on one wall for the bed, most of another wall for the kitchen, various outlines across the floor. Very handy. You wouldn't want a guest to be standing on the table when you expanded it.

I'd come here to get the feel of the place, to encourage a hunch, to see if I'd missed anything. Translation: I was playing. Playing, I reached through the control panel to find the circuits. The printed circuitry was too small and too detailed to tell me anything, but I ran imaginary fingertips along a few wires and found that they looped straight to their action points, no detours. No sensors to the outside. You'd have to be in the room to know what was expanded, what retracted.

So a supposedly occupied room had had its bed retracted for six weeks. But you'd have to be in the room to know it.

I pushed buttons to expand the kitchen nook and the reading chair. The wall slid out eight feet; the floor humped itself and took form. I sat down in the chair, and the kitchen nook blocked my view of the door.

Nobody would have seen Owen from the hall.

If only someone had noticed that Owen wasn't ordering food. That might have saved him.

I thought of something else, and it made me look around for the air conditioner. There was a grille at floor level. I felt behind it with my imaginary hand. Some of these apartment air-conditioning units go on when the CO_2 level hits half a percent. This one was geared to temperature and manual control.

With the other kind, our careful killer could have tapped the air-conditioner current to find out if Owen was still alive and present. As it was, 1809 had behaved like an empty room for six weeks.

I flopped back in the reading chair.

If my hypothetical killer had watched Owen, he'd done it with a bug. Unless he'd actually lived on this floor for the four or five weeks it took Owen to die, there was no other way.

Okay, think about a bug. Make it small enough and nobody would find it except the cleaning robot, who would send it straight to the incinerator. You'd have to make it big, so the robot wouldn't get it. No worry about Owen finding it! And then, when you knew Owen was dead, you'd use the self-destruct.

But if you burned it to slag, you'd leave a burn hole somewhere. Ordaz would have found it. So. An asbestos pad? You'd want the self-destruct to leave something that the cleaning robot would sweep up.

And if you'll believe that you'll believe anything. It was too chancy. *Nobody* knows what a cleaning robot will decide is garbage. They're made stupid because it's cheaper. So they're programed to leave large objects alone.

There had to be someone on this floor, either to watch Owen himself or to pick up the bug that did the watching. I was betting everything I had on a human watcher.

*   *   *

I'd come here mainly to give my intuition a chance. It wasn't working. Owen had spent six weeks in this chair, and for at least the last week he'd been dead. Yet I couldn't feel it with him. It was just a chair with two end tables. He had left nothing in the room, not even a restless ghost.

The call caught me halfway back to Headquarters.

"You were right," Ordaz told me over the wristphone. "We have found a locker at Death Valley Port registered to Cubes Forsythe. I am on my way there now. Will you join me?"

"I'll meet you there."

"Good. I am as eager as you to see what Owen Jennison left us."

I doubted that.

The Port was something more than two hundred thirty miles away, an hour at taxi speeds. It would be a big fare. I typed out a new address on the destination board, then called in at Headquarters. An ARM agent is fairly free; he doesn't have to justify every little move. There was no question of getting permission to go. At worst they might disallow the fare on my expense account.

"Oh, and there'll be a set of holos coming in from Monica Apartments," I told the man. "Have the computer check them against known organleggers and associates of Loren."

The taxi rose smoothly into the sky and headed east. I watched tridee and drank coffee until I ran out of coins for the dispenser.

If you go between November and May, when the climate is ideal, Death Valley can be a tourist's paradise. There is the Devil's Golf Course, with its fantastic ridges and pinnacles of salt; Zabriskie Point and its weird badlands topography; the old borax mining sites; and all kinds of strange, rare plants, adapted to the heat and the death-dry climate. Yes, Death Valley has many points of interest, and someday I was going to see them. So far all I'd seen was the spaceport. But the Port was impressive in its own way.

The landing field used to be part of a sizable inland sea. It is now a sea of salt. Alternating red and blue concentric circles mark the field for ships dropping from space, and a century's developments in chemical, fission, and fusion reaction motors have left blast pits striped like rainbows by esoteric, often radioactive salts. But mostly the field retains its ancient glare-white.

And out across the salt are ships of many sizes and many shapes. Vehicles and machinery dance attendance, and, if you're willing to wait, you may see a ship land. It's worth the wait.

The Port building, at the edge of the major salt flat, is a pastel green tower set in a wide patch of fluorescent orange concrete. No ship has ever landed on it—yet; the taxi dropped me at the entrance and moved away to join others of its kind. And I stood inhaling the dry, balmy air.

Four months of the year, Death Valley's climate is ideal. One August the Furnace Creek Ranch recorded 134° Fahrenheit shade temperature.

A man behind a desk told me that Ordaz had arrived before me. I found him and another officer in a labyrinth of pay lockers, each big enough to hold two or three suitcases. The locker Ordaz had opened held only a lightweight plastic briefcase.

"He may have taken other lockers," he said.

"Probably not. Belters travel light. Have you tried to open it?"

"Not yet. It is a combination lock. I thought perhaps . . ."

"Maybe." I squatted to look at it.

Funny: I felt no surprise at all. It was as if I'd known all along that Owen's suitcase would be there. And why not? He was bound to try to protect himself somehow. Through me, because I was already involved in the UN side of organlegging. By leaving something in a spaceport locker, because Loren couldn't find the right locker or get into it if he did, and because I would naturally connect Owen with spaceports. Under Cubes' name, because I'd be looking for that, and Loren wouldn't.

Hindsight is wonderful.

The lock had five digits. "He must have meant me to open it. Let's see . . ." and I moved the tumblers to 42217. April 22, 2117, the day Cubes died, stapled suddenly to a plastic partition.

The lock clicked open.

Ordaz went instantly for the manila folder. More slowly, I picked up two glass phials. One was tightly sealed against Earth's air, and half full of an incredibly fine dust. So fine was it that it slid about like oil inside the glass. The other phial held a blackened grain of nickel-iron, barely big enough to see.

Other things were in that case, but the prize was that folder. The story was in there . . . at least up to a point. Owen must have planned to add to it.

A message had been waiting for him in the Ceres mail dump when he returned from his last trip out. Owen must have laughed over parts of that message. Loren had taken the trouble to assemble a complete dossier of Owen's smuggling activities over the past eight years. Did he think he could ensure Owen's silence by threatening to turn the dossier over to the goldskins?

Maybe the dossier had given Owen the wrong idea. In any case, he'd decided to contact Loren and see what developed. Ordinarily he'd have sent me the entire message and let me try to track it down. I was the expert, after all. But Owen's last trip out had been a disaster.

His fusion drive had blown somewhere beyond Jupiter's orbit. No explanation. The safeties had blown his lifesystem capsule free of the explosion, barely. A rescue ship had returned him to Ceres. The fee had nearly broken him. He needed money. Loren may have known that, and counted on it.

The reward for information leading to Loren's capture would have bought him a new ship.

He'd landed at Outback Field, following Loren's instructions. From there, Loren's men had moved him about a good deal: to London, to Bombay, to Amberg, Germany. Owen's personal, written story ended in Amberg. How had he reached California? He had not had a chance to say.

But in between, he had learned a good deal. There were snatches of detail on Loren's organization. There was Loren's full plan for shipping illicit transplant materials to the Belt, and for finding and contacting customers. Owen had made suggestions there. Most of them sounded reasonable and would be unworkable in practice. Typically Owen. I could find no sign that he'd overplayed his hand.

But of course he hadn't known it when he did.

And there were holos, twenty-three of them, each a member of Loren's gang. Some of the pictures had markings on the back; others were blank. Owen had been unable to find out where each of them stood in the organization.

I leafed through them twice, wondering if one of them could be Loren himself. Owen had never known.

"It would seem you were right," said Ordaz. "He could not have collected such detail by accident. He must have planned from the beginning to betray the Loren gang."

"Just as I told you. And he was murdered for it."

"It seems he must have been. What motive could he have had for suicide?" Ordaz' round, calm face was doing its best to show anger. "I find I cannot believe in our inconsistent murderer either. You have ruined my digestion, Mr. Hamilton."

I told him my idea about other tenants on Owen's floor. He nodded. "Possibly, possibly. This is your department now. Organlegging is the business of the ARMs."

"Right." I closed the briefcase and hefted it. "Let's see what the computer can do with these. I'll send you photocopies of everything in here."

"You'll let me know about the other tenants?"

"Of course."

I walked into ARM Headquarters swinging that precious briefcase, feeling on top of the world. Owen had been murdered. He had died with honor, if not—oh, definitely not—with dignity. Even Ordaz knew it now.

Then Jackson Bera, snarling and panting, went by at a dead run.

"What's up?" I called after him. Maybe I wanted a chance to brag. I had twenty-three faces, twenty-three organleggers, in my briefcase.

Bera slid to a stop beside me. "Where *you* been?"

"Working. Honest. What's the hurry?"

"Remember that pleasure peddler we were watching?"

"Graham? Kenneth Graham?"

"That's the one. He's dead. We blew it." And Bera took off.

He'd reached the lab by the time I caught up with him.

Kenneth Graham's corpse was face up on the operating table. His long, lantern-jawed face was pale and slack, without expression: empty. Machinery was in place above and below his head.

"How you doing?" Bera demanded.

"Not good," the doctor answered. "Not your fault. You got him into the deepfreeze fast enough. It's just that the current—" He shrugged.

I shook Bera's shoulder. "What happened?"

Bera was panting a little from his run. "Something must have leaked. Graham tried to make a run for it. We got him at the airport."

"You could have waited. Put someone on the plane with him. Flooded the plane with TY-4."

"Remember the stink the last time we used TY-4 on civilians? Damn newscasters." Bera was shivering. I didn't blame him.

ARMs and organleggers play a funny kind of game. The organleggers have to turn their donors in alive, so they're always armed with hypo guns, firing slivers of crystalline anesthetic that melt instantly in the blood. We use the same weapon, for somewhat the same reason: a criminal has to be saved for trial, and then for the government hospitals. So no ARM ever expects to kill a man.

There was a day I learned the truth. A small-time organlegger named Raphael Haine was trying to reach a call button in his own home. If he'd reached it all kinds of hell would have broken loose. Haine's men would have hypoed me, and I would have regained consciousness a piece at a time, in Haine's organ-storage tanks. So I strangled him.

The report was in the computer, but only three human beings knew about it. One was my immediate superior, Lucas Carner. The other was Julie. So far, he was the only man I'd ever killed.

And Graham was Bera's first killing.

"We got him at the airport," said Bera. "He was wearing a hat. I wish I'd noticed that, we might have moved faster. We started to close in on him with hypo guns. He turned and saw us. He reached under his hat, and then he fell.''

"Killed himself?"

"Uh huh."

"How?"

"Look at his head."

I edged closer to the table, trying to stay out of the doctor's way. The doctor was going through the routine of trying to pull information from a dead brain by induction. It wasn't going well.

There was a flat oblong box on top of Graham's head. Black plastic, about half the size of a pack of cards. I touched it and knew at once that it was attached to Graham's skull.

"A droud. Not a standard type. Too big."

"Uh huh."

Liquid helium ran up my nerves. "There's a battery in it."

"Right."

"I often wonder what the vintners buy, et cetera. A cordless droud. Man, that's what *I* want for Christmas."

Bera twitched all over. "Don't *say* that."

"Did you know he was a current addict?"

"No. We were afraid to bug his home. He might have found it and been tipped. Take another look at that thing."

The shape was wrong, I thought. The black plastic case had been half melted.

"Heat," I mused. "Oh!"

"Uh huh. He blew the whole battery at once. Sent the whole killing charge right through his brain, right through the pleasure center of his brain. And, Jesus, Gil, the thing I keep wondering is, what did it feel like? Gil, what could it possibly have *felt* like?"

I thumped him across the shoulders in lieu of giving him an intelligent answer. He'd be a long time wondering. And so would I.

Here was the man who had put the wire in Owen's head. Had his death been momentary Hell, or all the delights of paradise in one singing jolt? Hell, I hoped, but I didn't believe it.

At least Kenneth Graham wasn't somewhere else in the world, getting a new face and new retinas and new fingertips from Loren's illicit organ banks.

"Nothing," said the doctor. "His brain's too badly burned. There's just nothing there that isn't too scrambled to make sense."

"Keep trying," said Bera.

I left quietly. Maybe later I'd buy Bera a drink. He seemed to need it. Bera was one of those with empathy. I knew that he could almost feel that awful surge of ecstasy and defeat as Kenneth Graham left the world behind.

The holos from Monica Apartments had arrived hours ago. Miller had picked not only the tenants who had occupied the eighteenth floor during the past six weeks, but tenants from the nineteenth and seventeenth floors too. It seemed an embarrassment of riches. I toyed with the idea of someone from the nineteenth floor dropping over his balcony to the eighteenth, every day for five weeks. But 1809 hadn't had an outside wall, let alone a window, not to mention a balcony.

Had Miller played with the same idea? Nonsense. He didn't even know the problem. He'd just overkilled with the holos to show how cooperative he was.

None of the tenants during the period in question matched known or suspected Loren men.

I said a few appropriate words and went for coffee. Then I remembered the twenty-three possible Loren men in Owen's briefcase. I'd left them with a programer, since I wasn't quite sure how to get them into the computer myself. He ought to be finished by now.

I called down. He was.

I persuaded the computer to compare them with the holos from Monica Apartments.

Nothing. Nobody matched anybody.

I spent the next two hours writing up the Owen Jennison case. A programer would have to translate it for the machine. I wasn't that good yet.

We were back with Ordaz' inconsistent killer.

That, and a tangle of dead ends. Owen's death had bought us a handful of new pictures, pictures which might even be obsolete by now. Organleggers changed their faces at the drop of a hat. I finished the case outline, sent it down to a programer, and called Julie. I wouldn't need her protection now.

Julie had left for home.

I started to call Taffy, stopped with her number half dialed. There are times not to make a phone call. I needed to sulk; I needed a cave to be alone in. My expression would probably have broken a phone screen. Why inflict it on an innocent girl?

I left for home.

It was dark when I reached the street. I rode the pedestrian bridge across the slidewalks, waited for a taxi at the intersection disk. Presently one dropped, the white FREE sign blinking on its belly. I stepped in and deposited my credit card.

Owen had collected his holos from all over the Eurasian continent. Most of them, if not all, had been Loren's foreign agents. Why had I expected to find them in Los Angeles?

The taxi rose into the white night sky. City lights turned the cloud cover into a flat white dome. We penetrated the clouds, and stayed there. The taxi autopilot didn't care if I had a view or not.

. . . So what did I have now? Someone among dozens of tenants was a Loren man. That, or Ordaz' inconsistent killer, the careful one, had left Owen to die for five weeks, alone and unsupervised.

. . . Was the inconsistent killer so unbelievable?

He was, after all, my own hypothetical Loren. And Loren had committed murder, the ultimate crime. He'd murdered routinely, over and over, with fabulous profits. The ARMs hadn't been able to touch him. Wasn't it about time he started getting careless?

Like Graham. How long had Graham been selecting donors among his customers, choosing a few nonentities a year? And then, twice within a few months, he took clients who were missed. Careless.

Most criminals are not too bright. Loren had brains enough; but the men on his payroll would be about average. Loren would deal with the stupid ones, the ones who turned to crime because they didn't have enough sense to make it in real life.

If a man like Loren got careless, this was how it would happen. Unconsciously he would judge ARM intelligence by his own men. Seduced by an ingenious plan for murder, he might ignore the single loophole and go through with it. With Graham to advise him, he knew more about current addiction than we did; perhaps enough to trust the effects of current addiction on Owen.

Then Owen's killers had delivered him to his apartment and never seen him again. It was a small gamble Loren had taken, and it had paid off, this time.

Next time, he'd grow more careless. One day we'd get him.

But not today.

The taxi settled out of the traffic pattern, touched down on the roof of my apartment building in the Hollywood Hills. I got out and moved toward the elevators.

An elevator opened. Someone stepped out.

Something warned me, something about the way he moved. I turned, quick-drawing from the shoulder. The taxi might have made good cover—if it hadn't been already rising. Other figures had stepped from the shadows.

I think I got a couple before something stung my cheek. Mercy-bullets, slivers of crystalline anesthetic melting in my bloodstream. My head spun, and the roof spun, and the centrifugal force dropped me limply to the roof. Shadows loomed above me, then receded to infinity.

Fingers on my scalp shocked me awake.

I woke standing upright, bound like a mummy in soft, swaddling bandages. I couldn't so much as twitch a muscle below my neck. By the time I knew that much it was too late. The man behind me had finished removing electrodes from my head and stepped into view, out of reach of my imaginary arm.

There was something of the bird about him. He was tall and slender, small-boned, and his triangular face reached a point at the chin. His wild, silken blond hair had withdrawn from his temples, leaving a sharp widow's peak. He wore impeccably tailored wool street shorts in orange and brown stripes. Smiling brightly, with his arms folded and his head cocked to one side, he stood waiting for me to speak.

And I recognized him. Owen had taken a holo of him, somewhere.

"Where am I?" I groaned, trying to sound groggy. "What time is it?"

"Time? It's already morning," said my captor. "As for where you are. I'll let you wonder."

Something about his manner . . . I took a guess and said, "Loren?"

Loren bowed, not overdoing it. "And you are Gilbert Hamilton of the United Nations Police. Gil the Arm."

Had he said Arm or ARM? I let it pass. "I seem to have slipped."

"You underestimated the reach of my own arm. You also underestimated my interest."

I had. It isn't much harder to capture an ARM than any other citizen, if you catch him off guard, and if you're willing to risk the men. In this case, his risk had cost him nothing. Cops use hypo guns for the same reason organleggers do. The men I'd shot, if I'd hit anyone in those few seconds of battle, would have come around long ago. Loren must have set me up in these bandages, then left me under "russian sleep" until he was ready to talk to me.

The electrodes were the "russian sleep." One goes on each eyelid, one on the nape of the neck. A small current goes through the brain, putting you right to sleep. You get a full night's sleep in an hour. If it's not turned off you can sleep forever.

So this was Loren.

He stood watching me with his head cocked to one side, birdlike, with his arms folded. One hand held a hypo gun, rather negligently, I thought.

What time was it? I didn't dare ask again, because Loren might guess something. But if I could stall him until 0945, Julie could send help . . .

She could send help where?

Finagle in hysterics! Where was I? If I didn't know that, Julie wouldn't know either!

And Loren intended me for the organ banks. One crystalline sliver would knock me out without harming any of the delicate, infinitely various parts that made me Gil Hamilton. Then Loren's doctors would take me apart.

In government operating rooms they flash-burn the criminal's brain for later urn burial. God knows what Loren would do with my own brain. But the rest of me was young and healthy. Even considering Loren's overhead, I was worth more than a million UN marks on the hoof.

"Why me?" I asked. "It was me you wanted, not just any ARM. Why the interest in me?"

"It was you who were investigating the case of Owen Jennison. *Much* too thoroughly."

"Not thoroughly enough, dammit!"

Loren looked puzzled. "You really don't understand?"

"I really don't."

"I find that highly interesting," Loren mused. "Highly."

"All right, why am I still alive?"

"I was curious, Mr. Hamilton. I hoped you'd tell me about your imaginary arm."

So he'd said Arm, not ARM. I bluffed anyway. "My *what?*"

"No need for games, Mr. Hamilton. If I think I'm losing I'll use this." He wiggled the hypo gun. "You'll never wake up."

Damn! He knew. The only things I could move were my ears and my imaginary arm, and Loren knew all about it! I'd never be able to lure him into reach.

Provided he knew *all* about it.

I had to draw him out.

"Okay," I said, "but I'd like to know how you found out about it. A plant in the ARMs?"

Loren chuckled. "I wish it were so. No. We captured one of your men some months ago, quite by accident. When I realized what he was, I induced him to talk shop with me. He was able to tell me something about your remarkable arm. I hope you'll tell me more."

"Who was it?"

"Really, Mr. Hamil—"

"*Who was it?*"

"Do you really expect me to remember the name of every donor?"

Who had gone into Loren's organ banks? Stranger, acquaintance, friend? Does the manager of a slaughterhouse remember every slaughtered steer?

"So-called psychic powers interest me," said Loren. "I remembered you. And then, when I was on the verge of concluding an agreement with your Belter friend Jennison, I remembered something unusual about a crewman he had shipped with. They called you Gil the Arm, didn't they? Prophetic. In port your drinks came free if you could use your imaginary arm to drink them."

"Then damn you. You thought Owen was a plant, did you? Because of me! Me!"

"Breast beating will earn you nothing, Mr. Hamilton." Loren put steel in his voice. "Entertain me, Mr. Hamilton."

I'd been feeling around for anything that might release me from my upright prison. No such luck. I was wrapped like a mummy in bandages too strong to break. All I could feel with my imaginary hand was cloth bandages up to my neck, and a bracing rod along my back to hold me upright. Beneath the swathing I was naked.

"I'll show you my eldritch powers," I told Loren, "if you'll loan me a cigarette." Maybe that would draw him close enough. . . .

He knew something about my arm. He knew its reach. He put one single cigarette on the edge of a small table-on-wheels and slid it up to me. I picked it up and stuck it in my mouth and waited hopefully for him to come light it. "My mistake," he murmured; and he pulled the table back and repeated the whole thing with a lighted cigarette.

No luck. At least I'd gotten my smoke. I pitched the dead one as far as it would go; about two feet. I have to move slowly with my imaginary hand. Otherwise what I'm holding simply slips through my fingers.

Loren watched in fascination. A floating, disembodied cigarette, obeying my will! His eyes held traces of awe and horror. That was bad. Maybe the cigarette had been a mistake.

Some people see psi powers as akin to witchcraft, and psychic people as servants of Satan. If Loren feared me, then I was dead.

"Interesting," said Loren. "How far will it reach?"

He knew that. "As far as my real arm, of course."

"But why? Others can reach much further. Why not you?"

He was clear across the room, a good ten yards away,

sprawled in an armchair. One hand held a drink, the other held the hypo gun. He was superbly relaxed. I wondered if I'd ever see him move from that comfortable chair, much less come within reach.

The room was small and bare, with the look of a basement. Loren's chair and a small portable bar were the only furnishings, unless there were others behind me.

A basement could be anywhere. Anywhere in Los Angeles, or out of it. If it was really morning, I could be anywhere on Earth by now.

"Sure," I said, "others can reach further than me. But they don't have my strength. It's an imaginary arm, sure enough, and my imagination won't make it ten feet long. Maybe someone could convince me it was, if he tried hard enough. But maybe he'd ruin what belief I have. Then I'd have two arms, just like everyone else; I'm better off . . ." I let it trail away, because Loren was going to take all my damn arms anyway.

My cigarette was finished. I pitched it away.

"Want a drink?"

"Sure, if you've got a jigger glass. Otherwise I can't lift it."

He found me a shot glass and sent it to me on the edge of the rolling table. I was barely strong enough to pick it up. Loren's eyes never left me as I sipped and put it down.

The old cigarette lure. Last night I'd used it to pick up a girl. Now it was keeping me alive.

Did I really want to leave the world with something gripped tightly in my imaginary fists? Entertaining Loren. Holding his interest until—

Where was I? Where?

And suddenly I knew. "We're at Monica Apartments," I said. "Nowhere else."

"I knew you'd guess that eventually." Loren smiled. "But it's too late. I got to you in time."

"Don't be so damn complacent. It was my stupidity, not your luck. I should have *smelled* it. Owen would never have come here of his own choice. You ordered him here."

"And so I did. By then I already knew he was a traitor."

"So you sent him here to die. Who was it that checked on him every day to see he'd stayed put? Was it Miller, the manager? He has to be working for you. He's the one who took the holographs of you and your men out of the computer."

"He was the one," said Loren. "But it wasn't every day. I had a man watching Jennison every second, through a portable camera. We took it out after he was dead."

"And then waited a week. Nice touch." The wonder was that it had taken me so long. The atmosphere of the place . . . what kind of people would live in Monica Apartments? The faceless ones, the ones with no identity, the ones who would surely be missed by nobody. They would stay put in their apartments while Loren checked on them, to see that they really did have nobody to miss them. Those who qualified would disappear, and their papers and possessions with them, and their holos would vanish from the computer.

Loren said, "I tried to sell organs to the Belters, through your friend Jennison. I know he betrayed me, Hamilton. I want to know how badly."

"Badly enough," He'd guess that. "We've got detailed plans for setting up an organ-bank dispensary in the Belt. It wouldn't have worked anyway, Loren. Belters don't think that way."

"No pictures."

"No." I didn't want him changing his face.

"I was sure he'd left something," said Loren. "Otherwise we'd have made him a donor. Much simpler. More profitable, too. I needed the money, Hamilton. Do you know what it costs the organization to let a donor go?"

"A million or so. Why'd you do it?"

"He'd left something. There was no way to get at it. All we could do was try to keep the ARMs from looking for it."

"Ah." I had it then. "When anyone disappears without a trace, the first thing any idiot thinks of is organleggers."

"Naturally. So he couldn't just disappear, could he? The police would go to the ARMs, the file would go to you, and you'd start looking."

"For a spaceport locker."

"Oh?"

"Under the name of Cubes Forsythe."

"I knew that name," Loren said between his teeth. "I should have tried that. You know, after we had him hooked on current, we tried pulling the plug on him to get him to talk. It didn't work. He couldn't concentrate on anything but getting the droud back in his head. We looked high and low—''

"I'm going to kill you," I said, and meant every word.

Loren cocked his head, frowning. "On the contrary, Mr. Hamilton. Another cigarette?"

"Yah."

He sent it to me, lighted, on the rolling table. I picked it up, holding it a trifle ostentatiously. Maybe I could focus his attention on it—on his only way to find my imaginary hand.

Because if he kept his eyes on the cigarette, and I put it in my mouth at a crucial moment—I'd leave my hand free without his noticing.

What crucial moment? He was still in the armchair. I had to fight the urge to coax him closer. Any move in that direction would make him suspicious.

What time was it? And what was Julie doing? I thought of a night two weeks past. Remembered dinner on the balcony of the highest restaurant in Los Angeles, just a fraction less than a mile up. A carpet of neon that spread below us to touch the horizon in all directions. Maybe she'd pick it up . . .

She'd be checking on me at 0945.

"You must have made a remarkable spaceman," said Loren. "Think of being the only man in the solar system who can adjust a hull antenna without leaving the cabin."

"Antennas take a little more muscle than I've got." So he knew I could reach through things. If he'd seen that far—"I should have stayed," I told Loren. "I wish I were on a mining ship, right this minute. All I wanted at the time was two good arms."

"Pity. Now you have three. Did it occur to you that using psi powers against men was a form of cheating?"

"What?"

"Remember Raphael Haine?" Loren's voice had become uneven. He was angry, and holding it down with difficulty.

"Sure. Small-time organlegger in Australia."

"Raphael Haine was a friend of mine. I know he had you tied up at one point. Tell me, Mr. Hamilton: if your imaginary hand is as weak as you say, how did you untie the ropes?"

"I didn't. I couldn't have. Haine used handcuffs. I picked

his pocket for the key . . . with my imaginary hand, of course.''

''You used psi powers against him. You had no right!''

Magic. Anyone who's not psychic himself feels the same way, just a little. A touch of dread, a touch of envy. Loren thought he could handle ARMs; he'd killed at least one of us. But to send warlocks against him was grossly unfair.

That was why he'd let me wake up. Loren wanted to gloat. How many men have captured a warlock?

''Don't be an idiot,'' I said. ''I didn't volunteer to play your silly game, or Haine's either. *My* rules make you a wholesale murderer.''

Loren got to his feet (what time was it?) and I suddenly realized my time was up. He was in a white rage. His silky blond hair seemed to stand on end.

I looked into the tiny needle hole in the hypo gun. There was nothing I could do. The reach of my TK was the reach of my fingers; I felt all the things I would never feel: the quart of Trastine in my blood to keep the water from freezing in my cells, the cold bath of half-frozen alcohol, the scalpels and the tiny, accurate surgical lasers. Most of all, the scalpels.

And my knowledge would die when they threw away my brain. I knew what Loren looked like. I knew about Monica Apartments, and who knew how many others of the same kind? I knew where to go to find all the loveliness in Death Valley, and someday I was going to go. What time was it? What time?

Loren had raised the hypo gun and was sighting down the stiff length of his arm. Obviously he thought he was at target practice. ''It really is a pity,'' he said, and there was only the slightest tremor in his voice. ''You should have stayed a spaceman.''

What was he waiting for? ''I can't cringe unless you loosen these bandages,'' I snapped, and I jabbed what was left of my cigarette at him for emphasis. It jerked out of my grip, and I reached and caught it and—

And stuck it in my left eye.

At another time I'd have examined the idea a little more closely. But I'd still have done it. Loren already thought of me as his property. As live skin and healthy kidneys and lengths of artery, as parts in Loren's organ banks, I was property worth a million UN marks. And I was destroying my eye! Organleggers are always hurting for eyes; anyone who wears glasses could use a new pair, and the organleggers themselves are constantly wanting to change retina prints.

What I hadn't anticipated was the pain. I'd read somewhere that there are no sensory nerves in the eyeball. Then it was my lids that hurt. Terribly!

But I only had to hold on for a moment.

Loren swore and came for me at a dead run. He knew how terribly weak was my imaginary arm. What could I do with it? He didn't know; he'd never known, though it stared him in the face. He ran at me and slapped at the cigarette, a full swing that half knocked my head off my neck and sent the now dead butt ricocheting off a wall. Panting, snarling, speechless with rage, he stood—within reach.

My eye closed like a small tormented fist.

I reached past Loren's gun, through his chest wall, and found his heart. And squeezed.

His eyes became very round, his mouth gaped wide, his larynx bobbed convulsively. There was time to fire the gun. Instead he clawed at his chest with a half-paralyzed arm. Twice he raked his fingernails across his chest, gaping upward for air that wouldn't come. He thought he was having a heart attack. Then his rolling eyes found my face.

My face. I was a one-eyed carnivore, snarling with the will to murder. I would have his life if I had to tear the heart out of his chest! How could he help but know?

He knew!

He fired at the floor, and fell.

I was sweating and shaking with reaction and disgust. The scars! He was all scars; I'd felt them going in. His heart was a transplant. And the rest of him—he'd looked about thirty from a distance, but this close it was impossible to tell. Parts were younger, parts older. How much of Loren was Loren? What parts had he taken from others? And none of the parts quite matched.

He must have been chronically ill, I thought. And the Board wouldn't give him the transplants he needed. And one day he'd seen the answer to all his problems. . . .

Loren wasn't moving. He wasn't breathing. I remembered the way his heart had jumped and wriggled in my imaginary hand, and then suddenly given up.

He was lying on his left arm, hiding his watch. I was all

alone in an empty room, and I still didn't know what time it was.

I never found out. It was hours before Miller finally dared to interrupt his boss. He stuck his round, blank face around the door jamb, saw Loren sprawled at my feet, and darted back with a squeak. A minute later a hypo gun came around the jamb, followed by a watery blue eye. I felt the sting in my cheek.

"I checked you early," said Julie. She settled herself uncomfortably at the foot of the hospital bed. "Rather, you called me. When I came to work you weren't there, and I wondered why, and *wham*. It was bad, wasn't it?"

"Pretty bad," I said.

"I've never sensed anyone so scared."

"Well, don't tell anyone about it." I hit the switch to raise the bed to sitting position. "I've got an image to maintain."

My eye and the socket around it were bandaged and numb. There was no pain, but the numbness was obtrusive, a reminder of two dead men who had become part of me. One arm, one eye.

If Julie was feeling that with me, then small wonder if she was nervous. She was. She kept shifting and twisting on the bed.

"I kept wondering what time it was. What time was it?"

"About nine-ten." Julie shivered. "I thought I'd faint when that—that vague little man pointed his hypo gun around the corner. Oh, don't! Don't, Gil. It's *over*."

That close? Was it *that* close? "Look," I said, "you go back to work. I appreciate the sick call, but this isn't doing either of us any good. If we keep it up we'll both wind up in a state of permanent terror."

She nodded jerkily and got up.

"Thanks for coming. Thanks for saving my life too."

Julie smiled from the doorway. "Thanks for the orchids."

I hadn't ordered them yet. I flagged down a nurse and got her to tell me that I could leave tonight, after dinner, provided I went straight home to bed. She brought me a phone, and I used it to order the orchids.

Afterward I dropped the bed back and lay there awhile. It was nice being alive. I began to remember promises I had made, promises I might never have kept. Perhaps it was time to keep a few.

I called down to Surveillance and got Jackson Bera. After letting him drag from me the story of my heroism, I invited him up to the infirmary for a drink. His bottle, but I'd pay. He didn't like that part, but I bullied him into it.

I had dialed half of Taffy's number before, as I had last night, I changed my mind. My wristphone was on the bedside table. No pictures.

"'Lo."

"Taffy? This is Gil. Can you get a weekend free?"

"Sure. Starting Friday?"

"Good."

"Come for me at ten. Did you ever find out about your friend?"

"Yah. I was right. Organleggers killed him. It's over now, we got the guy in charge." I didn't mention the eye. By Friday the bandages would be off. "About that weekend. How would you like to see Death Valley?"

"You're kidding, right?"

"I'm kidding, wrong. Listen—"

"But it's hot! It's dry! It's as dead as the moon! You did say Death Valley, didn't you?"

"It's not hot this month. Listen . . ." And she did listen. She listened long enough to be convinced.

"I've been thinking," she said then. "If we're going to see a lot of each other, we'd better make a—a bargain. No shop talk. All right?"

"A good idea."

"The point is, I work in a hospital," said Taffy. "Surgery. To me, organic transplant material is just the tools of my trade, tools to use in healing. It took me a long time to get that way. I don't want to know where the stuff comes from, and I don't want to know anything about organleggers."

"Okay, we've got a covenant. See you at ten hundred Friday."

A doctor, I thought afterward. Well. The weekend was going to be a good one. Surprising people are always the ones most worth knowing.

Bera came in with a pint of J&B. "My treat," he said. "No use arguing, 'cause you can't reach your wallet anyway." And the fight was on.

Un-man

by Poul Anderson

Un-man was a legend. Killed a thousand times, he never died.

1

They were gone, their boat whispering into the sky with all six of them aboard. Donner had watched them from his balcony—he had chosen the apartment carefully with a view to such features—as they walked out on the landing flange and entered the shell. Now their place was vacant and it was time for him to get busy.

For a moment hesitation was in him. He had waited many days for this chance, but a man does not willingly enter a potential trap. His eyes strayed to the picture on his desk. The darkly beautiful young woman and the child in her arms seemed to be looking at him, her lips were parted as if she were about to speak. He wanted to press the button that animated the film, but didn't quite dare. Gently, his finger stroked the glass over her cheek.

"Jeanne," he whispered. "Jeanne, honey."

He got to work. His colorful lounging pajamas were exchanged for a gray outfit that would be inconspicuous against the walls of the building. An ordinary featureless mask, its sheen carefully dulled to non-reflection, covered his face. He clipped a flat box of tools to his belt and painted his fingertips with collodion. Picking up a reel of cord in one hand, he returned to the balcony.

From here, two hundred and thirty-four stories up, he had a wide view of the Illinois plain. As far as he could see, the land rolled green with corn, hazing into a far horizon out of which the great sky lifted. Here and there, a clump of trees had been planted, and the white streak of an old highway crossed the field, but otherwise it was one immensity of growth. The holdings of Midwest Agricultural reached beyond sight.

On either hand, the apartment building lifted sheer from the trees and gardens of its park. Two miles long, a city in its own right, a mountain of walls and windows, the unit dominated the plain, sweeping heavenward in a magnificent arrogance that ended sixty-six stories above Donner's flat. Through the light prairie wind that fluttered his garments, the man could hear a low unending hum, muted pulsing of machines and life—the building—itself like a giant organism.

There were no other humans in sight. The balconies were so designed as to screen the users from view of neighbors on the same level, and anyone in the park would find his upward glance blocked by trees. A few brilliant points of light in the sky were airboats, but that didn't matter.

Donner fastened his reel to the edge of the balcony and took the end of the cord in his fingers. For still another moment he stood, letting the sunlight and wind pour over him, filling his eyes with the reaching plains and the high, white-clouded heaven.

He was a tall man, his apparent height reduced by the width of shoulders and chest, a curious rippling grace in his movements. His naturally yellow hair had been dyed brown, and contact lenses made his blue eyes dark, but otherwise there hadn't been much done to his face—the broad forehead, high cheekbones, square jaw, and jutting nose were the same. He smiled wryly behind the blank mask, took a deep breath, and swung himself over the balcony rail.

The cord unwound noiselessly, bearing him down past level after level. There was a risk involved in this daylight burglary—someone might happen to glance around the side wall of a balcony and spot him, and even the custom of privacy would hardly keep them from notifying the unit police. But the six he was after didn't time their simultaneous departures for his convenience.

The looming facade slid past, blurred a little by the speed of his descent. One, two, three—He counted as he went by, and at the eighth story down tugged the cord with his free hand. The reel braked and he hung in midair.

A long and empty way down— He grinned and began to swing himself back and forth, increasing the amplitude of each arc until his soles were touching the unit face. On the way back, he grasped the balcony rail, just beyond the screening side wall, with his free hand. His body jerked to a stop, the impact like a blow in his muscles.

Still clinging to the cord, he pulled himself one-armed past the screen, over the rail, and onto the balcony floor. Under the gray tunic and the sweating skin, his sinews felt as if they were about to crack. He grunted with relief when he stood freely, tied the cord to the rail, and unclipped his tool case.

The needle of his electronic detector flickered. So there was an alarm hooked to the door leading in from the balcony. Donner traced it with care, located a wire, and cut it. Pulling a small torch from his kit, he approached the door. Beyond its transparent plastic, the rooms lay quiet: a conventional arrangement of furniture, but with a waiting quality over it.

Imagination, thought Donner impatiently, and cut the lock from the door. As he entered, the autocleaner sensed his presence and its dust-sucking wind whined to silence.

The man forced the lock of a desk and riffled through the papers within. One or two in code he slipped into his pocket, the rest were uninteresting. There must be more, though. Curse it, this was their regional headquarters!

His metal detector helped him about the apartment, looking for hidden safes. When he found a large mass buried in a wall, he didn't trouble with searching for the button to open it, but cut the plastic facing away. The gang would know their place had been raided, and would want to move. If they took another flat in the same building, Donner's arrangement with the superintendent would come into effect; they'd get a vacancy which had been thoughtfully provided with all the spy apparatus he could install. The man grinned again.

Steel gleamed at him through the scorched and melted wall. It was a good safe, and he hadn't time to diddle with it. He plugged in his electric drill, and the diamond head gnawed a small hole in the lock. With a hypodermic he inserted a few cubic centimeters of levinite, and touched it off by a UHF beam. The lock jangled to ruin, and Donner opened the door.

He had only time to see the stet-gun within, and grasp the terrible fact of its existence. Then it spat three needles into his chest, and he whirled down into darkness.

II

Once or twice he had begun to waken, stirring dimly toward light, and the jab of a needle had thrust him back. Now, as his head slowly cleared, they let him alone. And that was worse.

Donner retched and tried to move. His body sagged against straps that held him fast in his chair. Vision blurred in a huge nauseous ache; the six who stood watching him were a ripple of fever-dream against an unquiet shadow.

"He's coming around," said the thin man unnecessarily.

The heavy-set, gray-haired man in the conservative blue tunic glanced at his timepiece. "Pretty fast, considering how he was dosed. Healthy specimen."

Donner mumbled. The taste of vomit was bitter in his mouth. "Give him some water," said the bearded man.

"Like hell!" The thin man's voice was a snarl. His face was dead white against the shifting, blurring murk of the room, and there was a fever in his eyes. "He doesn't rate it, the—Un-man!"

"Get him some water," said the gray-haired one quietly. The skeletal younger man slouched sulkily over to a chipped basin with an old-fashioned tap and drew a glassful.

Donner swallowed it greedily, letting it quench some of the dry fire in his throat and belly. The bearded man approached with a hypo.

"Stimulant," he explained. "Bring you around faster." It bit into Donner's arm and he felt his heartbeat quicken. His head was still a keen pulsing pain, but his eyes steadied and he looked at the others with returning clarity.

"We weren't altogether careless," said the heavy-set man. "That stet-gun was set to needle anybody who opened the safe without pressing the right button first. And, of course, a radio signal was emitted which brought us back in a hurry. We've kept you unconscious till now."

Donner looked around him. The room was bare, thick with the dust and cobwebs of many years, a few pieces of old-style wooden furniture crouched in ugliness against the cracked plaster walls. There was a single window, its broken glass panes stuffed with rags, dirt so thick on it that he could not be sure if there was daylight outside. But the hour was probably after dark. The only illumination within was from a single fluoro in a stand on the table.

He must be in Chicago, Donner decided through a wave of sickness. One of the vast moldering regions that encompassed the inhabited parts of the dying city—deserted, not worth destroying as yet, the lair of rats and decay. Sooner or later, some agricultural outfit would buy up the nominal title from the government which had condemned the place and raze what had been spared by fire and rot. But it hadn't happened yet, and the empty slum was a good hideaway for anybody.

Donner thought of those miles of ruinous buildings, wrapped in night, looming hollow against a vacant sky—dulled echoes in the cracked and grass-grown streets, the weary creak of a joist, the swift patter of feet and glare of eyes from the thick dark, menace and loneliness for further than he could run.

Alone, alone. He was more alone here than in the outermost reaches of space. He knew starkly that he was going to die.

Jeanne. O Jeanne, my darling.

"You were registered at the unit as Mark Roberts," said the woman crisply. She was thin, almost as thin as the bitter-eyed young man beside her. The face was sharp and hungry, the hair close-cropped, the voice harsh with purpose. "But your ID tattoo is a fake—it's a dye that comes off with acid. We got your thumbprint and that number on a check and called the bank central like in an ordinary verification, and the robofile said yes, that was Mark Roberts and the account was all right." She leaned forward, her face straining against the blur of night, and spat it at him. "Who are you really? Only a secret service man could get by with that kind of fake. Whose service are you in?"

"It's obvious, isn't it?" snapped the thin man. "He's not American Security. We know that. So he must be an Un-man."

The way he said the last word made it an ugly, inhuman sound. "*The* Un-man!" he repeated.

"Our great enemy," said the heavy-set one thoughtfully. "*The* Un-man—not just an ordinary operative, with human limitations, but the great and secret one who's made so much trouble for us."

He cocked his gray head and stared at Donner. "It fits what fragmentary descriptions we have," he went on. "But then, the U.N. boys can do a lot with surgery and cosmetics, can't they? And *the* Un-Man has been killed several times. An operator was bagged in Hong Kong only last month which the killer swore must be our enemy—he said nobody else could have led them such a chase."

That was most likely Weinberger, thought Donner. An immense weariness settled on him. They were so few, so desperately few, and one by one the Brothers went down into darkness. He was next, and after him—

"What I can't understand," said a fifth man—Donner recognized him as Colonel Samsey of the American Guard—"is why, if the U.N. Secret Services does have a corps of—uh—supermen, it should bother to disguise them to look all alike. So that we'll think we're dealing with an immortal?" He chuckled grimly. "Surely they don't expect us to be rattled by that!"

"Not supermen," said the gray-haired one. "Enormously able, yes, but the Un-men aren't infallible. As witness this one." He stood before Donner, his legs spread and his hands on his hips. "Suppose you start talking. Tell us about yourself.

"I can tell you about your own selves," answered Donner. His tongue felt thick and dry, but the acceptance of death made him, all at once, immensely steady. "You are Roger Wade, president of Brain Tools, Incorporated, and a prominent supporter of the Americanist Party." To the woman: "You are Marta Jennings, worker for the Party on a full-time basis. Your secretary, Mr. Wade"—his eyes roved to the gaunt young man—"is Rodney Borrow, Exogene Number—"

"Don't call me that!" Cursing, Borrow lunged at Donner. He clawed like a woman. When Samsey and the bearded man dragged him away, his face was death-white and he dribbled at the mouth.

"And the experiment was a failure," taunted Donner cruelly.

"Enough!" Wade slapped the prisoner, a ringing open-handed buffet. "We want to know something new, and there isn't much time. You are, of course, immunized against truth drugs—Dr. Lewin's tests have already confirmed that—but I assume you can still feel pain."

After a moment, he added quietly: "We aren't fiends. You know that we're patriots." *Working with the nationalists of a dozen other countries!* thought Donner. "We don't want to hurt or kill unnecessarily."

"But first we want your real identity," said the bearded

man, Lewin. "Then your background of information about us, the future plans of your chief, and so on. However, it will be sufficient for now if you answer a few questions pertaining to yourself, residence and so on."

Oh, yes, thought Donner, the weariness like a weight on his soul. *That'll do. Because then they'll find Jeanne and Jimmy, and bring them here, and—*

Lewin wheeled forth a lie detector. "Naturally, we don't want our time wasted by false leads," he said.

"It won't be," replied Donner. "I'm not going to say anything."

Lewin nodded, unsurprised, and brought out another machine. "This one generates low-frequency, low-voltage current," he remarked. "Quite painful. I don't think your will can hold out very long. If it does, we can always try prefrontal lobotomy; you won't have inhibitions then. But we'll give you a chance with this first."

He adjusted the electrodes on Donner's skin. Borrow locked his lips with a dreadful hunger.

Donner tried to smile, but his mouth felt stiff. The sixth man, who looked like a foreigner somehow, went out of the room.

There was a tiny receiver in Donner's skull, behind the right mastoid. It could only pick up messages of a special wave form, but it had its silencing uses too. After all, electric torture is a common form of inquisition, and very hard to bear.

He thought of Jeanne, and of Jimmy, and of the Brotherhood. He wished that the last air he was to breathe weren't stale and dusty.

The current tore him with a convulsive anguish. His muscles jerked against the straps and he cried out. Then the sensitized communicator blew up, releasing a small puff of fluorine.

The image Donner carried into death was that of Jeanne, smiling and bidding him welcome home.

III

Barney Rosenberg drove along a dim, rutted trail toward the sheer loom of the escarpment. Around its corner lay Drygulch. But he wasn't hurrying. As he got closer, he eased the throttle of his sandcat and the engine's purr became almost inaudible.

Leaning back in his seat, he looked through the tiny plastiglass cab at the Martian landscape. It was hard to understand that he would never see it again.

Even here, five miles or so from the colony, there was no trace of man save himself and his engine and the blurred track through sand and bush. Men had come to Mars on wings of fire, they had hammered out their cities with a clangorous brawl of life, mined and smelted and begun their ranches, trekked in sandcats and airsuits from the polar bogs to the equatorial scrubwoods—and still they had left no real sign of their passing. Not yet. Here a tin can or a broken tool, there a mummified corpse in the wreck of a burst sealtent, but sand and loneliness drifted over them, night and cold and forgetfulness. Mars was too old and strange for thirty years of man to matter.

The desert stretched away to Rosenberg's left, tumbling in steep drifts of sand from the naked painted hills. Off to the sharply curving horizon the desert marched, an iron barrenness of red and brown and tawny yellow, knife-edged shadows and a weird vicious shimmer of pale sunlight. Here and there a crag lifted, harsh with mineral color, worn by the passing of ages and thin wind to a fluted fantasy. A sandstorm was blowing a few miles off, a scud of dust hissing over stone, stirring the low gray-green brush to a sibilant murmur. On his right the hills rose bare and steep, streaked with blue and green of copper ores, gashed and scored and murmurous with wind. He saw life, the dusty thorn-bushes and the high gaunt cactoids and a flicker of movement as a tiny leaper fled. In one of the precipices, a series of carved, time-blurred steps went up to the ruin of a cliff dwelling abandoned—how long ago?

Overhead the sky was enormous, a reaching immensity of deep greenish blue-violet, incredibly high and cold and remote. The stars glittered faintly in its abyss, the tiny hurtling speck of a moon less bright than they. A shrunken sun stood in a living glory of corona and zodiacal light, the winged disc of royal Egypt lifting over Mars. Near the horizon a thin layer of ice crystals caught the luminescence in a chilly sparkle. There was wind, Rosenberg knew, a whimpering ghost of wind blowing through the bitter remnant of atmosphere, but he ouldn't hear it through the heavy plastiglass and somehow he felt that fact as a deeper isolation.

It was a cruel world, this Mars, a world of cold and ruin and soaring scornful emptiness, a world that broke men's hearts and drained their lives from them—rainless, oceanless, heatless, kindless, where the great wheel of the stars swung through a desert of millennia, where the days cried with wind and the nights rang and groaned with frost. It was a world of waste and mystery, a niggard world where a man ate starvation and drank thirst and finally went down in darkness. Men trudged through unending miles, toil and loneliness and quiet creeping fear, sweated and gasped, cursed the planet and wept for the dead and snatched at warmth and life in the drab colony towns. *It's all right when you find yourself talking to the sandbuggers—but when they start talking back, it's time to go home.*

And yet—and yet— The sweep of the polar moors, thin faint skirl of wind, sunlight shattered to a million diamond shards on the hoarfrost cap; the cloven tremendousness of Rasmussen Gorge, a tumbling sculptured wilderness of fairy stone, uncounted shifting hues of color and fleeting shadow; the high cold night of stars, fantastically brilliant constellations marching over a crystal heaven, a silence so great you thought you could hear God speaking over the universe; the delicate dayflowers of the Syrtis forests, loveliness blooming with the bitter dawn and dying in the swift sunset; traveling and searching, rare triumph and much defeat, but always the quest and the comradeship. Oh, yes, Mars was savage to her lovers, but she gave them of her strange beauty and they would not forget her while they lived.

Maybe Stef was the lucky one, thought Rosenberg. *He died here.*

He guided the sandcat over a razorback ridge. For a moment he paused, looking at the broad valley beyond. He hadn't been to Drygulch for a couple of years; that'd be almost four Earth years, he remembered.

The town, half underground below its doomed roof, hadn't changed much outwardly, but the plantations had doubled their area. The genetic engineers were doing good work, adapting terrestrial food plants to Mars and Martian plants to the needs of humans. The colonies were already self-supporting with regard to essentials, as they had to be considering the expense of freight from Earth. But they still hadn't developed a decent meat animal; that part of the diet had to come from yeast-culture factories in the towns and nobody saw a beef-steak on Mars. *But we'll have that too, one of these years.*

A worn-out world, stern and bitter and grudging, but it was being tamed. Already the new generation was being born. There wasn't much fresh immigration from Earth these days, but man was unshakably rooted here. Someday he'd get around to modifying the atmosphere and weather till humans could walk free and unclothed over the rusty hills—but that wouldn't happen till he, Rosenberg, was dead, and in an obscure way he was glad of it.

The cat's supercharging pumps roared, supplementing tanked oxygen with Martian air for the hungry Diesel as the man steered it along the precarious trail. It was terribly thin, that air, but its oxygen was mostly ozone and that helped. Passing a thorium mine, Rosenberg scowled. The existence of fission-ables was the main reason for planting colonies here in the first place, but they should be saved for Mars.

Well, I'm not really a Martian any longer. I'll be an Earthman again soon. You have to die on Mars, like Stef, and give your body back to the Martian land, before you altogether belong here.

The trail from the mine became broad and hard-packed enough to be called a road. There was other traffic now, streaming from all corners—a loaded ore-car, a farmer coming in with a truckful of harvested crops, a survey expedition returning with maps and specimens. Rosenberg waved to the drivers. They were of many nationalities, but except for the Pilgrims that didn't matter. Here they were simply humans. He hoped the U.N. would get around to internationalizing the planets soon.

There was a flag on a tall staff outside the town, the Stars and Stripes stiff against an alien sky. It was of metal—it had to be, in that murderous corroding atmosphere—and Rosenberg imagined that they had to repaint it pretty often. He steered past it, down a long ramp leading under the dome. He had to wait his turn at the airlock, and wondered when somebody would invent a better system of oxygen conservation. These new experiments in submolar mechanics offered a promising lead.

He left his cat in the underground garage, with word to the

attendant that another man, its purchaser, would pick it up later. There was an odd stinging in his eyes as he patted its scarred flanks. Then he took an elevator and a slideway to the housing office and arranged for a room; he had a couple of days before the *Phobos* left. A shower and a change of clothes were sheer luxury and he reveled in them. He didn't feel much desire for the cooperative taverns and pleasure joints, so he called up Doc Fieri instead.

The physician's round face beamed at him in the plate. "Barney, you old sandbugger! When'd you get in?"

"Just now. Can I come up?"

"Yeah, sure. Nothing doing at the office—that is, I've got company, but he won't stay long. Come right on over."

Rosenberg took a remembered route through crowded hallways and elevators till he reached the door he wanted. He knocked: Drygulch's imports and its own manufactures needed other things more urgently than call and recorder circuits. "Come in!" bawled the voice.

Rosenberg entered the cluttered room, a small leathery man with gray-sprinkled hair and a beaky nose, and Fieri pumped his hand enthusiastically. The guest stood rigid in the background, a lean ascetic figure in black—a Pilgrim. Rosenberg stiffened inwardly. He didn't like that sort, Puritan fanatics from the Years of Madness who'd gone to Mars so they could be unhappy in freedom. Rosenberg didn't care what a man's religion was, but nobody on Mars had a right to be so clannish and to deny cooperation as much as New Jerusalem. However, he shook hands politely, relishing the Pilgrim's ill-concealed distaste—they were anti-Semitic too.

"This is Dr. Morton," explained Fieri. "He heard of my research and came around to inquire about it."

"Most interesting," said the stranger. "And most promising, too. It will mean a great deal to Martian colonization."

"And surgery and biological research everywhere," put in Fieri. Pride was bursting from him.

"What is it, Doc?" asked Rosenberg, as expected.

"Suspended animation," said Fieri.

"Hm?"

"Uh-huh. You see, in what little spare time I have, I've puttered around with Martian biochemistry. Fascinating subject, and unearthly in two meanings of the word. We've nothing like it at home—don't need it. Hibernation and estivation approximate it, of course."

"Ummm . . . yes." Rosenberg rubbed his chin. "I know what you mean. Everybody does. The way so many plants and animals needing heat for their metabolisms can curl up and 'sleep' through the nights, or even through the whole winter. Or they can survive prolonged droughts that way, too." He chuckled. "Comparative matter, of course. Mars is in a state of permanent drought, by Earthly standards."

"And you say, Dr. Fieri, that the natives can do it also?" asked Morton.

"Yes. Even they, with a quite highly developed nervous system, can apparently 'sleep' through such spells of cold or famine. I had to rely on explorers' fragmentary reports for that datum. There are so few natives left, and they're so shy and secretive. But last year I did finally get a look at one in such a condition. It was incredible—respiration was indetectable, the heartbeat almost so, the encephalograph showed only a very slow, steady pulse. But I got blood and tissue samples, and was able to analyze and compare them with secretions from other life forms in suspension."

"I thought even Martians' blood would freeze in a winter night," said Rosenberg.

"It does. The freezing point is much lower than with human blood, but not so low that it can't freeze at all. However, in suspension there's a whole series of enzymes released. One of them, dissolved in the bloodstream, changes the characteristics of the plasma. When ice crystals form, they're *more* dense than the liquid, therefore cell walls aren't ruptured and the organism survives. Moreover, a slow circulation of oxygen-bearing radicals and nutrient solutions takes place even through the ice, apparently by some process analogous to ion exchange. Not much, but enough to keep the organism alive and undamaged. Heat, a sufficient temperature, causes the breakdown of these secretions and the animal or plant revives. In the case of suspension to escape thirst or famine, the process is somewhat different, of course, though the same basic enzymes are involved."

Fieri laughed triumphantly and slapped a heap of papers on his desk. "Here are my notes. The work isn't complete yet. I'm not quite ready to publish, but it's more or less a matter of detail now." A Nobel Prize glittered in his eye.

Morton skimmed through the manuscript. "*Very* interesting," he murmured. His lean, close-cropped head bent over a structural formula. "The physical chemistry of this material must be weird."

"It is, Morton, it is." Fieri grinned.

"Hmmm—do you mind if I borrow this to read? As I mentioned earlier, I believe my lab at New Jerusalem could carry out some of these analyses for you."

"That'll be fine. Tell you what, I'll make up a stat of this whole mess for you. I'll have it ready by tomorrow."

"Thank you." Morton smiled, though it seemed to hurt his face. "This will be quite a surprise, I'll warrant. You haven't told anyone else?"

"Oh, I've mentioned it around, of course, but you're the first person who's asked for the technical details. Everybody's too busy with their own work on Mars. But it'll knock their eye out back on Earth. They've been looking for something like this ever since—since the Sleeping Beauty story—and here's the first way to achieve it."

"I'd like to read this too, Doc," said Rosenberg.

"Are you a biochemist?" asked Morton.

"Well, I know enough biology and chemistry to get by, and I'll have leisure to wade through this before my ship blasts."

"Sure, Barney," said Fieri. "And do me a favor, will you? When you get home, tell old Summers at Cambridge—England, that is—about it. He's their big biochemist, and he always said I was one of his brighter pupils and shouldn't have switched over to medicine. I'm a hell of a modest cuss, huh? But damn it all, it's not everybody who grabs onto something as big as this!"

Morton's pale eyes lifted to Rosenberg's. "So you are returning to Earth?" he asked.

"Yeah. The *Phobos*." He felt he had to explain, that he didn't want the Pilgrim to think he was running out. "More or less doctor's orders, you understand. My helmet cracked open in a fall last year, and before I could slap a patch on I had a beautiful case of the bends, plus the low pressure and the cold and the ozone raising the very devil with my lungs." Rosenberg shrugged, and his smile was bitter. "I suppose I'm fortunate to be alive. At least I have enough credit saved to retire. But I'm just not strong enough to continue working on Mars, and it's not the sort of place where you can loaf and remain sane.''

"I see. It is a shame. When will you be on Earth, then?''

"Couple of months. The *Phobos* goes orbital most of the way—do I look like I could afford an acceleration passage?'' Rosenberg turned to Fieri. "Doc, will there be any other old sanders coming home this trip?''

'' 'Fraid not. You know there are darn few who retire from Mars to Earth. They die first. You're one of the lucky ones.''

"A lonesome trip, then. Well, I suppose I'll survive it.''

Morton made his excuses and left. Fieri stared after him. "Odd fellow. But then, all these Pilgrims are. They're anti almost everything. He's competent, though, and I'm glad he can tackle some of those analyses for me.'' He slapped Rosenberg's shoulder. "But forget it, old man! Cheer up and come along with me for a beer. Once you're stretched out on those warm white Florida sands, with blue sky and blue sea and luscious blondes walking by, I guarantee you won't miss Mars.''

"Maybe not.'' Rosenberg looked unhappily at the floor. "It's never been the same since Stef died. I didn't realize how much he'd meant to me till I'd buried him and gone on by myself.''

"He meant a lot to everyone, Barney. He was one of those people who seem to fill the world with life, wherever they are. Let's see—he was about sixty when he died, wasn't he? I saw him shortly before, and he could still drink any two men under the table, and all the girls were still adoring him.''

"Yeah. He was my best friend, I suppose. We tramped Earth and the planets together for fifteen years.'' Rosenberg smiled. "Funny thing, friendship. It has nothing to do with the love of women—which is why they never understand it. Stef and I didn't even talk much. It wasn't needed. The last five years have been pretty empty without him.''

"He died in a cave-in, didn't he?''

"Yes. We were exploring up near the Sawtooths, hunting a uranium lode. Our diggings collapsed, he held that toppling roof up with his shoulders and yelled at me to scramble out—then before he could get clear, it came down and burst his helmet open. I buried him on a hill, under a cairn, looking out over the desert. He was always a friend of high places.''

"Mmmmm—yes Well, thinking about Stefan Rostomily won't help him or us now. Let's go get that beer, shall we?"

IV

The shrilling within his head brought Robert Naysmith to full awareness with a savage force. His arm jerked, and the brush streaked a yellow line across his canvas.

"Naysmith!" The voice rattled harshly in his skull. "Report to Prior at Frisco Unit. Urgent. Martin Donner has disappeared, presumed dead. You're on his job now. Hop to it, boy."

For a moment Naysmith didn't grasp the name. He'd never met anyone called Donner. Then—yes, that was on the list, Donner was one of the Brotherhood. And dead now.

Dead— He had never seen Martin Donner, and yet he knew the man with an intimacy no two humans had realized before the Brothers came. Sharp in his mind rose the picture of the dead man, smiling a characteristic slow smile, sprawled back in a relaxer with a glass of Scotch in one strong blunt-fingered hand. The Brothers were all partial to Scotch, thought Naysmith with a twisting sadness. And Donner had been a mech-volley fan, and had played good chess, read a lot and sometimes quoted Shakespeare, tinkered with machinery, probably had a small collection of guns—

Dead. Sprawled sightlessly somewhere on the turning planet, his muscles stiff, his body already devouring itself in proteolysis, his brain darkened, withdrawn into the great night, and leaving an irreparable gap in the tight-drawn line of the Brotherhood.

"You might pick up a newscast on your way," said the voice in his head conversationally. "It's hot stuff."

Naysmith's eyes focused on his painting. It was shaping up to be a good one. He had been experimenting with techniques, and this latest caught the wide sunlit dazzle of California beach, the long creaming swell of waves, the hot cloudless sky and the thin harsh grass and the tawny-skinned woman who sprawled on the sand. Why did they have to call him just now?

"Okay, Sofie," he said with resignation. "That's all. I've got to get back."

The sun-browned woman rolled over on one elbow and

looked at him. "What the devil?" she asked. "We've only been here three hours. The day's hardly begun."

"It's gone far enough, I'm afraid." Naysmith began putting away his brushes. "Home to civilization."

"But I don't want to!"

"What has that got to do with it?" snorted the man. *Treat 'em rough and tell 'em nothing, and they'll come running. These modern women aren't as emancipated as they think.* He folded his easel.

"But why?" she cried, half getting up.

"I have an appointment this afternoon." Naysmith strode down the beach toward the trail. After a moment, Sofie followed.

"You didn't tell me that," she protested.

"You didn't ask me," he said. He added a "Sorry" that was no apology at all.

There weren't many others on the beach, and the parking lot was relatively uncluttered. Naysmith palmed the door of his boat and it opened for him. He slipped on tunic, slacks, and sandals, put a beret rakishly atop his sun-bleached yellow hair, and entered the boat. Sofie followed, not bothering to don her own clothes.

The ovoid shell slipped skyward on murmuring jets. "I'll drop you off at your place," said Naysmith. "Some other time, huh?"

She remained sulkily silent. They had met accidentally a week before, in a bar. Naysmith was officially a cybernetic epistemologist on vacation, Sofie an engineer on the Pacific Colony project, off for a holiday from her job and her free-marriage group. It had been a pleasant interlude, and Naysmith regretted it mildly.

Still—the rising urgent pulse of excitement tensed his body and cleared the last mists of artistic preoccupation from his brain. You lived on a knife edge in the Service, you drew breath and looked at the sun and grasped after the real world with a desperate awareness of little time. None of the Brotherhood were members of the Hedonists, they were all too well-balanced for that, but inevitably they were epicureans.

When you were trained from—well, from birth, even the sharpness of nearing death could be a kind of pleasure. *Besides*, thought Naysmith, *I might be one of the survivors.*

"You are a rat, you know," said Sofie.

"Squeak," said Naysmith. His face—the strange strong face of level fair brows and wide-set blue eyes, broad across the high cheekbones and in the mouth, square-jawed and crag-nosed—split in a grin that laughed with her while it laughed at her. He looked older than his twenty-five years. And she, thought Sofie with sudden tiredness, looked younger than her forty. Her people had been well off even during the Years of Hunger; she'd always been exposed to the best available biomedical techniques, and if she claimed thirty few would call her a liar. But—

Naysmith fiddled with the radio. Presently a voice came out of it; he didn't bother to focus the TV.

"—the thorough investigation demanded by finance minister Arnold Besser has been promised by President Lopez. In a prepared statement, the President said: 'The rest of the ministry, like myself, are frankly inclined to discredit this accusation and believe that the Chinese government is mistaken. However, its serious nature—' "

"Lopez, eh? The U.N. President himself," murmured Naysmith. "That means the accusation has been made officially now."

"What accusation?" asked the woman. "I haven't heard a 'cast for a week."

"The Chinese government was going to lodge charges that the assassination of Kwang-ti was done by U.N. secret agents," said Naysmith.

"Why, that's ridiculous!" she gasped. "The *U.N.?*" She shook her dark head. "They haven't the—right. The U.N. agents, I mean. Kwang-ti was a menace, yes, but assassination! I don't believe it."

"Just think what the anti-U.N. factions all over the Solar System, including our own Americanists, are going to make of this," said Naysmith. "Right on top of charges of corruption comes one of murder!"

"Turn it off," she said. "It's too horrible."

"These are horrible times, Sofie."

"I thought they were getting better." She shuddered. "I remember the tail-end of the Years of Hunger, and then the Years of Madness, and the Socialist Depression—people in rags, starving; you could see their bones—and a riot once, and the marching uniforms, and the great craters— No! The U.N.'s like a dam against all that hell. It *can't* break!"

Naysmith put the boat on automatic and comforted her. After all, anyone loyal to the U.N. deserved a little consideration.

Especially in view of the suppressed fact that the Chinese charge was absolutely true.

He dropped the woman off at her house, a small prefab in one of the colonies, and made vague promises about looking her up again. Then he opened the jets fully and streaked north toward Frisco Unit.

V

There was a lot of traffic around the great building, and his autopilot was kept busy bringing him in. Naysmith slipped a mantle over his tunic and a conventional half-mask over his face, the latter less from politeness than as a disguise. He didn't think he was being watched, but you were never sure. American Security was damnably efficient.

If ever wheels turned within wheels, he thought sardonically, modern American politics did the spinning. The government was officially Labor and pro-U.N., and was gradually being taken over by its sociodynamicists, who were even more in favor of world federation. However, the conservatives of all stripes, from the mildly socialist Republicans to the extreme Americanists, had enough seats in Congress and enough power generally to exert a potent influence. Among other things, the conservative coalition had prevented the abrogation of the Department of Security, and Hessling, its chief, was known to have Americanist leanings. So there were at least a goodly number of S-men out after "foreign agents"—which included Un-men.

Fourre had his own agents in American Security, of course. It was largely due to their efforts that the American Brothers had false IDs and that the whole tremendous fact of the Brotherhood had remained secret. But someday, thought Naysmith, the story would come out—and then the heavens would fall.

So thin a knife edge, so deep an abyss of chaos and ruin— Society was mad, humanity was a race of insane, and the few who strove to build stability were working against shattering odds. *Sofie was right. The U.N. is a dike, holding back a sea of radioative blood from the lands of men. And I,* thought Naysmith wryly, *seem to be the little boy with his finger in the dike.*

His boat landed on the downward ramp and rolled into the echoing vastness of the unit garage. He didn't quite dare land on Prior's flange. A mechanic tagged the vehicle, gave Naysmith a receipt, and guided him toward an elevator. It was an express, bearing him swiftly past the lower levels of shops, offices, service establishments, and places of education and entertainment, up to the residential stories. Naysmith stood in a crowd of humans, most of them masked, and waited for his stop. No one spoke to anyone else, the custom of privacy had become too ingrained. He was just as glad of that.

On Prior's level, the hundred and seventh, he stepped onto the slideway going east, transferred to a northbound strip at the second corner, and rode half a mile before he came to the alcove he wanted. He got off, the rubbery floor absorbing the very slight shock, and entered the recess. When he pressed the door button, the recorded voice said: "I am sorry, Mr. Prior is not at home. Do you wish to record a message?"

"Shut up and let me in," said Naysmith.

The code sentence activated the door, which opened for him. He stepped into a simply furnished vestibule as the door chimed. Prior's voice came over the intercom: "Naysmith?"

"The same."

"Come on in, then. Living room."

Naysmith hung up his mask and mantle, slipped off his sandals, and went down the hall. The floor was warm and resilient under his feet, like living flesh. Beyond another door that swung aside was the living room, also furnished with a bachelor austerity. Prior was a lone wolf by nature, belonging to no clubs and not even the loosest free-marriage group. His official job was semantic analyst for a large trading outfit; it gave him a lot of free time for his U.N. activities, plus a good excuse for traveling anywhere in the Solar System.

Naysmith's eyes flickered over the dark negroid face of his co-worker—Prior was not a Brother, though he knew of the band—and rested on the man who lay in the adjoining relaxer. "Are *you* here, chief?" He whistled. "Then it must be really big."

"Take off your clothes and get some sun-lamp," invited

Prior, waving his eternal cigaret at a relaxer. "I'll try to scare up some Scotch for you."

"Why the devil does the Brotherhood always have to drink Scotch?" grumbled Etienne Fourre. "Your padded expense accounts eat up half my budget. Or drink it up, I should say."

He was squat and square and powerful, and at eighty was still more alive than most boys. Small black eyes glistened in a face that seemed carved from scarred and pitted brown rock; his voice was a bass rumble from the shaggy chest, its English hardly accented. Geriatrics could only account for some of the vitality that lay like a coiled spring in him, for the entire battery of diet, exercise, and chemistry has to be applied almost from birth to give maximum effect and his youth antedated the science. *But he'll probably outlive us all*, thought Naysmith.

There was something of the fanatic about Etienne Fourre. He was a child of war whose most relentless battle had become one against war itself. As a young man he had been in the French Resistance of World War II. Later he had been high in the Western liaison with the European undergrounds of World War III, entering the occupied and devastated lands himself on his dark missions. He had fought with the liberals against the neofascists in the Years of Hunger and with the gendarmerie against the atomists in the Years of Madness and with U.N. troops in the Near East where his spy system had been a major factor in suppressing the Great Jehad. He had accepted the head of the secret service division of the U.N. Inspectorate after the Conference of Rio revised the charter and had proceeded quietly to engineer the coup which overthrew the anti-U.N. government of Argentina. Later his men had put the finger on Kwang-ti's faked revolution in the Republic of Mongolia, thus ending that conquest-from-within scheme; and he was ultimately the one responsible for the Chinese dictator's assassination. The Brotherhood was his idea from the beginning, his child and his instrument.

Such a man, thought Naysmith, would in earlier days have stood behind the stake and lash of an Inquisition, would have marched at Cromwell's side and carried out the Irish massacres, would have helped set up world-wide Communism—a sternly religious man, for all his mordant atheism, a living sword which needed a war. *Thank God he's on our side!*

"All right, what's the story?" asked the Un-man aloud.

"How long since you were on a Service job?" countered Fourre.

"About a year. Schumacher and I were investigating the *Arbeitspartei* in Germany. The other German Brothers were tied up in that Austrian business, you remember, and I speak the language well enough to pass for a Rhinelander when I'm in Prussia."

"Yes. I recall. You have been loafing long enough, my friend." Fourre took the glass of wine offered him by Prior, sipped it, and grimaced. "*Merde!* Won't these Californians ever give up trying?" Swinging back to Naysmith: "I am calling in the whole Brotherhood on this. I shall have to get back to Rio fast, the devil is running loose down there with those Chinese charges and I will be lucky to save our collective necks. But I have slipped up to North America to get you people organized and under way. I am pretty damn sure that the leadership of our great unknown enemy is down in Rio—probably with Besser, who is at least involved in it but has taken some very excellent precautions against assassination—and it would do no good to kill him only to have someone else take over. At any rate, the United States is still a most important focus of anti-U.N. activity, and Donner's capture means a rapid deterioration of things here. Prior, who was Donner's contact man, tells me that he was apparently closer to spying out the enemy headquarters for this continent than any other operative. Now that Donner is gone, Prior has recommended you to succeed in his assignment."

"Which was what?"

"I will come to that. Donner was an engineer by training. You are a cybernetic analyst, *hein?*"

"Yes, officially," said Naysmith. "My degrees are in epistemology and communications theory, and my supposed job is basic-theoretical consultant. Troubleshooter in the realm of ideas." He grinned. "When I get stuck, I can always refer the problem to Prior here."

"Ah, so. You are then necessarily something of a linguist too, eh? Good. Understand, I am not choosing you for your specialty, but rather for your un-specialty. You are too old to have had the benefit of Synthesis training. Some of the younger Brothers are getting it, of course—there is a lad in

Mexico, Peter Christian, whose call numbers you had better get from Prior in case you need such help.

"Meanwhile, an epistemologist or semanticist is the closest available thing to an integrating synthesist. By your knowledge of language, psychology, and the general sciences, you should be well equipped to fit together whatever information you can obtain and derive a large picture from them. I don't know." Fourre lit a cigar and puffed ferociously.

"Well, I can start anytime. I'm on extended leave of absence from my nominal job already," said Naysmith. "But what about this Donner? How far had he gotten, what happened to him, and so on?"

"I'll give you the background, because you'll need it," said Prior. "Martin Donner was officially adopted in Canada and, as I said, received a mechanical engineering degree there. About four years ago we had reason to think the enemy was learning that he wasn't all he seemed, so we transferred him to the States, flanged up an American ID for him and so on. Recently he was put to work investigating the Americanists. His leads were simple: he got a job with Brain Tools, Inc., which is known to be lousy with Party members. He didn't try to infiltrate the Party—we already have men in it, of course, though they haven't gotten very high—but he did snoop around, gather data, and finally put the snatch on a certain man and pumped him full of truth drug." Naysmith didn't ask what had happened to the victim: the struggle was utterly ruthless, with all history at stake. "That gave him news about the midwestern headquarters of the conspiracy, so he went there. It was one of the big units in Illinois. He got himself an apartment and disappeared. That was almost two weeks ago." Prior shrugged. "He's quite certainly dead by now. If they didn't kill him themselves, he'll have found a way to suicide."

"You can give me the dossier on what Donner learned and communicated to you?" asked Naysmith.

"Yes, of course, though I don't think it'll help you much." Prior looked moodily at his glass. "You'll be pretty much on your own. I needn't add that anything goes, from privacy violation to murder, but that with the Service in such bad odor right now you'd better not leave any evidence. Your first job, though, is to approach Donner's family. You see, he was married."

"Oh?"

"I don't mean free-married, or group-married, or trial-married, or any other version," snapped Prior impatiently. "I mean *married*. Old style. One kid."

"Hmmm—that's not so good, is it?"

"No. Un-men really have no business marrying that way, and most especially the Brothers don't. However—you see the difficulties, don't you? *If* Donner is still alive, somehow, and the gang traces his ID and grabs the wife and kid, they've got a hold on him that may make him spill all he knows. No sane man is infinitely loyal to a cause."

"Well, I suppose you provided Donner with a midwestern ID."

"Sure. Or rather, he used the one we already had set up—name, fingerprints, number, the data registered at Midwest Central. Praise Allah, we've got friends in the registry bureau! But Donner's case is bad. In previous instances where we lost a Brother, we've been able to recover the corpse or were at least sure that it was safely destroyed. Now the enemy has one complete Brother body, ready for fingerprinting, retinals, bloodtyping, Bertillion measurements, autopsy, and everything else they can think of. We can expect them to check that set of physical data against every ID office in the country. And when they find the same identification under different names and numbers in each and every file—all hell is going to let out for noon."

"It will take time, of course," said Fourre. "We have put in duplicate sets of non-Brother data too, as you know; that will give them extra work to do. Nor can they be sure which set corresponds to Donner's real identity."

In spite of himself, Naysmith grinned again. "Real identity" was an incongruous term as applied to the Brotherhood. However—

"Nevertheless," went on Fourre, "there is going to be an investigation in every country on Earth and perhaps the Moon and planets. The Brotherhood is going to have to go underground, in this country at least. And just now when I have to be fighting for my service's continued existence down in Rio!"

They're closing in. We always knew, deep in our brains, that this day would come, and now it is upon us.

"Even assuming Donner is dead, which is more likely," said Prior, "his widow would make a valuable captive for the gang. Probably she knows very little about her husband's Service activities, but she undoubtedly has a vast amount of information buried in her subconscious—faces, snatches of overheard conversation, perhaps merely the exact dates Donner was absent on this or that mission. A skilled man could get it out of her, you know—thereby presenting the enemy detectives with any number of leads—some of which would go straight to our most cherished secrets.''

"Haven't you tried to spirit her away?" asked Naysmith.

"She won't spirit," said Prior. "We sent an accredited agent to warn her that she was in danger and advise her to come away with him. She refused flat. After all, how can she be sure our agent isn't the creature of the enemy? Furthermore, she took some very intelligent precautions, such as consulting the local police, leaving notes in her bankbox to be opened if she disappears without warning, and so on, which have in effect made it impossibly difficult for us to remove her against her will. If nothing else, we couldn't stand the publicity. All we've been able to do is put a couple of men to watching her—and one of these was picked up by the cops the other day and we had hell's own time springing him.''

"She's got backbone," said Naysmith.

"Too much," replied Prior. "Well, you know your first assignment. Get her to go off willingly with you, hide her and the kid away somewhere, and then go underground yourself. After that, it's more or less up to you, boy.''

"But how'll I persuade her to—"

"Isn't it obvious?" snapped Fourre.

It was. Naysmith grimaced. "What kind of a skunk do you take me for?" he protested feebly. "Isn't it enough that I do your murders and robberies for you?''

VI

Brigham City, Utah, was not officially a colony, having existed long before the postwar resettlements. But it had always been a lovely town, and had converted itself almost entirely to modern layout and architecture. Naysmith had not been there before, but he felt his heart warming to it—*the same as Donner, who is dead now.*

He opened all jets and screamed at his habitual speed low

above the crumbling highway. Hills and orchards lay green about him under a high clear heaven, a great oasis lifted from the wastelands by the hands of men. They had come across many-miled emptiness, those men of another day, trudging dustily by their creaking, bumping, battered wagons on the way to the Promised Land. He, today, sat on plastic-foam cushions in a metal shell, howling at a thousand miles an hour till the echoes thundered, but was himself fleeing the persecutors.

Local traffic control took over as he intersected the radio beam. He relaxed as much as possible, puffing a nervous cigaret while the autopilot brought him in. When the boat grounded in a side lane, he slipped a full mask over his head and resumed, manually, driving.

The houses nestled in their screens of lawn and trees, the low half-underground homes of small families. Men and women, some in laboring clothes, were about on the slideways, and there were more children in sight, small bright flashes of color laughing and shouting, than was common elsewhere. The Mormon influence, Naysmith supposed; free-marriage and the rest hadn't ever been very fashionable in Utah. Most of the fruit-raising plantations were still privately owned small-holdings too, using cooperation to compete with the giant government-regulated agricultural combines. But there would nevertheless be a high proportion of men and women here who commuted to outside jobs by airbus—workers on the Pacific Colony project, for instance.

He reviewed Prior's file on Donner, passing the scanty items through his memory. The Brothers were always on call, but outside their own circle they were as jealous of their privacy as anyone else. It had, however, been plain that Jeanne Donner worked at home as a mail-consultant semantic linguist—correcting manuscript of various kinds—and gave an unusual amount of personal attention to her husband and child.

Naysmith felt inwardly cold.

Here was the address. He brought the boat to a silent halt and started up the walk toward the house. Its severe modern lines and curves were softened by a great rush of morning glory, and it lay in the rustling shade of trees, and there was a broad garden behind it. That was undoubtedly Jeanne's work; Donner would have hated gardening.

Instinctively, Naysmith glanced about for Prior's watchman. Nowhere in sight. But then, a good operative wouldn't be. Perhaps that old man, white-bearded and patriarchal, on the slideway; or the delivery boy whipping down the street on his biwheel; or even the little girl skipping rope in the park across the way. She might not be what she seemed: the biological laboratories could do strange things, and Fourre had built up his own secret shops—

The door was in front of him, shaded by a small vine-draped portico. He thumbed the button, and the voice informed him that no one was at home. Which was doubtless a lie, but— *Poor kid! Poor girl, huddled in there against fear, against the night which swallowed her man—waiting for his return, for a dead man's return.* Naysmith shook his head, swallowing a gorge of bitterness, and spoke into the recorder: "Hello, honey, aren't you being sort of inhospitable?"

She must have activated the playback at once, because it was only a moment before the door swung open. Naysmith caught her in his arms as he stepped into the vestibule.

"Marty, Marty, Marty!" She was sobbing and laughing, straining against him, pulling his face down to hers. The long black hair blinded his stinging eyes. "Oh, Marty, take off that blasted mask. It's been so long—"

She was of medium height, lithe and slim in his grasp, the face strong under its elfish lines, the eyes dark and lustrous and very faintly slanted, and the feel and the shaking voice of her made him realize his own loneliness with a sudden desolation. He lifted the mask, letting its helmet-shaped hollowness thud on the floor, and kissed her with hunger. *God damn it,* he thought savagely, *Donner would have to pick the kind I'm a sucker for! But then, he'd be bound to do so, wouldn't he?*

"No time, sweetheart," he said urgently, while she ruffled his hair. "Get some clothes and a mask—Jimmy too, of course. Never mind packing anything. Just call up the police and tell 'em you're leaving of your own accord. We've got to get out of here fast."

She stepped back a pace and looked at him with puzzlement. "What's happened, Marty?" she whispered.

"Fast, I said!" He brushed past her into the living room. "I'll explain later."

She nodded and was gone into one of the bedrooms,

bending over a crib and picking up a small sleepy figure. Naysmith lit another cigaret while his eyes prowled the room.

It was a typical prefab house, but Martin Donner, this other self who was now locked in darkness, had left his personality here. None of the mass-produced featureless gimmickry of today's floaters: this was the home of people who had meant to stay. Naysmith thought of the succession of apartments and hotel rooms which had been his life, and the loneliness deepened in him.

Yes—just as it should be. Donner had probably built that stone fireplace himself, not because it was needed but because the flicker of burning logs was good to look on. There was an antique musket hanging above the mantel, which bore a few objects: old marble clock, wrought-brass candlesticks, a flashing bit of Lunar crystal. The desk was a mahogany anachronism among relaxers. There were some animated films on the walls, but there were a couple of reproductions too—a Rembrandt rabbi and a Constable landscape—and a few engravings. There was an expensive console with a wide selection of music wires. The bookshelves held their share of microprint rolls, but there were a lot of old-style volumes too, carefully rebound. Naysmith smiled as his eye fell on the well-thumbed set of Shakespeare.

The Donners had not been live-in-the-past cranks, but they had not been rootless either. Naysmith sighed and recalled his anthropology. Western society had been based on the family as an economic and social unit: the first *raison d'être* had gone out with technology, the second had followed in the last war and the postwar upheavals. Modern life was an impersonal thing. Marriage—permanent marriage—came late, when both parties were tired of chasing, and was a loose contract at best; the crèche, the school, the public entertainment, made children a shadowy part of the home. And all of this reacted on the human self. From a creature of strong, highly focused emotional life, with a personality made complex by the interaction of environment and ego, Western man was changing to something like the old Samoan aborigines; easygoing, well-adjusted, close friendship and romantic love sliding into limbo. You couldn't say that it was good or bad, one way or the other; but you wondered what it would do to society.

But what could be done about it? You couldn't go back again, you couldn't support today's population with medieval technology even if the population had been willing to try. But that meant accepting the philosophical basis of science, exchanging the cozy medieval cosmos for a bewildering grid of impersonal relationships and abandoning the old cry of man shaking his fist at an empty heaven. *Why?* If you wanted to control population and disease (and the first, at least, was still a hideously urgent need) you accepted chemical contraceptives and antibiotic tablets and educated people to carry them in their pockets; but then it followed that the traditional relationships between the sexes became something else. Modern technology had no use for the pick-and-shovel laborer or for the routine intellectual; so you were faced with a huge class of people not fit for anything else, and what were you going to do about it? What your great, unbelievably complex civilization-machine needed, what it *had* to have in appalling quantity, was the trained man, trained to the limit of his capacity. But then education had to start early and, being free as long as you could pass exams, to be ruthlessly selective. Which meant that your first classes, Ph.D.'s at twenty or younger, looked down on the Second schools, who took out their frustration on the Thirds—intellectual snobbishness, social friction, but how to escape it?

And it was, after all, a world of fantastic anachronisms. It had grown too fast and too unevenly. Hindu peasants scratched in their tiny fields and lived in mud huts while each big Chinese collective was getting its own powerplant. Murderers lurked in the slums around Manhattan Crater while a technician could buy a house and furniture for six months' pay. Floating colonies were being established in the oceans, cities rose on Mars and Venus and the Moon while Congo natives drummed at the rain-clouds. Reconciliation—*how?*

Most people looked at the surface of things. They saw that the great upheavals, the World Wars and the Years of Hunger and the Years of Madness and the economic breakdowns, had been accompanied by the dissolution of traditional social modes, and they thought that the first was the cause of the second. "Give us a chance and we'll bring back the good old days." They couldn't see that those good old days had carried the seeds of death within them, that the change in technology had brought a change in human nature itself which would have deeper effects than any ephemeral transition period. War, depression, the waves of manic perversity, the hungry men and the marching men and the doomed men, were not causes, they were effects—symptoms. The world was changing and you can't go home again.

The psychodynamicists thought they were beginning to understand the process, with their semantic epistemology, games theory, least effort principle, communications theory— maybe so. It was too early to tell. The Scientific Synthesis was still more of a dream than an achievement, and there would have to be at least one generation of Synthesis-trained citizens before the effects could be noticed. Meanwhile, the combination of geriatrics and birth control, necessary as both were, was stiffening the population with the inevitable intellectual rigidity of advancing years, just at the moment when original thought was more desperately needed than ever before in history. The powers of chaos were gathering, and those who saw the truth and fought for it were so terribly few. *Are you absolutely sure you're right? Can you really justify your battle?*

"Daddy!"

Naysmith turned and held out his arms to the boy. A two-year-old, a sturdy lad with light hair and his mother's dark eyes, still half misted with sleep, was calling him. *My son—Donner's son, damn it!* "Hullo, Jimmy." His voice shook a little.

Jeanne picked the child up. She was masked and voluminously cloaked, and her tones were steadier than his. "All right, shall we go?"

Naysmith nodded and went to the front door. He was not quite there when the bell chimed.

"Who's that?" His ragged bark and the leap in his breast told him how strained his nerves were.

"I don't know. I've been staying indoors since—" Jeanne strode swiftly to one of the bay windows and lifted a curtain, peering out. "Two men. Strangers."

Naysmith fitted the mask on his own head and thumbed the playback switch. The voice was hard and sharp: "This is the Federal police. We know you are in, Mrs. Donner. Open at once."

"S-men!" Her whisper shuddered.

Naysmith nodded grimly. "They've tracked you down so soon, eh? Run and see if there are any behind the house."

Her feet pattered across the floor. "Four in the garden," she called.

"All right." Naysmith caught himself just before asking if she could shoot. He pulled the small flat stet-pistol from his tunic and gave it to her as she returned. He'd have to assume her training; the needler was recoilless anyway. " 'Once more unto the breach, dear friends—' We're getting out of here. Keep close behind me and shoot at their faces or hands. They may have breastplates under the clothes."

His own magnum automatic was cold and heavy in his hand. It was no gentle sleepy-gas weapon. At short range it would blow a hole in a man big enough to put your arm through, and a splinter from its bursting slug killed by hydrostatic shock. The rapping on the door grew thunderous.

She was all at once as cool as he. "Trouble with the law?" she asked crisply.

"The wrong kind of law," he answered. "We've still got cops on our side, though, if that's any consolation."

They couldn't be agents of Fourre's or they would have given him the code sentence. That mea..t they were sent by the same power which had murdered Martin Donner. He felt no special compunctions about replying in kind. The trick was to escape.

Naysmith stepped back into the living room and picked up a light table, holding it before his body as a shield against needles. Returning to the hall he crowded himself in front of Jeanne and pressed the door switch.

As the barrier swung open, Naysmith fired, a muted hiss and a dull thump of lead in flesh. That terrible impact sent the S-man off the porch and tumbling to the lawn in blood. His companion shot as if by instinct, a needle thunking into the table. Naysmith gunned him down even as he cried out.

Now—outside—to the boat and fast! Sprinting across the grass, Naysmith felt the wicked hum of a missile fan his cheek. Jeanne whirled, encumbered by Jimmy, and sprayed the approaching troop with needles as they burst around the corner of the house.

Naysmith was already at the opening door of his jet. He fired once again while his free hand started the motor.

The S-men were using needles. They wanted the quarry alive. Jeanne stumbled, a dart in her arm, letting Jimmy slide to earth. Naysmith sprang back from the boat. A needle splintered on his mask and he caught a whiff that made his head swoop.

The detectives spread out, approaching from two sides as they ran. Naysmith was shielded on one side by the boat, on the other by Jeanne's unstirring form as he picked her up. He crammed her and the child into the seat and wriggled across them. Slamming the door, he grabbed for the controls.

The whole performance had taken less than a minute. As the jet stood on its tail and screamed illegally skyward, Naysmith realized for the thousandth time that no ordinary human would have been fast enough and sure enough to carry off that escape. The S-men were good but they had simply been outclassed.

They'd check the house, inch by inch, and find his recent fingerprints, and those would be the same as the stray ones left here and there throughout the world by certain Un-man operatives—the same as Donner's. It was *the* Un-man, the hated and feared shadow who could strike in a dozen places at once, swifter and deadlier than flesh had a right to be, and who had now risen from his grave to harry them again. He, Naysmith, had just added another chapter to a legend.

Only—the S-men didn't believe in ghosts. They'd look for an answer. And if they found the right answer, that was the end of every dream.

And meanwhile the hunt was after him. Radio beams, license numbers, air-traffic analysis, broadcast alarms, ID files—all the resources of a great and desperate power would be hounding him across the world, and nowhere could he rest.

VII

Jimmy was weeping in fright, and Naysmith comforted him as well as possible while ripping through the sky. It was hard to be gay, laugh with the boy and tickle him and convince him it was all an exciting game, while Jeanne slumped motionless in the seat and the earth blurred below. But terror at such an early age could have devastating psychic effects and had to be allayed at once. *It's all I can do for you, son. The Brotherhood owes you that much, after the dirty trick it played in bringing you into this world as the child of one of us.*

When Jimmy was at ease again, placed in the back seat to watch a televised robotshow, Naysmith surveyed his situation. The boat had more legs than the law permitted, which was one good aspect. He had taken it five miles up, well above the lanes of controlled traffic, and was running northward in a circuitous course. His hungry engines gulped oil at a frightening rate; he'd have to stop for a refill two or three times. Fortunately, he had plenty of cash along. The routine identification of a thumbprint check would leave a written invitation to the pursuers, whereas they might never stumble on the isolated fuel stations where he meant to buy.

Jeanne came awake, stirring and gasping. He held her close to him until the spasm of returning consciousness had passed, and her eyes were clear again. Then he lit a cigaret for her and one for himself, and leaned back against the cushions.

"I suppose you're wondering what this is all about," he said.

"Uh-huh." Her smile was uncertain. "How much can you tell me?"

"As much as is safe for you to know," he answered. *Damn it, how much does she already know? I can't give myself away yet! She must be aware that her husband is— was—an Un-man, that his nominal job was a camouflage, but the details?*

"Where are we going?" she asked.

"I've got a hiding place for you and the kid, up in the Canadian Rockies. Not too comfortable, I'm afraid, but reasonably safe. If we can get there without being intercepted. It—"

"We interrupt this program to bring you an urgent announcement. A dangerous criminal is at large in an Airflyte numbered USA-1349-U-7683. Repeat, USA-1349-U-7683. This man is believed to be accompanied by a woman and child. If you see the boat, call the nearest police headquarters or Security office at once. The man is wanted for murder and kidnaping, and is thought to be the agent of a foreign power. Further announcements with complete description will follow as soon as possible."

The harsh voice faded and the robotshow came back on. "Man, oh man, oh man," breathed Naysmith. "They don't waste any time, do they?"

Jeanne's face was white, but her only words were: "How about painting this boat's number over?"

"Can't stop for that now or they'd catch us sure." Naysmith scanned the heavens. "Better strap yourself and Jimmy in, though. If a police boat tracks us, I've got machine guns in this one. We'll blast them."

She fought back the tears with a heart-wrenching gallantry. "Mind explaining a little?"

"I'll have to begin at the beginning," he said cautiously. "To get it all in order, I'll have to tell you a lot of things you already know. But I want to give you the complete pattern. I want to break away from the dirty names like spy and traitor, and show you what we're really trying to do."

"We?" She caressed the pronoun. No sane human likes to stand utterly alone.

"Listen," said the Naysmith. "I'm an Un-man. But a rather special kind. I'm not in the Inspectorate, allowed by charter and treaty to carry out investigations and report violations of things like disarmament agreements to the Council. I'm in the U.N. Secret Service—the *secret* Secret Service—and our standing is only quasi-legal. Officially we're an auxiliary to the Inspectorate; in practice we do a hell of a lot more. The Inspectorate is supposed to tell the U.N. Moon bases where to plant their rocket bombs; the Service tries to make bombardment unnecessary by forestalling hostile action."

"By assassinating Kwang-ti?" she challenged.

"Kwang-ti was a menace. He'd taken China out of the U.N. and was building up her armies. He'd made one attempt to take over Mongolia by sponsoring a phony revolt, and nearly succeeded. I'm not saying that he was knocked off by a Chinese Un-man, in spite of his successor government's charges. I'm just saying it was a good thing he died."

"He did a lot for China."

"Sure. And Hitler did a lot for Germany and Stalin did a lot for Russia, all of which was nullified, along with a lot of innocent people, when those countries went to war. Never forget that the U.N. exists first, last, and all the time to keep the peace. Everything else is secondary."

Jeanne lit another cigaret from the previous one. "Tell me more," she said in a voice that suggested she had known this for a long time.

"Look," said Naysmith, "the enemies the U.N. has faced

in the past were as nothing to what endangers it now. Because before the enmity has always been more or less open. In the Second War, the U.N. got started as a military alliance against the fascist powers. In the Third War it became, in effect, a military alliance against its own dissident and excommunicated members. After Rio it existed partly as an instrument of multilateral negotiation but still primarily as an alliance of a great many states, not merely Western, to prevent or suppress wars anywhere in the world. Oh, I don't want to play down its legal and cultural and humanitarian and scientific activities, but the essence of the U.N. was force, men and machines it could call on from all its member states— even against a member of itself, if that national were found guilty by a majority vote in the Council. It wasn't quite as large of the United States as you think to turn its Lunar bases over to the U.N. It thought it could still control the Council as it had done in the past, but matters didn't work out that way. Which is all to the good. We need a truly international body.

"Anyway, the principle of intervention to stop all wars, invited or not, led to things like the Great Jehad and the Brazil-Argentine affair. Small-scale war fought to prevent large-scale war. Then when the Russian government appealed for help against its nationalist insurgents, and got it, the precedent of active intervention within a country's own boundaries was set—much to the good and much to the distaste of almost every government, including the American. The conservatives were in power here about that time, you remember, trying unsuccessfully to patch up the Socialist Depression, and they nearly walked us out of membership. Not quite, though. And those other international functions, research and trade regulation and so on, have been growing apace.

"You see where this is leading? I've told you many times before"—a safe guess, that—"but I'll tell you again. The U.N. is in the process of becoming a federal world government. Already it has its own Inspectorate, its own small police force, and its Lunar Guard. Slowly, grudgingly, the nations are being induced to disarm—we abolished our own draft ten years or so back, remember? There's a movement afoot to internationalize the planets and the ocean developments, put them under direct U.N. authority. We've had international currency stabilization for a long time now; sooner or later, we'll adopt one money unit for the world. Tariffs are virtually extinct. Oh, I could go on all day.

"Previous proposals to make a world government of the U.N. were voted down. Nations were too short-sighted. But it is nevertheless happening, slowly, piece by piece, so that the final official unification of man will be only a formality. Understand? Of course you do. It's obvious. The trouble is, our enemies have begun to understand it too."

Naysmith lit a cigaret for himself and scowled at the blue cloud swirling from his nostrils. "There are so many who would like to break the U.N. There are nationalists and militarists of every kind, every country, men who would rise to power if the old anarchy returned. The need for power is a physical hunger in that sort. There are big men of industry, finance and politics, who'd like to cut their enterprises loose from regulation. There are labor leaders who want a return of the old strife which means power and profit for them. There are religionists of a dozen sorts who don't like our population-control campaigns and the quiet subversion of anti-contraceptive creeds. There are cranks and fanatics who seek a chance to impose their own beliefs, everyone from Syndics to Neo-communists, Pilgrims to Hedonists. There are those who were hurt by some or other U.N. action; perhaps they lost a son in one of our campaigns, perhaps a new development or policy wiped out their business. They want revenge. Oh, there are a thousand kinds of them, and if once the U.N. collapses they'll all be free to go fishing in troubled waters."

"Tell me something new," said Jeanne impatiently.

"I have to lead up to it, darling. I have to explain what this latest threat is. You see, these enemies of ours are getting together. All over the world, they're shelving their many quarrels and uniting into a great secret organization whose one purpose is to weaken and destroy the U.N. You wouldn't think fanatical nationalists of different countries could cooperate? Well, they can, because it's the only way they'll ever have a chance later on to attack each other. The leadership of this organization, which we Un-men somewhat inelegantly refer as to the gang, is brilliant; a lot of big men are members and the whole thing is beautifully set up. Such entities as the Americanist Party have become fronts for the gang. Whole governments are backing them, governments which are reluctant U.N. members only because of public opinion at home and the pressure that can be brought to bear on nonmembers. Kwang-ti's successors brought China back in, I'm sure, only to ruin us from within. U.N. Councillors are among their creatures, and I know not how many U.N. employees.''

Naysmith smiled humorlessly. "Even now, the great bulk of people throughout the world are pro-U.N., looking on it as a deliverer from the hell they've survived. So one way the enemy has to destroy us is by sabotage from inside. Corruption, arrogance, inefficiency, illegal actions—perpetrated by their own agents in the U.N. and becoming matters of public knowledge. You've heard a lot of that, and you'll hear still more in the months to come if this is allowed to go on. Another way is to ferret out some of our darker secrets— secrets which every government necessarily has—and make them known to the right people. All right, let's face it: Kwang-ti *was* assassinated by an Un-man. We thought the job had been passed off as the work of democratic conspirators, but apparently there's been a leak somewhere and the Chinese accusation is shaking the whole frail edifice of international cooperation. The Council will stall as long as possible, but eventually it'll have to disown the Service's action and heads will roll. Valuable heads.

"Now if at the proper moment, with the U.N. badly weakened, whole nations walking out again, public confidence trembling, there should be military revolutions within key nations—and the Moon bases seized by ground troops from a nearby colony— Do you see it? Do you see the return of international anarchy, dictatorship, war—and every Un-man in the Solar System hunted to his death?''

VIII

By a roundabout course avoiding the major towns and colonies, it was many hours even at the airboat's speed to Naysmith's goal. He found his powers of invention somewhat taxed enroute. First he had to give Jeanne a half-true account of his whereabouts in the past weeks. Then Jimmy, precociously articulate—as he should be, with both parents well into the genius class—felt disturbed by the gravity of his elders and the imminent re-disappearance of a father whom he obviously worshipped, and could only be comforted by Naysmith's long impromptu saga of Crock O'Dile, a green Irish alligator who worked at the Gideon Kleinmein Home for Helpless and Houseless Horses. Finally there were others to contend with, a couple of filling station operators and the clerk in a sporting goods store where he purchased supplies: they had to be convinced in an unobtrusive way that these were dully everyday customers to be forgotten as soon as they were gone. It all seemed to go off easily enough, but Naysmith was cold with the tension of wondering whether any of these people had heard the broadcast alarms. Obviously not, so far. But when they got home and, inevitably, were informed, would they remember well enough?

He zigzagged over Washington, crossing into British Columbia above an empty stretch of forest. There was no official reason for an American to stop, but the border was a logical place for the S-men to watch.

"Will the Canadian police cooperate in hunting us?" asked Jeanne.

"I don't know," said Naysmith. "It depends. You see, American Security, with its broad independent powers, has an anti-U.N. head. On the other hand, the President is pro-U.N. as everybody knows, and Fourre will doubtless see to it that he learns who this wanted criminal is. He can't actually countermand the chase without putting himself in an untenable position, but he can obstruct it in many ways and can perhaps tip off the Canadian government. All on the Q.T., of course."

The boat swung east until it was following the mighty spine of the Rockies, an immensity of stone and forest and snow turning gold with sunset. Naysmith had spent several vacations here, camping and painting, and knew where he was headed. It was after dark when he slanted the boat downward, feeling his way with the radar.

There was an abandoned uranium-hunting base here, one of the shacks still habitable. Naysmith bounced the boat to a halt on the edge of a steep cliff, cut the engines, and yawned hugely. "End of the line," he said.

They climbed out, burdened with equipment, food, and the sleeping child. Naysmith wheeled the vehicle under a tall pine and led the way up a slope. Jeanne drew a lungful of the sharp moonlit air and sighed. "Martin, it's beautiful! Why didn't you ever take me here before?"

He didn't answer. His flashlight picked out the crumbling face of the shack, its bare wood and metal blurred with many years. The door creaked open on darkness. Inside, it was bare, the flooring rotted away to a soft black mold, a few sticks of broken furniture scattered like bones. Taking a purchased ax, he went into the woods after spruce boughs, heaping them under the sleeping bags which Jeanne had laid out. Jimmy whimpered a little in his dreams, but they didn't wake him to eat.

Naysmith's watch showed midnight before the cabin was in order. He strolled out for a final cigaret and Jeanne followed to stand beside him. Her fingers closed about his.

The Moon was nearly full, rising over a peak whose heights were one glitter of snow. Stars wheeled enormously overhead, flashing and flashing in the keen cold air. The forests growing up the slant of this mountain soughed with wind, tall and dark and heady-scented, filled with night and mystery. Down in the gorge there was a river, a long gleam of broken moonlight, the fresh wild noise of its passage drifting up to them. Somewhere an owl hooted.

Jeanne shivered in the chill breeze and crept against Naysmith. He drew his mantle about both of them, holding her close. The little red eye of his cigaret waxed and waned in the dark.

"It's so lovely here," she whispered. "Do you have to go tomorrow?"

"Yes." His answer came harshly out of his throat. "You've supplies enough for a month. If anyone chances by, then you're of course just a camper on vacation. But I doubt they will, this is an isolated spot. If I'm not back within three weeks, though, follow the river down. There's a small colony about fifty miles from here. Or I may send one of our agents to get you. He'll have a password—let's see—'The crocodiles grow green in Ireland.' Okay?"

Her laugh was muted and wistful.

"I'm sorry to lay such a burden on you, darling," he said contritely.

"It's nothing—except that you'll be away, a hunted man, and I won't know—" She bit her lip. Her face was white in the streaming moon-glow. "This is a terrible world we live in."

"No, Jeanne. It's a—a potentially lovely world. My job is to help keep it that way." He chucked her under the chin, fighting to smile. "Don't let it worry you. Goodnight, sweet princess."

She kissed him with yearning. For an instant Naysmith hung back. *Should I tell her? She's safely away now—she has a right to know I'm not her husband—*

"What's wrong, Marty? You seem so strange."

I don't dare. I can't tell her—not while the enemy is abroad, not while there's a chance of their catching her. And a little longer in her fool's paradise—I can drop out of sight, let someone else give her the news— You crawling coward!

He surrendered. But it was a cruel thing to know, that she was really clasping a dead man to her.

They walked slowly back to the cabin.

Colonel Samsey woke with an animal swiftness and sat up in bed. Sleep drained from him as he saw the tall figure etched black against his open balcony door. He grabbed for the gun under his pillow.

"I wouldn't try that, friend." The voice was soft. Moonlight streamed in to glitter on the pistol in the intruder's hand.

"Who are you?" Samsey gasped it out, hardly aware of the incredible fact yet. Why—he was a hundred and fifty stories up. His front entrance was guarded, and no copter could so silently have put this masked figure on his balcony.

"Out of bed, boy. Fast! Okay, now clasp your hands on top of your head."

Samsey felt the night wind cold on his naked body. It was a helplessness, this standing unclothed and alone, out of his uniform and pistol belt, looking down the muzzle of a stranger's gun. His close-cropped scalp felt stubbly under his palms.

"How did you get in?" he whispered.

Naysmith didn't feel it necessary to explain the process. He had walked from the old highway on which he had landed his jet and used vacuum shoes and gloves to climb the sheer face of Denver Unit. "Better ask why I came," he said.

"All right, blast you! Why? This is a gross violation of privacy, plus menace and—" Samsey closed his mouth with a snap. Legality had plainly gone by the board.

"I want some information." Naysmith seated himself halfway on a table, one leg swinging easily, the gun steady in his right hand while his left fumbled in a belt pouch. "And you, as a high-ranking officer in the American Guard and a wellknown associate of Roger Wade, seemed likeliest to have it."

"You're crazy! This is— We're just a patriotic society. You know that. Or should. We—"

"Cram it, Samsey," said Naysmith wearily. "The American Guard has ranks, uniforms, weapons, and drills. Every member belongs to the Americanist Party. You're a private army. Nazi style, and you've done the murders, robberies, and beatings of the Party for the past five years. As soon as the government is able to prove that in court, you'll all go to the Antarctic mines and you know it. Your hope is that your faction can be in power before there's a case against you."

"Libel! We're a patriotic social group—"

"I regret my approach," said Naysmith sardonically. And he did. Direct attack of this sort was not only unlawful, it was crude and of very limited value. But he hadn't much choice. He *had* to get some kind of line on the enemy's plans, and the outlawing of the Brotherhood and the general suspicion cast on the Service meant that standard detective approaches were pretty well eliminated for the time being. Half a loaf— "Nevertheless, I want certain information. The big objective right now is to overthrow the U.N. How do you intend to accomplish that? Specifically, what is your next assignment?"

"You don't expect—"

Samsey recoiled as Naysmith moved. The Un-man's left hand came out of his pouch like a striking snake even as his body hurtled across the floor. The right arm grasped Samsey's biceps, twisting him around in front of the intruder, a knee in his back, while the hypodermic needle plunged into his neck.

Samsey struggled, gasping. The muscles holding him were like steel, cat-lithe, meeting his every wrench with practiced ease. And now the great wave of dizziness came. He lurched and Naysmith supported him, easing him back to the bed.

The hypo had been filled with four cubic centimeters of a neoscopaneurine mixture, very nearly a lethal dose. But it would act fast! Naysmith did not think the colonel had been immunized against such truth drugs. The gang wouldn't trust its lower echelons that much.

Moonlight barred the mindlessly drooling face on the pil-

low with a streak of icy silver. It was very quiet here, only
the man's labored breathing and the sigh of wind blowing the
curtains at the balcony door. Naysmith gave his victim a
stimulant injection, waited a couple of minutes, and began his
interrogation.

Truth drugs have been misnamed. They do not intrinsically
force the subject to speak truth; they damp those higher brain
centers needed to invent a lie or even to inhibit response. The
subject babbles, with a strong tendency to babble on those
subjects he has previously been most concerned to keep
secret. A skilled psychologist can lead the general direction
of the talk.

First, of course, the private nastinesses which every human
has buried within himself came out, like suppuration from an
inflamed wound. Naysmith had been through this before, but
he grimaced—Samsey was an especially bad sort. These
aggressively manly types often were. Naysmith continued
patiently until he got onto more interesting topics.

Samsey didn't know anyone higher in the gang than Wade.
Well, that was to be expected. In fact, Naysmith thought
scornfully, he, the outsider, knew more about the organization of the enemy than any one member below the very top
ranks. But that was a pretty general human characteristic too.
A man did his job, for whatever motives of power, profit, or
simple existence he might have, and didn't even try to learn
where it fitted into the great general pattern. The synthesizing
mentality is tragically rare.

But a free society at least permitted its members to learn,
and a rational society encouraged them to do so; whereas
totalitarianism, from the bossy foreman to the hemispheric
dictator, was based on the deliberate suppression of communications. Where there was no feedback, there could be no
stability except through the living death of imposed intellectual rigidity.

Back to business! Here came something he had been waiting for, the next task for the American Guard's thugs. The
Phobos was due in from Mars in a week. Guardsmen were
supposed to arrange the death of one Barney Rosenberg,
passenger, as soon as possible after his debarkation on Earth.
Why? The reason was not given and had not been asked for,
but a good description of the man was available.

Mars—yes, the Guard was also using a privately owned

spaceship to run arms to a secret base in the Thyle II country, where they were picked up by Pilgrims.

So! The Pilgrims were in on the gang. The Service had suspected as much, but here was proof. This might be the biggest break of all, but Naysmith had a hunch that it was incidental. Somehow, the murder of an obscure returnee from Mars impressed him as involving greater issues.

There wasn't more which seemed worth the risk of waiting. Naysmith had a final experiment to try.

Samsey was a rugged specimen, already beginning to pull out of his daze. Naysmith switched on a lamp, its radiance falling across the distorted face below him. The eyes focused blurrily on his sheening mask. Slowly, he lifted it.

"Who am I, Samsey?" he asked quietly.

A sob rattled in the throat. "Donner—but you're dead. We killed you in Chicago. You died, you're dead."

That settled that. Naysmith replaced his mask. Systematically, he repaired the alarms he had annulled for his entry and checked the room for traces of his presence. None. Then he took Samsey's gun from beneath the pillow. Silenced, naturally. He folded the lax fingers about the trigger and blew the colonel's brains out.

They'd suspect it wasn't suicide, of course, but they might not think of a biochemical autopsy before the drugs in the bloodstream had broken down beyond analysis. At least there was one less of them. Naysmith felt no qualms. This was not a routine police operation, it was war.

He went back to the balcony, closing the door behind him. Swinging over the edge as he adjusted his vacuum cups, he started the long climb earthward.

The Service could ordinarily have provided Naysmith with an excellent disguise, but the equipment needed was elaborate and he dared not assume that any of the offices which had it were unwatched by Security. Better rely on masks and the feeble observational powers of most citizens to brazen it out.

Calling Prior from a public communibooth, even using the scrambler, was risky too, but it had to be done. The mails were not to be trusted any more, and communication was an absolute necessity for accomplishment.

The voice was gray with weariness: "Mars, eh? Nice job, Naysmith. What should we do?"

"Get the word to Fourre, of course, for whatever he can make of it. And a coded radio message to our operatives on Mars. They can check this Pilgrim business and also look into Rosenberg's background and associates. Should be a lot of leads there. However, I'll try to snatch Rosenberg myself, with a Brother or two to help me, before the Americanists get him."

"Yeah, you'd better. The Service's hands are pretty well tied just now while the U.N. investigation of the Chinese accusations is going on. Furthermore, we can't be sure of many of our own people. So we, and especially the Brotherhood, will have to act pretty much independently for the time being. Carry on as well as you can. However, I can get your information to Rio and Mars all right."

"Good man. How are things going with you?"

"Don't call me again, Naysmith. I'm being watched, and my own men can't stop a really all-out assassination attempt." Prior chuckled dryly. "If they succeed, we can talk it over in hell."

"To modify what the old *cacique* said about Spaniards in Heaven—if there are nationalists in hell, I'm not sure if I want to go there. Okay, then. And good luck!"

It was only the next day that the newscasts carried word of the murder of one Nathan Prior, semanticist residing at Frisco Unit. It was believed to be the work of foreign agents, and S-men had been assigned to aid the local police.

IX

Most of the brothers had, of course, been given disguises early in their careers. Plastic surgery had altered the distinctive countenance and the exact height, false fingerprints and retinals been put in their ID records; each of them had a matching set of transparent plastic "tips" to put on his own fingers when he made a print for any official purpose. These men should temporarily be safe, and there was no justification for calling on their help yet. They were sitting tight and wary, for if the deadly efficiency of Hessling's organization came to suspect them and pull them in, an elementary physical exam would rip the masquerade wide open.

That left perhaps a hundred undisguised Brothers in the

United States when word came for them to go underground. Identical physique could be too useful—for example, in furnishing unshakable alibis, or in creating the legend of a superman who was everywhere—to be removed from all. Some of these would be able to assume temporary appearances and move in public for a while. The rest had to cross the border or hide.

The case of Juho Lampi was especially unfortunate. He had made enough of a name as a nucleonic engineer in Finland to be invited to America, and his disguise was only superficial. When Fourre's warning went out on the code circuit, he left his apartment in a hurry. A mechanic at the garage where he hired an airboat recognized the picture that had been flashed over the entire country. Lampi read the man's poorly hidden agitation, slugged him, and stole the boat, but it put the S-men on his trail. It told them, furthermore, that the identical men were not only American.

Lampi had been given the name and address of a woman in Iowa. The Brothers were organized into cells of half a dozen, each with its own rendezvous and contacts, and this was to be Lampi's while he was in the States. He went there after dark and got a room. Somewhat later, Naysmith showed up. Naysmith, being more nearly a full-time operative, knew where several cells had their meeting places. He collected Lampi and decided not to wait for anyone else. The *Phobos* was coming to Earth in a matter of hours. Naysmith had gone to Iowa in a self-driver boat hired from a careless office in Colorado; now, through the woman running the house, the two men rented another and flew back to Robinson Field.

"I have my own boat—repainted, new number, and so on—parked near here," said Naysmith. "We'll take off in it. If we get away."

"And then what?" asked Lampi. His English was good, marked with only a trace of accent. The Brothers were natural linguists.

"I don't know. I just don't know." Naysmith looked moodily about him. "We're being hunted as few have ever been hunted." He murmured half to himself:

"I heard myself proclaim'd;
And by the happy hollow of a tree
Escap'd the hunt. No port is free; no place,

That guard and most unusual vigilance
Does not attend my taking.''

They were sitting in the Moonjumper, bar and restaurant adjacent to the spaceport. They had chosen a booth near the door, and the transparent wall on this side opened onto the field. Its great pale expanse of concrete stretched under glaring floodlights out toward darkness, a gigantic loom of buildings on three sides of it. Coveralled mechanics were busy around a series of landing cradles. A uniformed policeman strolled by, speaking idly with a technician. Or was it so casual? The technie looked solemn.

"Oh, well," said Lampi. "To get onto a more cheerful subject, have you seen Warschawski's latest exhibition?"

"What's so cheerful about that?" asked Naysmith. "It's awful. Sculpture just doesn't lend itself to abstraction as he seems to think."

Though the Brothers naturally tended to have similar tastes, environment could make a difference. Naysmith and Lampi plunged into a stiff-necked argument about modern art. It was going at a fine pace when they were interrupted.

The curtains of the booth had been drawn. They were twitched aside now and the waitress looked in. She was young and shapely, and the skimpy playsuit might have been painted on. Beyond her, the bar room was a surge of people, a buzz and hum and rumble of voices. In spite of the laboring ventilators, there was a blue haze of smoke in the air.

"Would you like another round?" asked the girl.

"Not just yet, thanks," said Naysmith, turning his masked face toward her. He had dyed his yellow hair a mousy brown at the hideaway, and Lampi's was now black, but that didn't help much; there hadn't been time to change the wiry texture. He sat stooped, so that she wouldn't see at a casual glance that he was as big as Lampi, and hoped she wasn't very observant.

"Want some company?" she asked. "I can fix it up."

"No, thanks," said Naysmith. "We're waiting for the rocket."

"I mean later. Nice girls. You'll like them." She gave him a mechanically meretricious smile.

"Ummm—well—" Naysmith swapped a glance with Lampi, who nodded. He arranged an assignation for an hour after the landing and slipped her a bill. She left them, swaying her hips.

Lampi chuckled. "It's hardly fair to a couple of hardworking girls," he said. "They will be expecting us."

"Yeah. Probably supporting aged grandmothers, too." Naysmith grinned and lifted the Scotch to the mouth-slit of his mask. "However, it's not the sort of arrangement two fugitives would make."

"What about the American Guardsman?"

"Probably those burly characters lounging at the bar. Didn't you notice them as we came in? They'll have friends else-where who'll—"

"*Your attention, please. The first tender from the Phobos will be cradling in ten minutes, carrying half the passengers from Mars. The second will follow ten minutes alter. Repeat, the first—*"

"Which one is Rosenberg on?" asked Lampi.

"How should I know?" Naysmith shrugged. "We'll just have to take our chance. Drink up."

He patted his shoulder-holstered gun and loosened the tunic over it. He and Lampi had obtained breastplates and half-boots at the hideaway; their masks were needle-proof and an arm or groin or thigh was hard to hit when a knee-length cloak flapped around the body. They should be fairly well immune to stet-guns if they worked fast. Not to bullets—but even the Guardsmen probably wouldn't care to use those in a crowd.

The two men went out of the booth and mingled with the people swirling toward the passenger egress. They separated as they neared the gate and hung about on the fringe of the group. There were a couple of big hard-looking men in masks who had shouldered their way up next to the gate. One of them had been in the Moonjumper, Naysmith remembered.

He had no picture of Rosenberg, and Samsey's incoherent description had been of little value. The man was a nonentity who must have been off Earth for years. But presumably the Guardsmen knew what to look for. Which meant that—

There was a red-and-yellow glare high in the darkened heavens. The far thunder became a howling, bellowing, shaking roar that trembled in the bones and echoed in the skull. Nerves crawled with the nameless half terror of unheard subsonic vibrations. The tender grew to a slim spearhead, backing down with radio control on the landing cradle. Her chemical blasts splashed vividly off the concrete baffles. When she lay still and the rockets cut off, there was a ringing silence.

Endless ceremony—the mechanics wheeled up a stairway, the airlock ground open, a steward emerged, a medical crew stood by to handle space sickness—Naysmith longed for a cigaret. He shifted on his feet and forced his nerves to a semblance of calm.

There came the passengers, half a dozen of them filing toward the gateway. They stopped one by one at the clearance booth to have their papers stamped. The two Guardsmen exchanged a masked glance.

A stocky Oriental came through first. Then there was a woman engineer in Spaceways uniform who held up the line as she gathered two waiting children into her arms. Then—

He was a small bandy-legged man with a hooked nose and a leathery brown skin, shabbily clad, lugging a battered valise. One of the Guardsmen tapped him politely on the arm. He looked up and Naysmith saw his lips moving, the face etched in a harsh white glare. He couldn't hear what was said over the babble of the crowd, but he could imagine it. "Why, yes, I'm Barney Rosenberg. What do you want?"

Some answer was given him; it didn't really matter what. With a look of mild surprise, the little fellow nodded. The other Guardsman pushed over to him, and he went out of the crowd between them. Naysmith drew his stet-gun, holding it under his cloak, and cat-footed after. The Guardsmen didn't escort Rosenberg into the shadows beyond the field, but walked over toward the Moonjumper. There was no reason for Rosenberg to suspect their motives, especially if they stood him a drink.

Naysmith lengthened his stride and fell in beside the right-hand man. He didn't waste time: his gun was ready, its muzzle against the victim's hip. He fired. The Guardsman strangled on a yell.

Lampi was already on the left, but he'd been a trifle slow. That enemy grabbed the Finn's gun wrist with a slashing movement. Naysmith leaned over the first Guardsman, who clawed at him as he sagged to his knees, and brought the edge of his left palm down on the second one's neck, just at the base of the skull. The blow cracked numbingly back into his own sinews.

"What the blazes—" Rosenberg opened his mouth to shout. There was no time to argue, and Lampi needled him. With a look of utter astonishment, the prospector wilted. Lampi caught him under the arms and hoisted him to one shoulder.

The kidnaping had been seen. People were turning around, staring. Somebody began to scream. Lampi stepped over the two toppled men and followed Naysmith.

Past the door of the bar, out to the street, hurry!

A whistle skirled behind them. They jumped over the slideway and dashed across the avenue. There was a transcontinental Diesel truck bearing down on them, its lights one great glare, the roar of its engine filling the world. Naysmith thought that it brushed him. But its huge bulk was a cover. They plunged over the slideway beyond, ignoring the stares of passersby, and into the shadows of a park.

A siren began to howl. When he had reached the sheltering gloom thrown by a tree, Naysmith looked behind him. Two policemen were coming, but they hadn't spotted the fugitives yet. Naysmith and Lampi ducked through a formal garden, jumping hedges and running down twisted paths. Gravel scrunched underfoot.

Quartering across the park, Naysmith led the way to his airboat. He fumbled the door open and slithered inside. Lampi climbed in with him, tossing Rosenberg into the back seat and slamming the door. The boat slid smoothly out into passing traffic. There were quite a few cars and boats abroad, and Naysmith mingled with them.

Lampi breathed heavily in the gloom. A giant neon sign threw a bloody light over his mask. "Now what?" he asked.

"Now we get the devil out of here," said Naysmith. "Those boys are smart. It won't take them long to alert traffic control and stop all nearby vehicles for search. We have to be in the air before that time."

They left the clustered shops and dwellings, and Naysmith punched the board for permission to take off southbound. The automatic signal flashed him a fourth-lane directive. He climbed to the indicated height and went obediently south on the beam. Passing traffic was a stream of moving stars around him.

The emergency announcement signal blinked an angry red. "Fast is right," said Lampi, swearing in four languages.

"Up we go," said Naysmith.

He climbed vertically, narrowly missing boats in the higher levels, until he was above all lanes. He kept climbing till his vehicle was in the lower atmosphere. Then he turned westward at top speed.

"We'll go out over the Pacific," he explained. "Then we find us a nice uninhabited islet with some trees and lie doggo till tomorrow night. Won't be any too comfortable, but it'll have to be done and I have some food along." He grinned beneath his mask. "I hope you like cold canned beans, Juho."

"And then—"

"I know another island off the California coast," said Naysmith. "We'll disguise this boat at our first stop, of course, changing the number and recognition signal and so on. Then at the second place we'll refuel and I'll make an important call. You can bet your last mark the enemy knows who pulled this job and will have alerted all fuel station operators this time. But the man where we're going is an absentminded old codger who won't be hard to deceive." He scowled. "That'll take about the last of my cash money, too. Have to get some more somehow, if we're to carry on in our present style."

"Where do we go from there?" said Lampi.

"North, I suppose. We have to hide Rosenberg somewhere, and you—" Naysmith shook his head, feeling a dull pain within him. That was the end of the masquerade. Jeanne Donner would know.

At first Barney Rosenberg didn't believe it. He was too shocked. The Guardsmen had simply told him they were representatives of some vaguely identified company which was thinking of developments on Mars and wanted to consult him. He'd been offered a hotel suite and had been told the fee would be nice. Now he looked at his kidnapers with bewildered eyes and challenged them to say who they were.

"Think we'd be fools enough to carry our real IDs around?" snorted Naysmith. "You'll just have to take our word for it that we're U.N. operatives—till later, anyway, when we can safely prove it. I tell you, the devil is loose on Earth and you need protection. Those fellows were after your knowledge, and once they got that you'd have been a corpse."

Rosenberg looked from one masked face to the other. His head felt blurred, the drug was still in him and he couldn't think straight. But those voices—

He thought he remembered the voices. Both of them. Only they were the same.

"I don't know anything," he said weakly. "I tell you, I'm just a prospector, home from Mars."

"You must have information—that's the only possibility," said Lampi. "Something you learned on Mars which is important to them, perhaps to the whole world. What?"

Fieri in Drygulch, and the Pilgrim who had been so eager—

Rosenberg shook his head, trying to clear it. He looked at the two big cloaked figures hemming him in. There was darkness outside the hurtling airboat.

"Who are you?" he whispered.

"I told you we're friends. Un-men. Secret agents." Naysmith laid a hand on Rosenberg's shoulder. "We want to help you, that's all. We want to protect you, and whatever it is you know."

Rosenberg looked at the hand—strong, sinewy, blunt-fingered, with fine gold hairs on the knuckles. But no, no, no! His heart began thumping till he thought it must shatter his ribs.

"Let me see your faces," he gasped.

"Well—why not?" Naysmith and Lampi took off their masks. The dull panel light gleamed off the same features; broad, strong-boned, blue-eyed. There was a deep wrinkle above each jutting triangle of nose. The left ear was faintly bigger than the right. Both men had a trick of cocking their head a trifle sideways when listening.

We'll tell him we're twin brothers, thought Naysmith and Lampi simultaneously.

Rosenberg shrank into the seat. There was a tiny whimper in his throat.

"Stef," he murmured. "Stefan Rostomily."

X

The newscasts told of crisis in the U.N. Etienne Fourre, backed by its President, was claiming that the Chinese government was pressing a fantastic charge to cover up designs of its own. A full-dress investigation was in order. Only—as Besser, Minister of International Finance, pointed out—when the official investigating service was itself under suspicion, who could be trusted to get at the facts?

In the United States, Security was after a dangerous spy and public enemy. Minute descriptions of Donner-Naysmith-Lampi were on all the screens. Theoretically, the American President could call off the hunt, but that would mean an uproar in the delicately balanced Congress; there'd have been a vote of confidence, and if the President lost that, he and his cabinet would have to resign—and who would be elected to succeed? But Naysmith and Lampi exchanged grins at the interview statement of the President, that he thought this much-hunted spy was in Chinese pay.

Officially, Canada was cooperating with the United States in chasing the fugitive. Actually, Naysmith was sure it was bluff, a sop to the anti-U.N. elements in the Dominion. Mexico was doing nothing—but that meant the Mexican border was being closely watched.

It couldn't go on. The situation was so unstable that it would have to end, one way or another, in the next several days. If Hessling's men dragged in a Brother— Whether or not Fourre's organization survived, it would have lost its greatest and most secret asset.

But the main thing, Naysmith reflected grimly, was to keep Fourre's own head above water. The whole purpose of this uproar was to discredit the man and his painfully built-up service, and to replace him and his key personnel with nationalist stooges. After that, the enemy would find the next stages of their work simple.

And what can I do?

Naysmith felt a surge of helplessness. Human society had grown too big, too complex and powerful. It was a machine running blind and wild, and he was a fly caught in the gears.

There was one frail governor on the machine, only one, and if it were broken the whole thing would shatter. What to do? What to do?

He shrugged off the despair and concentrated on the next moment. The first thing was to get Rosenberg's information to his own side.

The island was a low sandy swell in an immensity of ocean. There was harsh grass on it, and a few trees gnarled by the great winds, and a tiny village. Naysmith dropped Lampi on the farther side of the island to hide till they came back for him. Rosenberg took the Finn's mask, and the two jetted across to the fuel station. While their boat's tanks were being filled, they entered a public communibooth.

Peter Christian, in Mexico City—Naysmith dialed the number given him by Prior. That seemed the best bet. Wasn't the kid undergoing Synthesis training? His logic might be able to integrate the meaningless flux of data.

No doubt every call across either border was being monitored, illegally but thoroughly. However, the booth had a scrambler unit. Naysmith fed it a coin, but didn't activate it immediately.

"Could I speak to Peter Christian?" he asked the servant whose face appeared in the screen. "Tell him it's his cousin Joe calling. And give him this message: 'The ragged scoundrel leers merrily, not peddling babies.' "

"Señor?" The brown face looked astonished.

"It's a private signal. Write it down, please, so you get it correct." Naysmith dictated slowly. " 'The ragged scoundrel—' "

"Yes, understand. Wait, please, I will call the young gentleman."

Naysmith stood watching the screen for a moment. He could vaguely make out the room beyond, a solid and handsomely furnished place. Then he stabbed at the scrambler buttons. There were eight of them, which could be punched in any order to yield 40,320 possible combinations. The key letters known to every Brother, were currently MNTSRPBL, and "the ragged scoundrel" had given Christian the order Naysmith was using. When Hessling's men got around to playing back their monitor tapes, the code sentence wouldn't help them unscramble without knowledge of the key. On the other hand, it wouldn't be proof that their quarry had been making the call; such privacy devices were not uncommon.

Naysmith blanked the booth's walls and removed his own

and Rosenberg's masks. The little man was in a state of hypnosis, total recall of the Fieri manuscript he had read on Mars. He was already drawing structural formulas of molecules.

The random blur and noise on the screen clicked away as Peter Christian set the scrambler unit at that end. It was his own face grown younger which looked out at Naysmith—a husky blond sixteen-year-old, streaked with sweat and panting a little. He grinned at his Brother.

"Sorry to be so long," he said. "I was working out in the gym. Have a new mech-volley play to develop which looks promising." His English was fluent and Naysmith saw no reason to use a Spanish which, in his own case, had grown a little rusty.

"Who're you the adoptive son of?" asked the man. Privacy customs didn't mean much in the Brotherhood.

"Holger Christian—Danish career diplomat, currently ambassador to Mexico. They're good people, he and his wife."

Yes, thought Naysmith, they would be, if they let their foster child, even with his obvious brilliance, take Synthesis. The multi-ordinal integrating education was so new and untried, and its graduates would have to make their own jobs. But the need was desperate. The sciences had grown too big and complex, like everything else, and there was too much overlap between the specialties. Further progress required the fully trained synthesizing mentality.

"And progress itself was no longer something justified only by Victorian prejudice. It was a matter of survival. Some means of creating a stable social and economic order in the face of continuous revolutionary change had to be found. More and more technological development was bitterly essential. Atomic-powered oil synthesis had come barely in time to save a fuel-starved Earth from industrial breakdown. Now new atomic energy fuels had to be evolved before the old ores were depleted. The rising incidence of neurosis and insanity among the intelligent and apathy among the insensitive had to be checked before other Years of Madness came. Heredity damaged by hard radiation had to be unscrambled, somehow, before dangerous recessive traits spread through the entire human population. Communications theory, basic to modern science and sociology, had to be perfected. There had to be. Why enumerate? Man had come too far and too fast. Now he was balanced on a knife edge over the red gulfs of hell.

When Peter Christian's education was complete, he would be one of Earth's most important men—whether he realized it himself or not. Of course, even his foster parents didn't know that one of his Synthesis instructors was an Un-man who was quietly teaching him the fine points of secret service. They most assuredly did not know that their so normal and healthy boy was already initiated into a group whose very existence was an unrecorded secret.

The first Brothers had been raised in the families of Un-man technies and operators who had been in on the project from the start. This practice continued on a small scale, but most of the new children were put out for adoption through recognized agencies around the world—having first been provided with a carefully faked background history. Between sterility and the fear of mutation, there was no difficulty in placing a good-looking man child with a superior family. From babyhood, the Brother was under the influence—a family friend or a pediatrician or instructor or camp counselor or minister, anyone who could get an occasional chance to talk intimately with the boy, would be a sparetime employee of Fourre's and helped incline the growing personality the right way. It had been established that a Brother could accept the truth and keep his secret from the age of twelve, and that he never refused to turn Un-man. From then on, progress was quicker. The Brothers were precocious: Naysmith was only twenty-five, and he had been on his first mission at seventeen; Lampi was an authority in his field at twenty-three. There should be no hesitation in dumping this responsibility on Christian, even if there had been any choice in the matter.

"Listen," said Naysmith. "You know all hell has broken loose and that the American S-men are out to get us. Specifically, I'm the one they think they're hunting. But Lampi, a Finnish Brother, and I have put the snatch on one Barney Rosenberg from Mars. He has certain information the enemy wants." The man knew that the boy must be thinking—in a way, those were his own thoughts—and added swiftly: "No, we haven't let him in on the secret, though the fact that he was a close friend of Rostomily's makes it awkward. But it also makes him trust us. He read the report of a Fieri on Mars, concerning suspended animation techniques. He'll give it to you now. Stand by to record.''

"Okay, *ja, si.*" Christian grinned and flipped a switch. He was still young enough to find this a glorious cloak-and-dagger adventure. Well, he'd learn, and the learning would be a little death within him.

Rosenberg began to talk, softly and very fast, holding up his structural formulas and chemical equations at the appropriate places. It took a little more than an hour. Christian would have been bored if he hadn't been so interested by the material; Naysmith fumed and sweated unhappily. Any moment there might come suspicion, discovery— The booth was hot.

"That's all, I guess," said Naysmith when the prospector had run down. "What do you make of it?"

"Why, it's sensational! It'll jump biology two decades!" Christian's eyes glowed. "Surgery—yes, that's obvious. Research techniques— *Gud Fader i himlen*, what a discovery!"

"And why do you think it's so important to the enemy?" snapped Naysmith.

"Isn't it plain? The military uses, man! You can use a light dose to immunize against terrific accelerations. Or you can pack a spaceship with men in frozen sleep, load 'em in almost like boxes, and have no supply worries enroute. Means you can take a good-sized army from planet to planet. And of course there's the research aspect. With what can be learned with the help of suspension techniques, biological warfare can be put on a wholly new plane."

"I thought as much." Naysmith nodded wearily. It was the same old story, the worn-out tale of hate and death and oppression. The logical end-product of scientific warfare was that *all* data became military secrets—a society without communication in its most vital department, without feedback or stability. That was what he fought against. "All right, what can you do about it?"

"I'll unscramble the record—no, better leave it scrambled—and get it to the right people. Hmmm—give me a small lab and I'll undertake to develop certain phases of this myself. In any case, we can't let the enemy have it."

"We've probably already given it to them. Chances are they have monitors on this line. But they can't get around to our recording and to trying all possible unscrambling combinations in less than a few days, especially if we keep them busy." Naysmith leaned forward, his haggard eyes probing into the screen. "Pete, as the son of a diplomat you must have a better than average notion of the overall politico-military picture. What can we do?"

Christian sat still for a moment. There was a curious withdrawn expression on the young face. His trained mind was assembling logic networks in a manner unknown to previous history. Finally he looked back at the man.

"There's about an eighty percent probability that Besser is the head of the gang," he said. "Chief of international finance, you know. That's an estimate of my own; I don't have Fourre's data, but I used a basis of Besser's past history and known character, his country's recent history, the necessary communications for a least-effort anti-U.N. setup on a planetary scale, the—never mind. You already know with high probability that Roger Wade is his chief for North America. I can't predict Besser's actions very closely, since in spite of his prominence he uses privacy as a cover-up for relevant psychological data. If we assume that he acts on a survival axiom, and logically apart from his inadequate grounding in modern socio-theory and his personal bias—hm."

"Besser, eh? I had my own suspicions, besides what I've been told. Financial integration has been proceeding rather slowly since he took office. Never mind. We have to strike at his organization. What to do?"

"I need more data. How many American Brothers are underground in the States and can be contacted?"

"How should I know? All that could would try to skip the country. I'm only here because I know enough of the overall situation to act usefully, I hope."

"Well, I can scare up a few in Mexico and South America, I think. We have our own communications. And I can use my 'father's' sealed diplomatic circuit to get in touch with Fourre. You have this Lampi with you, I suppose?" Christian sat in moody stillness for a while. Then:

"I can only suggest—and it's a pretty slim guess—that you two let yourselves be captured."

The man sighed. He had rather expected this.

Naysmith brought the boat whispering down just as the first cold light of sunrise crept skyward. He buzzed the narrow ledge where he had to land, swung back, and lowered the wheels. When they touched, it was a jarring, brutal contact that rattled his teeth together. He cut the motor and there was silence.

If Jeanne was alert, she'd have a gun on him now. He opened the door and called loudly: "The crocodiles grow green in Ireland." Then he stepped out and looked around him.

The mountains were a shadowy looming. Dawn lay like roses on their peaks. The air was fresh and chill, strong with the smell of pines, and there was dew underfoot and alarmed birds clamoring into the sky. Far below him, the river thundered and brawled.

Rosenberg climbed stiffly after him and leaned against the boat. Earth gravity dragged at his muscles, he was cold and hungry and cruelly tired, and these men who were ghosts of his youth would not tell him what the darkness was that lay over the world. Sharply he remembered the thin bitter sunup of Mars, a gaunt desert misting into life and a single crag etched against loneliness. Homesickness was an ache in him.

Only—he had not remembered Earth could be so lovely.

"Martin! Oh, Martin!" The woman came down the trail, running, slipping on the wet needles. Her raven hair was cloudy about the gallantly lifted head, and there was a light in her eyes which Rosenberg had almost forgotten. "Oh, my darling, you're back!"

Naysmith held her close, kissing her with hunger. One minute more, one little minute before Lampi emerged, was that too much?

He hadn't been able to leave the Finn anywhere behind. There was no safe hiding place in all America, not when the S-men were after him. There could be no reliable rendezvous later, and Lampi would be needed. He had to come along.

Of course, the Finn could have stayed masked and mute the entire while he was at the cabin. But Rosenberg would have to be left here, it was the best hideaway for him. The prospector might be trusted to keep secret the fact that two identical men had brought him here—or he might not. He was shrewd; Jeanne's conversation would lead him to some suspicion of the truth, and he might easily decide that she had been the victim of a shabby trick and should be given the facts. Then anything could happen.

Oh, with some precautions Naysmith could probably hide

his real nature from the girl awhile longer. Rosenberg might very well keep his mouth shut on request. But there was no longer any point in concealing the facts from her—she would not be captured by the gang before they had the Un-man himself. In any case, she must be told sooner or later. The man she thought was her husband was probably going to die, and it was as well that she think little of him and have no fears and sorrows on his account. One death was enough for her.

He laid his hands on the slim shoulders and stood back a bit, looking into her eyes. His own crinkled in the way she must know so well, and they were unnaturally bright in the dawn-glow. When he spoke, it was almost a whisper.

"Jeanne, honey, I've got some bad news for you."

He felt her stiffen beneath his hands, saw the face tighten and heard the little hiss of indrawn breath. There were dark rings about her eyes, she couldn't have slept very well while he was gone.

"This is a matter for absolute secrecy," he went on, tonelessly. "No one, repeat no one, is to have a word of it. But you have a right to the truth."

"Go ahead." There was an edge of harshness in her voice. "I can take it."

"I'm not Martin Donner," he said. "Your husband is dead."

She stood rigid for another heartbeat, and then she pulled wildly free. One hand went to her mouth. The other was half lifted as if to fend him off.

"I had to pretend it, to get you away without any fuss," he went on, looking at the ground. "The enemy would have— tortured you, maybe. Or killed you and Jimmy. I don't know."

Juho Lampi came up behind Naysmith. There was compassion on his face. Jeanne stepped backward, voiceless.

"You'll have to stay here," said Naysmith bleakly. "It's the only safe place. Here is Mr. Rosenberg, whom we're leaving with you. I assure you he's completely innocent of anything that has been done. I can't tell either of you more than this." He took a long step toward her. She stood her ground, unmoving. When he clasped her hands into his, they were cold. "Except that I love you," he whispered.

Then, swinging away, he faced Lampi. "We'll clean up

and get some breakfast here," he said. "After that, we're off."

Jeanne did not follow them inside. Jimmy, awakened by their noise, was delighted to have his father back (Lampi had reassumed a mask) but Naysmith gave him disappointingly little attention. He told Rosenberg that the three of them should stay put here as long as possible before striking out for the village, but that it was hoped to send a boat for them in a few days.

Jeanne's face was cold and bloodless as Naysmith and Lampi went back to the jet. When it was gone, she started to cry. Rosenberg wanted to leave and let her have it out by herself, but she clung to him blindly and he comforted her as well as he could.

XI

There was no difficulty about getting captured. Naysmith merely strolled into a public lavatory at Oregon Unit and took off his mask to wash his face; a man standing nearby went hurriedly out, and when Naysmith emerged he was knocked over by the stet-gun of a Unit policeman. It was what came afterward that was tough.

He woke up, stripped and handcuffed, in a cell, very shortly before a team of S-men arrived to lead him away. These took the added precaution of binding his ankles before stuffing him into a jet. He had to grin sourly at that, it was a compliment of sorts. Little was said until the jet came down on a secret headquarters which was also a Wyoming ranch.

There they gave him the works. He submitted meekly to every identification procedure he had ever heard of. Fluoroscopes showed nothing hidden within his body except the communicator, and there was some talk of operating it out; but they decided to wait for orders from higher up before attempting that. They questioned him and, since he had killed two or three of their fellows, used methods which cost him a couple of teeth and a sleepless night. He told them his name and address, but little else.

Orders came the following day. Naysmith was bundled into another jet and flown eastward. Near the destination, the jet was traded for an ordinary, inconspicuous airboat. They landed after dark on the grounds of a large new mansion in western Pennsylvania—Naysmith recalled that Roger Wade lived here—and he was led inside. There was a soundproofed room with a full battery of interrogation machines under the residential floors. The prisoner was put into a chair already equipped with straps, fastened down, and left for a while to ponder his situation.

He sighed and attempted to relax, leaning back against the metal of the chair. It was an uncomfortable seat, cold and stiff as it pressed into his naked skin. The room was long and low-ceilinged, barren in the white glare of high-powered fluoros, and the utter stillness of it muffled his breath and heartbeat. The air was cool, but somehow that absorbed quiet choked him. He faced the impassive dials of a lie detector and an electric neurovibrator, and the silence grew and grew.

His head ached, and he longed for a cigarette. His eyelids were sandy with sleeplessness and there was a foul taste in his mouth. Mostly, though, he thought of Jeanne Donner.

Presently the door at the end of the room opened and a group of people walked slowly toward him. He recognized Wade's massive form in the van. Behind him trailed a bearded man with a lean, sallow face; a young chap thin as a rail, his skin dead white and his hands clenching and unclenching nervously; a gaunt homely woman; and a squat, burly subordinate whom he did not know but assumed to be an S-man in Wade's pay. The others were familiar to Service dossiers: Lewin, Wade's personal physician; Rodney Borrow, his chief secretary; Marta Jennings, Americanist organizer. There was death in their eyes.

Wade proceeded quietly up toward Naysmith. Borrow drew a chair for him and he sat down in it and took out a cigaret. Nobody spoke till he had it lighted. Then he blew the smoke in Naysmith's direction and said gently: "According to the official records, you really are Robert Naysmith of California. But tell me, is that only another false identity?"

Naysmith shrugged. "Identity is a philosophical basic," he answered. "Where does similarity leave off and identity begin?"

"Mmmmmm-hm." Wade nodded slowly. "We've killed you at least once, and I suspect more than once. But are you Martin Donner, or are you his twin? And in the latter case, how does it happen that you two, or you three, four, five, ten thousand—are *completely* identical?''

"Oh, not quite," said Naysmith.

"No-o-o. There are the little scars and peculiarities due to environment—and habits, language, accent, occupation. But for police purposes you and Donner are the same man. How was it done?''

Naysmith smiled. "How much am I offered for that information?" he parried. "As well as other information you know I have?''

"So." Wade's eyes narrowed. "You weren't captured—not really. You gave yourself up.''

"Maybe. Have you caught anyone else yet?''

Wade traded a glance with the Security officer; then, with an air of decision, he said briskly: "An hour ago, I was informed that a man answering your description had been picked up in Minnesota. He admitted to being one Juho Lampi of Finland, and I'm inclined to take his word for it though we haven't checked port-of-entry records yet. How many more of you can we expect to meet?''

"As many as you like," said Naysmith. "Maybe more than that.''

"All right. You gave yourself up. You must know that we have no reason to spare your life—or lives. What do you hope to gain?''

"A compromise," answered Naysmith. "Which will, of course, involve our release.''

"How much are you willing to tell us now?''

"As little as possible, naturally. We'll have to bargain.''

Stall! Stall for time! The message from Rio has got to come soon. It's got to, or we're all dead men.

Borrow leaned over his master's shoulder. His voice was high and cracked, stuttering just a trifle: "How will we know you're telling the truth?''

"How will you know that even if you torture me?" shrugged Naysmith. "Your bird dogs must have reported that I've been immunized to drugs.''

"There are still ways," said Lewin. His words fell dull in the muffling silence. "Prefrontal lobotomy is usually effective.''

Yes, this is the enemy. These are the men of darkness. These are the men who in other days sent heretics to burning, or fed the furnaces of Belsen, or stuffed the rockets with

*radioactive death. Now they're opening skulls and slashing
brains across. Argue with them! Let them kick and slug and
whip you, but don't let them know—*

"Our bargain might not be considered valid if you do
that."

"The essential element of a bargain," said Wade pompously,
"is the free will and desire of both parties. You're not free."

"But I am. You've killed one of me and captured two
others. How do you know the number of me which is still
running loose, out there in the night?"

Borrow and Jennings flickered uneasy eyes toward the
smooth bare walls. The woman shuddered, ever so faintly.

"We needn't be clumsy about this," said Lewin. "There's
the lie detector, first of all. Its value is limited, but this man
is too old to have had Synthesis training, so he can't fool it
much. Then there are instruments that make a man quite
anxious to talk. I have a chlorine generator here, Naysmith.
How would you like to breathe a few whiffs of chlorine?"

"Or just a vise—applied in the right place," snapped
Jennings.

"Hold up a minute," ordered Wade. "Let's find out how
much he wants to reveal without such persuasion."

"I said I'd trade information, not give it away," said
Naysmith. He wished the sweat weren't running down his
face and body for all of them to see. The reek of primitive,
uncontrollable fear was sharp in his nostrils; not the fear of
death, but of the anguish and mutilation which were worse than
oblivion.

"What do *you* want to know?" snapped the Security officer contemptuously.

"Well," said Naysmith, "first off, I'd like to know your
organization's purpose."

"What's that?" Wade's heavy face blinked at him, and an
angry flush mottled his cheeks. "Let's not play crèche games.
You know what we want."

"No, seriously, I'm puzzled." Naysmith forced mildness
into his tones. "I realize you don't like the status quo and
want to change it. But you're all well off now. What do you
hope to gain?"

"What— That will do!" Wade gestured to the officer, and
Naysmith's head rang with a buffet. "We haven't time to
listen to your bad jokes."

Naysmith grinned viciously. If he could get them mad, play on those twisted emotions till the unreasoning thalamus controlled them—it would be hard on him, but it would delay their real aims. "Oh, I can guess," he said. "It's personal, isn't it? None of you really know what's driving you to this, except for the stupid jackals who're in with you merely because it pays better than any work they could get on their own merits. Like you, for instance." He glanced at the S-man and sneered deliberately.

"Shut up!" This time the blow was to his jaw. Blood ran out of his mouth, and he sagged a little against the straps that held him. But his voice lifted raggedly.

"Take Miss Jennings, for one. Not that I would, even if you paid me. You're all twisted up inside, aren't you? Too ugly to get a man, too scared of yourself to get a surgical remodeling. You're trying your clumsy damnedest to sublimate it into patriotism—and what kind of symbol is a flagpole? I notice it was you who made that highly personal suggestion about torturing me."

She drew back, the rage of a whipped animal in her. The S-man took out a piece of hose, but Wade gestured him away. The leader's face had gone wooden.

"Or Lewin—another case of psychotic frustration." Naysmith smiled, a close-lipped and unpleasant smile of bruised lips, at the doctor. "I warrant you'd work for free if you hadn't been hired. A two-bit sadist has trouble finding outlets these days.

"Now we come to Rodney Borrow."

"Shut up!" cried the thin man. He edged forward. Wade swept him back with a heavy arm.

"Exogene!" Naysmith's smile grew warm, almost pitying. "It's too bad that human exogenesis was developed during the Years of Madness, when moral scruples went to hell and scientists were as fanatical as everyone else. They grew you in a tank, Borrow, and your prenatal life, which every inherited instinct said should be warm and dark and sheltered, was one hell of study—bright lights, probes, microslides taken of your tissues. They learned a lot about the human fetus, but they should have killed you instead of letting such a pathetic quivering mass of engrammed psychoses walk around alive. If you could call it life, Exogene."

Borrow lunged past Wade. There was slaver running from

his lips, and he clawed for Naysmith's eyes. The S-man pulled him back and suddenly he collapsed, weeping hysterically. Naysmith shuddered beneath his skin. *There but for the grace of God—*

"And how about myself?" asked Wade. "These amateur analyses are most amusing. Please continue."

"Guilt drive. Overcompensation. The Service has investigated your childhood and adolescent background and—"

"And?"

"Come on, Roger, it's fun. It won't hurt a bit."

The big man sat stiff as an iron bar. For a long moment there was nothing, no sound except Borrow's sobs; no movement. Wade's face turned gray.

When he spoke, it was as if he were strangling: "I think you'd better start that chlorine generator, Lewin."

"With pleasure!"

Naysmith shook his head. "And you people want to run things," he murmured. "We're supposed to turn over a world slowly recovering its sanity to the likes of you."

The generator begin to hiss and bubble at his back. He could have turned his head to watch it, but that would have been a defeat. And he needed every scrap of pride remaining in this ultimate loneliness.

"Let me run the generator," whispered Borrow.

"No," said Lewin. "You might kill him too fast."

"Maybe we should wait till they bring this Lampi here," said Jennings. "Let him watch us working Naysmith over."

Wade shook his head. "Maybe later," he said.

"I notice that you still haven't tried to find out what I'm willing to tell you without compulsion," interrupted Naysmith.

"Well, go ahead," said Wade in a flat voice. "We're listening."

A little time, just a little more time, if I can spin them a yarn—

"Etienne Fourre has more resources than you know," declared Naysmith. "A counter blow has been prepared which will cost you dearly. But since it would also put quite a strain on us, we're willing to discuss—if not a permanent compromise, for there can obviously be none, at least an armistice. That's why—"

A chime sounded. "Come in," said Wade loudly. His voice activated the door and a man entered.

"Urgent call for you, Mr. Wade," he reported. "Scrambled."

"All right." The leader got up. "Hold off on that chlorine till I get back, Lewin." He went out.

When the door had closed behind him, Lewin said calmly: "Well, he didn't tell us to refrain from other things, did he?"

They took turns using the hose. Naysmith's mind grew a little hazy with pain. But they dared not inflict real damage, and it didn't last long.

Wade came back. He ignored Lewin, who was hastily pocketing the truncheon, and said curtly: "We're going on a trip. All of us. Now."

The word had come. Naysmith sank back, breathing hard. Just at that instant, the relief from pain was too great for him to think of anything else. It took him several minutes to start worrying about whether Peter Christian's logic had been correct, and whether the Service could fulfill its part, and even whether the orders that came to Wade had been the right ones.

XII

It was late afternoon before Barney Rosenberg had a chance to talk with Jeanne Donner, and then it was she who sought him out. He had wandered from the cabin after lunch, scrambling along the mountainside and strolling through the tall forest. But Earth gravity tired him, and he returned in a few hours. Even then, he didn't go back to the cabin, but found a log near the rim of the gorge and sat down to think.

So this was Earth.

It was a cool and lovely vision which opened before him. The cliffs tumbled in a sweep of gray and slate blue, down and down into the huge sounding canyon of the river. On the farther side, the mountain lifted in a mist of dim purple, up to its sun-blazing snow and the skyey vastness beyond. There were bushes growing on the slopes that fell riverward, green blurring the severe rock, here and there a cluster of firelike berries. Behind Rosenberg and on either side were the trees, looming pine in a cavern of shadow, slim whispering beech ash with the streaming, blinding, raining sunlight snared in its leaves. He had not remembered how much color there was on this planet.

And it was alive with sound. The trees murmured. Mosquitoes buzzed thinly around his ears. A bird was singing—he didn't know what kind of bird, but it had a wistful liquid trill that haunted his thoughts. Another answered in whistles, and somewhere a third was chattering and chirping its gossip. A squirrel darted past like a red comet, and he heard the tiny scrabble of its claws.

And the smells—the infinite living world of odors; pine and mould and wildflowers and the river mist! He had almost forgotten that he owned a sense of smell, in the tanked sterility of Mars.

Oh, his muscles ached and he was lonely for the grim bare magnificence of the deserts and he wondered how he would ever fit into this savage world of men against men. But still—Earth was home, and a billion years of evolution could not be denied.

Someday Mars would be a full-grown planet and its people would be rich and free. Rosenberg shook his head, smiling a little. Poor Martians!

There was a light footstep behind him. He turned and saw Jeanne Donner approaching. She had on a light blouse-and-slack outfit which didn't hide the grace of her or the weariness, and the sun gleamed darkly in her hair. Rosenberg stood up with a feeling of awkwardness.

"Please sit down." Her voice was grave, somehow remote. "I'd like to join you for a little while, if I may."

"By all means." Rosenberg lowered himself again to the mossy trunk. It was cool and yielding, a little damp, under his hand. Jeanne sat beside him, elbows on knees. For a moment she was quiet, looking over the sun-flooded land. Then she took out a pack of cigarets and held them toward the man. "Smoke?" she asked.

"Uh—no, thanks. I got out of the habit on Mars. Oxygen's too scarce, usually. We chew instead, if we can afford tobacco at all."

"M-hm." She lit a cigaret for herself and drew hard on it, sucking in her cheeks. He saw how fine the underlying bony structure was. Well—Stef had always picked the best women, and gotten them.

"We'll rig a bed for you," she said. "Cut some spruce boughs and put them under a sleeping bag. Makes a good doss."

"Thanks." They sat without talking for a while. The

cigaret smoke blew away in ragged streamers. Rosenberg could hear the wind whistling and piping far up the canyon.

"I'd like to ask you some questions," she said at last, turning her face to him. "If they get too personal, just say so."

"I've nothing to hide—worse luck." He tried to smile. "Anyway, we don't have those privacy notions on Mars. They'd be too hard to maintain under our living conditions."

"They're a recent phenomenon on Earth, anyway," she said. "Go back to the Years of Madness, when there was so much eccentricity of all kinds, a lot of it illegal. Oh, hell!" She threw the cigaret to the ground and stamped it savagely out with one heel. "I'm going to forget my own conditioning too. Ask me anything you think is relevant. We've got to get to the truth of this matter."

"If we can, I'd say it was a well-guarded secret."

"Listen," she said between her teeth. "My husband was Martin Donner. We were married three and a half years—and I mean married. He couldn't tell me much about his work. I knew he was really an Un-man and that his engineering work was only a blind, and that's about all he ever told me. Obviously, he never said a word about having—duplicates. But leaving that aside, we were in love and we got to know each other as well as two people can in that length of time. More than just physical appearance. It was also a matter of personality, reaction-patterns, facial expressions, word-configuration choices, manner of moving and working, the million little things which fit into one bit pattern. An overall *gestalt*, understand?

"Now this man—What did you say his name was?"

"Naysmith. Robert Naysmith. At least, that's what he told me. The other fellow was called Lampi."

"I'm supposed to believe that Martin died and that this—Naysmith—was substituted for him," she went on hurriedly. "They wanted to get me out of the home fast, couldn't stop to argue with me, so they sent in this ringer. Well, I saw him there in the house. He escaped with me and the boy. We had a long and uneasy flight together up here—you know how strain will bring out the most basic characteristics of a person. He stayed here overnight—" A slow flush crept up her cheeks and she looked away. Then, defiantly, she swung back on Rosenberg. "And he fooled me completely. Everything about him was Martin. *Everything!* Oh, I suppose there were minor variations, but they must have been very minor indeed. You can disguise a man these days, with surgery and cosmetics and whatnot, so that he duplicates almost every detail of physique. But can surgery give him the same funny slow way of smiling, the same choice of phrases, the same sense of humor, the same way of picking up his son and talking to him, the same habit of quoting Shakespeare, and way of taking out a cigaret and lighting it one-handed, and corner-cutting way of piloting an airboat—the same *soul?* Can they do that?''

"I don't know," whispered Rosenberg. "I shouldn't think so."

"I wouldn't really have believed it," she said. "I'd have thought he was trying to tell me a story for some unknown reason. Only there was that other man with him, and except for their hair being dyed I couldn't tell them apart—and you were along too, and seemed to accept the story." She clutched his arm. "Is it true? Is my husband really dead?"

"I don't know," he answered grayly. "I think they were telling the truth, but how can I know?"

"It's more than my own sanity," she said in a tired voice. "I've got to know what to tell Jimmy. I can't say anything now."

Rosenberg looked at the ground. His words came slowly and very soft: "I think your best bet is to sit tight for a while. This is something which is big, maybe the biggest secret in the universe. And it's either very good or very bad. I'd like to believe that it was good."

"But what do you know of it?" She held his eyes with her own, he couldn't look away, and her hand gripped his arm with a blind force. "What can you tell me? What do you think?"

He ran a thin, blue-veined hand through his grizzled hair and drew a breath. "Well," he said. "I think there probably are a lot of these identical Un-men. We know that there are—were—three, and I got the impression there must be more. Why not? That Lampi was a foreigner; he had an accent; so if they're found all over the world—"

"Un-men." She shivered a little, sitting there in the dappled shade and sunlight. "It's a hideous word. As if they weren't human."

"No," he said gently. "I think you're wrong there. They—well, I knew their prototype, and he was a *man*."

"Their—no!" Almost, she sprang to her feet. With an effort, she controlled herself and sat rigid. "*Who was that?*"

"His name was Stefan Rostomily. He was my best friend for fifteen years."

"I—don't know—never heard of him." Her tones were thick.

"You probably wouldn't have. He was off Earth the whole time. But his name is still a good one out on the planets. You may not know what a Rostomily valve is, but that was his invention. He tinkered it up one week for convenience, sold it for a good sum, and binged that away." Rosenberg chuckled dimly. "It made history, that binge. But the valve has meant a lot to Martian colonists."

"Who was he?"

"He never said much about his background. I gathered he was a European, probably Czech or Austrian. He must have done heroic things in the underground and guerrilla fighting during the Third War. But it kind of spoiled him for a settled career. By the time things began to calm a little, he'd matured in chaos and it was too late to do any serious studying. He drifted around Earth for a while, took a hand in some of the fighting that still went on here and there—he was with the U.N. forces that suppressed the Great Jehad, I know. But he got sick of killing, too, as any sane man would. In spite of his background, Mrs. Donner, he was basically one of the sanest men I ever knew. So at last he bluffed his way onto a spaceship—didn't have a degree, but he learned engineering in a hell of a hurry, and he was good at it. I met him on Venus, when I was prospecting around; I may not look it, but I'm a geologist and mineralogist. We ended up on Mars. Helped build Sandy Landing, helped in some of the plantation development work, prospected, mapped and surveyed and explored—we must've tried everything. He died five years ago. A cave-in. I buried him there on Mars."

The trees about them whispered with wind.

"And these others are—his sons?" she murmured. She was trembling a little now.

Rosenberg shook his head. "Impossible. These men are *him*. Stef in every last feature, come alive and young again. No child could ever be that close to his father."

"No. No, I suppose not."

"Stef was a human being, through and through," said Rosenberg. "But he was also pretty close to being a superman. Think of his handicaps: childhood gone under the Second War and its aftermath, young manhood gone in the Third War, poor, self-educated, uprooted. And still he was balanced and sane, gentle except when violence was called for—then he was a hellcat, I tell you. Men and women loved him: he had that kind of personality. He'd picked up a dozen languages, and he read their literatures with more appreciation and understanding than most professors. He knew music and composed some good songs of his own—rowdy but good. They're still being sung out on Mars. He was an artist, did some fine murals for several buildings, painted the Martian landscape like no camera has ever shown it, though he was good with a camera too. I've already told you about his inventiveness, and he had clever hands that a machine liked. His physique stood up to anything—he was almost sixty when he died and could still match any boy of twenty. He—why go on? He was everything, and good at everything."

"I know," she answered. "Martin was the same way." Her brief smile was wistful. "Believe me, I had the devil's own time hooking him. Real competition there." After a moment she added thoughtfully: "There must be a few such supermen walking around in every generation. It's just a matter of a happy genetic accident, a preponderance of favorable characteristics appearing in the same zygote, a highly intelligent mesomorph. Some of them go down in history. Think of Michelangelo, Vespucci, Raleigh—men who worked at everything: science, politics, war, engineering, exploration, art, literature. Others weren't interested in prominence, or maybe they had bad luck. Like your friend."

"I don't know what the connection is with these Un-men," said Rosenberg. "Stef never said a word to me—but of course, he'd've been sworn to secrecy, or it might even have been done without his knowledge. Only what was done? Matter duplication? I don't think so. If the U.N. had matter duplication, it wouldn't be in the fix it is now. What was done—and *why?*"

Jeanne didn't answer. She was looking away now, across the ravine to the high clear beauty of mountains beyond. It was blurred in her eyes. Suddenly she got up and walked away.

XIII

There was a night of stars and streaming wind about the jet. The Moon was low, throwing a bridge of broken light across the heaving Atlantic immensity. Once, far off, Naysmith saw a single meteoric streak burning upward, a rocket bound for space. Otherwise he sat in darkness and alone.

He had been locked into a tiny compartment in the rear of the jet. Wade and his entourage, together with a pilot and a couple of guards, sat forward; the jet was comfortably furnished, and they were probably catching up on their sleep. Naysmith didn't want a nap, though the weakness of hunger and his injuries was on him. He sat staring out of the port, listening to the mighty rush of wind and trying to estimate where they were.

The middle Atlantic, he guessed, perhaps fifteen degrees north latitude. If Christian's prognosis of Besser's reactions was correct, they were bound for the secret world headquarters of the gang, but Wade and the others hadn't told him anything. They were over the high seas now, the great unrestful wilderness which ran across three-fourths of the planet's turning surface, the last home on Earth of mystery and solitude. Anything could be done out here, and when fish had eaten the bodies who would ever be the wiser?

Naysmith's gaze traveled to the Moon, riding cold above the sea. Up there was the dominion over Earth. Between the space-station observatories and the rocket bases of the Lunar Guard, there should be nothing which the forces of sanity could not smash. The Moon had not rained death since the Third War, but the very threat of that monstrous fist poised in the sky had done much to quell a crazed planet. If the Service could tell the Guard where to shoot—

Only it couldn't. It never could, because this rebellion was not the armed uprising of a nation with cities and factories and mines. It was a virus within the body of all humankind. You wouldn't get anywhere bombing China, except to turn four hundred million innocent victims who had been your friends against you—because it was a small key group in the Chinese government which was conspiring against sanity.

You can blast a sickness from outside, with drugs and antibiotics and radiation. But the darkness of the human mind can only be helped by a psychiatrist; the cure must come from within itself.

If the U.N. were not brought tumbling down, but slowly eaten away, mutilated and crippled and demoralized, what would there be to shoot at? Sooner or later, official orders would come disbanding its police and Lunar Guard. Or there were other ways to attack those Moon bases. If they didn't have the Secret Service to warn them, it would be no trick for an enemy to smuggle military equipment to the Moon surface itself and blow them apart from there.

And in the end—what? Complete and immediate collapse into the dog-eat-dog madness which had come so close once to ruining civilization? (*Man won't get another chance. We were luckier than we deserved the last time.*) Or a jerry-built world empire of oppression, the stamping out of that keen and critical science whose early dawn-light was just beginning to show man a new path, a thousand-year nightmare of humanity turned into an ant-hill? There was little choice between the two.

Naysmith sighed and shifted on the hard bare seat. They could have had the decency to give him some clothes and a cigaret. A sandwich at the very least. Only, of course, the idea was to break down his morale as far as possible.

He tried again, for the thousandth time, to evaluate the situation, but there were too many unknowns and intangibles. It would be stupid to insist that tonight was a crisis point in human history. It could be—then again, if this attempt of the Brotherhood ended in failure, if the Brothers themselves were hunted down, there might come some other chance, some compensating factor. *Might!* But passive reliance on luck was ruin.

And in any case, he thought bleakly, tonight would surely decide the fate of Robert Naysmith.

The jet slanted downward, slowing as it wailed out of the upper air. Naysmith leaned against the wall, gripping the edge of the port with manacled hands, and peered below. Moonlight washed a great rippling mass of darkness, and in the center of it something which rose like a metal cliff.

A sea station!

I should have guessed it, thought Naysmith wildly. His brain felt hollow and strange. *The most logical place; accessible, mobile, under the very nose of the world but hidden all the same. I imagine the Service has considered this possibility—only how could it check all the sea stations in existence? It isn't even known how many there are.*

This one lay amidst acres of floating weed. Probably one of the specially developed sea plants with which it was hoped to help feed an overcrowded planet; or maybe this place passed itself off as an experiment station working to improve the growth. In either case, ranch or laboratory, Naysmith was sure that its announced activities were really carried out, that there was a complete working staff with all equipment and impeccable dossiers. The gang's headquarters would be underneath, in the submerged bowels of the station.

An organization like this had to parallel its enemy in most respects. Complex and world-wide—no. System-wide, if it really included Pilgrim fanatics who wanted to take over Mars. It would have to keep extensive records, have some kind of communications center. *This is it! By Heaven, this is their brain!*

The shiver of excitement faded into a hard subsurface tingle. A dead man had no way of relaying his knowledge to Fourre.

There was a landing platform at one end of the great floating structure. The pilot brought his jet down to a skillful rest, cut the motors, and let silence fall. Naysmith heard the deep endless voice of the sea, rolling and washing against the walls. He wondered how far it was to the next humanity. Far indeed. Perhaps they were beyond the edge of death.

The door opened and light filtered into the compartment. "All right, Naysmith," said the guard. "Come along."

Obediently, the Un-man went out between his captors to stand on the platform. It was floodlit, cutting off the view of the ocean surging twenty or thirty feet under its rails. The station superstructure, gimbal-mounted and gyro-stabilized above its great caissons, wouldn't roll much even in the heaviest weather. There were two other jets standing nearby. No sign of armament, though Naysmith was sure that missile tubes were here in abundance and that each mechanic carried a gun.

The wind was chill on his body as he was led toward the main cabin. Wade strode ahead of him, cloak flapping wildly in the flowing, murmuring night. To one side, Naysmith saw Borrow's stiff white face and the sunken expressionlessness of Lewin. Perhaps those two would be allowed to work him over.

They entered a short hallway. At the farther end, Wade pressed his hand to a scanner. A panel slid back in front of an elevator cage. "In," grunted one of the S-men.

Naysmith stood quietly, hemmed into a corner by the wary bodies of his guards. He saw that Borrow and Jennings were shivering with nervous tension. A little humorless smile twisted his mouth. Whatever else happened, the Brotherhood had certainly given the enemy a jolt.

The elevator sighed to a halt. Naysmith was led out, down a long corridor lined with doors. One of them stood ajar, and he saw walls covered with micro-file cabinets. Yes, this must be their archive. A besmocked man went the other way, carrying a computer tape. Unaided human brains were no longer enough even for those who would overthrow society. Too big, too big.

At the end of the hall, Naysmith was ushered into a large room. It was almost as if he were back in Wade's torture chamber—the same bright lights, the same muffling walls, the same instruments of inquisition. His eyes swept its breadth until they rested on the three men who sat behind a rack of neuroanalyzers.

The Brothers could tell each other apart; there were enough subtle environmental differences for that. Naysmith recognized Lampi, who seemed undamaged except for a black eye; he must have been taken directly here on orders. There was also Carlos Martinez of Guatemala, whom he had met before, and a third man whom he didn't recognize but who was probably South American.

They smiled at him, and he smiled back. Four pairs of blue eyes looked out of the same lean muscular faces, four blond heads nodded, four brains flashed the same intangible message: *You too, my Brother? Now we must endure.*

Naysmith was strapped in beside Martinez. He listened to Wade, speaking to Lucientes, who had been suspected of being the Argentine sector chief of the rebels: "Besser hasn't come yet?"

"No, he is on his way. He should be here very soon."

Besser is the real head, then, the organizing brain—and he is on his way! The four Brothers held themselves rigid, four identical faces staring uncannily ahead, not daring to move or exchange a glance. *Besser is coming!*

Wade took a restless turn about the room. "It's a weird business," he said thinly. "I'm not sure I like the idea of having all four together—in this very place."

"What can they do?" shrugged Lucientes. "My men captured Villareal here in Buenos Aires yesterday. He had been an artist, supposedly, and dropped out of sight when word first came about a fugitive Un-man answering that description. But he made a childish attempt to get back to his apartment and was arrested without difficulty. Martinez was obtained in Panama City with equal ease. If they are that incompetent—"

"But they aren't! They're anything but!" Wade glared at the prisoners. "This was done on purpose, I tell you. Why?"

"I already said—" Naysmith and Villareal spoke almost simultaneously. They stopped, and the Argentine grinned and closed his mouth. "I told you," Naysmith finished. "We wanted to bargain. There was no other quick and expedient way of making the sort of contact we needed."

"Were four of you needed?" snapped Wade. "Four valuable men?"

"Perhaps not so valuable," said Lewin quietly. "Not if there are any number of them still at large."

"They are not supernatural!" protested Lucientes. "They are flesh and blood. They can feel pain, and cannot break handcuffs. I know! Nor are they telepaths or anything equally absurd. They are—" His voice faltered.

"Yes?" challenged Wade. "They are what?"

Naysmith drew into himself. There was a moment of utter stillness. Only the heavy breathing of the captors, the captors half terrified by an unknown, and all the more vicious and deadly because of that, had voice.

The real reason was simple, thought Naysmith—so simple that it defeated those tortuous minds. It had seemed reasonable, and Christian's logic had confirmed the high probability, that one man identical with the agent who had been killed would be unsettling enough, and that four of them, from four different countries, would imply something so enormous that the chief conspirator would want them all together in his own strongest and most secret place, that he himself would want to be there at the questioning.

Only what happened next?

"They aren't human!" Borrow's voice was shrill and wavering. "They can't be. Not four or five or a thousand identical men. The U.N. has its own laboratories. Fourre could easily have had secret projects carried out."

"So?" Lewin's eyes blinked sardonically at the white face.

"So they're robots—androids—synthetic life—whatever you want to call it. Test-tube monsters!"

Lewin shook his head, grimly. "That's too big a stride forward," he said. "No human science will be able to do that for centuries to come. You don't appreciate the complexity of a living human being—and our best efforts haven't yet synthesized even one functioning cell. I admit these fellows have something—superhuman—about them. They've done incredible things. But they can't be robots. It isn't humanly possible."

"Humanly!" screamed Borrow. "Is man the only scientific race in the universe? How about creatures from the stars? Who's the real power behind the U.N?"

"That will do," snapped Wade. "We'll find out pretty soon." His look fastened harsh on Naysmith. "Let's forget this stupid talk of bargaining. There can be no compromise until one or the other party is done for."

That's right. The same thought quivered in four living brains.

"I"—Wade stopped and swung toward the door. It opened for two men who entered.

One was Arnold Besser. He was a small man, fine-boned, dark-haired, still graceful at seventy years of age. There was a flame in him that burned past the drab plainness of his features, the eerie light of fanaticism deep within his narrow skull. He nodded curtly to the greetings and stepped briskly forward. His attendant came after, a big and powerful man in chauffeur's uniform, cat-quiet, his face rugged and expressionless.

Only—only—Naysmith's heart leaped wildly within him. He looked away from the chauffeur-guard, up into the eyes of Arnold Besser.

"Now, then." The chief stood before his prisoners, hands on hips, staring impersonally at them but with a faint shiver running beneath his pale skin. "I want to know you people's real motive in giving yourselves up. I've studied your 'vised dossiers, such as they are, on the way here, so you needn't repeat the obvious. I want to know everything else."

" 'The quality of mercy is not strained,' " murmured Lampi. Naysmith's mind continued the lovely words. He needed their comfort, for here was death.

"The issues are too large and urgent for sparring," said Besser. There was a chill in his voice as he turned to Lewin. "We have four of them here, and presumably each of them knows what the others know. So we can try four different approaches. Suggestions?"

"Lobotomy on one," answered the physician promptly. "We can remove that explosive detonator at the same time, of course. But it will take a few days before he can be questioned, even under the best conditions, and perhaps there has been some precaution taken so that the subject will die. We can try physical methods immediately on two of them, in the presence of each other. We had better save a fourth—just in case."

"Very well." Besser's gaze went to a white-jacketed man behind the prisoners. "You are the surgeon here. Take one away and get to work on his brain."

The doctor nodded and began to wheel Martinez' chair out of the room. Lewin started a chlorine generator. The chauffeur-guard leaned against a table, watching with flat blank eyes.

The end? Goodnight, then, world, sun and moon and wind in the heavens. Goodnight, Jeanne.

A siren hooted. It shrilled up and down a saw-edged scale, ringing in metal and glass and human bones. Besser whirled toward a communicator. Wade stood heavy and paralyzed. Jennings screamed.

The room shivered, and they heard the dull crumping of an explosion. The door opened and a man stumbled in, shouting something. His words drowned in the rising whistle and bellow of rocket missiles.

Suddenly there was a magnum gun in the chauffeur's hand. It spewed a rain of slugs as he crouched, swinging it around the chamber. Naysmith saw Besser's head explode. Two of the guards had guns halfway out when the chauffeur cut them down.

The communicator chattered up on the wall, screaming something hysterical about an air attack. The chauffeur was already across to the door switch. He closed and locked the barrier, jumped over Wade's body, and grabbed for a surgical saw. It bit at the straps holding Naysmith, drawing a little blood. Lampi, Martinez, and Villareal were whooping aloud.

The chauffeur spoke in rapid Brazilo-Portuguese: "I'll get you free. Then take some weapons and be ready to fight. They may attack us in here, I don't know. But there will be paratroops landing as soon as our air strength has reduced their defenses. We should be able to hold out till then."

It had worked. The incredible, desperate, precarious plan had worked. Besser, in alarm and uncertainty, had gone personally to his secret headquarters. He had been piloted by his trusted gunman as usual. Only—Fourre's office would long have known about that pilot, studied him, prepared a surgically disguised duplicate from a Brazilian Un-man and held this agent in reserve. When Christian's message came, the chauffeur had been taken care of and the Un-man had replaced him—and been able to slip a radio tracer into Besser's jet—a tracer which the Rio-based U.N. police had followed.

And now they had the base!

Naysmith flung himself out of the chair and snatched a gun off the floor. He exchanged a glance with his rescuer, a brief warm glance of kinship and comradeship and belongingness. Even under the disguise and the carefully learned mannerisms, there had been something intangible which he had known—or was it only the fact that the deliverer had moved with such swift and certain decision?

"Yes," said the Brazilian unnecessarily. "I too am a Brother."

XIV

There was one morning when Naysmith came out of his tent and walked down to the sea. This was in Northwest National Park, the new preserve which included a good stretch of Oregon's coast. He had come for rest and solitude, to do some thinking which seemed to lead nowhere, and had stayed longer than he intended. There was peace here, in the great rocky stretch of land, the sandy nooks between, the loneliness of ocean, and the forest and mountains behind. Not many people were in the park now, and he had pitched his tent remote from the camping grounds anyway.

It was over. The job was finished. With the records of

Besser's headquarters for clues and proof, Fourre had been in a position to expose the whole conspiracy. Nobody had cared much about the technical illegality of his raid. Several governments fell—the Chinese had a spectacularly bloody end—and were replaced with men closer to sanity. Agents had been weeded out of every regime. In America, Hessling was in jail and there was talk of disbanding Security altogether. The U.N. had a renewed prestige and power, a firmer allegiance from the people of the world. Happy ending?

No. Because it was a job which never really ended. The enemy was old and strong and crafty, it took a million forms and it could never quite be slain. For it was man himself—the madness and sorrow of the human soul, the revolt of a primitive animal against the unnatural state called civilization and freedom. Somebody would try again. His methods would be different, he might not have the same avowed goal, but he would be the enemy and the watchers would have to break him. *And who shall watch the watchmen?*

Security was a meaningless dream. There was no stability except in death. Peace and happiness were not a reward to be earned, but a state to be maintained with toil and grief.

Naysmith's thinking at the moment concerned personal matters. But there didn't seem to be any answer except the one gray command: Endure.

He crossed the beach, slipping on rocks and swearing at the chill damp wind. His plunge into the water was an icy shock which only faded with violent swimming. But when he came out, he was tingling with wakefulness.

Romeo, he thought, toweling himself vigorously, *was an ass. Psychological troubles are no excuse for losing your appetite. In fact, they should heighten the old reliable pleasures. Mercutio was the real hero of that play.*

He picked his way toward the tent, thinking of bacon and eggs. As he mounted the steep, rocky bank, he paused, scowling. A small airboat had landed next to his own. *Damn! I don't feel like being polite to anybody.* But when he saw the figure which stood beside it, he broke into a run.

Jeanne Donner waited for him, gravely as a child. When he stood before her, she met his gaze steadily, mute, and it was he who looked away.

"How did you find me?" he whispered at last. He thought

the fury of his heartbeat must soon break his ribs. "I dropped out of sight pretty thoroughly."

"It wasn't easy," she answered, smiling a little. "After the U.N. pilot took us back to the States, I pestered the life out of everyone concerned. Finally one of them forgot privacy laws and told me—I suppose on the theory that you would take care of the nuisance. I've been landing at every isolated spot in the park for the last two days. I knew you'd want to be alone."

"Rosenberg—?"

"He agreed to accept hypno-conditioning for a nice payment—since he was sure he'd never learn the secret anyway. Now he's forgotten that there ever was another Stefan Rostomily. I refused, of course."

"Well—" His voice trailed off. Finally he looked at her again and said harshly: "Yes, I've played a filthy trick on you. The whole Service has, I guess. Only it's a secret which men have been killed for learning."

She smiled again, looking up at him, with a lilting challenge in her eyes. "Go ahead," she invited.

His hands dropped. "No. You've got a right to know this. I should never have—oh, well, skip it. We aren't complete fanatics. An organization which drew the line nowhere in reaching its aims wouldn't be worth having around."

"Thank you," she breathed.

"Nothing to thank me for. You've probably guessed the basis of the secret already, if you know who Rostomily was."

"And what he was. Yes, I think I know. But tell me."

"They needed a lot of agents for the Service—agents who could meet specifications. Somebody got acquainted with Rostomily while he was still on Earth. He himself wasn't trained, or interested in doing such work, but his heredity was wanted—the pattern of genes and chromosomes. Fourre had organized his secret research laboratories. That wasn't hard to do, in the Years of Madness. Exogenesis of a fertilized ovum was already an accomplished fact. It was only one step further to take a few complete cells from Rostomily and use them—as a chromosome source for undifferentiated human tissue. Proteins are autocatalytic, you know, and a gene is nothing but a set of giant protein molecules.

"We Brothers, all of us, we're completely human. Except

that our hereditary pattern is derived entirely from one person instead of from two and, therefore, duplicates its prototype exactly. There are thousands of us by now, scattered around the Solar System. I'm one of the oldest. There are younger ones coming up to carry on.''

"Exogenesis——" She couldn't repress a slight shudder.

"It has a bad name, yes. But that was only because of the known experiments which were performed, with their prenatal probing. Naturally that would produce psychotics. *Our* artificial wombs are safer and more serene even than the natural kind.''

She nodded then, the dark wings of her hair falling past the ivory planes of her cheeks. "I understand. I see how it must be—you can tell me the details later. And I see why. Fourre needed supermen. The world was too chaotic and violent—it still is—for anything less than a brotherhood of supermen.''

"Oh—look now!''

"No, I mean it. You aren't the entire Service, or even a majority of it. But you're the crack agents, the sword-hand.'' Suddenly she smiled, lighting up the whole universe, and gripped his arm. Her fingers were cool and slender against his flesh. "And how wonderful it is! Remember *King Henry the Fifth?*''

The words whispered from him:

"And Crispin Crispian shall ne'er go by,
From this day to the ending of the world,
But we in it shall be remembered,
We few, we happy few, we band of brothers—''

After a long moment, he added wryly: "But we can't look for fame. Not for a long time yet. The first requirement of a secret agent is secrecy, and if it were known that our kind exists half our usefulness would be gone.''

"Oh, yes. I understand.'' She stood quiet for a while. The wind blew her dress and hair about her, fluttering them against the great clean expanse of sea and forest and sky.

"What are you going to do now?'' she asked.

"I'm not sure. Naturally, we'll have to kill the story of a wanted murderer answering our description. That won't be hard. We'll announce his death resisting arrest, and after that—well, people forget. In a year or two the memory will be gone. But of course several of us, myself included, will need new identities, have to move to new homes. I've been thinking of New Zealand.''

"And it will go on. Your work will go on. Aren't you ever lonely?''

He nodded, then tried to grin. "But let's not go on a crying jag. Come on and have breakfast with me. I'm a helluvva good egg frier.''

"No, wait.'' She drew him back and made him face her. "Tell me—I want the truth now. You said, the last time, that you loved me. Was that true?''

"Yes,'' he said steadily. "But it doesn't matter. I was unusually vulnerable. I'd always been the cat who walks by himself, more so even than most of my Brothers. I'll get over it.''

"Maybe I don't want you to get over it,'' she said.

He stood without motion for a thunderous century. A sea gull went crying overhead.

"You are Martin,'' she told him. "You aren't the same, not quite, but you're still Martin with another past. And Jimmy needs a father, and I need you.''

He couldn't find words, but they weren't called for anyway.

Muse

by Dean R. Koontz

*The world had never seen a finer talent. But did he have an
ugly habit?*

Her hair tumbled over her breasts like burned butter, darkly
yellow, darkly gleaming with reflected bits of the dim amber
ceiling light, parting now and again to bare the greater wonders beneath that it was attempting to conceal. She came out
of the bathroom, blotting her frosty lipstick, and said, "What?"

I stretched out on the couch, half of my face buried in it,
flat on my stomach, also naked from the waist up, and
pointed to the jug on the floor. "Put Icky on for me, Lynda."

She came across the floor on dancer's toes like a leaf
blown through the windless chamber of the grav-plane, a
wonder of curves and indentations, mounds and recesses. She
sat on the edge of the couch, her hair dancing to conceal her
treasures and only partially succeeding, and dipped her hands
into the wide-mouthed jug, lifting Icky out and holding him
like he was an unmolded jello serving or a hunk of raw liver.

"Careful," I said.

"You shut up, now. Icky and I know what we're doing."

"Just the same—"

"Shush!"

She placed the slug on my back, directly between my
shoulders, pressing it gently to get its adhesive layer firmly
attached. Then she pried up the anterior end of it and tucked
its sensory flap under so that the porous side was against my
skin and so that Icky would not have to do the job himself
with a lot of unpleasant, wet squirming and wriggling. As
much as I thought of Icky, I didn't much care for it when he
began to twitch, slipping and sliding over my skin. But
Lynda had the flap under and the slug on properly. She was
experienced, as she said. But I still worried about Icky.

"All's in place," she said, signaling the finish of the ritual.

I felt the hair-fine tendrils probing through my flesh, snaking painlessly through my skull and making gentle contact with my brain in all the necessary places. Icky was with me. Icky was *in* me. A peculiar sense of well-being swept over me, filled me to the center of my body. My muscles felt better toned, and my senses were sharper just as they always were immediately after contact. My hands itched to hold the guitar, to finger the strings, to throb the chords from the shallow wooden box, to play the latest numbers so that Icky could experience them.

"We land in fifteen minutes," Lynda said, slapping me on the ass. "You better finish getting dressed." She stood and returned to the bathroom, shaking every ounce of her slim body with every step she took.

"If there were time—" I began.

"But there isn't," she said, winking. "So hurry up."

Homecoming. Lynda stood beside me, holding my hand in hers, fingering my fingers with her tiny ones, and Icky was on my shoulder, concealed beneath my black leather suit. No, not concealed, really, for the lump of his jelly body rounded my back where it ought to be concave, thickened my neck where it normally would have been straight and thin. Lynda was comforting me, petting my arm, winking, whispering things that she knew made me feel good, things about how good a musician I was, about how everyone loved me, about what she would do with me if she could ever—for a change—get me alone for a moment without having to rush. She was great. There was confidence in her eyes that gave me confidence too. There was love in them that calmed me. Icky (his real name is unpronounceable outside his own star system) comforted me with his tendrils, with the wordless discussions we carried on inside my head. He projected images of assurance to me, mellowed me, prepared me for what was to come.

Lynda took the last private moment we had to squeeze my hand again.

Icky touched me reassuringly with feathers of protoplasm.

And the doors opened before us like the shutters being thrown wide on a window. Beyond lay the airport.

And the people . . .

There was at least eight thousand, maybe ten thousand there. They stretched away in all directions, people of all ages—but mostly the young—waving, holding up banners that said LOVE YOU, LEONARD CHRIS and WELCOME HOME, LEO!, cheering, cheering, cheering. Nine years had passed, and I had climbed a ladder out of obscurity to become the most famous musician in the galaxy, known not only to the race calling itself Mankind but to the Seven Races, understood best by my own and by Icky's, but listened to by all. Still, it was a revelation that a backwater city the size of Harrisburg, Pennsylvania, could turn out something like this crowd to meet me. I began, I think, to tremble.

Guards moved up the platform, surrounded us, moved us down toward the limousine that waited below. It wasn't a grav car, but an honest-to-God museum-piece Ford with tires and everything. We were ushered into the back seat while two motorcyclists pulled in front of us on real, vintage motorcycles. They were going all out.

"Not bad, is it?" Lynda asked.

Icky asked something similar that had no words.

The crowd was unwilling to let us pass easily. They pressed close, anxious to touch the glass through which they could see me. They screamed my name.

"Mostly girls," Lynda noted.

"Jealous?"

"No. They don't want you. At least not all of you. They just want a scrap to take home as souvenir."

After the crowds had passed, we sped on toward the hotel, our cyclists pressing on their sirens. I reached into my jacket pocket and took out my father's letter once more. It was wrinkled from previous readings, but I had to see it again, to know I had interpreted it correctly. Really, there was no mistaking what it said: "Son," it said plainly, "son, don't try to bring It with you. Come by yourself, and you'll be made welcome, very welcome. But if you bring along that goddamned worm, if you bring along that puppet master that rides you like a demon, that perverts your body and contaminates the thing that makes you a man, then stay the hell away. If you bring It with you, son, then stay in some damn hotel somewhere. But don't come home. And if you bring It with you, if you insist on carrying It along, then I don't want to see you. I don't want to be reminded of what It has done to you."

But of course I had to bring Icky. And now I was returning home triumphant, but I was denied entrance to my own home, the place of my childhood, to the garden I had immortalized in *Childflowers*. I bit my teeth together, ground them against one another, trying to recall my anger from the depths where it had settled since my last reading of the letter. At first, I had gotten strength from my fury, from anger at the names my father had called Icky. But that was all gone now. It was impossible to stir anger at simple, brutal ignorance. The only things left were pity and disgust, and neither one could sustain my anger. I choked as I reread the last line of the letter, swore I would not cry for my father's stupidity.

Lynda took my hand.

Icky touched my mind and soothed me some. . . .

Once in the city proper, the driver fooled the crowd at the hotel by driving the limousine down a side street and through an alleyway, bringing us into the hotel through a service entrance. Only half a dozen people waited there, and the police used diluted chemical mace on these, rushed us through into safety.

We stood in a room full of produce and cartons of canned and jarred food. A row of garbage cans lined the left wall, and the aroma from these was extremely rotten. Standing well away from the filthy containers was the manager. He wore a black suit (not leather) and a white carnation on his lapel. He also wore a smile as broad as a jack-o'-lantern's—and just as fake. He came to us, took Lynda's hand and squeezed it lightly. He dropped it, shook mine politely. I could tell he was reluctant to touch the hand of a human-slug symbiote, but he overcame that magnificently (apparently reminding himself of the publicity his hotel was receiving) and kept his smile intact.

"Such a pleasure, Mr. Chris. My name is Cavander. Harold."

"Mr. Cavander," I said politely enough, considering what I was thinking about him. "Could we be shown to our rooms, please. I must rest for the concert tonight." I was quite sufficiently rested, but I wanted out of the garbage room and out of this fellow's sight. The way he eyed my hump gave me chills.

"Uh—" he said, suddenly embarrassed.

"Yes?" I asked impatiently.

"The Grande Suite—"

"Yes?"

"Well, the fact is that we got our schedules a little confused, and we now find that we booked two parties into the Grande Suite—"

"A normal suite will do," I said, getting his point. Once it was known that a human-slug symbiote had stayed in his precious Grande Suite, most honeymooners and most "aristocrats" would not consider it fit for lovemaking and aristocrating. He was only protecting his business. Still, I hated him for it.

He seemed relieved and almost managed to smile a genuine smile. But he checked himself just in time and pasted the phony one back on. "This way, then. And I do hope you will excuse this terrible inconvenience. I don't know how we could have been so stupid as to—"

When Cavander had overseen the deposition of our luggage (a car had followed with it, and he stood talking with us until that car arrived) and had ascertained that we had sufficient towels, soap and toilet paper, I bid him goodbye and closed the door hard behind him.

"The little creep," Lynda hissed, plopping down in an overstuffed leather easy chair and kicking off her shoes.

I opened my guitar case and took out my beautiful Trevelox Electro and set about hooking up the amplifiers. I could pay back pudgy Harold Cavander for what he had done. I could blast the ears out of the entire floor. And I didn't think he would have enough guts to ask me to stop. He might be afraid I would go elsewhere for accommodations. And though his prejudices kept him from serving us well, he would not want to throw away all that publicity by refusing to serve us at all.

"What should it be?" I asked Lynda.

She scrunched her toes into the deep pile carpet. "The one you wrote last night, *Mind Dark*."

"Yeah. That fits," I said.

I played a few chords tentatively. The music welled through my bones, slithered over my fingers and punctuated the rooms with nearly tactile sound. I went back to the beginning and started again, full volume this time. I felt good. Icky felt good. He rejoiced, touching my mind to tell me that it was a

good thing, this *Mind Dark*. I sang the words throatily like I
would sing them tonight on the big stage. And for a minute,
the room and Lynda receded and I *was* on the big stage,
seated on a stool before five thousand enthralled fans, Icky
humped between my shoulders. I played like I had never
played before, but in my vision, the people began leaving,
drifting out as I started the second song. And as they left, I
saw why they would not stay: each of the five thousand was
my father, each had his face. . . .

"This is your dressing room," the man said, pointing in a
cubbyhole where a dresser and full-length mirror were the
only furnishings. But I was not so concerned with the room.
It was good enough. I was more interested in the fact that the
little man was a human-slug symbiote with a hump on his
shoulders where his own Icky rested.

"How long have you had him?" I asked.

He looked perplexed for a minute, then brightened and
smiled. "Icky?" He grinned broader, and I could see that he
was even now in some sort of delicate communication with
his symbiote partner. "Oh, going on three years now."

"What is the give-take?" Lynda asked.

"Icky's a romantic. He likes to travel. He wants to see
parts of this world. He'll stay with me until I die, then move
on to someone else, always looking, always taking things in."

"And you?" I asked.

"Same thing. I can't go to Icky's home planet, to his star
system. But he can give me visions of every world he has
ever seen simply by touching parts of my brain with his
filaments. I guess you'd say I'm a romantic too."

"You're the first symbiote I've seen since we arrived," I
said.

He frowned. "There aren't many here. Small-city pro-
vincialism. This is in the Bible Belt, you know. The conservative Cumberland Valley. Maybe a few hundred here, that's
all. But there must be thousands in the cities—the big cities."

"Eleven million symbiotes," Lynda said. "I just read that
somewhere."

"I envision a day," the little man said, "when— Oh, your
mother is waiting to see you. I left her out by the office. You
want me to show her back?"

I looked at Lynda. "Yes," I said. "Please."

*   *   *

Later, after my mother had come, subdued, and gone, I sat on the bare stage, looking at the back of the curtain, my guitar across my lap. In moments, that velveteen monstrosity would part, revealing the audience to me and me to the audience. I would make no remarks but begin immediately with *Childflowers*. I felt good. *Childflowers* would mean something, for my father had relented, had asked to see me after all. True, the message my mother had delivered was terse and unemotional. He wanted to see me backstage an hour after the performance, after everyone was gone and he would not be seen conversing with me. He was still prejudiced. I was prepared for one of his persuasive arguments to try to get me to give up Icky. But I was also confident that I might get him, at least in some small degree, to accept the symbiote relationship. He would have to accept it someday, for it would never be my choice to break it off.

Then the curtains opened.

And I was scared.

Like always.

Childflowers spun from my toiling fingers like golden threads from a magic loom. I did a double rendition of it, bringing the entire length to something just over fourteen minutes. When I finished, I was dripping sweat, and the audience was applauding wildly. Icky touched my mind, and some of my nervousness was gone. I played *Mind Dark* next, my song about prejudice, and I played it with conviction.

Lynda and Icky and I waited on the dimly lighted stage. The audience was gone now. The clamorous boom of applause had whispered off through the rows of seats. The echo of my music had been stilled. We were waiting for my father.

When he came, it was with friends.

He came down the center aisle, a big man, clean-shaven and dressed in a gray suit. Behind him came two friends, apparently. This was some consolation. It wasn't to be an entirely confidential tête-à-tête. He was not so ashamed that he had to hide the meeting entirely from the eyes of the public. I sat on the stool, Lynda on a chair beside me, waiting for him to mount the stage.

The three of them came up and stood by the right proscenium pillar, the two men still behind my father. ''Len,'' he said, nodding his gray head, his hands held at his sides, his entire posture one of stiffness and uneasiness.

"Hello, Dad." Lynda said it first. I followed her example. There was still pity in me.

"It was a good show," he said awkwardly.

"I'm glad you came."

One of the men walked across the front of the stage and stood against the left proscenium pillar.

Walter Chris came toward me, an older version of myself. His friends remained at each side of the stage like bodyguards. "Why, Len?" he asked simply, opening his palms in the gesture I was so familiar with. Always when I had done something wrong as a child, he had opened his hands in wonderment just that way, had shrugged his shoulders just so.

"Why what?" I asked. I was trembling. I wanted to make him understand Icky, but I was determined he should open the subject.

"Why bring It. I asked you not to bring It."

"I had to, Dad."

"But why?"

"A slug," I explained patiently, "requires a host. It would die in twenty-four hours if I should take it off. I usually leave Icky off for no more than twelve hours at a time. I had to bring him."

"You've got everything. You've got money, fame. Why did you have to humiliate your mother and me with It? That wasn't right, Len. It wasn't right to humiliate us like that."

He came towards me then with something more than fatherly concern in his eyes, twisting his face into a leer. The two friends advanced from the proscenium pillars.

"What is this?" I asked, starting off the stool.

"We have a little group—" my father started.

"What kind of little group?" Lynda was off her chair too.

"That doesn't like the sort of thing that's been happening—all these symbies, all these puppet masters."

"They aren't puppet masters!" I protested. I felt like I was shouting down a deep well, so deep that not even my own echoes returned to me. "They take, yes. But they also give!"

"It's the sign of a weak character," one of the other men said. "Only a weakling needs boosting by an alien worm like that thing you're wearing."

"Dad," Lynda said. "Dad, stay away from him."

"You stay out of this, honey."

I was backing toward the rear of the stage, toward the brilliantly colored flats that had backed me during the performance. They were closing in from three sides, each one with some degree of determination lining his face like a death mask.

"What are you going to do?" I asked, backing against the flats.

"Help you," Walter Chris said.

My fingers found the edge of a glow-blue flat on my left. I swung, wrenched at it, sent it toppling to the left, the canvas striking the man on that side and carrying him to the door. But the other two were on me. I heard Lynda scream. But screams weren't stopping them. Walter Chris had set out on a holy crusade to redeem his son, to reclaim what he fancied had been taken from him, and he would not stop until he had killed Icky.

I kicked upward with a knee, caught the remaining accomplice in the crotch. He rolled off, gagging.

I shouted at my father.

But he had sealed his ears.

He drove a big fist into my face. For a moment, everything swam about me. I could see Lynda leaving the stage, running for help, but she was bobbing wildly up and down. Blackness swept toward me, but I fought it off. I had to fight it off. If I passed out, it would be the end for Icky—and, consequently, an end of sorts for me.

I tried driving a knee into his crotch, but he had learned from what I had done to the other fellow. He blocked the blow, struck me again.

I swung a fist, pounded helplessly against his side. He was a bigger man than I, and he had not gone to fat.

The fellow I had kneed stood and came to the old man's aid, pinning my shoulders with his knees while my father worked me over. My face was swelling and bleeding, and one eye had already swollen shut. With every blow, strength drained from me. The knees hurt where they dug into my shoulders. I writhed, trying to break free. I could not. Icky was excited, but he managed to sooth my panic and keep me acting rationally. I could only hope now that Lynda would return in time with help.

But she didn't.

When he had dealt the punishment he thought I deserved, he and his accomplice rolled me over, pinned me on my stomach, and worried up my coat and shirt until they had uncovered Icky.

I screamed.

But there was no one to hear.

I writhed and kicked.

But I was tired, and they were two.

They stuck fingers under the pulpy bulk of the slug. Icky quickly retracted his filaments so that my brain would not be damaged when they yanked him away. Then they tore him loose. I was still screaming. My throat was raw. I rolled over as they stood, grabbed at my father's ankles. But he had Icky raised over his head. He threw the slug to the floor. It hit with a sickening splashing noise and wriggled helplessly. The other man snatched it up before I could grasp it, threw it down again. And again. Then my father had it once more. They exchanged Icky until he had been thrown too often. He was mangled and did not move any more.

I was crying. The stage was as something seen through a rain-splattered window. They tried to help me to my feet, but I struck out weakly at them and drove them back. I stood, weaving, feeling the stage dance beneath my feet. I remember that my father was smiling.

"Now you—" he started to say.

The third man had found his way out of the blue flat.

"You sons of bitches!" I snapped. The words were strained between my teeth so that nothing but hatred and bitterness came out. It hissed like escaping steam.

"Now, Len, simmer down a little."

But I could only curse. Every foul thing I could think of, every four-letter word I had ever heard came bubbling out in a torrent of rage.

"Wait," my father said. "Now wait just a damn minute. We got rid of it for you. We're trying to help you see you can do without the slug for a crutch. Whatever it is you need, son, we can give you. Come to us. If it's love or appreciation, we've got more than enough for you."

"You stupid damn wretch," I hissed. I was still crying, and the words were interspersed with sobs, I guess. "I have nothing now. You can't give me what Icky gave me. Never!"

"Just give us time to—"

"Time, hell. Icky gave me my talent, you damn fool!"

He stood, stunned, working his mouth without managing to make anything come out of it.

"That's it; that's right! He could not make music through his own body, since he had no fingers, and no 'ears' to appreciate Earth music. But he had a perfect understanding of what made a song. It was Icky who composed *Childflowers* and everything else. He took my memory and made beauty with it. I got the money and fame. He got the satisfaction of creation. It was a mutual agreement. It was symbiosis. And I got more than the money and the fame. I got to be a part of that creativity, got to work with it, to offer suggestions to it. I was in a world of poetry, a world of loveliness. The things I wanted to say he said for me. He vented the ache in me. Without him, my soul would never have found release, and I would have contained it and rotted with it as you and your goddamned friends have. Can you really replace what Icky gave me? Not a fraction of it, you can't!"

He turned from me, turned toward the steps.

I took a few steps, grabbed my Trevelox Electro and brought it down on his shoulders.

I was still sobbing.

He took the blows without resistance.

When the other two tried to come near to stop me, I swung furiously at them. They backed off to let me return to my father. I brought the instrument up and down, over and over. I might have killed him had not Lynda arrived with the help that was too late for Icky. They pulled me off him. I remember that. Then, until I woke in the hospital, recovering from shock, I remember nothing.

I have a new Trevelox Electro, just like the one I splintered and ruined. But there is no second Icky, no slug I have found with his same abilities. So I play the old songs, though I never play *Childflowers,* and Lynda sits with me by the window, watching the dark to whom I sing.

Resurrection

by A. E. van Vogt

The aliens wondered why man had died. Good thing they didn't know about curiosity and the cat.

The great ship poised a quarter of a mile above one of the cities. Below was a cosmic desolation. As he floated down in his energy bubble, Enash saw that the buildings were crumbling with age.

"No sign of war damage!" The bodiless voice touched his ears momentarily. Enash tuned it out.

On the ground he collapsed his bubble. He found himself in a walled enclosure overgrown with weeds. Several skeletons lay in the tall grass beside the rakish building. They were of long, two-legged, two-armed beings with the skulls in each case mounted at the end of a thin spine. The skeletons, all of adults, seemed in excellent preservation, but when he bent down and touched one, a whole section of it crumbled into a fine powder. As he straightened, he saw that Yoal was floating down nearby. Enash waited till the historian had stepped out of his bubble, then he said:

"Do you think we ought to use our method of reviving the long-dead?"

Yoal was thoughtful. "I have been asking questions of the various people who have landed, and there is something wrong here. This planet has no surviving life, not even insect life. We'll have to find out what happened before we risk any colonization."

Enash said nothing. A soft wind was blowing. It rustled through a clump of trees nearby. He motioned towards the trees. Yoal nodded.

"Yes, the plant life has not been harmed, but plants after all are not affected in the same way as the active life forms."

There was an interruption. A voice spoke from Yoal's

receiver, "A museum has been found at approximately the center of the city. A red light has been fixed to the roof."

Enash said, "I'll go with you, Yoal. There might be skeletons of animals and of the intelligent being in various stages of his evolution. You didn't answer my question: Are you going to revive these beings?"

Yoal said slowly, "I intend to discuss the matter with the council, but I think there is no doubt. We must know the cause of this disaster." He waved one sucker vaguely to take in half the compass. He added as an afterthought, "We shall proceed cautiously, of course, beginning with an obviously early-development. The absence of the skeletons of children indicates that the race had developed personal immortality."

The council came to look at the exhibits. It was, Enash knew, a formal preliminary only. The decision was made. There would be revivals. It was more than that. They were curious. Space was vast, the journeys through it long and lonely, landing always a stimulating experience, with its prospect of new life forms to be seen and studied.

The museum looked ordinary. High-domed ceilings, vast rooms. Plastic models of strange beasts, many artifacts—too many to see and comprehend in so short a time. The life span of a race was imprisoned here in a progressive array of relics. Enash looked with the others, and was glad when they came to the line of skeletons and preserved bodies. He seated himself behind the energy screen, and watched the biological experts take a preserved body out of a stone sarcophagus. It was wrapped in windings of cloth, many of them. The experts did not bother to unravel the rotted material. Their forceps reached through, pinched a piece of the skull—that was the accepted procedure. Any part of the skeleton could be used, but the most perfect revivals, the most complete reconstructions, resulted when a certain section of the skull was used.

Hamar, the chief biologist, explained the choice of body. "The chemicals used to preserve this mummy show a sketchy knowledge of chemistry; the carvings of the sarcophagus indicate a crude and unmechanical culture. In such a civilization there would not be much development of the potentialities of the nervous system. Our speech experts have been analyzing the recorded voice mechanism which is a part of each exhibit, and though many languages are involved—

evidence that the ancient language spoken at the time the body was alive has been reproduced—they found no difficulty in translating the meanings. They have now adapted our universal speech machine, so that anyone who wishes to, need merely speak into his communicator, and so will have his words translated into the language of the revived person. The reverse, naturally, is also true. Ah, I see we are ready for the first body.''

Enash watched intently with the others, as the lid was clamped down on the plastic reconstructor, and the growth processes were started. He could feel himself becoming tense. For there was nothing haphazard about what was happening. In a few minutes a full-grown ancient inhabitant of this planet would sit up and stare at them. The science involved was simple and always fully effective.

. . . Out of the shadows of smallness life grows. The level of beginning and ending, of life and—not life; in that dim region matter oscillates easily between old and new habits. The habit of organic, or the habit of inorganic.

Electrons do not have life and un-life values. Atoms know nothing of inanimateness. But when atoms form into molecules, there is a step in the process, one tiny step, that is of life—if life begins at all. One step, and then darkness. Or aliveness.

A stone or a living cell. A grain of gold or a blade of grass, the sands of the sea or the equally numerous animalcules inhabiting the endless fishy waters—the difference is there in the twilight zone of matter. Each living cell has in it the whole form. The crab grows a new leg when the old one is torn from its flesh. Both ends of the planarian worm elongate, and soon there are two worms, two identities, two digestive systems, each as greedy as the original, each a whole, unwounded, unharmed by its experience.

Each cell can be the whole. Each cell remembers in a detail so intricate that no totality of words could ever describe the completeness achieved.

But—paradox—memory is not organic. An ordinary wax record remembers sounds. A wire recorder easily gives up a duplicate of the voice that spoke into it years before. Memory is a physiological impression, a mark on matter, a change in the shape of a molecule, so that when a reaction is desired the *shape* emits the same rhythm of response.

Out of the mummy's skull had come the multi-quadrillion

memory shapes from which a response was now being evoked. As ever, the memory held true.

A man blinked, and opened his eyes.

"It is true, then," he said aloud, and the words were translated into the Ganae tongue as he spoke them. "Death is merely an opening into another life—but where are my attendants?" At the end, his voice took on a complaining tone.

He sat up, and climbed out of the case, which had automatically opened as he came to life. He saw his captors. He froze—but only for a moment. He had a pride and a very special arrogant courage, which served him now.

Reluctantly, he sank to his knees, and made obeisance, but doubt must have been strong in him. "Am I in the presence of the gods of Egypt?"

He climbed to his feet. "What nonsense is this? I do not bow to nameless demons."

Captain Gorsid said, "Kill him!"

The two-legged monster dissolved, writhing, in the beam of a ray gun.

The second man stood up palely, and trembled with fear. "My God, I swear I won't touch the stuff again. Talk about pink elephants—"

Yoal was curious. "To what *stuff* do you refer, revived one?"

"The old hooch, the poison in the old hip pocket flask, the juice they gave me at that speak . . . my lordie!"

Captain Gorsid looked questioningly at Yoal. "Need we linger?"

Yoal hesitated: "I am curious." He addressed the man. "If I were to tell you that we were visitors from another star, what would be your reaction?"

The man stared at him. He was obviously puzzled, but the fear was stronger. "Now, look," he said, "I was driving along, minding my own business. I admit I'd had a shot or two too many, but it's the liquor they serve these days. I swear I didn't see the other car—and if this is some new idea of punishing people who drink and drive, well, you've won. I won't touch another drop as long as I live, so help me."

Yoal said, "Drives a 'car' and thinks nothing of it. Yet we saw no cars; they didn't even bother to preserve them in the museum."

Enash noticed that everyone waited for everyone else to comment. He stirred as he realized the circle of silence would be complete unless he spoke. He said, "Ask him to describe the car. How does it work?"

"Now you're talking," said the man. "Bring on your line of chalk, and I'll walk it, and ask any questions you please. I may be so tight that I can't see straight, but I can always drive. How does it work? You just put her in gear, and step on the gas."

"Gas," said engineering officer Veed. "The internal combustion engine. That places him."

Captain Gorsid motioned to the guard with the ray gun.

The third man sat up, and looked at them thoughtfully. "From the stars?" he said finally. "Have you a system, or was it blind chance?"

The Ganae councilors in that doomed room stirred uneasily in their curved chairs. Enash caught Yoal's eye on him; the shock in the historian's eyes alarmed the meteorologist. He thought: "The two-legged one's adjustment to a new situation, his grasp of realities, was unnormally rapid. No Ganae could have equaled the swiftness of the reaction."

Hamar, the chief biologist, said, "Speed of thought is not necessarily a sign of superiority. The slow, careful thinker has his place in the hierarchy of intellect."

But, Enash found himself thinking, it was not the speed; it was the accuracy of the response. He tried to imagine himself being revived from the dead, and understanding instantly the meaning of the presence of aliens from the stars. He couldn't have done it.

He forgot his thought, for the man was out of the case. As Enash watched with the others, he walked briskly over to the window and looked out. One glance, and then he turned back.

"Is it all like this?" he asked.

Once again, the speed of his understanding caused a sensation. It was Yoal who finally replied.

"Yes. Desolation. Death. Ruin. Have you any idea as to what happened?"

The man came back and stood in front of the energy screen that guarded the Ganae. "May I look over the museum? I have to estimate what age I am in. We had certain possibilities of destruction when I was last alive, but which one was realized depends on the time elapsed.''

The councilors looked at Captain Gorsid, who hesitated; then: "Watch him," he said to the guard with the ray gun. He faced the man. "We understand your aspirations fully. You would like to seize control of this situation, and insure your own safety. Let me assure you. Make no false moves, and all will be well.''

Whether or not the man believed the lie, he gave no sign. Nor did he show by a glance on a movement that he had seen the scarred floor where the ray gun had burned his two predecessors into nothingness. He walked curiously to the nearest doorway, studied the other guard who waited there for him, and then, gingerly, stepped through. The first guard followed him, then came the mobile energy screen, and finally, trailing one another, the councilors. Enash was the third to pass through the doorway. The room contained skeletons and plastic models of animals. The room beyond that was what, for want of a better term, Enash called a culture room. It contained the artifacts from a single period of civilization. It looked very advanced. He had examined some of the machines when they first passed through it, and had thought: Atomic energy. He was not alone in his recognition.

From behind him, Captain Gorsid said, "You are forbidden to touch anything. A false move will be the signal for the guards to fire.''

The man stood at ease in the center of the room. In spite of a curious anxiety, Enash had to admire his calmness. He must have known what his fate would be, but he stood there thoughtfully, and said finally, deliberately:

"I do not need to go any farther. Perhaps you will be able better than I to judge of the time that has elapsed since I was born and these machines were built. I see over there an instrument which, according to the sign above it, counts atoms when they explode. As soon as the proper number have exploded it shuts off the power automatically, and for just the right length of time to prevent a chain explosion. In my time we had a thousand crude devices for limiting the size of an atomic reaction, but it required two thousand years to develop those devices from the early beginnings of atomic energy. Can you make a comparison?''

The councilors glanced at Veed. The engineering officer

hesitated. At last, reluctantly: "Nine thousand years ago we had a thousand methods of limiting atomic explosions." He paused, then even more slowly, "I have never heard of an instrument that counts out atoms for such a purpose."

"And yet," murmured Shuri, the astronomer breathlessly, "the race was destroyed."

There was silence—that ended as Gorsid said to the nearest guard, "Kill the monster!"

But it was the guard who went down, bursting into flame. Not just one guard, but the guards! Simultaneously down, burning with a blue flame. The flame licked at the screen, recoiled, and licked more furiously, recoiled and burned brighter. Through a haze of fire, Enash saw that the man had retreated to the far door, and that the machine that counted atoms was glowing with a blue intensity.

Captain Gorsid shouted into his communicator, "Guard all exits with ray guns. Spaceships stand by to kill alien with heavy guns."

Somebody said, "Mental control. Some kind of mental control. What have we run into?"

They were retreating. The blue fire was at the ceiling, struggling to break through the screen. Enash had a last glimpse of the machine. It must still be counting atoms, for it was a hellish blue. Enash raced with the others to the room where the man had been resurrected. There another energy screen crashed to their rescue. Safe now, they retreated into their separate bubbles and whisked through the outer doors and up to the ship. As the great ship soared, an atomic bomb hurtled down from it. The mushroom of flame blotted out the museum and the city below.

"But we still don't know why the race died," Yoal whispered into Enash's ear, after the thunder had died from the heavens behind them.

The pale yellow sun crept over the horizon on the third morning after the bomb was dropped—the eighth day since the landing. Enash floated with the others down on a new city. He had come to argue against any further revival.

"As a meteorologist," he said, "I pronounce this planet safe for Ganae colonization. I cannot see the need for taking any risks. This race has discovered the secrets of its nervous system, and we cannot afford—"

He was interrupted. Hamar, the biologist, said dryly, "If they knew so much why didn't they migrate to other star systems and save themselves?"

"I will concede," said Enash, "that very possibly they had not discovered our system of locating stars with planetary families." He looked earnestly around the circle of his friends. "We have agreed that was a unique accidental discovery. We were lucky, not clever."

He saw by the expressions on their faces that they were mentally refuting his arguments. He felt a helpless sense of imminent catastrophe. For he could see that picture of a great race facing death. It must have come swiftly, but not so swiftly that they didn't know about it. There were too many skeletons in the open, lying in the gardens of the magnificent homes, as if each man and his wife had come out to wait for the doom of his kind.

He tried to picture it for the council, that last day long, long ago, when a race had calmly met its ending. But his visualization failed somehow, for the others shifted impatiently in the seats that had been set up behind the series of energy screens, and Captain Gorsid said:

"Exactly what aroused this intense emotional reaction in you, Enash?"

The question gave Enash pause. He hadn't thought of it as emotional. He hadn't realized the nature of his obsession, so subtly had it stolen upon him. Abruptly, now, he realized.

"It was the third one," he said slowly. "I saw him through the haze of energy fire, and he was standing there in the distant doorway watching us curiously, just before we turned to run. His gravery, his calm, the skillful way he had duped us—it all added up."

"Added up to his death?" said Hamar. And everybody laughed.

"Come now, Enash," said vice-captain Mayad good-humoredly, "you're not going to pretend that this race is braver than our own, or that, with all the precautions we have now taken, we need fear one man?"

Enash was silent, feeling foolish. The discovery that he had had an emotional obsession abashed him. He did not want to appear unreasonable. One final protest he made.

"I merely wish to point out," he said doggedly, "that this

desire to discover what happened to a dead race does not seem absolutely essential to me."

Captain Gorsid waved at the biologist. "Proceed," he said, "with the revival."

To Enash, he said, "Do we dare return to Gana, and recommend mass migrations—and then admit that we did not actually complete our investigations here? It's impossible, my friend."

It was the old argument, but reluctantly now Enash admitted there was something to be said for that point of view.

He forgot that, for the fourth man was stirring.

The man sat up—and vanished.

There was a blank, startled, horrified silence. Then Captain Gorsid said harshly, "He can't get out of there. We know that. He's in there somewhere."

All around Enash, the Ganae were out of their chairs, peering into the energy shell. The guards stood with ray guns held limply in their suckers. Out of the corner of his eye, he saw one of the protective screen technicians beckon to Veed, who went over—and came back grim.

"I'm told the needles jumped ten points when he first disappeared. That's on the nucleonic level."

"By ancient Ganae!" Shuri whispered. "We've run into what we've always feared."

Gorsid was shouting into the communicator. "Destroy all the locators on the ship. Destroy them, do you hear?"

He turned with glary eyes. "Shuri," he bellowed, "they don't seem to understand. Tell those subordinates of yours to act. All locators and reconstructors must be destroyed."

"Hurry, hurry!" said Shuri weakly.

When that was done they breathed more easily. There were grim smiles and a tensed satisfaction. "At least," said vice-captain Mayad, "he cannot now ever discover Gana. Our great system of locating suns with planets remains our secret. There can be no retaliation for—" He stopped, said slowly, "What am I talking about? We haven't done anything. We're not responsible for the disaster that has befallen the inhabitants of this planet."

But Enash knew what he had meant. The guilt feelings came to the surface at such moments as this—the ghosts of all the races destroyed by the Ganae, the remorseless will that had been in them, when they first landed, to annihilate whatever was here. The dark abyss of voiceless hate and terror that lay behind them; the days on end when they had mercilessly poured poisonous radiation down upon the unsuspecting inhabitants of peaceful planets—all that had been in Mayad's words.

"I still refuse to believe he has escaped." That was Captain Gorsid. "He's in there. He's waiting for us to take down our screens, so he can escape. Well, we won't do it."

There was silence again, as they stared expectantly into the energy shell—into the emptiness of the energy shell. The reconstructor rested on its metal supports, a glittering affair. But there was nothing else. Not a flicker of unnatural light or shade. The yellow rays of the sun bathed the open spaces with a brilliance that left no room for concealment.

"Guards," said Gorsid, "destroy the reconstructor. I thought he might come back to examine it, but we can't take a chance on that."

It burned with a white fury; and Enash, who had hoped somehow that the deadly energy would force the two-legged thing into the open, felt his hopes sag within him.

"But where can he have gone?" Yoal whispered.

Enash turned to discuss the matter. In the act of swinging around, he saw that the monster was standing under a tree a score of feet to one side, watching them. He must have arrived *that* moment, for there was a collective gasp from the councilors. Everybody drew back. One of the screen technicians, using great presence of mind, jerked up an energy screen between the Ganae and the monster. The creature came forward slowly. He was slim of build, he held his head well back. His eyes shone as from an inner fire.

He stopped as he came to the screen, reached out and touched it with his fingers. It flared, blurred with changing colors; the colors grew brighter, and extended in an intricate pattern all the way from his head to the ground. The blur cleared. The colors drew back into the pattern. The pattern faded into invisibility. The man was through the screen.

He laughed, a soft sound; then sobered. "When I first wakened," he said, "I was curious about the situation. The question was, what should I do with you?"

The words had a fateful ring to Enash on the still morning air of that planet of the dead. A voice broke the silence, a voice so strained and unnatural that a moment passed before he recognized it as belonging to Captain Gorsid.

"Kill him!"

When the blasters ceased their effort, the unkillable thing remained standing. He walked slowly forward until he was only half a dozen feet from the nearest Ganae. Enash had a position well to the rear. The man said slowly:

"Two courses suggest themselves, one based on gratitude for reviving me, the other based on reality. I know you for what you are. Yes, *know* you—and that is unfortunate. It is hard to feel merciful.

"To begin with," he went on, "let us suppose you surrender the secret of the locater. Naturally, now that a system exists, we shall never again be caught as we were—"

Enash had been intent, his mind so alive with the potentialities of the disaster that was here that it seemed impossible he could think of anything else. And yet, now a part of his attention was stirred.

"What did happen?"

The man changed color. The emotions of that far day thickened his voice. "A nucleonic storm. It swept in from outer space. It brushed this edge of our galaxy. It was about ninety light-years in diameter, beyond the farthest limits of our power. There was no escape from it. We had dispensed with spaceships, and had no time to contruct any. Cator, the only star with planets ever discovered by us, was also in the path of the storm."

He stopped. "The secret?" he said.

Around Enash, the councilors were breathing easier. The fear of race destruction that had come to them was lifting. Enash saw with pride that the first shock was over, and they were not even afraid for themselves.

"Ah," said Yoal softly, "you don't know the secret. In spite of all your great development, we alone can conquer the galaxy."

He looked at the others, smiling confidently. "Gentlemen," he said, "our pride in a great Ganae achievement is justified. I suggest we return to our ship. We have no further business on this planet."

There was a confused moment while their bubbles formed, when Enash wondered if the two-legged one would try to stop their departure. But the man, when he looked back, was walking in a leisurely fashion along a street.

That was the memory Enash carried with him, as the ship began to move. That and the fact that the three atomic bombs they dropped, one after the other, failed to explode.

"We will not," said Captain Gorsid, "give up a planet as easily as that. I propose another interview with the creature."

They were floating down again into the city, Enash and Yoal and Veed and the commander.

Captain Gorsid's voice tuned in once more: ". . . As I visualize it"—through mist Enash could see the transparent glint of the other three bubbles around him—"we jumped to conclusions about this creature, not justified by the evidence. For instance, when he awakened, he vanished. Why? Because he was afraid, of course. He wanted to size up the situation. He didn't believe he was omnipotent."

It was sound logic. Enash found himself taking heart from it. Suddenly, he was astonished that he had become panicky so easily. He began to see the danger in a new light. One man, only one man, alive on a new planet. If they were determined enough, colonists could be moved in as if he did not exist. It had been done before, he recalled. On several planets, small groups of the original populations had survived the destroying radiation, and taken refuge in remote areas. In almost every case, the new colonists gradually hunted them down. In two instances, however, that Enash remembered, native races were still holding small sections of their planets. In each case, it had been found impractical to destroy them because it would have endangered the Ganae on the planet. So the survivors were tolerated.

One man would not take up very much room.

When they found him, he was busily sweeping out the lower floor of a small bungalow. He put the broom aside, and stepped onto the terrace outside. He had put on sandals, and he wore a loose-fitting robe made of very shiny material. He eyed them indolently but he said nothing.

It was Captain Gorsid who made the proposition. Enash had to admire the story he told into the language machine. The commander was very frank. That approach had been decided on. He pointed out that the Ganae could not be expected to revive the dead of this planet. Such altruism would be unnatural considering that the ever-growing Ganae hordes had a continual need for new worlds. Each vast new population increment was a problem that could be solved by one method only. In this instance, the colonist would gladly respect the rights of the sole survivor of the—

It was at that point the man interrupted. "But what is the purpose of this endless expansion?" He seemed genuinely curious. "What will happen when you finally occupy every planet in this galaxy?"

Captain Gorsid's puzzled eyes met Yoal's, then flashed to Veed, then Enash. Enash shrugged his torso negatively, and felt pity for the creature. The man didn't understand, possibly never could understand. It was the old story of two different viewpoints, the virile and the decadent, the race that aspired to the stars and the race that declined the call of destiny.

"Why not," urged the man, "control the breeding chambers."

"And have the government overthrown!" said Yoal.

He spoke tolerantly, and Enash saw that the others were smiling at the man's naïveté. He felt the intellectual gulf between them widening. The man had no comprehension of the natural life forces that were at work. He said now:

"Well, if you don't control them, we will control them for you."

There was silence.

They began to stiffen. Enash felt it in himself, saw the signs of it in the others. His gaze flicked from face to face, then back to the creature in the doorway. Not for the first time Enash had the thought that their enemy seemed helpless.

"Why," he almost decided, "I could put my suckers around him and crush him."

He wondered if mental control of nucleonic, nuclear and gravitonic energies included the ability to defend oneself from a macrocosmic attack. He had an idea it did. The exhibition of power two hours before might have had limitations, but, if so, it was not apparent.

Strength or weakness could make no difference. The threat of threats had been made: "If you don't control—we will."

The words echoed in Enash's brain, and, as the meaning penetrated deeper, his aloofness faded. He had always regarded himself as a spectator. Even when, earlier, he had argued against his revival, he had been aware of a detached part of himself watching the scene rather than being part of it.

He saw with a sharp clarity that that was why he had finally yielded to the conviction of the others.

Going back beyond that to remoter days, he saw that he had never quite considered himself a participant in the seizure of the planets of other races. He was the one who looked on, and thought of reality, and speculated on a life that seemed to have no meaning.

It was meaningless no longer. He was caught by a tide of irresistible emotion, and swept along. He felt himself sinking, merging with the Ganae mass being. All the strength and all the will of the race surged up in his veins.

He snarled, "Creature, if you have any hopes of reviving your dead race, abandon them now."

The man looked at him, but said nothing.

Enash rushed on, "If you could destroy us, you would have done so already. But the truth is that you operate within limitations. Our ship is so built that no conceivable chain reaction could be started in it. For every plate of potential unstable material in it there is a counteracting plate, which prevents the development of a critical pile. You might be able to set off explosions in our engines, but they, too, would be limited, and would merely start the process for which they are intended—confined in their proper space."

He was aware of Yoal touching his arm. "Careful," warned the historian. "Do not in your just anger give away vital information."

Enash shook off the restraining sucker. "Let us not be unrealistic," he said harshly. "This thing has divined most of our racial secrets, apparently merely by looking at our bodies. We would be acting childishly if we assumed that he has not already realized the possibilities of the situation."

"Enash!" Captain Gorsid's voice was imperative.

As swiftly as it had come Enash's rage subsided. He stepped back.

"Yes, Commander."

"I think I know what you intended to say," said Captain Gorsid. "I assure you I am in full accord, but I believe also that I, as the top Ganae official, should deliver the ultimatum."

He turned. His horny body towered above the man.

"You have made the unforgivable threat. You have told

us, in effect, that you will attempt to restrict the vaulting Ganae spirit—''

"Not the spirit," said the man. He laughed softly. "No, not the spirit."

The commander ignored the interruption. "Accordingly, we have no alternative. We are assuming that, given time to locate the materials and develop the tools, you might be able to build a reconstructor.

"In our opinion it will be at least two years before you can complete it, *even if you know how*. It is an immensely intricate machine not easily assembled by the lone survivor of a race that gave up its machines millennia before disaster struck.

"You did not have time to build a spaceship.

"We won't give you time to build a reconstructor.

"Within a few minutes our ship will start dropping bombs. It is possible you will be able to prevent explosions in your vicinity. We will start, accordingly, on the other side of the planet. If you stop us there, then we will assume we need help.

"In six months of traveling at top acceleration, we can reach a point where the nearest Ganae planet would hear our messages. They will send a fleet so vast that all your powers of resistance will be overcome. By dropping a hundred or a thousand bombs every minute we will succeed in devastating every city, so that not a grain of dust will remain of the skeletons of your people.

"That is our plan.

"So it shall be.

"Now, do your worst to us who are at your mercy."

The man shook his head. "I shall do nothing—now!" he said. He paused, then thoughtfully, "Your reasoning is fairly accurate. Fairly. Naturally, I am not all-powerful, but it seems to me you have forgotten one little point.

"I won't tell you what it is.

"And now," he said, "good day to you. Get back to your ship, and be on your way. I have much to do."

Enash had been standing quietly, aware of the fury building up in him again. Now, with a hiss, he sprang forward, suckers outstretched. They were almost touching the smooth flesh—when something snatched at him.

He was back on the ship.

He had no memory of movement, no sense of being dazed or harmed. He was aware of Veed and Yoal and Captain Gorsid standing near him as astonished as he himself. Enash remained very still, thinking of what the man had said: ". . . *Forgotten one little point.*" Forgotten? That meant they knew. What could it be? He was still pondering about it when Yoal said, "We can be reasonably certain our bombs alone will not work."

They didn't.

Forty light-years out from Earth, Enash was summoned to the council members.

Yoal greeted him wanly, "The monster is aboard."

The thunder of that poured through Enash, and with it came a sudden comprehension. "That was what he meant we had forgotten," he said finally, aloud and wonderingly, "that he can travel through space at will within a limit—what was the figure he once used—of ninety light-years."

He sighed. He was not surprised that the Ganae, who had to use ships, would not have thought immediately of such a possibility. Slowly. he began to retreat from the reality. Now that the shock had come, he felt old and weary, a sense of his mind withdrawing again to its earlier state of aloofness.

It required a few minutes to get the story. A physicist's assistant, on his way to the storeroom, had caught a glimpse of a man in a lower corridor. In such a heavily manned ship, the wonder was that the intruder had escaped earlier observation. Enash had a thought.

"But after all we are not going all the way to one of our planets. How does he expect to make use of us to locate it if we only use video—" He stopped. That was it, of course. Directional video beams would have to be used, and the man would travel in the right direction the instant contact was made.

Enash saw the decision in the eyes of his companions, the only possible decision under the circumstances. And yet—it seemed to him they were missing some vital point.

He walked slowly to the great video plate at one end of the chamber. There was a picture on it, so vivid, so sharp, so majestic that the unaccustomed mind would have reeled as from a stunning blow. Even to him, who knew the scene, there came a constriction, a sense of unthinkable vastness. It was a video view of a section of the milky way. Four hundred *million* stars as seen through telescopes that could pick up the light of a red dwarf at thirty thousand light-years.

The video plate was twenty-five yards in diameter—a scene that had no parallel elsewhere in the plenum. Other galaxies simply did not have that many stars.

Only one in two hundred thousand of those glowing suns had planets.

That was the colossal fact that compelled them now to an irrevocable act. Wearily, Enash looked around him.

"The monster has been very clever," he said quietly. "If we go ahead, he goes with us—obtains a reconstructor and returns by his method to his planet. If we use the directional beam, he flashes along it, obtains a reconstructor and again reaches his planet first. In either event, by the time our fleets arrived back there, he would have revived enough of his kind to thwart any attack we could mount."

He shook his torso. The picture was accurate, he felt sure, but it still seemed incomplete. He said slowly, "We have one advantage now. Whatever decision we make, there is no language machine to enable him to learn what it is. We can carry out our plans without his knowing what they will be. He knows that neither he nor we can blow up the ship. That leaves us one real alternative."

It was Captain Gorsid who broke the silence that followed. "Well, gentlemen, I see we know our minds. We will set the engines, blow up the controls—and take him with us."

They looked at each other, race pride in their eyes. Enash touched suckers with each in turn.

An hour later, when the heat was already considerable, Enash had the thought that sent him staggering to the communicator, to call Shuri, the astronomer.

"Shuri," he cried, "when the monster first awakened—remember Captain Gorsid had difficulty getting your subordinates to destroy the locaters. We never thought to ask them what the delay was. Ask them . . . ask them—"

There was a pause, then Shuri's voice came weakly over the roar of static, "They . . . couldn't . . . get . . . into . . . the . . . room. The door was locked."

Enash sagged to the floor. They had missed more than one point, he realized. The man had awakened, realized the situation; and, when he vanished, he had gone to the ship, and there discovered the secret of the locator and possibly the secret of the reconstructor—if he didn't know it previously. By the time he reappeared, he already had from them what he wanted. All the rest must have been designed to lead them to this act of desperation.

In a few moments, now, *he* would be leaving the ship secure in the knowledge that shortly no alien mind would know his planet existed. Knowing, too, that his race would live again, and this time never die.

Enash staggered to his feet, clawed at the roaring communicator, and shouted his new understanding into it. There was no answer. It clattered with the static of uncontrollable and inconceivable energy.

The heat was peeling his armored hide, as he struggled to the matter transmitter. It flashed at him with purple flame. Back to the communicator he ran shouting and screaming.

He was still whimpering into it a few minutes later when the mighty ship plunged into the heart of a blue-white sun.

Pseudopath

by Philip E. High

He was not a telepath. But the scope of his power was beyond words.

Welling paced restlessly up and down his office. He was not exactly frightened but he was near enough to it to be jumpy and over-tense. One expected casualties in a war, but this one—Soames was dead, losing Soames was like losing a brilliant tactical general, one couldn't afford to lose a man like that, particularly now.

Welling stopped pacing and stared out of the window at the city below. A beautiful city of delicate pastels and architectural perfection, humming with life. Yet, down there, beneath the untroubled surface of normal life was war. A war as brutal, as vicious as any in the world's history, a new kind of war.

Meeker came into the office silently and joined him at the window. "Deceptive, isn't it?" Meeker seemed to be reading his thoughts. "The enemy walks beside you in the street, he brushes against you in the park, speaks to you in a public conveyance and you do not know he is your enemy."

Welling nodded and made an angry gesture. "How did they miss this? Why didn't they see it coming? The trends were there, centuries ago, but never seen, never prepared for. Now that we're in it up to our necks, all we get from H.Q. are reports on enemy weapons which they don't attempt to counter." He sighed abruptly and changed the subject. "You heard about Soames?"

Meeker nodded. His face in the sunlight had a waxy look which emphasized the lines about his mouth and the pouches of weariness beneath his eyes. "How did they get him?"

Welling shrugged. "Does it matter?"

"I suppose not." Meeker fumbled a cigarette from his pocket, sucked it alight, hungrily, and stared out over the city. "It just means that it's our turn next, yours or mine. One day we'll walk out of this building and—phut!"

'Fatalistic,' thought Welling, tiredly. An almost calm acceptance of a sudden and violent death. An acknowledgment that the enemy were lying in wait, biding their time for the moment you were off guard. The enemy could afford to wait, they could almost announce victory with a fanfare of trumpets. When the balance, in terms of numerical superiority, was about two million to one, you could afford to dictate tactics. God! If only they could get Magnesta; if they could do that, they could split the enemy into warring factions and then . . .

Welling scowled at himself mentally. He was daydreaming, wasn't he? They had about as much chance of getting Magnesta as they had of spitting at the moon and hitting it.

"Oh, I brought this." Meeker laid a folder on the desk. "You should read it, you really should. I think H.Q. or the psych labs are really scraping the bottom of the barrel, all we need after this is a man with two heads."

Welling sat down slowly at the desk and opened the folder. It contained a long and unnecessarily wordy report on a new officer. He turned the pages indifferently, reading only a few words here and there until a phrase at the foot of the third page brought him up short—*to be regarded as a telepath*.

"What the hell do they mean by that?" he said, aloud.

"Yes," said Meeker, "what?"

Welling ran a tired hand over his face. "What do they think we want—freaks?" With only eighty-five trained men and nineteen women to hold down a city of twenty million, they send me *this*. God, they must be mad. Listen to this: *'Although this officer's talents are strictly nontelepathic, on no account should enemy intelligence be allowed to discover this. On the contrary, enemy intelligence should be discreetly advised that a telepath is now operating against them.'* My God!" Welling's voice was almost an explosion. "Even if this man is a telepath which, according to the reports, he isn't, the enemy would blast this building wide open to get him if they thought it was true. Now they're asking us to stick our necks out and say we have one."

"There are no telepaths," said Meeker mildly. "They've been trying for years and even neurosurgery can't make one that works."

"They've got themselves a dummy one." Welling tossed the folder angrily to one side. "They're sending it to us to operate—and note this, Meeker—under the direct orders of H.Q. In short, although I outrank him, he does as he likes. On the other hand, if he gets his fool head blown off, they'll ask me, as the superior officer, why I didn't take more care of him. Hell, haven't we enough on our hands?"

"Officer Lott, reporting for duty, sir."

Welling returned the smart salute casually. "We don't bother with stuff here, Lott. This is the front line, we try and save our energy for other matters."

"I'm sorry, sir, I—"

"Never mind, you'll know next time, won't you?" He smiled. He was too good an officer to let his irritation become personal. After all, it wasn't Lott's fault that Headquarters had singled him out to do a specific job in a particularly idiotic way, the fault lay, as usual, with those at the top.

"Sit down, Lott." He introduced Meeker casually and picked up the folder. "Your training reports seem particularly good, we can use a man with brains and ability but, candidly I can't see any use for your—ah—talents, as yet."

Lott smiled. He was a slight, pleasant-faced man of thirty with amused blue eyes which concealed considerable ability. Those eyes, Welling was to learn, missed nothing. Further, although the man's movements appeared slow, there was a suggestion of power and control which was unmistakable. Welling cursed again inwardly, this was first-class fighting material and H.Q. had thrown it away on some wild scheme or other which would never work.

Lott said, quietly, "With due respect, sir, you can use those talents now."

Welling sighed, he supposed he'd have to explain it all. "We haven't the time to try, we're practically besieged in here. Every time we go out we take our lives in our hands, every flyer from the roof is tracked by enemy instruments—"

"I'm sorry, sir." Lott was interrupting, firmly but politely. "My instructions are to use my talents, they're there, they don't have to be tried, sir."

Welling opened his mouth but the caller at his elbow interrupted him. "Yes?"

Meeker watched, letting the smoke trickle from his nostrils, ready to act if action was called for, ready to relax again if the call was routine.

Welling looked up, he had forgotten Lott. "Mottram," he said softly. "Mottram got Soames and that's official."

Meeker ground out the spent cigarette. "Who does it?"

Welling shrugged. "Roberts or Judy, maybe both, it's their district."

"The enemy will expect it," said Meeker in a detached voice. "They'll be ready and waiting."

"It's still got to be tried, perhaps two of them may bring it off."

Meeker nodded. He didn't believe it and Welling didn't expect him to. In Welling's place, he would have to give exactly the same order which was virtually sending two agents to their deaths with no assurance of success to justify it, yet it had to be done, Meeker saw that. It was like the days of the old wars when retreating armies sent suicide detachments in the form of rearguards. There was little hope of the detachments returning alive but they had to be sent to give the army time to withdraw in order. It was even more important now, if they became wholly ineffectual they were lost. Nevertheless he was acutely conscious of the fact that Welling felt like a murderer every time he was forced to issue such an order. He realized suddenly that Lott and Welling were arguing bitterly.

"Don't be a damn fool." Welling banged his fist angrily on the desk. "At least Roberts knows some of the enemy, he has a chance of recognizing some but you'd be completely in the dark."

"No." Lott's voice was stubborn. "I can detect the enemy."

"Heavens, man, listen to reason, we'd have won the war if we could do that, but we can't, we can't distinguish them from friend or neutral, no one can."

"*I* can," said Lott.

Welling paused, his clenched fist raised above the desk. "You mean you actually can read minds or something?"

Lott smiled gently. "Let's just say I have something—"

Roberts was a tall pale man with the bright, deeply sunken eyes of one who has lived on his nerves too long. He was breaking up fast and he knew it. He still walked with the springy step of a trained athlete but shoulders were inclined to slump and the strong hands were never still. Trigger-twitch they called it back at base and he knew it would not be long before he would be forever sliding his hand into his gun pocket to assure himself the weapon was still there.

He met Lott in a small downtown eating house and introduced himself with the correct gestures. "Welling says you can help us. We need help." He sat down at the table and glanced quickly over his shoulder. "I was tailed at first but I think I threw them. The real trouble is that there are so few of us, they know us by sight." He stirred his coffee absently, staring unseeingly at the dark liquid. "Mottram frequents the *Blue Grass Tavern*, usually gets there around ten." He paused to sip his coffee.

"What's the set-up?" Lott toyed with a meal he didn't really want.

Roberts shrugged. "Purely tentative. Judy will be drinking by the bar, maybe she can create some kind of diversion and in the general excitement—" He shrugged again and said, bitterly, "Candidly it would be easier for us to cut our own throats here and now, save a lot of trouble. Mottram won't be alone, the place will be packed with neutrals and guards we can't identify." He pushed his cup away irritably. "Why did they have to drag Judy in? She's a nice kid, pretty, bags of courage but they'll kill her, too, with less compunction than a bedbug."

"I take it we don't stand much chance."

"If we get Mottram, which is unlikely, we'll come out feet first."

Lott said: "Thanks," drily. He leaned a little forward over his plate and began to cut at the cheap syntha-steak. "Welling tell you anything about me?"

"Oh, he said something about you being able to identify enemy personnel, but I'm afraid we won't have time to find out."

Lott was still cutting industriously and did not raise his eyes. "Two men just came in, they're standing by the autoserve, they're both enemy units."

Roberts lit a cigarette and looked without appearing to do so. "You're sure?"

"Dead sure."

"Looking for us?"

"You, anyway, they're not sure about me."

Roberts flicked ash at the table disposal slot. "Are they going to start something in here do you think?"

"Yes." Lott's voice was detached. "They're working up to a drunken fight, there'll be a struggle, shots, and somehow you'll get killed."

"Thank you," said Roberts, bitterly.

"Skip it." Lott pushed away his plate. "I can use another coffee." He rose before Roberts could stop him and crossed to the counter. "Excuse me," he said politely. Then there were two plopping explosions, so close they sounded like a single report.

Roberts turned just in time to see one of the men, face blank with surprise, clutch at his chest and fall slowly backwards. The other was already face down on the floor and very still.

"Let's get out of here." Lott's voice was quite calm and his hands were empty.

Roberts waited until they were a mile away and had changed air-taxis three times before he said anything. "My God, I thought you were green."

Lott shrugged. "Special training. The enemy concentrates on new weapons, we're concentrating on special type personnel to use the ones we have—reflex fighters."

"And I thought I was fast." Roberts stared unseeingly in front of him. "The first two enemy units in four months, knocked out by a recruit. If we're lucky enough to get Mottram, too, they'll think we're getting reinforcements somewhere."

"Or perhaps," said Lott, "they'll start worrying how we managed to hit them so hard after all this time."

Roberts looked at him sharply. "Just what are your talents?"

"I can identify enemy units, even in a crowd of neutrals." He grinned faintly. "My file says I can read minds too."

"And can you?"

"No, but in due course, the enemy will probably think I can."

Roberts did not pursue the subject, he could see that Lott did not intend to commit himself and he probably had direct orders not to. Nevertheless something damn funny was going on. How had Lott *known* that the two men in the eating house were the enemy? There was no doubt that he was right, as they had left Roberts had noticed that one of the dead men had a Geeson pistol half drawn from his pocket. How had Lott known? The implications struck Roberts suddenly and he stiffened. With the ability to detect the enemy, they stood a chance. Not just a sea of faces in a night spot, any one of which might belong to the enemy but a few, identified, pinpointed and allowed for by a man who had—what? If he didn't read minds, he got damn close to it. "What the hell do you call yourself?" he asked. "If you're not a telepath, what are you?"

Lott rubbed his chin and frowned. "I suppose," he said, after some thought, "you'd call me a pseudopath."

The *Blue Grass Tavern* was enemy-controlled but designed to attract the neutrals. It was, therefore, outwardly respectable and prohibitively expensive. Real waiters, instead of table-dials, accepted orders and delivered meals, even the near-nude floor show was flesh and blood and not the usual solidex transmission. Between shows, tables were pleasantly intimate islands of shadows and artificial moonlight, made even more subtle and romantic by the new half-heard melody-projectors.

Roberts looked about him as they entered and said: "Damn!" under his breath. The lighting set-up was going to make shooting difficult, and, further, the place was packed with neutrals. Neutrals, the blind innocents of society who lived their comparatively normal lives unaware that around them was being fought one of the most savage wars in history. The ironic aspect of the war was that neither side told them it was going on. On the one side were the defenders, who for many reasons couldn't, they didn't control public news services any more and without those they were mute. Second, they had been maneuvered into fighting a guerrilla war and could not tell too much without betraying both their strength and, possibly, their sources of supply and revenue.

The enemy, on the other hand, was striving for complete domination and you can't cook your goose until you've caught it. In point of fact, the enemy went to considerable lengths to convince the neutrals that all was well with the world while they skillfully undermined it from within.

Roberts looked around again, shrugged, and allowed a smooth waiter to guide them to a center table. He studied the wine list and menu with some care, ordered the meal and waited until the man had gone before he spoke. "Judy's at the bar, blue dress, dark, shoulder-length hair—got her?"

"Got her," said Lott without appearing to look.

"Mottram is in the corner by the pillar, heavy, dark hair parted in the center."

Lott saw a heavy-faced man with small but alert dark eyes. It had always troubled him that enemy units looked so normal, he felt that they should look tight-mouthed, expressionless and vaguely furtive but they never did. This man had a heavy, full-lipped mouth and, when he smiled, which was frequently, he displayed large but very white teeth. In the peculiar vernacular of the enemy he was a Top Torp and would be addressed as 'Gun' which was roughly equivalent to a specialist officer in a normal army.

"He hasn't seen us yet, I think," said Roberts softly. "Not that it matters, someone knows we're here. They never take chances and this place has talents of its own. There are little probes dotted around, so sensitive they can register a metal filling in an eyetooth." He smiled without humor. "That means they know all they need to know, they know two men have come in with weapons, they know about the tiny spitrod between Judy's breasts, the only thing they don't know is when we're going to start. They could, of course, start the ball rolling themselves but they like to play it cat-and-mouse with the additional advantage of making it look like self-defense."

The waiter arrived with the order and Roberts discussed sport until he was out of hearing. He scowled briefly at his plate then drew it slightly towards him. "Damn it, I'm going to enjoy this, it's probably my last." He grinned twistedly at the other. "Don't imagine I'm joking heroically, will you? If it wasn't for the Andrabenze tablets they issue I'd never have got in here."

Lott made no comment, outwardly he was calm but inside he was like a coiled spring. He could well imagine what one felt like after one mission too many, the inevitable day when one was compelled to fall back on the Andrabenze tablets in order to complete that mission without cracking.

He appeared to be eating quietly and steadily but he was watching, measuring distances, checking angles and noting exits. He pushed his plate a little to one side and toyed with his wine glass. "Four," he said casually. "The big man with bald head by the bar—he's there to cover Judy. Then there's the barman, watch him, he doesn't have to draw, his weapon is just below the level of the counter. Then on the opposite side of the room, two men in evening dress by the table near the wall.''

After a few seconds Roberts said: "Got 'em." Then bitterly, "They're not taking any chances are they?" He sipped his wine, studying the situation. "Think you and Judy can keep those gentry occupied while I try and take Mottram?"

Lott was bending slightly over his plate and did not look up. When he spoke, his voice was almost inaudible. "You won't take Mottram, you'll never get the gun out of your pocket. There'll be a hole burned through to your spine before your fingers touch the butt.''

"What are you trying to do—unnerve me?" Roberts sounded angry and bitter.

"No." Lott was still bent over his plate. "You see that fork he keeps playing with, sort of toys with and waves in tune to the music? Well, it's not a fork, it's a spit rod.''

"My God!" For the first time Roberts paled slightly. "I could have walked right into it thinking I had a chance." He frowned and said: "Clever," bitterly. "All he has to do is aim.'' He looked at Lott with a new respect. "Perhaps it would be better if we thought out some other idea between us, any suggestions?"

Lott drained his wine glass. "If I can take those two characters in evening dress by the wall, I might have a chance of swinging around and knocking out our bald friend before he knows quite where it's coming from—"

Roberts nodded quickly. "Go on, I'm listening—" When Lott had finished, he considered carefully before answering. "Yes, yes, it might work but you'll have to be devilish fast." He lit a cigar with some care and exhaled smoke.

Lott watched, the cigar was a signal. It was one thing which the enemy did not know and had probably never suspected. The enemy were probably waiting for him or Roberts to confer with Judy and then to act. A cigar might be a signal for that act but it never occurred to them that the conference was already in progress. Roberts made casual gestures, he toyed with a knife, he studied the contents of his wallet, he rubbed his chin. The gesture-code was vastly superior, at least for close work, than the enemy's micro-transmitters insofar that it could be neither jammed nor tapped and was almost unbreakable.

Judy raised her wine glass to the level of her eyes as if studying the wine and put it down again. The gesture meant: 'Message received and understood.'

Lott pushed his empty plate to one side. "Okay?"

Roberts nodded. "Good luck."

Lott rose. They were watching him, he could feel them. He sensed, rather than saw, the indicative sliding of hands, the sudden blanking of faces, the tensing of muscles. They expected him to approach the bar to contact Judy or, alternatively, to try and get behind Mottram. He did neither, he walked easily and steadily towards the door marked 'Washroom.'

He felt the tension drain from the watchers, the spurious fork in Mottram's hand, which had steadied drooped slightly towards the table again.

Inside, Lott felt a knot of coldness which seemed to fill his stomach and invade his heart and lungs. This was his first real taste of action, the culmination of nearly seven years intensive training and, at the moment, the seven years didn't help. He was a soldier going into action for the first time and he was scared. Would the reflex action be automatic now? Would his body, his brain, his judgment react as they had reacted under laboratory test? 'If they don't,' he told himself, suddenly fatalistic, 'this is goodbye.'

Four more paces towards the door and action. Was everything clear in his mind? The two enemy units were in front, slightly to his right. Behind him, also to his right, was the bar, raised some two feet above the floor. Judy was there, the big bald man just behind her, his hand casually, too casually, in his jacket pocket. Mottram of course would be invisible behind the decorative pillar. Pray to God some fool neutral doesn't decide to stand up in the line of fire just as you turn—*now!*

Roberts, watching, had never seen anything quite so fast in his life. One minute Lott was walking unhurriedly towards the washroom, and the next, the tiny electric machine-pistol was spluttering redly in his hand.

The two enemy units never stood a chance, a line of black spots cut across the immaculate shirt fronts before they knew what had hit them.

Lott spun round, and, at the same moment, Judy dropped flat. The second burst knocked the bald man off his stool and back against the bar.

Mottram half rose then fell forward across the table. Judy had shot him neatly between the eyes as she went flat.

Roberts fired once and the barman toppled from sight before his bewildered fingers could grasp the weapon concealed beneath the counter . . .

"They screamed the place down, milled around like sheep. We got out before anyone could figure quite what had happened." Roberts leaned back tiredly in his chair, he was shaking unashamedly from reaction and wanted nothing better than to sleep.

"So Lott did identify the enemy units, he actually does have some faculties for recognizing them?" Welling was leaning tensely over his desk.

"If he hadn't we wouldn't be here now, they were all set to shoot us to pieces at the first move." He reached in his pocket and tossed something on the desk. "Judy scooped that up as we broke for the exits. Now how the hell did Lott know it was a spit rod?"

Welling examined the 'fork' with interest. "Very neat." He frowned. "Yes, how did Lott know?"

Meeker, puffing the inevitable cigarette, said: "Hadn't we better concentrate on the immediate danger? They won't like this, seven of their units knocked out in a day is going to shake them and they'll react fast. They'll be drafting exterminator units for all their worth and in our honor. In four days this city will be hotter than a frying pan."

Roberts said, wearily: "Can I sleep until I feel the heat?"

"Sure, sure." Welling's voice was very understanding. "Room 229 is all ready for you." He smiled. "Hurry along, we brought your wife and kids in for safety."

"That's damn decent of you." Roberts' eyes misted a little. "You don't often do that, do you?"

"It's not because we don't want to, it's because we haven't the room. In this case we daren't take chances. False names and spurious backgrounds may not be enough to protect them." He made an abrupt gesture as if to brush aside further thanks. "Tell Lott I want to see him as you go out, please."

* * *

Lott looked tired but still very alert. He looked inquiringly from one to the other but did not speak.

Welling waved him to a chair and poured out the customary after-mission drink. "You did damn well, exceptionally well. I've no word of criticism to make." He paused, looking unhappily at the younger man, not knowing quite how to put it. How could you tell a man that a soldier in this war who was too successful automatically signed his own death warrant. This war was a personal war. It was like the old stories of air warfare when an ace flyer was a natural target for every aspiring pilot in the opposing squadrons. Yes, it was like that only more so. In this case the whole potential of the enemy would be directed on getting that ace, only there would be no chivalry, no chance of survival and no warning.

"You've stirred up a hornets' nest," said Meeker, trying to help.

Lott nodded. "Thank you. I know what you're both trying to say but you see H.Q. wanted it this way. They *wanted* me to do rather well. You see, they want Magnesta rather badly."

"Would you mind," said Meeker, in a carefully controlled voice, "explaining that."

Lott smiled. "I did put that rather badly, didn't I? What I mean is that we know nothing about Magnesta, he's a complete enigma. One day there is no Magnesta and the next he is in supreme command. Who is he? Where did he come from? All we know is that he exists, that somehow or other he unseated the previous commander and assumed absolute power. We have seen his picture and heard his voice but there has never been any actual contact, nothing we can use to draw up a psych chart. We know he is vain, hypno-educated, and a natural leader and tactician but beyond that—" Lott spread his hands in an almost Latin gesture of helplessness.

Welling nodded then frowned suddenly. "You're trying to provoke him, the recent success, the whispers about a telepath— what do you hope to gain?"

Lott laughed softly. "We're hoping he'll be vain enough and, incidentally, stupid enough to come through on the Solidex where I can work on him."

"You mean you can actually get something from a three-dimensional transmission?" said Meeker. "You see a moving picture and read its mind?"

Welling was rubbing his chin thoughtfully. "We could add to this." he said before Lott could answer the question.

"We still have one or two reliable contacts with courage enough to drop hints, we could start a crop, say that someone betrayed the enemy units, lots of things." He pressed a button. "Get me Hambling—"

Meeker stared unseeingly before him, thinking of Magnesta. The man who had welded the enemy into a complex but unified fighting machine which threatened to throw the race back to barbarism and had already brought it to the brink of economic and cultural collapse.

Magnesta who lived in a house which was half mansion, half fortress and cunningly erected in the heart of the city. It was mansion enough to deceive the neutrals, fortress enough to stop a restricted-fission grenade and yet too densely surrounded to try anything bigger without loss of life.

Magnesta, the most powerful dictator of all time who, but for a handful of devoted fighters, was complete master of the world. What could they use against him? The army? The army was rotten with enemy units and they could never bring it near enough to him without interiorly inspired mutiny.

What did Lott hope to gain? Certainly knowledge was power but you had to have a means of applying that power or it was useless. Probably H.Q. had something up their sleeve but, apart from Lott, they were keeping very quiet about it.

Meeker wondered if the provocation and bluff would work and, if so, how long it would take.

It took exactly seventeen hours.

"Mr. Magnesta calling on Solidex, sir." The operator's voice sounded almost awed.

Welling snapped his fingers and grinned savagely. "Hooked! Come on, Lott."

In the reception room, light flickered mistily about a receptor chair, light which seemed to plane sideways into shadow and solidify . . .

"Good day, Mr. Welling," said the projected image, politely.

"You want something, Magnesta?" Welling's voice was cold.

"But of course, why else should I call?" The voice was smooth like the man, cultured, gentle almost, but not quite;

oily. Brown bright eyes in a sallow face, dark hair, inclined to curl, small almost chubby hands but nothing to suggest the arrogance of power.

Welling said, "What makes you think you'll get what you want?"

Magnesta shrugged. "Deals and negotiations are not new."

"Between opposing armies?" inquired Welling, sharply.

Magnesta smiled, showing very white almost feminine teeth. "You asked before thinking, Welling. Are not the exchange of sick prisoners deals between opposing armies?"

"They might be if you took prisoners—what sort of deal had you in mind?"

Magnesta smiled again. "Let us try and understand each other first, then, perhaps, negotiations."

Welling laughed. "Really, Magnesta, I am not a fool." His voice was almost gentle. "You called because you heard whispers; you heard that, perhaps, someone betrayed your units, or, maybe that we had a telepath. You called yourself because, in your heart, you trust no one." He paused. "Would you like the answer?"

"If you give me the answer so easily then, obviously, it is not true. I, also, am not a fool."

Lott leaned slightly forward in his chair. "Suppose we can prove our answer?"

Magnesta only shifted his eyes slightly in the other's direction. "This is your new officer, Welling?"

"Yes, he is also our telepath, you may have heard about that."

A slight flush appeared in Magnesta's cheeks. "You think I am a damned idiot?"

"Lott reads minds well enough to identify your units." Welling's voice was even, almost detached. "You can dismiss it as fantasy or you can prove it. Call in some of your units, call in some neutrals, Lott can tell you which is which."

"Yes?" Obviously Magnesta was debating inwardly, then he frowned. "Very well."

The test was a pure triumph for Lott. Of the forty people, enemy and neutral, who entered the projection room, he identified them all.

"You are a clever man." Magnesta's expression was a controlled blank. "You can identify friend from enemy but this does not mean you can read minds."

Lott smiled. "Would I tell you if I could read yours? I would keep it to myself and use it later. Don't make too many plans, here, Magnesta."

The other shrugged. "You are all fools. With a thousand such men you might have achieved victory. With one—pouf!" The image shimmered and began to fade.

"Any help?" said Welling later.

"Maybe." Lott was noncommittal. "Excuse me, while I check World Army regulations." He was back ten minutes later, holding a slip of paper and grinning faintly. "*A deserter, or suspected deserter. Shall be taken into custody irrespective of civil law and, in the face of resistance, the officer-in-charge shall take such action as seems necessary insofar as he safeguards civilian life and property.*" He quoted from the paper.

Welling said: "So?" blankly.

Lott lit a cigarette. "Magnesta is a deserter from World Army, section seventy-four. As you know, all service personnel are marked with a red spot on the ball of the thumb on discharge. Short of removing the thumb altogether, this spot cannot be erased. Magnesta has no such spot, therefore he deserted."

"How did you know that he was in the army in the first place—no don't answer that, you read his mind." Welling sighed. "I wish I knew just what your talents were." He stopped, frowning. "If you think the army can arrest him, think again. The army does what Magnesta tells it."

Lott exhaled smoke. "If you lack power, use a lever." He rose. "What I want now is an officer of fairly high rank with a reputation for honesty and conscientious devotion to duty. No doubt a few such officers remain."

"Only neutrals."

"When I've finished with him, he fights for us. If he exists, records will find him with their classification computers."

"And then?"

"Then Judy and I will talk to him. I take it there's a way of getting out of here without being noticed.

"We can do that, but why take Judy?"

Lott grinned. "Why not, I need her for the psychological side, not that you'll believe me."

"I don't," said Welling flatly. He paused. "We can smuggle you out, Lott, but you can't hide forever. Keep low and stay low, once they spot you you're a dead duck."

*   *   *

Colonel Wintering was a tall, graying man with tired faded blue eyes, slightly sagging cheeks but a firm chin. "Security? What the devil has World Security to do with the army?" He looked from one to the other in a puzzled way. "Why come to me?" He had checked their credentials carefully and there was no doubt who they were.

Lott said, directly. "We have access to army records, Colonel. We were seeking a particular type of officer and the classification computers selected you."

"You require some kind of assistance?"

"Perhaps a little more than assistance." Lott paused. "This may stagger you, Colonel, but the race is at war."

"I beg your pardon." Wintering stared at him blankly. "This is some joke perhaps?"

"No joke, Colonel, this is a war that has been going on a very long time and we're losing it."

"Really?" Wintering's voice was remote.

Lott sighed inwardly. He didn't want to be brutal but he saw he had no choice, the Colonel was disinterested and only half listening.

Fortunately, Judy softened the blow. "You had a daughter, Colonel, a girl about my age—she died in this war."

Colonel Wintering stiffened and the faded blue eyes grew suddenly cold. "I consider that remark uncalled-for and in extremely bad taste." He rose from behind his desk. "Would you be good enough to leave now. Any assistance you may require should be forwarded through the proper channels."

Judy didn't move. "Your daughter was killed by a stray bullet in a street battle. An innocent bystander shot by an enemy unit trying to get one of us."

"If you do not leave," began the Colonel, stiffly—

Lott interrupted him, angrily. "Colonel Wintering, when the forces of organized crime become greater and more powerful than the forces of law and order then one is at war."

Wintering slowly resumed his seat, his face was pale but there were twin spots of color in the cheeks. "You are serious? You do not exaggerate?"

Lott shook his head. "World Security is all that is left. The last barrier against chaos."

Wintering stared at him blankly. "I don't understand. Why

is it not known, why is not something done? If this is war, why is it not fought like one, by armies?"

"In the first place politicians control the army and crime controls the politicians. In the second, the army itself is lousy with enemy units."

"It seems incredible, how did this start?"

"It dates as far back as the twentieth century when crime became organized by syndicates who conducted their affairs behind legitimate business fronts. A situation which slowly began to undermine society and force the cost of living to dangerous levels. In Paris, a determined Prefect of Police succeeded in breaking up one of the syndicates but the resulting exposure resulted in a change of government. An unbelievable state of corruption existed, reaching almost to the heads of state themselves. Crime had almost succeeded in completely dictating city policy. High officials were found guilty of taking bribes or admitted that they had been intimidated by threats, either to themselves or those dearest to them, into acting for the syndicate."

Lott paused to light a cigarette. "The result, of course, was to cause similar crusading elsewhere with the same evidence of corruption in high places. The repercussions, however, were unfortunate. Some of the syndicates were nationwide, some international, and the present purge threatened to break them up and seal off their immense illegal revenues from such undertakings as work unions, vice, protective associations and narcotics. For years, the syndicates had been at each other's throats, now, in self-defense they combined. They were not fools, not stupid criminals, but astute tacticians skilled in administration. Their first move was to enroll an immense army of lawyers whose business it was to circumvent and corrupt the law. The corruption and intimidation of those in high places was resumed with skill and subtlety and very soon the law became a mockery. Corrupt judges, intimidated juries, bribed officials—"

Lott ground out the cigarette and laughed without humor. "Under criminal administration the situation seemed outwardly to improve. Crime had learned a great deal and there was a great show of purges, police action and so on for the benefit of the masses. All that stood between crime and complete domination of public administration was World Security. And

World Security found itself deprived of its only weapon—law. It could arrest, only to have the criminal released by a corrupt court. Crime on the other hand had begun a private war of its own against Security, and Security in self-defense had to fight back and already they were at a disadvantage. If crime could corrupt the law, it could also intimidate or manipulate science to fight in its favor and the battle became not a clash of arms but a retreat—'' Lott, leaned back tiredly in his chair. ''Do I have to say more?''

Wintering drummed nervous fingers on the edge of his desk. ''You have some proof of these assertions, I take it?''

Lott had. The Colonel studied the figures, the tapes, the view-shots and grew slowly paler. ''It's unbelievable! Why couldn't I see it myself?''

''Neutrals seldom can, they are wrapped up in their work and, at a glance, all seems well with the world. Some, of course, suspect but have heard of enemy reprisals and deliberately bury their heads in the sand.''

Wintering nodded, his mind evidently made up. ''What do you want me to do?''

''Quite a lot. First, access to secret records, inductions, section seventy-four.''

The Colonel lit a cigarette. ''That can be arranged.''

''I want to pick, unseen—incidentally, about forty men from your best combat troops. Lastly and most important, I want the troops under your command ready to march at a moment's notice. Now, before you say it, I know you can't move ten men and a sergeant from one place to another without authority from Army Council. Bluntly, they take their orders from the politicians who, in turn, receive them from Magnesta.'' Lott smiled, it was almost a feline grimace. ''It has been proposed from H.Q. that coming from you, we might get sanction for moving a large body of troops and equipment. Now here's what they had in mind—''

Wintering nodded, almost boyishly, when he had finished. ''Yes, yes, on the basis of recruiting figures alone, they would probably sanction it without a thought.''

Lott stood up. ''Thank you, Colonel.'' He paused. ''You realize there is considerable personal risk, this is after all, war.''

''No, Lott.'' Wintering shook his head. ''I am not a religious man but I would call it something more than war. I would call it—Armaggedon.''

* * *

Welling stared moodily from the window at the streets below, for reasons he could only half-explain, he felt strangely depressed. It was irritating to realize that this was H.Q.'s first major counterattack and that they had left him in the dark. He liked Lott but he found it infuriating that the fellow could apparently read minds and promptly turn around and say he couldn't. H.Q. always fed you bits and pieces and left you to guess the grand strategy.

Judy standing beside him, turned. "Do you think it will work?"

"If we can get them there, yes."

"It could be the decisive battle couldn't it?"

"If we win this one, it *is* the decisive battle, it's the turn of the tide." He laughed briefly. "God, in ten years we might be able to arrest someone and make the charge stick."

"Instead of having to kill one of them when they kill one of us." She turned away from him. "Could you go for a girl you'd seen shoot a man between the eyes?"

He laid his hand gently on her shoulder. "We're soldiers, Judy, and this is war. Maybe he wonders if you could go for a man who can read minds."

Meeker came in. "How do I look?"

Welling studied him carefully. "Colonel Wintering will probably have apoplexy," he said, unkindly, "but I guess you'll pass in a crowd."

"The Advocats have started," said Judy tensely, "they're on their way."

Welling turned and gazed down into a street empty of traffic, but lined with sightseers. Above their heads the advocats tossed their bright luminous words like bunting. THE ARMY IS COMING . . . THE ARMY IS A *MAN'S* LIFE . . . JOIN THE MODERN ARMY.

In the distance could be heard the faint strains of a military band and the rumble of armored vehicles. DON'T JUST WATCH IT, said the advocats, JOIN IT—*NOW*.

"I must be going," said Meeker. He held out his hand. "Wish us luck."

Welling watched the parade pass, obsolete, he realized, but still stirring and impressive, the launchers, the armored vehicles, the rumbling land monitors, the lines of marching men. JOIN THE ARMY NOW.

He watched it until it was out of sight, then picked it up again on the telecasts. He watched it march to the center of the city, encircle the private Green Tree park and stop.

Welling grinned savagely. In the center of Green Tree park was a white ornate building which was half fortress and half mansion.

"Blast!" He punched angrily at the switch. "What the hell's the matter with the damn thing?" The screen had gone black. He punched the switch again and slowly vision returned but it did not show the progress of the recruiting parade. In the screen was the face of a man Welling knew almost as well as his own.

"Attention, please, attention. This is Douglas Monkton, Director of World Security calling you from Command Headquarters . . ."

Welling sank a little shakily into the nearest chair. This was tantamount to a mass assault and they must have been preparing it for years. Adding to it piece by piece and keeping those pieces in the dark until they found a weakness they could exploit. Now they'd found it, they were throwing everything they had at it. This broadcast, for example, they must have been holding that in readiness until they could really use it. He'd always considered it virtually impossible to jam the immensely powerful enemy-controlled newscasts but they'd not only succeeded in jamming them but had imposed their own transmission without a flicker of distortion.

"God," he said suddenly and aloud. "It looks as if we might win."

Magnesta said, wearily: "Because I sanctioned this damn recruiting parade, it doesn't mean I have to look at it. If you've seen one soldier, you've seen them all. Turn it off, Morden."

His lawyer did so. "A lot of people seem to like it."

"Yeah, yeah, stops them worrying their M.P.'s, or senators or whoever they think represents them, about what they call gang war." He laughed abruptly. "Hell, this marching stuff may even hook a recruit or two."

A section of the wall, close to his chair, glowed briefly and he pressed his hand to the contact pad. "Yes? What is it?" He listened. "Are you insane, Condor?" He punched the vision switch angrily and found himself looking into the face of a uniformed man. "Yes?"

Wintering played it strictly according to the book. "Auguste Magnesta?"

"Yes."

"We have reasons for supposing that your real name is Otto Linz, and, as such, you are a deserter from World Army. I am, therefore, instructed to place you under close arrest until said charges are proved or disproved."

Magnesta stared at him, blinking. "Are you out of your mind?" Aside, he said, "Call Morris, get this damn parade pulled out of town, fast."

"I can't, I've been trying." The lawyer's eyes were furtive and frightened. "We're surrounded, Magnesta, and every damn truck must be full of jamming equipment. I can't call anyone."

Magnesta saw one of the uniformed figures behind the Colonel step forward. "Are you coming out, Magnesta, or do we have to come in and get you?"

He stared, recognizing both the face and the voice. "Meeker, you're a fool. If you take me, even you can't visualize the reprisals. You won't be tolerated, you won't be permitted slow liquidation because of neutral alarm, the whole lot of you will be hunted down and destroyed within a week and that goes for the toy soldiers with you."

"Magnesta, you're the fool. Linker and Moran will be close in line to take your place and they hate each other's guts. Without you in the saddle to hold them apart, they'll be daggers drawn and we're still smart enough to set them at each other's throats. Your pet boast is that you're a general, that you've studied history and this is a case of divide and destroy. I think your units will be too busy liquidating each other to bother about us." Meeker smiled, almost beatifically. "May I add, it gives me infinite satisfaction, Magnesta, that you unwittingly sanctioned the entry into this city of your own execution squad."

"You come in and get me, eh?" Magnesta showed his teeth.

"We don't have to." Meeker raised his arm in a signal and the firing ports of one of the land monitors clanged open. He didn't wait. "All right, let them have it."

The disrupter cannon was already obsolete and misleadingly named, its effect, however, was spectacular and wholly terrifying. It literally hosed its near-microscopic pellets down the projector beam. With each pellet containing the destructive power of the old-time six-inch artillery shell, the weapon's misnomer was almost justified. Magnesta's mansion simply vomited skywards in a column of red flame and spinning black dust . . .

"The broadcast was the final blow, it really scared the neutrals and already they're clearing things up for themselves." Welling leaned back comfortably in his chair and puffed smoke. He had unearthed a box of enormous cigars from somewhere and a long-hoarded bottle of brandy.

"I suppose," said Meeker, "H.Q. has been working on this for years while we held the fort." He looked at Lott. "And you, of course, were the prime weapon."

Lott shook his head. "To be perfectly honest no. I was one of many experiments and only thrown in for a test. When it looked as if my presence might produce some results, H.Q. hastily adapted one of many plans to exploit the enemy weakness."

Welling studied the tip of his cigar. "I suppose you couldn't tell us just what your talents are now?"

Lott grinned. "I'm afraid this is going to shake you. I haven't any. I don't read minds, I interpret gestures. My talents are nothing more than acute observation and the ability to interpret what I see."

"You wouldn't," said Meeker, carefully, "care to enlarge on that would you?"

Lott lit a cigar. "Remember the trend of employment psychology, when a man applying for an important post was interviewed by a psychiatrist. The psych could tell by the way the man sat, used his hands, position of his feet and voice inflection, whether or not the applicant was suited to the position, without asking a single direct or personal question. We carried this technique a great deal further until we were able to interpret from a man's actions, if not his thoughts, at least his general way of life and, more important, his immediate intentions. This gave us the advantage of being able to distinguish enemy from neutral. Violence writes its intentions plainly in a man's actions and, in moments of tension—such as in the *Blue Grass Tavern*—to me the enemy might just as well have worn a uniform."

''We, too,'' Welling reminded him, ''have also lived by violence for a very long time.''

''With a different motivation,'' said Lott quickly. ''That also is detectable to a trained observer.''

Welling sighed. ''Without undue sarcasm, just what did you get from Magnesta? Are there certain gestures which say, 'Look, boy, I'm a deserter from World Army'?''

Lott laughed, good-naturedly. ''I wish it had been that easy. No, Magnesta had gone to considerable lengths to cover his past. He'd had his face remolded—detectable to a trained observer—had his fingerprints, the shape of his ears and the color of his eyes changed. In fact, he had even gone to the lengths of surgical operation to change his walk but there are certain things one cannot alter. Word pronunciation placed him as having lived most of his life in mid-Europe and there were certain vocal mannerisms which one only acquires in military training.

''In the first place, as I have mentioned, there was no red discharge spot on the ball of the thumb and in the second he was inordinately proud of his teeth, even a casual observer would have noticed that by the way he smiled. I noticed, however, that the eyeteeth were small and undeveloped which, of course, would be noted on an army dental chart. I figured that a man so vain about his teeth would probably leave them untouched. It was then only a question of getting the sorters to work on the charts and having them re-sorted in relation to height, shape of head, etc.''

''Sherlock,'' said Meeker, but there was no malice in his voice. ''And Mottram's spurious fork?''

Lott shrugged. ''That was an easy one. Mottram was waving it around, toying with it, beating it on the table in time to the music but every time one of us made the slightest movement, his hand lifted and the end came up. The only possible weapon which could be adapted to look like a fork was a spit rod and, in any case, the man's every gesture was literally shouting: 'This is a weapon.' ''

''Just one question more,'' said Meeker. ''Just how did you know when you were in the eating house with Roberts, that those two were going to start a drunken fight?''

For the first time Lott looked slightly uncomfortable. ''I lip-read too,'' he said, sheepishly.

After the Myths Went Home

by Robert Silverberg

Our dreams provide us power. We may be lost without them.

For a while in those years we were calling great ones out of the past, to find out what they were like. This was in the middle twelves—12400 to 12450, say. We called up Caesar and Antony, and also Cleopatra. We got Freud and Marx and Lenin into the same room and let them talk. We summoned Winston Churchill, who was a disappointment (he lisped and drank too much), and Napoleon, who was magnificent. We raided ten millennia of history for our sport.

But after half a century of this we grew bored with our game. We were easily bored, in the middle twelves. So we started to call up the myth people, the gods and the heroes. That seemed more romantic, and this was one of Earth's romanticist eras we lived in.

It was my turn to serve as curator of the Hall of Man, and that was where they built the machine, so I watched it going up from the start. Leor the Builder was in charge. He had made the machines that called the real people up, so this was only slightly different, no real challenge to his talents. He had to feed in another kind of data, full of archetypes and psychic currents, but the essential process of reconstruction would be the same. He never had any doubt of success.

Leor's new machine had crystal rods and silver sides. A giant emerald was embedded in its twelve-angled lid. Tinsel streamers of radiant platinum dangled from the ebony struts on which it rose.

"Mere decoration," Leor confided to me. "I could have made a simple black box. But brutalism is out of fashion."

The machine sprawled all over the Pavilion of Hope on the north face of the Hall of Man. It hid the lovely flicker-mosaic flooring, but at least it cast lovely reflections into the mirrored surfaces of the exhibit cases. Somewhere about 12570, Leor said he was ready to put his machine into operation.

We arranged the best possible weather. We tuned the winds, deflecting the westerlies a bit and pushing all clouds far to the south. We sent up new moons to dance at night in wondrous patterns, now and again coming together to spell out Leor's name. People came from all over Earth, thousands of them, camping in whisper-tents on the great plain that begins at the Hall of Man's doorstep. There was real excitement then, a tension that crackled beautifully through the clear blue air.

Leor made his last adjustments. The committee of literary advisers conferred with him over the order of events, and there was some friendly bickering. We chose daytime for the first demonstration, and tinted the sky light purple for better effect. Most of us put on our youngest bodies, though there were some who said they wanted to look mature in the presence of these fabled figures out of time's dawn.

"Whenever you wish me to begin—" Leor said.

There were speeches first. Chairman Peng gave his usual light-hearted address. The Procurator of Pluto, who was visiting us, congratulated Leor on the fertility of his inventions. Nistim, then in his third or fourth successive term as Metabolizer General, encouraged everyone present to climb to a higher level. Then the master of ceremonies pointed to me. No, I said, shaking my head, I am a very poor speaker. They replied that it was my duty, as curator of the Hall of Man, to explain what was about to unfold.

Reluctantly I came forward.

"You will see the dreams of old mankind made real today," I said, groping for words. "The hopes of the past will walk among you, and so, I think, will the nightmares. We are offering you a view of the imaginary figures by means of whom the ancients attempted to give structure to the universe. These gods, these heroes, summed up patterns of cause and effect, and served as organizing forces around which cultures could crystallize. It is all very strange to us and it will be wonderfully interesting. Thank you."

Leor was given the signal to begin.

"I must explain one thing," he said. "Some of the beings you are about to see were purely imaginary, concocted by tribal poets, even as my friend has just told you. Others, though, were based on actual human beings who once walked the Earth as ordinary mortals, and who were transfigured, given more-than-human qualities, raised to the pantheon. Until they actually appear, we will not know which figures belong to which category, but I can tell you how to detect their origin once you see them. Those who were human beings before they became myths will have a slight aura, a shadow, a darkness in the air about them. This is the lingering trace of their essential humanity, which no mythmaker can erase. So I learned in my preliminary experiments. I am now ready.''

Leor disappeared into the bowels of his machine. A single pure note, high and clean, rang in the air. Suddenly, on the stage looking out to the plain, there emerged a naked man, blinking, peering around.

Leor's voice, from within the machine, said, "This is Adam, the first of all men.''

And so the gods and the heroes came back to us on that brilliant afternoon in the middle twelves, while all the world watched in joy and fascination.

Adam walked across the stage and spoke to Chairman Peng, who solemnly saluted him and explained what was taking place. Adam's hand was outspread over his loins. "Why am I naked?" Adam asked. "It is wrong to be naked.''

I pointed out to him that he had been naked when he first came into the world, and that we were merely showing respect for authenticity by summoning him back that way.

"But I have eaten the apple,'' Adam said. "Why do you bring me back conscious of shame, and give me nothing to conceal my shame? Is this proper? Is this consistent? If you want a naked Adam, bring forth an Adam who has not yet eaten the apple. But—''

Leor's voice broke in: "This is Eve, the mother of us all.''

Eve stepped forth, naked also, though her long silken hair hid the curve of her breasts. Unashamed, she smiled and held out a hand to Adam, who rushed to her, crying, "Cover yourself! Cover yourself!''

Surveying the thousands of onlookers, Eve said coolly, "Why should I, Adam? These people are naked too, and this must be Eden again.''

"This is not Eden," said Adam. "This is the world of our children's children's children's children."

"I like this world," Eve said. "Relax."

Leor announced the arrival of Pan the Goat-footed.

Now, Adam and Eve both were surrounded by the dark aura of essential humanity. I was surprised at this, since I doubted that there had ever been a First Man and a First Woman on whom legends could be based; yet I assumed that this must be some symbolic representation of the concept of man's evolution. But Pan, the half-human monster, also wore the aura. Had there been such a being in the real world?

I did not understand it then. But later I came to see that if there had never been a goat-footed man, there nevertheless had been men who behaved as Pan behaved, and out of them that lusty god had been created. As for the Pan who came out of Leor's machine, he did not remain long on the stage. He plunged forward into the audience, laughing and waving his arms and kicked his cloven hooves in the air. "Great Pan lives!" he cried. "Great Pan lives!" He seized in his arms Milian, the year-wife of Divud the Archivist, and carried her away toward a grove of feather-trees.

"He does me honor," said Milian's year-husband Divud.

Leor continued to toil in his machine.

He brought forth Hector and Achilles, Orpheus, Perseus, Loki, and Absalom. He brought forth Medea, Cassandra, Odysseus, Oedipus. He brought forth Thoth, the Minotaur, Aeneas, Salome. He brought forth Shiva and Gilgamesh, Viracoha and Pandora, Priapus and Astarte, Diana, Diomedes, Dionysus, Deucalion. The afternoon waned and the sparkling moons sailed into the sky, and still Leor labored. He gave us Clytemnestra and Agamemnon, Helen and Menelaus, Isis and Osiris. He gave us Damballa and Guede-nibo and Papa Legba. He gave us Baal. He gave us Samson. He gave us Krishna. He woke Quetzalcoatl, Adonis, Holger Dansk, Kali, Ptah, Thor, Jason, Nimrod, Set.

The darkness deepened and the creatures of myth jostled and tumbled on the stage, and overflowed onto the plain. They mingled with one another, old enemies exchanging gossip, old friends clasping hands, members of the same pantheon embracing or looking warily upon their rivals. They mixed with us, too, the heroes selecting women, the monsters trying to seem less monstrous, the gods shopping for worshipers.

Perhaps we had enough. But Leor would not stop. This was his time of glory.

Out of the machine came Roland and Oliver, Rustum and Sohrab, Cain and Abel, Damon and Pythias, Orestes and Pylades, Jonathan and David. Out of the machine came St. George, St. Vitus, St. Nicholas, St. Christopher, St. Valentine, St. Jude. Out of the machine came the Furies, the Harpies, the Pleiades, the Fates, the Norns. Leor was a romantic, and he knew no moderation.

All who came forth wore the aura of humanity.

But wonders pall. The Earthfolk of the middle twelves were easily distracted and easily bored. The cornucopia of miracles was far from exhausted, but on the fringes of the audience I saw people taking to the sky and heading for home. We who were close to Leor had to remain, of course, though we were surfeited by these fantasies and baffled by their abundance.

An old white-bearded man wrapped in a heavy aura left the machine. He carried a slender metal tube. "This is Galileo," said Leor.

"Who is he?" the Procurator of Pluto asked me, for Leor, growing weary, had ceased to describe his conjured ghosts.

I had to request the information from an output in the Hall of Man. "A latter-day god of science," I told the Procurator, "who is credited with discovering the stars. Believed to have been an historical personage before his deification, which occurred after his martyrdom by religious conservatives."

Now that the mood was on him, Leor summoned more of these gods of science, Newton and Einstein and Hippocrates and Copernicus and Oppenheimer and Freud. We had met some of them before, in the days when we were bringing real people out of lost time, but now they had new guises, for they had passed through the mythmakers' hands. They bore emblems of their special functions, and they went among us offering to heal, to teach, to explain. They were nothing like the real Newton and Einstein and Freud we had seen. They stood three times the height of men, and lightnings played around their brows.

Then came a tall, bearded man with a bloodied head. "Abraham Lincoln," said Leor.

"The ancient god of emancipation," I told the Procurator, after some research.

Then came a handsome young man with a dazzling smile and also a bloodied head. "John Kennedy," said Leor.

"The ancient god of youth and springtime," I told the Procurator. "A symbol of the change of seasons, of the defeat of winter by summer."

"That was Osiris," said the Procurator. "Why are there two?"

"There were many more," I said. "Baldur, Tammuz, Mithra, Attis."

"Why did they need so many?" he asked.

Leor said, "Now I will stop."

The gods and heroes were among us. A season of revelry began.

Medea went off with Jason, and Agamemnon was reconciled with Clytemnestra, and Theseus and the Minotaur took up lodgings together. Others preferred the company of men. I spoke awhile with John Kennedy, the last of the myths to come from the machine. Like Adam, the first, he was troubled at being here.

"I was no myth," he insisted. "I lived. I was real. I entered primaries and made speeches."

"You became a myth," I said. "You lived and died and in your dying you were transfigured."

He chuckled. "Into Osiris? Into Baldur?"

"It seems appropriate."

"To you, maybe. They stopped believing in Baldur a thousand years before I was born."

"To me," I said, "you and Osiris and Baldur are contemporaries. You are of the ancient world. You are thousands of years removed from us."

"And I'm the last myth you let out of the machine?"

"You are."

"Why? Did men stop making myths after the twentieth century?"

"You would have to ask Leor. But I think you are right: your time was the end of the age of mythmaking. After your time we could no longer believe such things as myths. We did not *need* myths. When we passed out of the era of troubles, we entered a kind of paradise where every one of us lived a myth of his own, and then why should we have to raise some men to great heights among us?"

He looked at me strangely. "Do you really believe that? That you live in paradise? That men have become gods?"

"Spend some time in our world," I said, "and see for yourself."

He went out into the world, but what his conclusions were I never knew, for I did not speak to him again. Often I encountered roving gods and heroes, though. They were everywhere. They quarreled and looted and ran amok, some of them, but we were not very upset by that, since it was how we expected archetypes out of the dawn to act. And some were gentle. I had a brief love affair with Persephone. I listened, enchanted, to the singing of Orpheus. Krishna danced for me.

Dionysus revived the lost art of making liquors, and taught us to drink and be drunk.

Loki made magics of flame for us.

Taliesin crooned incomprehensible, wondrous ballads to us.

Achilles hurled his javelin for us.

It was a season of wonder, but the wonder ebbed. The mythfolk began to bore us. There were too many of them, and they were too loud, too active, too demanding. They wanted us to love them, listen to them, bow to them, write poems about them. They asked questions—some of them, anyway—that pried into the inner workings of our world, and embarrassed us, for we scarcely knew the answers. They grew vicious, and schemed against each other, sometimes causing perils for us.

Leor had provided us with a splendid diversion. But we all agreed it was time for the myths to go home. We had had them with us for fifty years, and that was quite enough.

We rounded them up, and started to put them back into the machine. The heroes were the easiest to catch, for all their strength. We hired Loki to trick them into returning to the Hall of Man. "Mighty tasks await you there," he told them, and they hurried thence to show their valor. Loki led them into the machine and scurried out, and Leor sent them away, Heracles, Achilles, Hector, Perseus, Cuchulainn, and the rest of that energetic breed.

After that many of the demonic ones came, and said they were as bored with us as we were with them, and went back into the machine of their free will. Thus departed Kali, Legba, Set, and many more.

Some we had to trap and take by force. Odysseus disguised himself as Breel, the secretary to Chairman Peng, and would have fooled us forever if the real Breel, returning from a holiday in Jupiter, had not exposed the hoax. And then Odysseus struggled. Loki gave us problems. Oedipus launched blazing curses when we came for him. Daedalus clung touchingly to Leor and begged, "Let me stay, brother! Let me stay!" and had to be thrust within.

Year after year the task of finding and capturing them continued, and one day we knew we had them all. The last to go was Cassandra, who had been living alone in a distant island, clad in rags.

"Why did you send for us?" she asked. "And, having sent, why do you ship us away?"

"The game is over," I said to her. "We will turn now to other sports."

"You should have kept us," Cassandra said. "People who have no myths of their own would do well to borrow those of others, and not just as sport. Who will comfort your souls in the dark times ahead? Who will guide your spirits when the suffering begins? Who will explain the woe that will befall you? Woe! Woe!"

"The woes of Earth," I said gently, "lie in Earth's past. We need no myths."

Cassandra smiled and stepped into the machine. And was gone.

And then the age of fire and turmoil opened, for when the myths went home, the invaders came, bursting from the sky. And our towers toppled and our moons fell. And the cold-eyed strangers went among us, doing as they wished.

And those of us who survived cried out to the old gods, the vanished heroes.

Loki, come!

Achilles, defend us!

Shiva, release us!

Heracles! Thor! Gawain!

But the gods are silent, and the heroes do not come. The machine that glittered in the Hall of Man is broken. Leor its maker is gone from this world. Jackals run through our gardens, and our masters stride in our streets, and we are made slaves. And we are alone beneath the frightful sky. And we are alone.

Before the Talent Dies

by Henry Slesar

Because he was a mutant, the Government decided he must die. They forgot about his power living on.

It was a prison.

It had carpeted floors and Queen Anne furniture. There was a high wall of leather-bound books, a humidor of fine cigars on the desk, a high-fidelity phonograph with a library of excellent recordings.

But Wayne Harkavy knew it was a prison. There were bars outside the narrow, heavy-draped windows, blurring the view of Pennsylvania Avenue and the Capitol dome. Outside the room's only door stood a civilian guard with a shoulder holster. Harkavy had been a well-privileged prisoner for six days. He had had few visitors, and most of them the medical officers assigned to perform the examinations. His needs were swiftly attended to; every meal he took was splendidly prepared, and expertly served inside the room.

He leaned back now and pushed aside the plate on the serving trolley. Then he poured himself a second cup of coffee, and sipped it thoughtfully.

Harkavy was a young man, with smooth blond hair and a sensitive, long-featured face. His skin was unlined and pale, and he didn't give the impression of physical strength. He was someone easy to ignore on a street or in a crowd, unless you happened to notice his eyes. The pupils were so dark and enlarged that he appeared to have no eyes at all, but almond-shaped, cavernous pits of strangely compelling darkness.

He was lonely, he was unhappy, and he was bored.

Yet even now, Harkavy didn't regret the decision that had brought him to Washington, D.C. Even now, when he sensed that the official attitude towards him was merely polite and slightly amused interest—perhaps even a touch of fear. The Medical Commission which had undertaken to investigate his extraordinary claims had gone about their examinations briskly and meticulously. But he had probed into the minds behind the gray hairs and gleaming spectacles and serene brows, and he knew that in the beginning they regarded him as nothing more than a somewhat gifted lunatic. He wondered how much they believed him now. Enough, at least, to have learned to shield some of their thoughts.

He smiled to himself, not humorously, and picked up the folded newspaper lying beside him.

The newspapers had been his greatest ally. Their lurid feature stories concerning his telepathic powers contained untruths and exaggerations, but they had served the purpose. They had made him a public figure, someone to be reckoned with. They had made it mandatory for some sort of official attention to be paid to his demands.

Harkavy unfolded the paper. His photograph was on the bottom of Page One, and the caption read: "COMMISSION REPORT DUE ON HARKAVY TOMORROW." The likeness was good; his eyes burned out of the newsprint. The story beneath the photo was less faithful. It hinted that the government was considering Harkavy with a view to national defense; that his sensational talents were being studied and catalogued for some vague military or espionage purposes.

He snorted, and dropped the paper to the floor.

When he heard the bolt sliding on the door, he turned to face his visitor. It was Dr. Esmond, the short, smooth-cheeked medical man who had been conducting his examinations. He was grinning, and Harkavy gently probed into his mind for the emotion that was pleasing him so much. He pulled away in disgust when he determined what it was.

"Well!" Esmond said, pulling up a chair. "Didn't mean to interrupt you at your meal, Mr. Harkavy."

"That's quite all right. I've finished. Perhaps you'd like a cup of coffee?"

"No, thanks," Esmond said quickly. "But I have good news for you this time."

"Oh? On my proposal?"

"I'm afraid I can't speak on that subject, Mr. Harkavy. As I've told you, the right people know all about the purpose of your visit, and keep daily contact with the reports of the Medical Commission. But whether or not they'll agree to your proposals about this eugenic foundation—well, that's a matter of state. I'm only a poor physician.'' He laughed.

"I see. Then how much longer must I stay here?"

"That's the good news I was talking about. We've completed our study, and you're free to leave anytime you wish. Tonight, if you like.''

Harkavy sighed.

"I thought you'd be pleased," Esmond said. "You've been something of a prisoner here, but I trust it wasn't too unpleasant. I'm sure you'll be hearing in a matter of a few weeks—"

Harkavy was startled. The smooth rhythm of the doctor's emotional pulse had suddenly broken as he spoke the last sentence. Lightly, Harkavy probed at Esmond's mind, but it seemed well-sealed against intrusion.

"Of course, no one doubts your ability as a telepath any longer, Mr. Harkavy. Your demonstrations have been most convincing. We're not equipped to explain them any more than you have been yourself, but I think you'd find our brainwave studies interesting. The output of electrical energy is astonishing; they would indicate that you have many times the active brain cell capacity of the, er, normal mind.''

Harkavy folded his hands in his lap. "I'm not interested in diagnosis, Doctor. I'm interested in application.''

"Exactly so, exactly so," Esmond beamed. "Well, you've probably read the articles about making you a spy, that sort of thing.'' He chuckled.

"I'm not interested in such things. There's more than mind-reading involved, Doctor. There's—understanding. If every human in the world had this talent of mine, the world might change overnight. Change for the better. That's what I've been trying to tell you. That's what I've been trying to tell the newspapers, too, but they preferred to feature the more sensational aspects.''

"You can't really blame them," Esmond said tolerantly. "Especially this transformation business. There's precedent for telepathy, Mr. Harkavy. But this other claim of yours, this power to change form—that's rather incredible.''

"I can do it," Harkavy said tonelessly. "It's merely another aspect of the talent. It's purely an hypnotic effect. By intensifying the strength of my probe, I can convince you or any other human being that I'm someone else. In every detail, every physical feature.''

"If you would only permit a demonstration—''

"I've explained that—I realize that if I demonstrate such a power, I would make myself a kind of monster in the eyes of the world . . . I would become something loathsome and nonhuman, something not to be trusted, something to be destroyed like a mythological demon—''

Again, a throb of ugly emotion came from the placid-faced medical man, and Harkavy looked at him sharply.

"You exaggerate,'' Esmond said smoothly. "You underestimate the intelligence of modern man. We're no longer stumbling in medieval darkness, Mr. Harkavy—we are ready to accept far more than you give us credit for.'' He laughed pleasantly, and stroked his chin.

Harkavy said: "I'd like to believe it.''

He picked up his coffee, sipped it.

Esmond watched him, and smiled.

Once more, Harkavy caught the erratic jump in the pulsations of the doctor's mind. He probed again, but Esmond's thoughts were still barred to him.

"And what about my proposals?'' Harkavy said. "Are they taking them seriously?''

"It's really not my province—''

"Don't tell me that, Doctor. This is your decision. If your Commission decides against my recommendation, it will not be forwarded to a proper Government agency. I can only hope your judgment will be based on the evidence, and not influenced by the opinions of certain pompous Senator friends of yours looking for publicity.''

Esmond flushed. "That's unjustified. But you'll have to understand that your request is an unusual one. It might result in much criticism if adopted without the most careful study—''

"Study?'' Harkavy slammed his cup down, his face showing anger for the first time. "What more study do you need? I'm not asking you for anything, Doctor. I'm offering you something! I'm offering continuation of a talent, a vital talent, a talent that may change this cockeyed world someday, if put to the right use.''

His face changed, and the anger in his voice was replaced with earnestness.

"Look, I realize I'm some kind of freak, Dr. Esmond. Just

like my father was. We were both born with this twist in us, and it made us different. But we can't afford to let the talent die, just because I will some day. Some kind of eugenic foundation *must* be formed to carry it on, to nurture it, to—" He stopped.

"It's a laudable idea," Esmond smiled. "Believe me, Mr. Harkavy, I'm sure you mean well. But exactly how practical this all is—" He spread his hands.

Harkavy stood up.

"I'd like to leave now."

"Very well. But you're sure you won't satisfy my curiosity about this transformation business? Surely you don't think *I'll* regard you as a monster."

The blond man looked at the doctor, and there was a new interest in his cavernous eyes.

"Perhaps I will," he said. "But in order to perform for you, Doctor, I'll need your complete cooperation."

"Of course!"

"Then you must release the tight rein you have on your mind."

"I don't understand."

"Of course you do. You've built a barrier against me, ever since you learned my telepathic talents were real. But if you wish to see me transformed, you must relinquish it."

Esmond looked doubtful, but his curiosity was too great. "All right," he said. "I'll do as you say."

Harkavy probed—gently, then more forcibly. Slowly, the patterns of thought in the physician's brain were exposed.

Death . . . said Esmond's mind . . . *Five or six days, aluminate metathycoline, indetectable . . . never notice it . . . coffee . . . inexorable process . . . superb plan, neatly executed . . . death by natural causes, five or six days . . . finis would-be superman . . . for the good of the world . . . death . . . good job . . . congratulations . . .*

Harkavy shut his eyes.

"What is it?" Esmond said. "What's wrong?"

"Nothing . . ."

Suspicious? said Esmond's mind. *Impossible . . . no way of detecting . . . tasteless . . . result heart disease . . . irreversible . . . no antidote . . . Harkavy . . . Harkavy . . . five to six days . . . death . . .*

Harkavy opened his eyes, and his mouth was grim. Then

he let the total impact of his probe take possession of Esmond's mind, until the physician cried out in shock and pain.

"Oh, God!" he said. "God, no!"

Harkavy smiled, with Esmond's mouth.

"You're *me*!" Shakily, the physician got to his feet. "You're me, Harkavy! Don't do this. Don't do it!"

"Don't do what?" Harkavy said, in Esmond's voice. "I mean you no harm, Doctor. I'm merely demonstrating, as you asked me to. Now see yourself as others see you."

"It's horrible! Change back, Harkavy, for God's sake, change back!"

"I could cause you a great deal of trouble, couldn't I, Doctor? I could kill you, for instance, and go on living your life. However, that may not be very long . . ."

"What do you mean?"

"Nothing," Harkavy said wearily. "Nothing at all." He probed again towards the short man with the sweating, smooth-shaven cheeks, breaking the hypnotic hold.

"Satisfied?" he said.

Esmond fell heavily into the chair, his trembling hands in his lap. "Yes," he said. "Now please go, Mr. Harkavy. Please go!"

The blond man looked at him for a moment, and then went to the door.

The guard outside tipped his hat. "Goodbye, Mr. Harkavy."

"Yes," Harkavy said. "Goodbye."

When he reached the street, he was surprised to find the April air warm, even sultry, as if Summer had come upon the city suddenly during his six-day confinement.

There was a small patch of greenery a few blocks away. Harkavy went to it, and sat down on a bench to let the sun warm his face and hands. He began to think.

The message he had read in Esmond's mind was clear. He had been officially executed. In five to six days, he would be dead. . . . Five to six days!

He must live them well.

Then Harkavy knew what he had to do. He was so convinced of its rightness that he spoke the words aloud.

"I must have a child," he said.

Laura

She woke up with a headache, and the blurred memory of an unpleasant dream. She sat on the edge of the bed and put her hands to her throbbing temples, debating whether she should ask her husband for an Empirin. Then she remembered that Gil wasn't in the opposite bed.

She went into the kitchen of her four-room apartment and made coffee. From the window, she saw that the weather had turned fair and warmer, but the sunshine failed to improve her spirits. The argument with Gil last night still rankled within her.

At ten-thirty, the doorbell sounded. She went to answer it.

"Hello, Laura."

"Gil! What are *you* doing home? I thought you were on the plane to Denver?"

"I called it off." Her husband came inside, avoiding her eyes.

"That's funny. You acted as if it was the most important business deal of the century, yesterday."

He smiled wryly. "I guess I was wrong."

"I was just having some breakfast," Laura said. "Would you like a cup of coffee?"

"That would be fine."

In the kitchen, Laura watched him from the corner of her eyes. He seemed oddly shy, or maybe the word was chastened. She felt sorry for him suddenly. She touched his hand tenderly and said, "Gil, I'm sorry. About those things I said last night."

His face was blank.

"I just couldn't help myself," Laura said. "We've only been married six months, Gil. Yet you've been away so often, I feel as if we don't even know each other yet. And when you told me about this Denver trip today—well, I suppose I just lost my head."

"Sure." He sipped his coffee.

"I always thought that a husband and wife—well, that after a while they wouldn't *need* words for them to know how they felt. I guess that's what's wrong with us, Gil. We just don't *know* each other well enough. . . ."

"I guess you're right," Gil said. He looked up suddenly and caught her eyes. They held her strangely, with a power she had never noticed before. "Sometimes, people need more than words, Laura. Do you know anything about this fellow Harkavy? He claims to be a telepath, that kind of thing."

"Oh, yes, I remember. That mind-reader—"

"No!" Gil spoke sharply. "It's not that crude, Laura. Harkavy is—well, he thinks the talent has a deeper meaning than just mind-reading. He thinks it's a way for people to understand each other as they never did before. . . ."

Laura laughed. "That doesn't sound like you, Gil."

Her husband put down the cup, and it rattled against the saucer. "Just one of my deeper moods, Laura. I won't let it happen again."

"No, Gil." She squeezed his hand. "Let it happen. I like you this way."

"Look," he said. "It's really a beautiful day. What say we have ourselves an outing? Walk around the park, maybe, or go sit by the river and watch the ships pass. Then we can just talk. Would you like that, Laura?"

"I'd love it!"

They kissed at the doorway before they went out, and she had the flushed, spirited look of a schoolgirl.

It was a magnificent day for an outing. They walked slowly through the sunlit park for two hours, and stopped for a late lunch at an outdoor restaurant. Then they walked westwards across the city streets towards the river, and sat on a bench and talked until the sun descended spectacularly into the water. Then they had a romantic dinner in a candlelit restaurant downtown.

By the time they returned to their east side apartment, it was after ten-thirty.

They sat on the sofa and sipped brandy from highball glasses. Gil put his arm around her, and she leaned against his shoulder.

After a while, he reached up and turned off the end-table lamp. She whispered: "I love you, Gil. . . ."

He put down his glass and kissed her. Then he took her in his arms, and picked her up from the sofa. She felt small and frail, and laughed sleepily, nuzzling her head against his chest.

He carried her to the bedroom door, kicked it open with his foot, and took her inside.

When he put her gently on the bed, the telephone rang.

"Damn!" Laura whispered.

"Ignore it," Gil said. "Just let it ring."

"Oh, Gil, I can't—"

"Please, Laura."

"You know how it'll bother me," Laura said, and reached over to pick up the receiver.

"Hello?"

The voice said: "Laura? You weren't sleeping, were you?"

"No. Who's this?"

"What do you mean, who's this? It's Gil, of course. I'm calling from the Statler, in Denver. Listen, honey, that damn fight we had keeps bothering me—"

She stared at the receiver, and then turned a wild eye to the man standing beside her.

"Hello?" The receiver quivered. "Hey, are you listening?"

"What is it?" the man by her bed said, putting his hand on her shoulder. "Who's calling?"

She handed him the instrument.

"Hello, Laura?" the voice said. "You're not still *sore*, are you? The least you can do is *talk* to me, for God's sake; these calls cost money—"

The man hung up.

"I'm sorry," he said.

She stared at him, without words.

"I met him at the airport," the man said. "That's how I knew about you. I had my reasons for this, believe me."

She began to scream, and Harkavy sent out a probe from his mind to hers, to stop the terror that was gripping her brain. He held her mind as a doctor holds a struggling patient, until it became quiescent.

Then he turned and left.

Bettina

The soft lights of the cafeteria were kind to the small diamond that flashed on Peggy's finger. Bettina bent over to examine the stone, her pretty red mouth an O, her eyes shining with either awe or envy or both.

Peggy waggled her fingers and said: "Of course, we probably won't get married until Fall. Ralph's got his pre-med to finish, and we want to make sure that there's some money in the bank in case of—'' She blushed.

Bettina, her slightly stringy red hair falling over her valentine-shaped face, said: "I'm really happy for you, Peggy. Honest I am."

"Thanks. But if *you* were a little smarter about men, Bettina, you'd be wearing a diamond, too. Ernie's diamond. If you only didn't waste so much time moonin' over Rex Corrigan and those other movie heroes of yours. Honest to God, for a girl *your* age—"

"Please!" Bettina said, her face a study in patient suffering. "I'm sure you'll be very happy with Ralph. But I'm going to wait until I meet somebody *I* can be happy with. It's as simple as that."

"And what about Ernie? He's been hanging around you now for two years—"

"Ernie's a nice boy," Bettina said.

"But he's no Rex Corrigan, is that it? Or haven't you been able to make up his mind for him?"

"Peggy—"

"Hey," her friend said. "Did you notice? He's gone."

"Who is?"

"That blond guy who was sitting at the next table. Didn't you see him? He was looking you over, but good. Looked pretty nice, too. No Rex Corrigan either, but kinda cute."

"Now you stop it, Peggy!"

"Okay, honey, okay. I'm just trying to get you to be realistic, that's all. There's a hell of a lot more Ernies than Rexes in the world, that's all I'm trying to say. But suit yourself." She shrugged and dug into her purse for her lipstick. . . .

Bettina walked towards home alone, enjoying the unusual warmth of the April air, feeling as if summer had come to the city. She even strolled three blocks out of her way to pass the Cameo Theatre, where Rex Corrigan's newest movie was being offered to public view. She had seen the film twice, and was almost tempted to see it again.

She stood in front of the six-foot cardboard display that featured the star in a characteristically dashing pose. His dark narrow eyes seemed to burn into her own, his handsome, humorous mouth was turned up in an understanding smile that might have been meant just for her.

Bettina sighed.

"I beg your pardon—"

She barely turned her head to face the man who had spoken to her. "Yes?"

"Have you seen this picture?"

The question was a leading one, and Bettina's automatic masher-defense was quickly organized. She turned and started to walk off. Sure enough, he followed her.

"I'm sorry," the man said. "I didn't mean to frighten you. If you'll just let me explain—"

"Say, listen," Bettina said, and turned.

When she saw the man's face, its effect, Medusa-like, was to freeze solid her expression of indignation and surprise.

"My name's Corrigan," the man smiled—a smile on a handsome, humorous mouth, with an understanding that was unquestionably meant only for her. "Rex Corrigan. That's why I was curious about your reaction to the movie."

"Rex Corrigan," Bettina repeated.

"Yes. Listen, this is rather difficult to explain. But perhaps we can go somewhere and talk. It's really very important to me."

"Talk?" Bettina said stupidly, her mouth open.

"Yes. There are some questions I'd like to ask you, as part of a personal survey I'm making. I guess you could call it that. Would you mind very much?"

"Oh, no. No, I wouldn't mind."

"Fine," Rex Corrigan grinned.

She didn't recall how they finally arrived at the corner bar, didn't remember the contact of her high heels upon the pavement, or what the waiter looked like, or even the name of the dimlit cocktail lounge they were in.

"I feel like I'm dreaming," Bettina said. "I know that sounds corny, Mr. Corrigan, but that's just how I feel."

"You're just being flattering," he said. "But as you can see, I'm no phantom. I'm just another guy." He smiled engagingly.

"But you're not. Oh, but you're not! You're *Rex Corrigan*. Why, Peggy and I were just *talking* about you. I was just telling her how much I—" She stopped.

"I know this is presumptuous of me," the man said. "As a

matter of fact, it was my agent's idea. He felt that I was getting too far removed from the public, that I should go out and talk to them myself. That's what I've been doing for the past few days. But I must admit—this is the most pleasant part of the assignment yet—"

He reached across the table and held her hand. "You're a lovely girl, Bettina. Did you know that?"

"How did you know my name?"

"Oh, didn't you mention it?"

"I guess I did. It's Bettina Anderson."

"Pretty name. Do you live in the city, Bettina?"

"Oh, yes. Down on 12th Street. It's a sort of a rooming house, but very nice."

"Can we go down there and talk? I'd really like to know you better, Bettina. Of course, if you don't think it would be proper—"

"Oh, no!" Bettina said quickly. "It's perfectly all right, Mr. Corrigan. I'd love to have you!"

"Good. But you'll have to forget about that Mr. Corrigan stuff. My name's Rex."

"Rex," Bettina breathed. "I'll be ready to go in a minute. I just want to go and freshen up—"

She was gone ten minutes. When she returned, her red mouth was redder, her curly red hair more neatly arranged, her cheeks glowing under the retouched makeup.

Bettina's apartment on 12th Street was very much like Bettina. It was small, sweetly attractive, and perhaps too overdecorated.

She found it incredible that Rex Corrigan himself was seated on her sofa, thanking her cordially for the glass of warm wine she offered him, patting the plump cushion beside him and inviting her to sit beside him.

She accepted the invitation, and didn't even murmur when Corrigan's arm slipped easily around her shoulder.

"Of course I meet a lot of women," he said, in answer to her question. "Perhaps that's just the trouble. Or maybe I meet too many women who've forgotten who and what they really are. But you're someone different, Bettina. Different for me, anyway. You're someone I can find very appealing. . . ."

"Oh, Rex!" Bettina said. "You can't really mean that."

"Of course I mean it." His hand moved across the back of

her dress. She hardly felt the light pressure of his fingers as he undid the top button.

Corrigan moved his other hand to encircle her waist.

"Rex . . ." Bettina breathed.

He kissed her, and she appeared to swoon.

The sound that came at the door wasn't a knock—it was an assault. Bettina jumped, and looked at Corrigan in surprise. The hammering noise continued, and then the unlocked door was flung open, to slam against the wall with an alarming explosion of wood on plaster.

"What the hell!" Corrigan said.

"Ernie!" Bettina cried.

The assailant of the door was a young man with a round, bespectacled face and unruly red hair. The face had a quality of homely innocence that even the scowl couldn't conceal. It was a black scowl, a murderous scowl, and his head was lowered like an enraged bull.

"For heaven's sake, Ernie," Bettina said primly. "What are *you* doing here? I *told* you I was busy tonight. I called you *especially* to tell you I was having a guest."

"Some guest!" Ernie spluttered.

Corrigan said: "Now look, friend—"

"You shut up!" The redhead swallowed hard and turned to the girl. "Who do you think you are? Betty Grable or something?"

"Ernie!"

"Now wait a minute," Corrigan said. "When did Bettina call you?"

"About an hour ago. Said she was coming here with Rex Corrigan. I thought she was off her nut, only now I see what's going on. You thought because you were a big-shot movie star—"

"An hour ago?" Corrigan frowned and looked at Bettina. "I thought you went to powder your nose?"

"I just had to call Ernie," she sniffed. "I wanted him to know about it."

"So that was the idea." Corrigan smiled wryly. "All right," he said. "I'm glad I could help, Bettina. In any way."

He got up and went to the door.

"And don't come back!" Ernie yelled after him. "Don't come bothering my girl! You hear that, big shot?"

"I heard you," Wayne Harkavy said. Gently, he probed at Bettina's mind, and was sadly amused by the emotion he read there.

Della

When her father began rattling his newspaper and clearing his throat, Della sighed wearily, knowing what was coming next. It was the Senator's preamble to a pronouncement, and he would expect her to agree with him. She looked towards the mahogany doors of the library and thought about making a tactful escape, but the Senator was already turning around in the big leather chair near the fireplace and saying:

"Of all the damnable things. You been reading about this Harkavy character, Della?"

"Yes, father."

"A madman, no doubt of it."

"I suppose so," Della said. She ran her fingers over the blond streak in her black hair. The fingers were thin and fragile, like fine porcelain. They were like the rest of Della; beautiful and breakable.

"And the worst part is," the Senator said, "the press is taking him seriously!"

"Yes, father."

"Say." He stood up and came to her side. "Shouldn't you be getting dressed? Or aren't you going to that party with Freddy?"

"I'm trying to make up my mind," Della said.

"Want to see the paper?"

"No, thanks."

"You ought to read it. A lot of crazy things are happening in this world, and you just don't seem to care."

She smiled up at him, but not in the way a daughter should.

"The new rebels, father?"

"All right, the new rebels." His broad face flushed. "I know what you're thinking, Della. You think I'm nothing but a political posturer. But you're wrong. I'm serious about this new rebels business. I think it's a great threat to this country.

I'll keep on fighting 'em as long as I've got a place to stand on Capitol Hill.''

"Is Harkavy one of your new rebels?"

"Maybe he is! How should I know? As I pointed out in my remarks to the press, he's got crackpot ideas, and we don't have time these days for crackpot ideas. There are all kinds of rebels around, and we've got to flush 'em out. Whatever disguise they're wearing.''

She took the paper from his hand. There was a photo of Wayne Harkavy on the second page, his cavernous eyes staring out from the paper.

"And what kind of rebel is he?" she said.

"I don't know. But just read his statements about this telepathy business. Wants to start some kind of government foundation, continuation of his powers, something like that. Wants to make the whole damn country telepathic, so we can all go around reading each other's minds.''

"Sounds like fun." She laughed.

"It's all nonsense. Oh, not that he can't do what he claims. That seems to be well-documented. Our friend Esmond headed up a medical commission to examine him; they say he's genuine enough. But when a man with a power like that gets ideas, he's dangerous! Listen, what's more important than the privacy of the mind? How would you like somebody sneaking around in your thoughts?''

Della considered it. "Not much," she said. She got up from the chair and smoothed her skirt over her flat hips. "Maybe I will go to the party," she said. "I feel stifled—''

"Splendid," the Senator said. "I was hoping you would, Della. Do you a world of good. Now go call Freddy before he gets himself another girl.''

"All right, father.''

Della went to the door and opened it. Sherry, her father's new wife, was just coming in, her mink coat swirling around her young body.

"Oh, hello," she said airily, with a toss of her blond curls. "Going out, Della? How nice. . . . Your father inside?"

"I'm here," the Senator said.

"Have a good time, dear." Sherry planted a sisterly kiss on her cheek. She was two years younger than Della.

"I will," Della said.

*   *   *

She went up the graceful marble stairway to the second floor. In her bedroom, Della sat at the dressing table and stared at her white, thin-featured face in the mirror for a long time. Then she caught her breath, and went to the window to let in some of the balmy April air. She breathed deeply.

After a while, she lifted the white telephone by her bedside and dialed Freddy's number.

"Hello, Freddy? This is Della. Look, I've got this awful headache, and I don't think I can make the party tonight. Do you mind very much?"

She listened patiently to his protests.

"I'm sorry," she said. "Call me tomorrow, if you can. I'm going to try and sleep it off."

When she hung up, she went to her closet, and changed her dress for a black turtle-neck sweater and plaid skirt. Then she sat at the dressing table and put light dabs of color on her pale face.

Her father and Sherry were still behind the closed doors of the library, so she had no trouble in making the front door without being seen. She walked briskly to the garage in back of the house, and got into the low-slung Italian-built roadster that had been last year's birthday gift.

She drove at a moderate speed until she reached the city limits. She drove faster after that, until the growl of the foreign car became a constant roar. She only slowed down when the red glow of a neon sign appeared in the distance. The sign said: Gentleman Jack's.

The main room of the roadhouse was cluttered with chrome-plated tables, with soft lights set into the centers. The bar was like the prow of an ocean liner. There weren't many patrons.

She went up to the bar and sat on a stool. The barman was at the other end, pouring a drink for a blond man with dark eyes and a long, sensitive face.

When it was her turn she said, "Hello, Gus. Is Jack around?"

"I saw him upstairs an hour ago, Miss. You want I should call upstairs?"

"In a minute. Give me a drink first. Martini."

She drank her drink, conscious of the blond man's eyes on her. She ignored him, busy with her own thoughts. When she was finished, she nodded at the bartender.

"All right. Maybe you better call him. Tell him Miss D. is here."

"Okay, Miss." He picked up one of the two bar telephones and spoke quietly. He put it down with a sigh. "Sorry, Miss. Mr. Collins says he's busy."

"What does that mean?"

"Search me, Miss."

She glared at him, and hopped off the stool. She threaded her way past the tables to the front, not noticing that the blond man was gone.

There was a man sitting in her car.

"Jack!"

"Hello, baby."

"But I just had the bartender call you. He said you were busy."

He grinned at her. His face would have been handsome, but too many of the bones showed beneath the thin, dry skin. "I just didn't want to advertise," he said. "We don't need publicity, do we?"

"No, I guess not." She climbed into the driver's seat.

"Let's go to my place," Jack said. "You know the way."

She nodded, and turned the ignition key. They drove for ten minutes, in silence. When they pulled up at the small, ranch-style house off the main road, he had some trouble locating his key, so she used her own, the little gold key he had made for her.

"That's the first time, baby," he grinned. "First time you ever used that key. Had a change of heart?"

"Let's go inside."

They sat on the curved sofa in front of the false fireplace, and Jack made them both a drink. When he sat down, he slipped his arm around her shoulder, and she pushed it away.

"Don't—"

"What's the matter? I thought maybe we were getting someplace."

"You thought wrong," Della said tightly. "I just wanted to ask you a favor, Jack."

"Sure, anything."

"I want you to help me locate somebody, somebody important—"

"I don't get you."

"There's a man named Harkavy, maybe you've read about

him. He came to Washington a few days ago. He's a sort of mind-reader.''

Jack looked at her with narrowed eyes. "So what? You know this guy?"

"No. But I want to, Jack. I want to a lot."

"Why?"

"I can't explain. Maybe I don't know why myself. But I have to meet him—"

He looked at her.

"I'm Harkavy," he said.

"What?"

"I'm not Jack, Della. I'm Wayne Harkavy. I've made you think I'm Jack, because I thought I saw something in your mind—"

"What are you talking about?"

He probed out and enveloped her mind, gently at first, and then with graduated force. The shock of it jolted her and she screamed, shutting her eyes and putting her balled fists to her face.

"Oh, my God!" she said, staring at the blond man.

"I'm sorry," Harkavy said. "I had to do it this way, Della. I didn't want to trick you, but I have so little time."

"You were at the bar—"

"That's right. I left when I realized that Jack wouldn't be coming downstairs, that he was tired of trying to break down your resistance. I saw that in the bartender's thoughts when he picked up the telephone."

She smiled bitterly. "I thought it would happen. But I don't care."

"You know," Harkavy said, "your father doesn't approve of me. And I suddenly got the idea I'd like to see if his daughter agreed with him. . . . But I wonder why you wanted to meet me."

"I don't know." She looked into the fireplace. "I just had to find you, talk to you. I've been reading about you, saw your picture in the paper."

"And what do you think about what you've read?"

"I don't know what to think. It bothered me, all those things you said. I wanted to find out more, find out all about you, what made you the way you are—"

"I don't know myself," Harkavy said. "I just don't know, Della." He touched her hand. This time, she didn't resist.

"You're so strange," she said. "Your eyes . . ."

"I'm a freak."

"No!"

He pulled her to him, and she didn't resist.

"You're reading my mind," she said.

"Yes," Harkavy answered, gently.

Esmond

Dr. Esmond stepped out of the taxi in front of Jefferson Hospital, and his tip to the driver was generous. He was feeling particularly well today. The weather was balmy, the cherry blossoms were burdening the Washington trees, and his good friend the Senator had honored him by letting him be among the first to know about the Senator's new grandchild.

The hospital staff recognized him as he entered the front lobby, and bowed him into the elevator that led to the maternity floor. The Senator himself was the first to greet him as he stepped off the car.

"Nice of you to come," the Senator said. "I believe you've met my son-in-law, Freddy Holmes."

"How do you do," Esmond beamed, pumping the hand of the vacuous-faced young man by the Senator's side. "And congratulations. Understand you have a fine, bouncing baby boy."

Freddy giggled. "I dunno. I haven't seen him bounce yet, but I guess he's okay."

Esmond chuckled. "And how is Mrs. Holmes?"

"She's fine," the Senator said gruffly. "Della's fine. A little depressed, maybe, but that's only natural. You know how it is—"

"Of course, exactly so."

"They'll be showing the infants in about five minutes," the Senator said. "We can go have a look at him. He's the image of Della."

"Oh, I dunno," Freddy said, looking injured. "I sort of thought he looked like me, a little."

The Senator laughed, and pounded his son-in-law's back.

"Let's say he favors you both. Now if you'll excuse us for a moment, Freddy . . . I want to speak to Dr. Esmond. Alone."

Freddy got the hint, slowly. "Oh, certainly."

When he was gone, the Senator growled: "Nincompoop!"

Esmond said, "Something you wanted to tell me, Senator?"

"Nothing very important. It's this Harkavy business. Since his death last year, there've been some questions concerning that proposition of his. The issue is still unresolved, and it's leading to criticism. I think the best thing we can do is for the Senate to hold a brief, formal hearing on the matter, get a report from the Medical Commission, and close the books for good."

"Very well," Esmond sighed. "If you think that's necessary, Senator. You'll have my full cooperation."

"Good!" The Senator lost his businesslike manner and became the proud grandparent again. "Now I think we ought to take a look at the new baby. You go first, Doctor; it's right down that way. I want to stop in and say hello to Della."

Esmond went down the hall in the direction of the Senator's gesture. There was a clean sheet of glass facing the hospital nursery, and a nurse wheeled a crib with leather sides to the glass, and then reached in to remove the bundle it held.

The tiny face that appeared at the window had a startling effect upon the doctor. He didn't know why; the features of infants always struck him as gross distortions of humanity. But this face was different, with its black, cavernous, almost adult eyes, its long features, its straggly blond hair.

He stared at it, and saw no resemblance to the sandy-haired, gray-eyed, vacuous-faced Freddy, or to the black-haired, fragile Della. There was a resemblance to another face he knew; a face he saw in brief, unpleasant dreams.

He looked away, troubled by his irrational thoughts, and was glad to see the Senator coming his way.

"Well, Doctor? What do you think of my grandson?"

"Lovely child," Esmond said feebly. "Very lovely."

The Senator put his face to the glass and made silly noises at the infant.

"I think he looks like Della, don't you? Thank God for that, anyway. Couldn't stand another Freddy around the house."

"What?" Esmond turned around.

"I said he looks like Della. Same blue eyes, same dark hair. What do you think?"

Esmond looked again, and there was ice in his spine. The baby's hair was curly and black. Its features were round. It's eyes were somewhat small and brilliantly blue, and before they closed in sleep, they seemed infinitely wise. . . .

Brood World Barbarian

by Perry A. Chapdelaine

*Captured as a youth, this barbarian became Earth's champion.
Then he found his fight had just begun.*

I

Sand, fear, blood and gawkers—the trivia of a thousand
arenas on a thousand planets in a thousand ages. I am an
athlete of great proportions, strength and skill—one who kills
by order of the gawkers or my master, whichever calls first—
and I am one soon to be killed.

She came yesterday on the day of the games after I had
neatly decapitated the former champion of the Sabre worlds
by means of wrist pressors only. Declared the season's Grand
Champion, head garlanded with red-brandy vines, chest proudly
extended against chest band, I swaggered away from the
game's space on wrist pressors only, as if to say, *Look at me,
you weaklings. I have bested your best. Now who is master
and who is slave?*

Their sun of a thousand yellow rays beat down on my back
as I pushed my way across the game's space into the lower
ramp to my cage, expecting there to relax with wine, song
and the caress of the opposite sex, as, I suppose, has been
done by my kind for ages past.

Then she came. The lights burned brightly as the crowd
surged past our flux cages. The public was not satisfied with
the death, pain and sadism of the arena, but demanded that
my cage—all our cages—be kept open to public gathering.
Like my cellmates I was a freakish one-G animal, trained by
means of gravitylike pressor and tractor beams to tear and
hew at others.

She walked with her father. He, merely a seven-tenths-G
animal, was human and shaped like myself. He had a strong
smile, cropped gray hair and rugged features set off by

317

sunken eyes, a bulbous nose and bright, straight teeth. Oh God! How I hated that animal—that all-powerful, all-great leader of the Sabre planets. Trevic Strenger and his family walked in public gathering to view *me*, this season's Grand Champion, in my "natural" habitat!

First came the retinue of sycophants and guards. Cloaked in tight plastic of weblon to nullify pressor and tractor rays, they stationed themselves to one side of my cage, holding the crowded path open for the dictator Strenger and his family.

I threw my wine outward to vent my disgust and anger, helplessly watching as it struck the surrounding magnetic field, to be sucked inward and downward instantaneously as the powerful field latched onto minute iron particles in the liquid.

They didn't yield an inch nor did they acknowledge my act by even a twitch of the mouth—except Trevic Strenger. He passed his hand back to his beautiful wife and gently tugged her forward so as not to miss the show, just as he did the night I was taken, five years ago, on my rocky planet.

I came from an unusual brood and, had I known then what I now know, even their fleetest hunters would have gone back to the ship empty. My brood cell—brothers, sisters, mother and father—had left me for the day. I tossed rocks at the passing pack animals below our cave, not aware of the hunters swooping over me, preparing to entangle me in their rays and beams. I spat at Trevic with the thought, and he pulled his head back to laugh, just as he had the day I was brought, bound and struggling before him.

Oh, I was more than a barbarian from the Planet of Rocks. I was an educated barbarian, for their pleasure would not be enough unless they knew that inside of each gladiator lay a trapped, cunning and scheming modern mind—a mind equal perhaps even to their own in knowledge, yet trapped by their science and their orders to fight on a barbaric level of their choice. I spat again when I thought of their educators and how facts were poured into my animal brain day and night, indiscriminate facts. Did you know that a man named Plato once said, "Know thyself"?

I spat again in honor of such useless information.

His wife's face strained at her husband's sadistic laughter and I imagined that she disapproved. Then I vowed some day to kill Trevic Strenger with my own bare hands. I watched the daughter.

She pushed through the crowd and I saw perfection. I had known many other women, slave women thrown to us along with victory wines and victory songs. I had seen none with the grace, the litheness, the color, the shadows of this one. Daughter of a mad king and a radiant slave-queen, she was— and her eyes seemed to glow with a kind of empathy for me I had never before known outside of the brood chamber.

I opened my gnarled fists, dropping my cups, and sprang to the field's side. My chest band pulsed with heat as its magnetic field fought against the lines of force. I strained my body mightily to bring it closer to her side until only inches separated us and my metal chest-belt glowed cherry red from hysteresis.

Across those billions of lines of flux sprang the stronger invisible rays of my love. Her blue eyes met my gray ones and mine clung while the world dissolved around us. Though worlds of differing customs and a powerful kingdom lay between us, I vowed to reach her as deeply and strongly as I had just vowed to kill her father.

Would Patricia Strenger respond to me? Could a barbaric brood-world creature reach her more refined heart? Though doubt assailed my thoughts, I clung to my twin emotions of hate for her father and my newborn love for her.

"Barbarian," he said, "you must come to terms with your simple emotions. In you lie only the pure emotions—hate, love, anger—not any refined, civilized, subtle and complex ones."

Snarling, I threw my drinking vessel at him, only to see it stop in midair, then retreat backward from the invisible wall. He did not even laugh at my anger.

"Our people crave heroes," he continued evenly. "You may be a great one. With gladiator success come civilized opportunities which would normally be denied one of your kind. You may soon see complete freedom, then complete citizenship with all the rights and privileges of a Sabre citizen. Shall we drop this silly feud now?"

Hate boiled in me like a hidden volcano and I did not answer.

Trevic Strenger paused silently to watch my heaving chest,

then added: "After all, barbarian, had it not been you who was captured, another from your brood world would now be standing where you are—another would now be offered full education, citizenship and opportunity for worldwide adulation."

I could not control my emotions. So complete was my hatred for this man who had torn me from brood home that my whole muscular body convulsed as I spat directly at his face.

Without change of tone in his voice he said, "Tomorrow I will introduce you to Urut of Ewit, a two-point-five-G champion."

I sneered, as I had yet to learn of either Ewit or Urut of Ewit and therefore lacked comprehension of his plans for the morrow.

Trevic narrowed his browless eyes to watch as he bored in with his varied rapierlike pieces of knowledge, "Urut can crush rocks on your planet between his two hands. On his world a day lasts seven of yours. A day's work to him means seven times twenty-four or one hundred and sixty-eight of your hours. Can you fight him even one of his days, Grand Champion?"

I knew the answer. Urut's skin would be as tough as rock, his stamina far beyond any normal one-G human's bounds, and his strength would be like ordinary muscle taut against the pressure of invariant hydraulic presses. I would most surely die tomorrow. I knew it and Trevic Strenger knew it. But I spat again in barbaric defiance.

II

I awoke in the morning to the sounds of tractor and pressor duels around me and knew I had overslept on this, my last day. According to my educated brain, thousands of years before a certain B. Franklin had said, *Early to bed and early to rise will make a man healthy, wealthy and wise.*

I paused briefly in disgust at giving thought to such revolting associations. Why had not my mind been permitted to remain that of a normal brood-world barbarian?

I bound my two pressor beams to my wrists and my two tractor beams to my ankles and gyrated my body through the endless contortions of tension and countertension so necessary to the modern gladiator.

I pulled my leg muscles to their limit of endurance, slowly but surely overcoming the tractor-versus-tractor configuration. Then, and so rapidly that the eye would be unable to follow, I twisted my body muscles to push pressor against pressor until, biceps bulging, I heard the faint clink of wrist plate against wrist plate, signifying I had once again overcome the hidden power of my death machinery.

Only then did I eat lightly, my good nature returning slowly as I felt a sense of well-being.

Again I passed my body through every one of the hard-learned exercises designed to test to the utmost one muscle against another, passing through the last just as the aurora at the side of my cage indicated that I was to move out into the arena.

To avoid death from chest-band pressure, as my cell slowly contracted around me, I moved forward, following the energy glow. There, under the beat of their merciless sun, was the open arena, its sand, its hate-driven gawkers, its blood of the past and psychic blood yet to flow.

Pushing my way toward the ellipsoid's nearest focus, I then squinted to see the squat hulk of Urut of Ewit at the far end.

The crowd of blood-mongers surrounding our large cage, except at floor level, howled on my entry. Knowing I was the handicapped, they screamed for Urut's blood which, could I but arrange it, would be most happily furnished them—for it was his blood or mine.

Almost I felt sorry for that hulk—short, broad of torso, leg and arm; flat-headed with parrotlike lips; humanoid of form and lizard-hided of skin.

My survival was at stake and my mind swiveled back to life-and-death calculations. He had the sun. Trevic Strenger would have seen to that. He had more. As strong as I was, my muscles were but one-G-trained. As quick as I was, he would act faster. Very probably I would not find any weak spot in his natural armor, whereas to him I was but an anthropomorphic jellyfish.

In a gladiator's daze I calculated my survival paths

overlong—already he was swimming toward me with tractors and pressors working together.

No sooner had I tensed to meet his first attack than he was beyond me, already rebounding from the magnetic wall.

I pushed both tractors outward at the widest angle of my legs, unconsciously reaching for the bedrock which I knew to exist there. Both arms were folded against my chest band to place pressors in their firmest position. He struck like a ten-ton boulder rolling down the mountainside. My muscle-banded legs vibrated with the pressure and my reserves soon evaporated.

His right tractor could reach around to the side of my head to hold while his left reached to my right side and I knew scant instants stood between me and decapitation.

More in instinctive desperation than for any reason I switched pressors down low and slipped my body under his. He rocketed overhead to slam mightily against the far side of the arena's shield, chest band glowing red, while I twisted around from back to belly on the sand floor.

Still no strategy came to my mind. Can a pygmy subdue the elephant? Can the ant topple the pedestrian? Can a simple one-G human resist for long the heavy-planet man under one-G conditions?

I concentrated every bit of thought and will on my survival. Brute force against inhuman force was my only strategy.

He sliced through the air again and I dodged. He brought both legs into play to cut me in two and I again dodged. He tried the ploy of alternating leg tractors and arm pressors and I eluded him. Not until he sat above me in the overhead tractor-look position did my strategy bloom. Though only tiny moments of time were involved, my thoughts ran as follows.

Why can I dodge this lightninglike man so easily? How is it he misuses his speed so much? Could it be that he is unused to fighting in a one-G environment—that this is his first experience on such a light world? If so, his timing must be too fast and I am not really eluding him. He misses me and then I dodge.

Using tractors, pressors, fingers and toes, I crawled excruciatingly slowly across the bottom until his tractors caught bedrock below and I could slide out from under.

He jabbed down with pressors but this time I was ready. I kicked my tractors into his squat belly and followed behind his moving arms with my own pressors. He somersaulted then and pinwheeled before catching himself.

Now I had the trick. Every time he moved I swung either tractor or pressor, catching his motion from behind and enforcing it. I used his own strength and speed against him until finally, during one complex maneuver where his tractors reinforced his pressor movement, I doubly reinforced his action with my pressors and tractors and his two arms snapped.

The gawkers screamed and howled for blood but I had other ideas. Already exhausted, I doubted my ability to penetrate his thick hide, though he lay helpless. More important to me than his destruction were the death of another and the love of a third.

Urut floated around and around on tractors, frantically twisting his body to redirect his dangling arms and their pressors. I shot forward and spoke for the first time.

"Urut. Cooperate with me and live to fight another day."

In a high, squeaking voice he warily asked, "What is it you want?"

"I want out of this cage and you can help. What they do to me outside and where I go should be of no concern to anyone but me—and no one will suspect your help in what will follow."

"What do I do?"

"I am going to use both pressors and tractors to propel myself through the cage. Only if I go very quickly will my chest band remain sufficiently cool for me to survive. I am going to place myself within range of your tractors and with their help, and the quickness of your legs, I can crash through. Will you do this, Urut?"

"But you will die if we are not quick enough. Why should you place yourself within my control when you have already won?"

"Urut, my friend, you and I have no quarrel. We have never had. We fight only to survive—now let us help each other live. I want freedom and revenge. You want your life. Why should we not bargain?"

The crowd began the death chant.

"Blood—blood! Kill the hulk! Kill the hulk—"

I could tell from their frenzy that soon something must be done or their passion would be on all of us. Urut could also sense it. The idea of mutual help was not yet fully integrated in his mind but he nodded.

"May your mud-nest be pleasing!"

I swung to the other side of the arena to begin my plan.

From hundreds of previous fights I knew every inch of arena bedrock and I used the knowledge to advantage. I flung wrist pressors at each point behind me and ankle tractors ahead of me, accelerating swiftly in line with Urut. The crowd hushed and Urut patiently moved his hulk into position for the throw.

I swung past his body swiftly. More swiftly still he lashed onto me with both tractors webbed together. I felt the fringe of their beams pass my arms, then my head and thick neck absorbed the pull and I was flung up to and against the magnetic field surrounding us.

My chest band glowed and part of my body tried to wrench itself backward—but still onward and through I passed. I flew over the heads of those in the first tiers, then plowed into the next ranks.

Heads popped; chest, arm and leg bones snapped. I arose amidst the gore of dead and dying gawkers. Their hush changed to screams. Pandemonium reigned.

A small number in the crowd rushed to the exits but the majority stood shouting, "Champion! Champion! Champion!"

Over and over again their acknowledgment echoed—like the beating of surf on the rocky shores—until my very bones vibrated with the chant. Never before had one escaped the magnetic arena and the crowd was wild with enthusiasm.

I should have trusted to my judgment of their emotion. My next move was utterly foolish. I swung out to reach for Trevic Strenger, hoping to crush his thick neck between my pressors. Above and below and all around me flew his weblon-encased protectors.

High over me were the platforms of heavy rays, while on each side were the smaller hand weapons—but I had agility, speed and coordination far beyond those of any group of Strenger guards. I had one tactic which would catch them by surprise. My muscles were trained to use beams but my mind was trained to use muscles. With those I bowled over the first group, tumbling weapon and guard onto the tiers below.

III

Fighting one-G animals in an open environment and with full knowledge of their beams and rays, I was more than a match for them all. But no matter how I hacked and hewed, how cleverly I spilled their heavy weapons, I still could not reach Strenger. I can see him yet in my memory, sitting back, watching with faint amusement as I tossed his guards here and there like feathers—only to find more guards taking their places.

The gawkers shrieked with pleasure over this new form of entertainment and I turned and ran, dashing up beyond the seat rims, finding space between the roof and two structural pressor beams to squeeze my bulky body through.

Outside the arena I fell several hundred feet before my rays caught bedrock below and I could twist myself across the pylons and roadways of this ungodly civilization to search for the city's end and silent peace.

Behind me, perhaps a mile away, the guards boiled out from the arena area and I swept down low below their sight level. Another mile and another and another—when would the city end?

Then little by little trees, parks and farms replaced city blocks, until only farm land and tall mountains lay ahead. That first night I slept in peace among the wild foothills of this strange world, free for the first time since being taken from my brood world. In my dreams lived the face of Strenger—but also in my dreams was the sad, melancholy face of Patricia and my body longed for both in their proper place.

The morning sun no longer seemed so hot and sultry. The air seemed fresher and the planet, even with its strange flora and fauna, appeared friendly. I speared a small carnivore with a tractor beam, drank fresh water and ate the raw meat, then washed and rested while I thought.

Were I to go back to the city my large bulk would easily identify me as the Champion. My muscles would be impossible to hide in this civilization.

Farmers I knew about because of my helter-skelter education—I knew, for example, that some Sabre planet genius had called farmers stewards of the state. Could I trust the farmer not to turn me in for one of Strenger's high rewards? I thought not.

Though I searched my brain for other informative tidbits on this society, I concluded that only the mountains and hills would hide me.

I removed my tractors and pressors, fastening them to my chest band by means of twisted fibers, then unhesitatingly I strode off toward the snow-capped mountains ahead.

Day followed day and night followed night. I easily speared game with tractor or pressor while I followed the animal trails from elevation to elevation. My body stayed in trim and my hate gradually oozed outward as my path came closer to the appearance of rocky plateaus similar to my brood world—all, that is, except the tiny, reserved corner of my emotions which repeated my need over and over.

Kill Strenger.

The rocky path wound upward and I trod closer to the snowy peaks, my body now covered with animal skins for warmth. Slowly the rock turned to snow, then snow to mixed snow and ice, glazing white while I moved onward and upward, never hurrying, never slowing.

Miles of ice were crossed and only once did I have to pull myself from a deep crevice by means of a tractor beam. Finally the downslope snow line was reached on the mountain's other side. I stepped with relief into familiar rocky plateaus, fully expecting a similar leisurely pace downward. Then it happened.

It was Strenger again. I was caught. His men dropped the cage neatly over my body and turned the field on high. He came from behind the rocks, with his bold smile and just looked, hands folded against his chest.

"The gawkers now love you, barbarian, and we can still make a truce. Come, I invite you to bury your hatred. You are one of the greatest of our world's champions—over all time—and it saddens me, your waste. By popular demand I can now release you from gladiator status to become a free citizen. But how can I permit a hate-driven barbarian to roam free among us?"

I showed my feeling by emitting a low growl. I clenched my fists, imagining his thick neck in my hands.

Trevic beckoned his retainers to lower the cage. He found

a convenient rock upon which to sit while he pleaded his case again with me.

"Know this, barbarian. Your use of tractor and pressor beams can be traced wherever you go on the Sabre planets. Even so, you have no further need for them, no matter what your decision."

He motioned with his finger and my cage began to tighten until my chest band squeezed me from all directions. Weblon-encased tools drove through my shield and skillfully cut my beams from my chest band, after which the cage was restored in size.

"Your chest band is made of the world's strongest metal. It cannot be removed without special scientific tools. Wherever you wear it, you are subject to immediate seizure and capture. Do you still wish these marks of the gladiator?"

My tongue finally loosed.

I spoke in an angry voice. "You tore me from my brood world without my permission, mad king, and I shall one day kill you!"

Unable to reason with me further, he beckoned his men forward. My cage was lifted by weblon devices and I continued my trans-mountain flight as his captive.

IV

They towed me farther into the mountains, disregarding any inconvenience inertia might make to my caged body. My chest band glowed again and again as my body bounced off the cage's sides.

Perhaps fifty miles inward, we followed another rocky path down to the valley of our destination. Below us, laid out in neat geometrical array, were the energy cages of thousands of humans.

Walking like tiny bugs between each cage were the weblon-protected guards who passed out either food or water or else the whip—whichever seemed most appropriate for the moment.

A scrap of random information forced its way into my conscious mind—forced, I suppose, by the association of the antlike men far below. Only a century ago someone named G. Harcel had said, "Men are tiny bugs once they have seen their souls."

Could any information be more useless at a time like this?

High on one side were the mine tailings, glistening red from the evening sun. Immediately behind those tailings stood the factory, puffing out streamers of noxious gases which, I eventually learned, represented part of the physical and chemical wastes resulting from separating weblon metal from the ores found deep in the planet's crust.

My cage was tugged next to a larger one. The aurora along the side, signifying an opening in my cage, burned brightly and I hurried across into the larger. Trevic Strenger paid his last respects then.

"Enjoy your new lessons, barbarian. When you have learned more, find a way to contact me. Perhaps we may yet be friends."

He walked away and I flung myself furiously at my magnetic shield.

My routine was simple. Each day, every day, I was chained to a row of ten other prisoners who walked two miles along the valley floor and three miles downward on sloping shafts to our work area. Here alternating tractor-pressor beams were given to us, each a model considered too large for a single human to support.

Two of us would hold the mining tool, aiming it at the green streak of weblon metal running throughout the enormous, partly natural and partly man-made caverns. The alternating tractor-pressor forces acted swiftly on the cavern walls, grinding all but the impervious weblon metal to thin mono-molecular layers.

Follow-up crews sucked up the dust-mixed metal and transported it back to the surface, where further chemical and physical processes separated the pure weblon metal from the mono-molecular dust layers. Large ships transported the purified weblon to other industrial locations for treatment into forms and shapes for use wherever beam neutrality was required.

It was obvious from the beginning that I was different from the others. Most were political prisoners with only puny muscles. Most were gregarious creatures, friendly with one another, some counting days until their release while others were hopelessly resigned to making the best of a lifetime under lock and chain.

Though I was as sociable as anyone on my brood world, here I snarled and spat until, like one with a great scabrous disease, I was avoided by all.

Enemies were easy to make. The chip on my shoulder was as big as a sturdy oak, balanced precariously and waiting patiently for anyone to tip its trunk toward the ground.

It took only one or two short tussles for my strength, agility and training to show.

We were fed in line and normally the distance between my chained figure and others in my line was the maximum length of chain between us. One day a particularly fast, aggressive person bumped against my broad body in his eagerness to get nourishment. I swung around snarling, grabbed his neck between my giant paws and began to squeeze the life from him.

Only the whips of the guards and the combined pulls of other prisoners dragged me from his body while life still throbbed on him.

Another day my reflexes were sufficiently quick to grab the whip from a guard as he swung its tip toward me. I turned the whip around and nearly lacerated the guard to death before others could stop me.

That was the day all of them, prisoners and guards alike, combined positive efforts against me. That I was not only asocial but beyond the restraints of any ordinary prison had now become obvious.

In the first attempt at my life one of the heavy tractor-pressor beam generators was tipped on me from a height of about fifteen feet. Fortunately my gladiator-honed senses caught the movement and I easily sidestepped and safely evaded what seemed to me was the generator's slow fall. I didn't catch on then.

The next time a small, wiry prisoner pushed his body against mine in such a way that I tumbled backward into the yawning black chasm below us. I twisted and caught the edge of the chasm's rim and quickly drew myself upward.

Already the guards had moved my attacker beyond reach, passing him quickly to the surface to become part of a different and unreachable work crew. It was then I began to suspect.

One day the guards left our work crew. All became quiet and I looked up from my work to see every eye staring at me.

Some had grasped rocks and stones while others grabbed the neck chains lying nearby. Slowly the group closed in on me, eyes glazed and muscles taut.

I moved swiftly to my gladiator's stance and waited quietly. Every sense on the alert, I could place every one of the nine around me. How little they knew of my training. None had access to gladiator power beams and I was now faced with a purely two-dimensional problem.

The rocks came first and I easily dodged them. Then, in quick resolve, all nine swooped in toward me. I rushed through the circle, grabbing the nearest one holding the chain. Lifting him from the ground I flailed the group, though the chain was still held by two others. Those poor misguided point-seven-G fools had no concept of a gladiator's training and strength.

I flailed until it seemed that none survived. But two had climbed above me during the melee to redirect the mining beam at my body.

I am quick and well coordinated but even I could not move as fast as their fingers on the machine's switch.

Quite probably the alternating tractor-pressor beam had never been used on human flesh around these prisoners before. They certainly had no knowledge of the effect of the beams when used this way. I stood my ground and let the waves of current ripple through my body, neither resisting nor helping the flow of alternate tugs and pulls, and my gladiator-trained body as well as my water-based tissue withstood the strains well. Every piece of metal I wore—including my hated chest band and the newly attached neck band—disintegrated into mono-molecular powder as fine as any created in the weblon mines. I was truly free of their hated instruments of capture now.

I leaped to the machine's top and from there crushed any attackers' heads like eggshells. Now only I, the mining machine and the solitude of the caverns remained in this branch of the tunnel. I wondered how long I had before the guards returned.

Behind me lay certain capture. Directly ahead of me lay granitic rock, but to my side lay the deep, perhaps more dangerous chasm. What choice did I have?

I picked up the mining tool and chain, using the latter to tie the tool to my back. Then slowly, using trained fingers and toes, I picked up my way down the steep crevice's side, using the slightest of indentations along the wall to support my own two hundred pounds and the additional two hundred on my back.

Down I crawled. Down until my fingers and toes were sore beyond description—down until I reached the first ledge. Here I rested, conserving my strength for the next lap downward. Again and yet again I traveled downward, resting from ledge to ledge, sometimes finding one only when it seemed that my last reserves of strength had been reached. Would I never reach the bottom?

I dropped pebbles down the long, dark, silent tube, hearing only the sibilance of air sweeping around its path—never hearing splash or bounce of its final strike. It was then I paused to consider.

It was highly doubtful that I could go up again, and going farther down seemed useless. Now was the time to unlimber my mining instrument.

Then I pointed the alternating tractor-pressor inward against the chasm's wall and powdered my way forward. The first layer powdered at my feet and swept outward into the chasm below. Soon I was scrabbling with hands and knees to force the dust backward behind me. Fortunately the mono-molecular layers filled less space than their more complex forms and air from the chasm swept in behind me as the stone ahead powdered to the floor.

Mile after mile I bored ahead. When tired, I rested. Then I bored again for miles. Days passed. Even my gladiator's physique suffered from lack of nourishment. My body became sluggish, my mind tormented by memories of the sneering laughter and red-spurting throat of Trevic Strenger and by the graceful body and full lips of his daughter. The latter vision filled my mind to overflowing until my muscles responded.

I pressed on, even forgetting which way was up and which down and distrusting my fatigued senses for knowledge of either direction.

Dust filled my mouth, my eyes, my ears and, it seemed, even my mind, until I could go no farther. With one last effort at survival I shoved my poundage, and my machine against the wall, lurched forward. Under sudden acceleration both the machine and my body fell outward and down as the thin wall between my tunnel and the opening broke through.

My body revolved around and around. Centrifugal force flung my arms and legs outward as I plunged through a narrow fissure.

I strained my back, neck and belly muscles to bring my turning to a stop but did not succeed. Light glimmered several hundred feet below and my frustrated mind focused on it until my spinning made it appear a whole galaxy of light particles swinging around me in tighter and tighter circles. My mind let go.

My back and head hit the water first. To this day, I am unaware of the extent of the true damage done to me in the fall.

V

How long did I lie there? Weeks? Days? Minutes? No one will ever know. I do know that hundreds of thousands of scraps of their educative process passed through my mind, only one of which I remembered on regaining consciousness.

" 'The time has come,' the Walrus said, 'to talk of many things: Of shoes—and ships—and sealing wax—Of cabbages—and kings—' "

Could any thought have been more out of place and foolish or less useful?

On returning to consciousness, I found my body to be whole and undamaged but bruised terribly. Water was washing over me. Some trickled into my open mouth and some laved my nose and ears, trailing my hair downstream like fine wires extended.

My right arm lay under me, touching the rocky stream bed below. My left arm lay partially submerged, the hand resting on a shallow bank.

My legs were upstream, resting on rock. My eyes were pasted shut by the dust around their rims. Soon I became aware of the mining tool's soft hum and the gentle tugging and pulling of my flesh under its influence.

I waved my right hand around in a circle and felt the broken chain with which I had attached the mining tool to my chest. I scraped mud from my swollen eyes, opened them and found I could see. Phosphorescent particles emitted sufficient photons for me to view my surroundings dimly. The mining instrument was on and pointed steadily in my direction.

I drank until my shrunken belly was fully distended, then lay back to rest and to sleep peacefully under the gentle vibration and hum of the tractor-pressor beam. Probably never before in history had a human being been subjected so long to the rapid alternate pull and push of the tractor-pressor beam. Would its effect be harmful? I didn't know.

When I awoke I crawled again to the stream, taking my fill. Below me I could see the shining shapes of water creatures, among them the unmistakably welcome shape of a fish. I struck with my right hand and grabbed the unwary creature tightly. Its cold flesh furnished my first nourishment in what seemed like months but may have been only days.

Again I slept, then ate and slept again. Later I walked over to my mining instrument and turned it off.

I felt light-headed, but oddly healthy and not in the least tired. I attributed this to the effect of poisons manufactured by my own system under unusual stress and at the time had no idea of the damage done to my body. I could have acted no differently under the conditions. Suffice it to say that I felt unusually alert and full of a sense of well-being, though attributing all of these characteristics to normal results of excessive stress.

I began my long walk along the stream hopefully toward light, air and freedom, packing the mining instrument on my back once more. The walls of the stream bed became narrower. Soon they reached a point where my broad shoulders could no longer squeeze through. My way forward was finally halted by granite blocks.

With almost a swagger of confidence, certainly more than the moment warranted, I unlimbered the tractor-pressor and blasted my way out.

The ship waited for me at my exit point. Of course—use of tractor or pressor beams anywhere on the planet could be easily followed by Strenger and his men.

I turned too late to reenter my cavern retreat. A rock bounded from my head and I fell forward to lie unconscious once again.

When I gained consciousness, my feet were trussed together, my arms tied behind my back and my head ached. I was in a cabin. Two gnarled men sat in front of me, alternately eating and gawking. Was I back in the arena? Were these my new keepers?

I strained at the bonds on my hands and feet but the ties were stronger than I. I humped my body to a sitting position and looked at my two captors, hatred washing through me in waves.

"Pretty, ain't he?" the one on my left said to the other.

"Needs a bath though. Think we could oblige him?"

Both stopped eating. One tied a drag rope to my legs and hauled me outside the cabin to a nearby spring. My flesh was torn and bleeding from the sharp rocks and sticks over which I was dragged and my head was still dizzy from the blow on my head, but I uttered no complaint.

They pulled the rope end over an overhanging rock until I was dangling upside down over the water, my head scant inches from its surface. I took a deep breath, expecting the worst. It came. I was dunked under water seven or eight times, probably saved from drowning only by my one-G physique and high lung capacity.

I was dragged back into the cabin, trussed up against the post and forgotten for the time being.

They finished their dinner, checked various instruments lying around the cabin, then turned back to me. The older one—gray-haired and with a stubble-covered chin—was the first to speak directly to me.

"You might as well tell us why you were snooping around our private weblon mine. It's your only chance of saving your life."

My mind, now quite confused, failed to function as quickly as it might have under gladiator conditions. I said nothing.

The one with black hair and coal-black eyes bent his bulk over me and said, "If you are a government agent we will let you go free on another planet. It's to your advantage to tell us the truth."

I coughed some water from my burning lungs and said, "I am a gladiator. I have no name."

"All gladiators have names," the first one said. "Besides, what would a gladiator be doing using pressor-tractor equipment in these mountains? Come on, fellow—if you value your life—tell us the truth."

I strained every muscle of my body to burst the bonds. At last my body sagged. I knew a spasm of futility before I lost consciousness again.

I came to inside their ship. The interior was pure luxury and there I learned how the gawkers had searched for me in vain. I was one of the most popular heroes of all Sabre history—my life was public property and not even Trevic Strenger, dictator over all, would dare to violate it openly.

But no trace of me was found until my mining equipment had been sensed by these law-violating miners near their illegal mine.

I was kept bound inside their ship while they checked and double-checked my now clean-shaven features with pictures taken during my gladiator days. Convinced I was truly the escaped Grand Champion, they struck my bonds, not knowing how close they were to true death at the moment.

I soon learned that everywhere I was loved by the people. But I felt certain that I would still be unsafe anywhere on a planet ruled by Trevic Strenger and his type.

I stayed with the mining ship, hoping to get back to my brood world one day. But how could I flee when my two goals of hate and love were here? Not only would deserting them be unnatural to my brood training—it was unnatural to the unusual state of my biology, still deeply hidden from my conscious processes.

Still, in violation of every instinct, I left civilization behind to flee toward the Planet of Rocks of my birth. Seven long light-years lay ahead, meaning months of travel. Hundreds of thousands of strange worlds would be silently, unknowingly passed as we sped onward. How many contained brood worlds? How many had produced two-and-a-half-G monstrosities like Urut of Ewit? How many contained Patricia Strengers or Trevic Strengers? How many had educated barbarian champions and how many even held the humanoid form?

The days passed slowly. I became acquainted with the two outlaws. An objective study of their patterns of behavior gave me a certain recognition of their finer shadings of emotions. All three of us were outside the law but these two still subscribed to certain ethics and species-assisting patterns of behavior—much as each of the brood helps another for the sake of survival of the whole.

Unlike the brood, they had days when their minds were dominated by mixtures of pure emotions. They certainly exhibited pure forms of overt anger and calm complacency but they also showed fine shadings of moroseness and languor. I began to recognize emotional subtleties and, for the first time, began to question my pure hatred response to Trevic Strenger. Was he really as bad as I had projected or did he, too, have comprehensible feelings and behavior-motives mixed into his treatment of me?

One day I noted the outlaws' deep concern for one dial on the ships's panel. Daily the dial's indicator swung upward and daily other instruments were checked and rechecked against it. Presently I read their concern—patrols were on our path. A whole fleet crawled toward us, closing in slowly.

There are no maneuvers that can deceive a determined fleet. Our only hope lay in an act of some god who, out of the goodness of his being and the emptiness of space, would reach outward and hand us some device or means by which to escape.

To make matters worse, I had no place to stand and make the fight mine, using my gladiator's training. I felt trapped like an animal and could almost feel civilization's magnetic cages crush through my bones again. My chest, where I had worn the metal band of servitude, had healed and was covered with keloids. I wanted no more slavery.

One slim hope remained to me. My captors searched the directory for any kind of planet with breathable air. Then they began long-range perturbation analysis of surrounding stars, hoping to spot planets within range.

One bright yellow sun on our pathway seemed to offer hope and they quickly adjusted our route slightly to pass near its planets. We swung inward in a giant cycloidal loop, and an automatic analysis assured us that one planet, fourth from center, had breathable, oxidizing air.

But now our range was within the patrol's striking power and their beams reached out for hundreds of thousands of miles to vibrate our craft ceaselessly.

Though weakened structurally, we recklessly approached the planet's atmosphere, dropping swiftly into its density to skip and skip again as the craft was buffeted by the force of its own passage. Now weakened further and red from heat, it plunged at even sharper angles until its tail section broke off and our front portion spun uncontrolled toward the water below.

VI

The miners must surely have been killed in the plunge. At the time I attributed my survival to my gladiator's training and my powerful physique. I had bunched my muscles together and dived out of the ship an instant before it splashed.

I hit hard, maybe as hard as Urut had hit me. Maybe a little harder—I don't know. In any case my body sustained the shock and I swam to the surface, spotting land perhaps ten miles away. Toward this I swam and just before sundown reached the sandy beach where I lay in exhausted stupor.

The jungle ahead of me was unrecognizable. Whether fern or animal, flora or fauna, I could not tell. Only experience would show.

Food was my immediate concern. Next came shelter and water. I rose, rather unnaturally recovered, and strode confidently into the strange organic configurations ahead.

Suddenly my emotional complex dropped from open elation and overwhelming optimism to complete apathy. Death would have seemed a pleasant release. Striving always with my gladiator's training and the stubbornness born of brood world, I consciously searched everywhere without success—no recognizable cause was creating my emotional void.

Down the scale of emotions my feelings plummeted—and slowly and silently the fibrous matting of the jungle undulated toward me. It was white with streaks of gray running through it and gave the appearance of some broad-patterned, supine foliage which moved like a leech. Who could tell what it really was? I wanted to back away but my apathy was too deep. I stood in an abandonment of despair, even squatting so the slimy thing could more easily flow up my body.

My apathy was dense—as dense as thick glue—and the thing nearly covered my back. I squatted lower to let it cover more of me, then felt its acid trickle over my skin. Apathy prevailed—nonetheless, under the stimulus of pain, my gladiator's instinct snapped my body erect and my hands and feet flung the horrible thing from me.

Acid had etched the skin all over my back, neck, arms and shoulders. Just as suddenly as the skin had been destroyed my body began its preconditioned, rapid repairs, though at the time I was too busy to give the phenomenon thought.

It was not yet safe, however. The things flowed toward me as before and my apathy was as leaden as before. Why should I move when all of life seemed so useless, so hopeless? W. Shakespeare did not quite say it, but my mind, sunken in depths beyond conscious control and mired in the facts of the educators, paraphrased it as: "O mighty barbarian—dost thou lie low? Are all thy conquests, glories, triumphs, spoils, shrunk to this little measure?"

I will say this about the paraphrase—at least there was some relation between its semantics and my condition of the moment, though there was little else to recommend it.

Yet my fighting instinct had been aroused and at another level of my being I exploringly fought back. First I strove for excitement and the adrenaline lift which accompanies it. Then I strove to force enthusiasm into the cellular portions of my body—to no avail. Whatever force the thing had, my manufactured enthusiasm was not the answer.

I let my body freely wage swift endocrine war as my emotions tore from cheerfulness through antagonism, overt anger, covert anger, resentment, fear, grief and apathy. Nothing manufactured by my body for my body helped.

As the thing crawled closer I switched my endocrine war outward against the whole world of loops and snakelike whorls around me, raging within my soul but nonetheless subtly spouting torrents of emotion outward through some unseen orifice of my stilled body.

It was when I again hit the apathy band that the thing stilled. Each time my body broadcast apathy, it retreated a little farther. My body had instinctively found the key to survival on this planet. The thing's emotional load lifted from my body. Again I felt lighthearted and full of a sense of health, though I still poured tons of black apathy at the crawling thing now scurrying away so rapidly.

I turned back to the tangle of organic misshapes and little by little ferreted out its secrets. The ropy black serpentlike form dangling from above responded to fear. The flapping fanlike objects responded to overt anger and the other dangers responded to other emotions either singly or in combination.

No single entity could easily be identified as food, but now that I was learning to walk through the jungle by casting my emotions externally here and there, I followed the first stream upward with hopes of learning what was edible and what was not. Clearly the acid- and base-forming entities were inedible. Time after time I succumbed to all their emotional complexities, learning only after their acidic or basic sting to fling them off and redirect my emotions outward. Time after time, my skin rapidly healed itself.

Order began to appear from the chaos surrounding me. I watched the slinker root, a slob of jellylike flesh that looked like a weathered tree-root from my Planet of the Rocks, as it flushed out its quarry, a small blob of milksac covered with horny projections.

Using almost pure fear, its emotion swept outward to cover growths of pink and purple velvety layers of some vertical materials. From the bottom of this growth the milksac animals—if that's what they were—rushed directly toward the jellylike growth.

There they were easily held until the chemical base dissolved their vital layers, after which they were absorbed into the attacker's system.

For lack of better hunch, I followed the next jellylike sack. It captured a victim. I tore it away from its grasp, using my hands for the act of tearing and my emotions for the act of neutralizing the strange beast.

I placed the juices of the injured beast on my tongue and found them sweet—but some poisons are sweet. I didn't know the difference but my body did—or so I thought at the time.

I chewed and swallowed and stayed healthy. Looking back on the experience now, I wonder. Did my body adapt to the alien food or did my instinct determine what was food and what was not?

I ate my way across thousands of miles of outrageous growths and forms as I traveled from coast to coast across one great continent. Occasionally I hid from search ships— the Patrol would not rest until our bodies were discovered, I reasoned. I left no daily trail by use of tractor or pressor beam and my human body could hide among the fibrous, gelatinous, oozing, slinking, stinking mess around me.

I crossed two mountain ranges, walking high above the life-plateau, living for weeks on air, water, fat and determination. Lonely pools of water were to be found at these higher levels.

The longer I survived in that emotional jungle the more grip I had on my own emotions—until I could instantly turn up the emotion of hate against Trevic Strenger or the passion and hunger of love for his daughter.

I soon was aware of his ships less often and rightly assumed their surveillance of the planet to be more or less precautionary and automatic.

Now I wanted the ships down, but only under my own terms. The problem was to attract their attention in order to make them a bit suspicious—but not overly so—and to trap the trappers.

Fire is common to most planets—but during a year's survival on this one, I had never seen a conflagration. I assumed that the patrol would also have observed this obvious fact. Could I make the unnatural happen by natural means?

The unnatural did happen but in a different way. I found a large piece of metal with fused pieces and burned spots. Either our ship or another had caused this piece to be flung across the continent where it burned and fused on entry into the atmosphere; but whatever the true case, I had the part I needed to attract Strenger's persistent watchers.

Above the organic line, which is also above the rain line, are mountains, thin dry air and pools of water resting in bowls of rock lined with streaks of nearly pure lead. No weather or natural disturbance occurs at these heights or does so only occasionally. The pools are remnants of another era in the planet's ecology.

Before placing my plan into action, I had much work ahead and hoped my body was equal to its task. First, I found the pool nearest to the organic growth line. The pool I chose featured rocks jutting overhead. From one of these overhangs I tossed in more stones until the pile below the water's level was nearly to its surface.

I then lowered a large organic membrane to this new rock

level under the surface, folding it into a kind of loosely formed bag with its corners and sides above water. I tied the corners together loosely and tied the other end to a rock overhead.

Within the newly separated layer of water I slowly lowered the spaceship's metal part, keeping one end high above the rock projection and lowering the other end to the bottom of the water-filled bag.

I tied another piece of organic rope to the top of the metal structure and looped its end to a rock some seven feet back from the water's edge. Then, carefully, I pulled on the metal, bending it farther and farther until it just touched a streak of partially oxidized lead jutting from the banks of the pool. Again and again I pulled the metal until I was in absolute control of its motion and could touch the lead streak with the ease of long practice.

The next day I drove hundreds of organic entities ahead of me, using only the apathy band, for I had learned that this emotion was associated with acid-bearing life. Up the rocks they tumbled and rolled, gyrated, squirmed and crawled until the pool was reached.

When the pool was made sufficiently acid by these monsters, I went after the base-bearing kind, using covert hostility for the drive, and I also drove them into the pool without qualms. There the the bases partially neutralized the acids, forming a serviceable electrolyte.

How many beasts of which kind should I drive to create the huge battery I wanted? I did not know. Neither did I know about the permeability of the membrane sectioning off some liquid from the rest, nor the difference in electrolytic potential between the streaks of partially oxidized lead crawling along the pond's basin and the unknown metal now jutting above the pond's surface. With so many unknowns I could only try—perhaps to fail and try again.

After rest I pulled the metal down to the lead streak by means of the attached rope and was rewarded by observing a weak spark as the gap nearly closed. I returned to the herding of more creatures. Night came and the following day and I still herded creatures to the pond, testing the spark size with every new batch.

I hoped that the spark of light could be seen from a

spaceship at night—or at least that the electromagnetic waves radiating from the source would alert the patrolling monitors. I had not figured on the quick response which actually occurred.

I was driving my last batch of creatures ahead when the ship came. I crouched behind the rocks to watch when the rays hit and I was stuck rigid to the spot.

Through instruments of science or intellect, possibly both, they had outwitted me again. I was incapable of moving a muscle.

The ship I had seen was the decoy. Another one had landed somewhat earlier to trap me.

VII

There were two of them, one on either side of me, and they held me fast with heavy portable pressors. I strained with every bit of muscle tissue to no useful end.

All around me the life I had driven from the jungle below boiled in confusion and from that movement came my idea. I summoned my energy and emoted apathy, driving the group toward one of the men. He faltered, then fell under the onslaught. The other also slumped. The pressors slipped from me and I ran to each man in turn. One pressor I threw into the acid pond. The second I focused on the ship, wedging it between two rocks.

I turned to the fallen men. One was encrusted with an acid which had eaten deeply. Almost dead, he would be of no help to me. The other was visibly shaken. I ran my own emotional output back up and down the scale several times until I could key into his basic confusion, then brought him up to a comfortable emotional level.

"How many are in the ship?" I quietly asked.

"Three. But who are you? What are you doing alone on this surrealistic planet?"

Now it's strange, but up to that point I had not thought of myself as a name. On the planet of my birth I was just one of the brood and could easily be identified by smell or appearance. On the Sabre planet I was known as barbarian or Champion or Grand Champion. Here on an alien planet, under an alien sun, I was again being asked a most fundamental question whose answer I could not give.

"Are you on regular patrol around this planet?" I asked.

"Yes."

"What are your duties?"

"We are to observe and report any slightest irregularity in shape or phenomenon or behavior over the whole planet's surface."

"How long has your patrol had the planet under surveillance?"

"Better than a year. Ever since outlaws were seen to approach the planet."

I moved the patrolman closer to the pressor beam so that I could more quickly reach its controls if I needed to.

"What did you expect to find here?" I asked.

"None of us knows. We merely take orders. We sighted the pond's heat activity by auto-infrared surveillance and watched you at work. It was then we laid our trap to capture you and find out what was happening."

"Are you a follower of the gladiators?" I asked.

"Who isn't?" he replied. He looked up expectantly.

"Then you are familiar with the disappearance of your Grand Champion over a year and a half ago?"

He looked me over from top to bottom before answering, then said excitedly, "Why, I believe you are he. Yes—you must be—"

His emotions bounced from my artificially maintained level to his interest and sincerity.

"If you are indeed the Grand Champion of a year ago— you should know that your status is that of a free man. After your successful fight with Urut of Ewit and your escape from the arena you were declared free by the enthusiasm and will of all the people. How did you get here?"

At one time I might have snarled and growled at this representative of their civilization. Now my mind froze as my conscious portion became aware of my own lack of emotional response to him. I listened politely and rationally to his talk. My mind, though, buzzed with consternation. Was I wrong to hate Trevic Strenger so? Was their world really all bad? Would I have been better off on the Planet of Rocks, chasing rock wolves and fighting with others of the brood?

Then, against all the instincts which make up a brood-world barbarian, I freed the man and docilely followed him to his ship.

The way back to Sabre planet was filled with wining and dining in the best of the patrol tradition. Word went out that the Grand Champion had survived shipwreck on a horribly inimical planet, and space for parsecs around was charged with the news.

My fame had spread—and my prowess increased. I had been the Greatest of Grand Champions and had so been declared on official gladiator roles. And only Trevic Strenger knew my true status but even he was not certain how I had come to be found on the forlorn Planet of Emotion.

VIII

We were like two giant computers battling one another. Trevic Strenger knew that every move I made might lead inevitably to his death—for I still meant to keep my vow. I knew that anything he did might cause my destruction directly or indirectly. He held the power, the education and the experience.

I was the Great Grand Champion, beloved of the people and not entirely unused to facing the thought of daily danger. Urut of Ewit was now champion, for no ordinary one-G humanoid had been able to withstand his stamina, strength and speed once he had grown experienced in one-G conditions. Between Urut and myself the people gawked as only gawkers can.

When I entered the gladiator stands, the gawkers stood and cheered for fifteen minutes. On the other side, far away from my grasping hands, Trevic Strenger sat surrounded by his sycophants and guards. Did I still wish him ill? I genuinely did not know. I knew only that I meant to kill him.

Urut entered and the crowd applauded with enthusiasm. Today was his show as well as mine. Then Trevic began his clever move against me. He arose, stilled the crowd, announced that it was only fitting that the newest and best of champions, Urut of Ewit, be challenged by the world's Great Grand Champion.

As he knew it would, the idea caught the gawkers' imagination and they howled their approval. I was committed before my barbaric wits could form a defensive reply.

Only by sustaining the people's good will could I be safe from Trevic, and he had cleverly made use of the situation. I had to fight. I flung off my civilized accouterments and leaped into the arena, no longer bound by chest band, free to enter and leave whenever I wished.

I caught the tractor and pressor beams, tying them quickly to my ankles and wrists, and waited for Urut to move. He looked at me sadly from his heavy-lidded eyes and parrot-shaped mouth and I knew he had no desire for what he felt was sure to come.

His first blow, with pressor, was light and I knew he was pulling his attack. As any other one-G gladiator would be, I was clumsy, slow and weak compared to Urut. I was also out of training. At any time he could have decapitated me or ripped my body to shreds, for his timing was perfect.

For purpose of show, I'm sure, he let me cartwheel him several times and the gawkers thought my response would soon build in duration and quality. I knew and he knew that we were mismatched and that he had the advantage. Survival on the Planet of Emotion had taught me that emotion, too, can be a club if only one knows how to generate it. I had much practice and while Urut had his will with me—now under tractor lock, then under pressor throw—I sought the key to the emotions in his humanoid bulk.

My endocrine system worked rapidly, generating pure emotions from apathy to grief, resentment to fear, boredom to happiness. None worked. I then tried combinations as I had learned to do on the Planet of Emotions. Once I saw Urut falter briefly and pause to stare from glazed eyes. I thought then I had the key but lost the combination.

My powerful physique was tiring fast. Urut had pressors on opposite sides of my body and tractors at right angles, on opposite sides. I was being simultaneously squeezed and pulled on different body sections. I could almost feel cartilage tear and muscle tissues pop.

The gawkers were yelling for blood as I continued my search.

I caught the emotional combination to his alien form and Urut paused again briefly. I drove my emotional wedge in and he faltered. He stumbled and fell to his chest as I slowly rose from the sand, giving every appearance of pushing back on pressors and pulling back from tractors still clinging to me.

The gawkers screamed.

As my body strengthened, my emotional output rose and Urut twitched in agony. I have no idea what the emotional content meant to his way of life; but it was a powerful antidote to his physical superiority.

By the time I reached his side, my body was fully recovered and, using every ounce of my two hundred pounds of muscle, I might have been able to decapitate him. I looked to the crowd and asked their pleasure and I thanked the great brood-God that nearly all screamed for his release.

The gawkers yelled, stamped their feet and clapped their hands together. For them the solution had the appeal of a well-laid plot. How else could they have both their Great Grand Champion and the newest Champion to carry on with their future entertainment?

The day of Strenger's trap ended and I rested in my public-donated apartment that was lined with trophies of my earlier slave-status wins. Now, I thought, it was my turn against Strenger. My plan took form.

During my planning stages and the impasse to follow the faulty educative process to which I had been subjected caused A. Zlinsky's phrase to repeat through my mind. It ran: "To the wise go words!" A meaningless utterance. I tried to suppress it. It wouldn't go away, so I found myself trying to rationalize it. I did need a true and honest education to compete with Strenger—maybe that was what Zlinsky's silly quotation meant. I don't know. But eventually it led me directly to more efficient and better organized educators.

The habit pattern my mind had developed of tracing all knowledge through quotations or simulated quotations whenever possible was disturbing. My new educators explained that I would slowly lose the habit with time if I made a conscious effort to do so and that it arose from faulty use of the educator when I was a gladiator trainee.

Time passed. I became more acclimated to civilized behavior patterns. My emotional control was nearly perfect and I could more easily read the emotional patterns of others. Were it not for my vow against Strenger's life, I might have learned to enjoy my new free status.

When I was invited to attend the annual fealty procession and to serve as one of many state showpieces for public consumption, I could not help but suspect that Trevic Strenger's next trap was ready. My own plan was shelved and I prepared myself to look for any opening, regardless of cost to myself.

Since our procession was to approach Trevic Strenger's seat within a matter of feet, I knew our day of confrontation had come and that I was being baited. He couldn't know of my new ability to manipulate emotion, with which I would trap trapper.

I took his challenge. On each leg and arm I attached secret pressor and tractor beams and joined the grand procession. Behind the others, I slowly approached his position to give my symbol of fealty to the state. I could sense Trevic's muscles tighten as I approached him. His emotions became snarled and bent by covert hostility.

I grabbed his emotions by means of my new talents and twisted them down through grief and apathy. Downward they went until his face became placid, his arms and neck muscles relaxed and his whole stance presented a hopelessness.

Only one person stood between Trevic and me and that one quickly left, urged on by another emotional impulse from my hulking body.

I faced Strenger as if he and I were alone in the world. His eyes seemed to plead and I scorned him, for what power could this emotional invalid have over me?

And then I knew that my hate for him was over and I dropped my long vow of hate and vengeance.

Suddenly the floor dropped from under me. Instantly my reflexes snapped on tractors and pressors and I curved my body into the best stance to slow my fall.

Slow it would not! Somewhere above me automatics caught and sheared off my powers. No matter how I scrambled and twisted my body, the machinery kept up with my efforts, seeming to anticipate every one of my merely human emotions.

The fall was not far. I landed catlike on all fours and bounded up to my feet again. Automatic machinery continued to nullify my pressors and tractors and steel bars surrounded me. Light came from the walls outside my new steel cage.

I heard a door open in the outside wall and then Trevic Strenger's careful tread. He did not smile; neither did he frown. I reached forward with my emotions to engulf him in apathy again but he spoke quickly.

"Turn off your machinery, barbarian. Throw out your tractor and pressor beams, too. I expect you to try for my life again and, as you can see, your attempt has not and cannot succeed. Face up to the fact that your machine-built education is only veneer-deep, your emotional control is uncivilized and your continuous attempts to kill me are more barbaric than our gladiator's arena. At least, there you know the rules."

I threw the pressor and tractors outward but remained silent. "That's better," he said. "At least you are intelligent enough to know when you are captured. That's more than I could say for you when I first caught you on your Planet of the Rocks. You fought until exhaustion then. Why not now?"

I remained quiet but watchful. I read less emotional hatred in his voice and actions than before, perhaps because I projected less of my own thoughts into the situation.

"I don't know what mutational talent you used to control my emotions to such a deep apathy before I triggered your fall into this chamber," he continued, "but I can assure you, you are here to stay until this senseless hatred of me is gone or—as is most likely from your stubborn character—you die of old age. Which shall it be?"

Unbidden to my mind came Farragut's thought, "Damn the torpedoes! Go ahead!" I pushed it below my conscious level and spoke to Trevic for the first time since his capture of me.

"I thought to kill you upstairs but then realized its futility just before your trap door opened. My hate has burned itself out."

He smiled and I noted how pleasant the smile was—not at all malevolent as I had believed for so long.

"How can I believe your statement now?" he asked.

"You have urged me to accept the civilization you represent. What guarantee do I have that it consists of the advantages you have told me about?"

"Try it," he said instantly.

"Then try me," I also said instantly.

He laughed at my answer and seemed to consider my

request quite seriously. He reflected only minutes, however, then bravely motioned to his retainers.

"Free him."

The bars around me rose and I faced Trevic Strenger, separated by only feet. I could easily have killed him at that moment.

IX

Years had passed since Trevic's momentous decision to free me. Sitting at the helm of this tiny empire known as the Sabre planets I looked back with nostalgia at my innocent entrance into its society.

Man had gone to the stars and returned, gone again. And those remaining at home had formed a weakened gene reservoir. Noting this state of affairs, man had returned the gladiator games to his home planet and then had forcibly invited back the barbaric and the humanoid—any mutational sports or freaks bearing new and untested genes were brought to Earth as gladiators.

Here in the arena of strength, agility, intelligence and courage the long screening took place—its purpose to find new blood for the human race. Those freed, like myself, were the backbone of humanity's new drive outward and inward. Slowly man returned his genetic protoplasm to an honored, aggressive, survival status.

I'll not forget the day of my final release from both the steel cell and my own inward-driven emotions. Trevic Strenger stood before me, bravely waiting for me to call his bluff—to kill him suddenly or to accept his offer for civilized peace. He waited. Then suddenly he tore off his shirt and I could see the thickened keloids around his chest where his gladiator band had once burned into him.

Patricia Strenger, hair now grayed, skin wrinkled, figure long gone, sat by my side. She crushed my hand in thoughtful empathy as I looked down on the newcomer from far beyond the Sabre planets. His hatred of me was volatile and could have exploded at any moment, were it a gaseous compound.

I could have dulled the edge of his emotions with my own freakish control over external emotions, of course, but this would also crush his spirit. Who knew? Perhaps the young barbarian below me would be my replacement. I smiled at the thought, all the time knowing that he would interpret my brief flicker as a sneering grin of hatred.

To my mind came unbidden phrases from quotes of our ancient past and I had finally learned to reconcile my thoughts to their contents. J. Christ had said, "And ye shall know the truth, and the truth shall make you free."

I signaled to have the snarling barbarian thrown into our ship and prepared myself for our long trek home.